SLOW SEDUCTION

Rory shifted, letting his arm play out gradually along the back of the swing behind Norah until his fingertips grazed the line of her shoulder. She was wearing her nightclothes, silk over silk, and the heat of his hand scorched with promise.

"I missed you, Norah."

"Really?" She couldn't help that. There was too much bitterness to just brush it away as if it had never existed. "I'm surprised you noticed we were gone."

"That's not fair."

To ease the spark of flint and fire from her words, his hand strayed lower. Her response was instinctive, slight but significant. His touch was maddeningly light, just a whisper of sensation.

"I remember a night like this, me jus' minding my own business when this here lovely looking lady strolled out and commenced to provoking me something fierce by pretending not to care. 'Member what she said to me, Norah-honey?"

She leaned into the circle of his arm, her head resting on his shoulder, her breath pulsing rapidly against his neck. Her voice was hoarse.

"I want you." Then she said again, "I want you, Rory." Her body moved against him in helpless abandon, her fingers gathering in the fabric of his shirt, tangling in the hair at the back of his head.

DANA RANSOM

DAKOTA PROMISES

ZEBRA BOOKS
KENSINGTON PUBLISHING CORP.

ZEBRA BOOKS are published by

Kensington Publishing Corp.
475 Park Avenue South
New York, NY 10016

First printing: August, 1993

Printed in the United States of America

Chapter One

A glimpse. Just a brief snatch of recognition through a crowded room. That was all it took to reduce three years of her life into a helpless sham.

"What do you think, my darling?"

Norah Prescott was jerked back to the present. She turned to her escort with a blank gaze, the way one would confront a stranger. And for one startled moment, she was taken with an absolutely paralyzing thought. *This isn't the man I should be with.*

But then, Trevor Samuels took up her chilled hand and pressed an adoring kiss upon it, melting her panic with the warmth of his care. Of course, he was. Trevor Samuels was everything she wanted: Strong, powerful, kind. He had the money and influence of position to secure her place in society. And that was what she wanted. No ghost from the past was going to shake her from the new and satisfying world she'd made for herself.

Norah forced a smile for her companion and fought to still the clutch of anxiety within her breast as she canted a nervous gaze about the room. Instinct told her to run, to escape quickly before unpleasantness was at hand. Then a colder reason settled and a

7

shoring sense of pride. She had no cause to flee this room filled with her new friends, her new life. She had nothing to be ashamed of. So what if he was here, this shadow from a life she'd fought so hard to put behind her? What could he do? Make a scene? She didn't think so. That wasn't his style. He possessed a polished veneer of sophistication. Few in this gilded room would believe her if she told them of the savage lurking beneath that smooth facade. Stealth and lethal surprise were his weapons, not head-on confrontation.

Where had he disappeared to? Her gaze scanned the mob of Baltimore's wealthy art patrons for the striking figure. Losing him in the crowd was almost as disturbing as coming upon him with a shock of hurtful memory. The shock of it, that's what it was, she told herself staunchly. That's what had staggered her composure.

"Norah?"

"I'm sorry, Trevor. You were saying?"

"Are you all right, my dear? You're looking very peculiar."

Norah smiled to ease the creases of concern lining her escort's noble brow. "Just a little tired, perhaps."

"Would you like me to see you home?"

Before she could agree, a soft drawling voice dragged her back three years in the space of a second.

"You weren't planning to leave before we had a chance to say hello, were you, Norah?"

The quiet threat of those seemingly harmless words slipped between her ribs with the deadly ease of the big knife he probably carried even beneath his evening wear. However, part of Norah Prescott's past had molded her into a competent actress when the situation demanded it. She had brazened her way through many a danger worse than meeting this

8

sleek enemy from South Dakota who had the power to jerk her conscience to its knees. Her instinct for self-preservation screamed, *Don't let him know you're afraid.*

With a smile as chill as the coming months, Norah turned to face the fearsome challenge. "No," she purred silkily, bracing for the clash of wills. She stared him down, never betraying how her emotions had bobbed up into her throat to choke her. "How very nice to see you again."

"I'll just bet it is," he murmured with a smile of his own, a slick surface smile that was in glaring contrast to the molten fires of his gaze. How he hated her, that golden glare stated plainly while his smile assumed the proper bend of formality. That look was as roasting as the fires of hell and Norah struggled not to writhe beneath its condemnation. She knew a moment of relief as his attention shifted to the man at her side. She grasped for the distraction.

"I'd like you to meet—"

"I know who he is." A dark bronze-colored hand thrust out. "The name's Prescott."

Trevor's gasp was audible. His eyes darted to Norah for explanation. *Is this man your husband?* she read in that distressed gaze.

"Trevor Samuels, Scott Prescott. My husband's brother," she summed up tersely.

As if that could explain the complexity of what Scott Prescott was. Part Harvard lawyer. Part Dakota Sioux warrior. A part of the same proud Kincaid blood that flowed through Rory Prescott. A part of the past she thought she'd put behind her. Until this minute.

The two men shook hands with a stiff politeness, each sizing up the other through wary eyes. Trevor Samuels saw a man of compact build, sharply

9

handsome, with shrewdly intelligent eyes and skin of gold. There was a dangerous tautness about Scott Prescott that was immediately apparent despite the bland smile and dapper black attire. A man you wouldn't turn your back on.

From Samuels, Scott observed just the opposite. Here was a man you'd trust to take your wife to dinner. His hazel-green eyes held complete candor, a simmer of sincerity. He sensed an innate honesty in Trevor Samuels and that bothered him. Because he knew who and what the man was.

"So, Scott, what brings you so far from home?" Norah's voice almost broke. Home. Why did she still think of it as her home, too? It wasn't. Not anymore.

"I've been in Washington for over three months now lobbying for changes in the Burke Act." His gaze cut subtly to Trevor to gage his reaction. There was none, so he continued smoothly. "I was invited here by a friend, Charles Bonaparte. We met at Harvard. He thought I might mingle with some influential voting parties.

Trevor raised a sandy brow. Bonaparte's was a name with considerable clout. Everyone in Baltimore knew the "Peacock of Park Avenue," mostly by reputation since his aloof manner and acid wit didn't invite close confidants. He, like Trevor, was born into his wealth and was an avid reformer. And he, to Trevor's envy, had the ear of President Roosevelt. If Scott Prescott claimed a friendship with the man, he was moving in high circles, indeed.

"Are you a Republican, too, Mr. Prescott?"

"I'm not a political man, Mr. Samuels. I only want to take care of my own. Family means more to me than a lot of empty ideals." He looked at Norah then, right through her, twisting those words like the blade of his knife to see if she would wince. Her composure

10

never altered. At least, not outwardly.

Damn you, Scott, don't do this. But what else could she expect from him? A fond reunion? Not hardly. How strange to speak to him with the polite distance of mere acquaintances. To speak of surface things when what burned inside was the want to know about those she still considered family. She didn't care about Indian policies. She wanted to ask him about Gena and their daughter, about his parents. And about Rory. A great wave of yearning threatened her cool resolve. Only sensibility kept her quiet. Not here. Not in front of Trevor.

"I think I'd like to take in some air. Scott, would you walk with me? Excuse us, Trevor, won't you?"

Trevor couldn't very well refuse. Smiling rather stiffly, he released her arm and let her brother-in-law's dark fingers assume his place at the bend of her elbow. Politeness demanded he make no objection. But he didn't like it. Not at all.

The night was brisk and deeply starred. Winter beckoned with every breath of chilly air. But Norah was grateful for its bite. She needed its reviving snap to sharpen her wits if she were to deal with Scott Prescott.

The minute they were out of sight of the others, Scott dropped his hand from her arm and much of his genial pretense. He continued to walk across the terraced grounds with her, drawn by curiosity, yet so very cautious she could feel the tension vibrate from him. Not exactly a heartening atmosphere.

"I'm surprised you would want to risk a walk in the darkness with me."

The fierce quiet of his words crept over her skin like a shiver. "I'm not afraid of you, Scott. Should I be worried for my hair?"

"Maybe." There was no humor in that, and she

experienced an odd tightening along her scalp.

"Nonsense. You're much too civilized when in these surroundings."

"Am I?" He stopped abruptly and Norah had time to utter a soft gasp as his fingers encircled her throat. "Too civilized to want to break your pretty neck?" The pressure increased, intimidating but not painful. When Norah held his glare without signs of distress, his grip eased. "Perhaps I am."

He released her and moved away. Norah was careful not to sound her thanksgiving too loudly. She might not have been afraid of him, but she was sensible enough to be rightly wary. She watched him stalk across the patio with his light, cat-like step, hating the way more memories dredged up with every second she spent in his presence. She couldn't separate them from the man. But then, perhaps perversely, she longed for that feeling of sweet anguish swelling within her breast. Oh, how she cherished those memories, and having Scott here brought them into such clear, almost tangible focus. Almost as if she were back on the clean-smelling Dakota plain where any minute she would hear the brash tones of Rory Prescott's voice from behind her, whiskey-warm with intimate suggestion. Breath trembling, she closed her eyes tight. She tried to ignore the pooling of moisture forced out to rim her lashes as she embraced the agony of remembrance.

Norah-honey, I just love you so much.

Rory . . .

"What do you want, Norah?"

The harshness of Scott Prescott's words cut through her reverie. Blinking quickly to clear her eyes of betraying sentiment, Norah spoke with candor, knowing if she made an honest appeal, she would have a better chance with Rory's guarded brother. "How's Gena?"

He turned toward her and before he could catch it, Norah saw his taut features soften to a poignant misery. Three months without his wife beside him. Norah could read the pain of missing her etched upon his face. Then that trace of vulnerability was gone as he recalled who was asking. And his reply was brutally stingy with the personal details Norah ached to hear.

"She's fine."

"And Dawn?"

"Eight-years old."

Emotion squeezed about her chest as she thought of the flame-haired child she and Rory had helped bring into the world in the back of a buckboard. Eight years ago. Yet the experience was so close, so fresh, more recent then those of a week gone by. She could see the squalling babe red and wriggling in Rory's big hands as he settled her into her mother's arms for the first time. And she could feel the caress of his eyes as he looked up at her then, could recall again the sweet promise held in that dark, compelling gaze. That same day, she'd agreed to marry him.

And he'd vowed she would never regret it.

Hoping to coax her stoic brother-in-law from his incommunicative stand, she prompted softly, "And Ethan and Aurora? How are they?" Before he could answer with a flat monotone, she interjected crisply, "And don't tell me they're fine. I want to hear it in more than two words."

"You want?" Scott's gaze narrowed fiercely. "If you cared so much about my family, you wouldn't have run off and left them without a word. They're angry and hurt and confused. How did you think they'd be?"

"I don't know what Rory told you," she began in

13

her own defense, but he cut her off tersely.

"He didn't tell me anything. What's to tell? You left him. You tore the heart out of him. And you expect me to be civilized about it? Sorry, Norah." He started to storm past her and she saw her last chance for news leaving with him. Suddenly, she couldn't bear not knowing.

"Scott." She grabbed his arm and he jerked up short, going rigid as one of his beloved Dakota pines. She couldn't keep the husky plea from her voice. "How is he?"

Scott drew in a long, hissing breath between clenched teeth. When he spoke, his words were brittle as thin glass. "He's surviving. It's what we Prescotts do best. Now, if that's all you wanted to know, let go of me."

"He never came after me, Scott. He never once wrote or sent word." She didn't know why she bothered to tell him these things. They weren't reasonable excuses. Not to him.

"Why would he? You just disappeared. None of us knew where. Did you think he'd just up and leave the ranch to go chasing after you when you left a trail too cold to follow? I'll say this for you, you sure learned how to cover your tracks well. Guess you'd have to with the business you were in."

She did wince at that. She couldn't help it. It had been so long since anyone had thrown that particular piece of hurtful fact into her face. She recovered the only way she knew how, by drawing in tight to protect her fragile feelings, by shoving up a shield of indifference to hide behind. Her reply was so cold it would have frozen over a Dakota stream in summer.

"No, I never thought he'd leave the Bar K. Not for me. Not for anyone. He wouldn't neglect his precious ground even to save his marriage." She

14

paused, nearly smothered by the pent up scorch of jealousy. Had it been another woman, she could have understood. But for acres of grass, for that damned Dakota dirt. That, she had never understood and she was furious and frustrated all over again. "When you see your brother, you tell him that I'm—fine. You tell him I hope he's very happy with all his pastures and his fat Kincaid cows. And that I hope he can keep his promise to his grandfather better than he could to me."

Scott disengaged her hold on him with the pry of surprisingly gentle fingers. His answer was equally disturbing for its quiet cadence.

"I'll tell him, Norah."

And abruptly, the heating anger was gone, replaced by the lifeless cold that had been her constant companion for almost three years. Since the second her buggy wheels crossed from Kincaid property.

From his impersonal distance across the room, Martin Samuels watched his son as the younger man paced in well-bred agitation. The elder's eyes missed nothing—not the arrival of the swarthy stranger, not the shock on Trevor's companion's lovely features, not his son's distress over her absence. As he was not a man to be left adrift when a current of dismay disturbed his boy, he motioned impatiently for the little man lurking near by.

"Yes, Mr. Samuels. What is it you need?"

Samuels didn't spare his assistant a glance. He didn't need to. Carter Clemens was as familiar to him as the cane he leaned upon. Both gave unfaltering support without question. Both had their unbending strength taken for granted by the one using them. But

15

unlike the silver-topped staff of mahogany, Carter Clemens knew with smug certainty that Martin Samuels couldn't get far without him.

"Who is the man the Prescott woman took outside?"

"I don't know, sir."

"Why don't you know? I pay you to know everything that concerns my son. Find out!"

"Yes, sir."

Samuels waited, his shrewd gaze passing between the closed terrace doors and his son's pinched features. In less than a minute, his aide was sidling up next to him.

"Well?"

"Prescott, sir. Scott Prescott. He's her brother-in-law. A lawyer, Harvard-schooled, from South Dakota. An Indian rights advocate who's been giving us a bit of trouble in Washington. He's protesting the Commission's right to sell off allotment lands held in trust for the Sioux."

"And is anyone listening to him?" Who he was wasn't as important as whom he knew.

"He's here as Bonaparte's guest."

Samuels frowned. "I think it's time Trevor distanced himself from Norah Prescott."

"But sir—"

"I don't want to hear it, Carter. I had your assurance that he would not be sullied by the association. I trusted your judgment. It would seem I was in error."

"Please, sir," his assistant wheezed in an irritating whine. "I wasn't wrong. The woman can be of use to us. Even more so, now. Please, sir, have I ever let you down before?"

Martin Samuels flicked an irritated glance at the nervous little man. Carter Clemens was everything

16

his own son was not. He was small, fragile-looking with his narrow shoulders and unproportionately long arms. Watery blue eyes blinked in rapid earnest behind the thick lenses of his pince-nez spectacles as he ran bony fingers back through the thinning threads of his lusterless dark hair. The scars left by a childhood illness had a more marked appearance upon his face when it was drawn by anxiety as it was now. But despite his homely looks, his timid manner, his high-pitched voice, and his spindly frame, Carter Clemens was something else his son was not. He was ruthlessly clever.

Carter had been with Samuels since his rescue from a failing law practice, applying his unscrupled intelligence wherever it was directed. He managed to keep all of his employer's activities above reproach. Clemens's suggestion that he back the rebuilding of the city after its devastating fire in '04 with his own considerable fortune had ultimately helped him survive the crackdown on the controlling bosses targeted by those shrieking for social justice. He never once worried about placing his son's hopeful political future in the little man's capable hands. Trevor had all the outward signs of political greatness: Fine looks, insurmountable charm, polished poise that was still approachable, and the mellifluous voice of a natural orator. But he lacked the instinct to achieve greatness, the ambition to overlook his surroundings in favor of himself. That necessary remorselessness was supplied by Carter Clemens.

When Trevor began escorting the yet-married Norah Prescott about town, Carter assured him there was no danger there. Mrs. Prescott was a powerful voice in the Progressive movement and they needed friends in that circle. She was an intimate of Miss Mary Garrett, daughter of the president of the

Baltimore & Ohio Railroad who brought Women's Suffrage to the attention of the social elite and of Elizabeth Ellicott, Baltimore clubwoman par excellence. Mrs. Prescott was a symbol of the nation's New Woman: independent of means, intelligent of mind, bold of spirit, and possessed of a cool, untouchable beauty. Though half the country separated her from her rancher-husband, she was careful to keep even a hint of scandalous talk from tainting her behavior. She graced Trevor's arms with her perfect poise and cultivated wit without encouraging any salacious gossip which might have injured the young man's future. Carter insisted the woman had no designs upon the affections of his son, but it would seem he misjudged the intensity of Trevor's intentions. He made no secret that he would wed Mrs. Prescott in a second should she be free for him to do so. And that made Martin Samuels uncomfortable. No matter how respected Norah Prescott was within the social circles, the wife of a politician could not survive the stigma of divorce, not even in this enlightened century. So it was Carter Clemens' added duty to see that the relationship did not progress in that threatening direction.

"All right, Carter. I will allow it for now. But keep your eyes open. I have plans for my son. I'll not have a moment's indiscretion ruin the promise of his future."

Carter supplied a self-effacing smile while eyes magnified to an unnatural degree behind his rimless spectacles canted toward Trevor Samuels. It was the hard, calculating look of secret ambition.

"Yes, sir, Mr. Samuels. I'll take care of everything. Don't you worry."

*   *   *

18

The moment Scott and Norah returned to the noise and glare of the party, they were approached by a breathless boy.

"Mr. Prescott? I have a telegram for you."

After fishing out an appropriate coin, Scott took the missive and broke the seal. Norah was standing close enough to hear his sudden intake of breath. There was no change in his expression. The muscles of his face hardened to hold it firm. The only thing that betrayed him was the rattle of the page within his white-knuckled grasp.

"Scott?"

It was as if he hadn't heard her. Without so much as a parting word, Scott strode rapidly away, thrusting through the crowded room as if nothing existed to him beyond the words on the page. Norah hurried after him. Something was wrong. Something terrible. Only one thing could shake the unflappable Scott Prescott and that was something affecting his family. Her family. That knowledge beat frantically along her pulse points as she turned into the quiet coat room to find him there in the secluded shadows. The sight drew her up with a soft gasp.

He was on his knees, bent over double so that his forehead brushed the floor. An immediate image struck her with a breath-stealing force—of Scott Prescott kneeling in a sun-washed Dakota yard lacerating his flesh with steely purpose after his wife had been thrown from a speeding buggy. He'd been calling to the spirit world of his father's ancestors to save the soul of his wife and unborn child. He made those same low, wailing sounds of Lakota mourning now; and, as it had then, an awful prickling ran along her skin.

"Oh, God, Scott. What's happened? Is it Gena? Dawn?

The soft, undulating moan was her only answer. That and the piece of paper clenched in his outflung fists. Norah knelt down in the awkward confines of her narrow skirt to place a comforting hand upon his shoulder. He flinched away.

"Don't." That single word tore from him, harsh and raw.

"Scott, tell me," she demanded, truly frightened now by whatever mystery had crumpled his reserve so completely. "What's wrong?" *Not Rory,* she prayed in a panic. *Please, God, don't let it be Rory.* Needing to know the worst, she reached for the damning bit of news, wrestling it from the desperate cramp of his fingers. It wasn't Rory, a quick scan of the message told her. However, that relief was short-lived. Not Rory, but his father.

The message from his mother was terse, to the point with an almost savage bluntness. Ethan Prescott had suffered a serious concussion and had yet to regain consciousness. The prognosis wasn't good. Come home.

Norah sank to the floor in a twist of satin. "Oh, no. Oh, Scott, I'm so sorry." Ethan Prescott. The big, strapping Texan. Neither heart nor mind could comprehend it. Compassionately, she touched the short black hair of his adopted son. For a moment, Scott allowed it, then he gave a jerk of awareness—recalled to where he was, to who she was. He pulled away, rolling to one side until he was sitting on the floor across from her. Clearly struggling for control, he ground the heels of his hands over eyes brimming with the evidence of his grief. And with the long pull of one unsteady breath, he was himself once more. He glanced at Norah, uncomfortable that she'd witnessed his private pain. Even if it weren't the first time she'd seen his soul stripped bare, he didn't like it. Especially now, when she'd thrown away the right to share in his distress.

Norah read all those things in his aloof gaze and she fought not to recoil. She did have the right to grieve for Ethan Prescott. They had been—they still were—family. And she resented the isolating chill of Scott's stare.

"When will you leave?" she asked softly. What was this crazy insistent voice inside that cried out for her to pack her bags and go with him?

His reply was shockingly brief. "I can't."

"Can't?" Norah stared at him, incredulous. "Scott, your father could be dying. You may never get the chance to see him again."

"I know that," he hissed at her. "Don't you think I know that?"

"Then why—"

"I can't go back just now. I can't leave. I have a meeting in Washington tomorrow. I've been trying to arrange it for months. I can't just cancel. Daddy would understand." He added that defensively, forcefully, as if trying to convince himself.

"Your mother won't. And neither do I." She saw him stiffen and withdraw behind that solemn, unemotional mask he'd inherited from the Sioux. But no, she realized, looking closer. It wasn't from the Sioux that he drew that fierce determination. It was from Garth Kincaid, his and Rory's grandfather. She'd seen that look before. That same staunch, unswerving glaze of purpose. She'd seen it in Rory's face the day she'd left him. That single-minded devotion to one goal, excluding and surpassing all others, even family. For Scott Prescott, it was the welfare of the Lakota. To his brother, it was the resurrection of his grandfather's ranch. She knew better than to think an impassioned plea could sway

21

either of them from their chosen course. And suddenly, Norah was furious with both of them. She struggled to stand but the tangle of her narrow skirt conspired against her. Angrily, she depended upon the gallant offer of Scott's hand and immediately jerked free when she'd gained her feet.

"I hope your father lives long enough for your mother to forgive you," she told the impassive, hard-eyed man before her. "I know I never would."

With that, she whirled away, trying to force the Prescotts from her mind.

And failing.

Hours later, in a darkened bedroom in her fashionable townhouse, she gave up the fight. The pull upon her heart and soul was too strong. Admitting it to herself, she was committed to action. With a soft sigh, she settled on the edge of the bed and smiled down upon the sleeping figure nestled in it. Gently, she brushed back the dark auburn hair curling over a smooth brow and placed a kiss upon it.

"We're going home, Jacob," she whispered softly so as not to wake him. "Home to see your father."

Chapter Two

It wasn't the cross-country travel that wore her to the point of exhaustion. It was the worrying. With every mile, there was a new question, with every minute a new doubt. Was she crazy? What was she hoping to find in South Dakota that she didn't have in Baltimore? Was she foolish enough to think there was some kind of magic to heal the horrendous split in her marriage? Some charm that would lift the sting of parting words or soothe the hurt of broken promises? There were no such things. She was making this trip out of obligation, not optimism. Ethan Prescott had opened his home to her and, for a few years, had embraced her into his family. Her fondness and gratitude hadn't diminished because she was separated from his son.

And then there was Jacob to consider. She glanced down at the dark burnished head burrowed into her side and knew a wistful pang. He had the right to know his father. He'd been little more than a babe when she'd taken him from the Bar K, four-years-old. She wasn't sure how much he actually remembered, if any of the impressions had remained. Jacob never spoke of his father. He never asked questions about their home in South Dakota. And she hadn't been able to press the subject upon him. She wasn't certain what he thought about the trip west. He'd kept his feelings buttoned up as tight as the coat of his Buster Brown suit.

One person hadn't been so silent about his reservations. Norah could still hear every one of Trevor's protests. His objections had been eloquent. Why did she have to go? Why did she feel it necessary to reconnect ties she'd severed years ago? She had her own life, a life he hoped included him. He'd thought she'd come to care for him. He'd hoped something would come of their association. Something beyond friendship. That's when Norah had stopped his poetic oration. She was married. She couldn't entertain such words from him. It wasn't fair to either of them. And that's when Trevor had asked her.

He'd asked her to divorce her husband and marry him. To put aside Mrs. Rory Prescott and become Mrs. Trevor Samuels.

She'd been stunned at first. But was it really a surprise? She had known how Trevor felt about her. He was just too much of a gentleman to press the issue beyond the proper. And there had been times she'd wished he would. Times when she was so lonely, she ached clear to the soul. Times when she missed a man's touch so badly it was like a consuming madness burning in her veins. On those nights that went on forever, she made herself think about Trevor Samuels. About inviting him to share her life, to reignite her passions. She was only twenty-eight. Hardly ready for a celibate existence. She had a lot of prime years ahead of her, years meant to be spent with a companion of the mind, soul, and body.

She enjoyed sharing her mind with Trevor. He was

24

well-read, inquisitive as a child, and incredibly open to new ideas. He wanted to share all those new things with her. That was his greatest appeal. Trevor treated her as an equal, as a partner. He made no secret of respecting her opinion on everything from the color of his dinner jacket to the content of lectures they attended. He was wonderful with Jacob. The little boy looked up to him with admiration and, more disturbingly, with the affection that should have been reserved for a father figure. Jacob had no trouble casting the handsome Easterner in that mold. He was a fine example for a boy to follow: strong, kind, stable. And more than willing to give of his time and his tenderness.

Time and tenderness. Oh, how she'd missed receiving those precious gifts. Perhaps she was ready to encourage Trevor Samuels to appreciate more than her mind. She'd liked his careful overtures well enough. She'd allowed him a few brief kisses, a few restless caresses. He was more than anxious to continue but had stopped when she'd pulled away. It wasn't the fact she wore a gold ring upon her left hand that held her back from seeking pleasure in Trevor Samuels's arms. It was the too-apparent truth—that she couldn't share her body with Trevor when her soul was held far away, out where the grass stretched to the horizons, where there was nothing to make a shadow for mile after majestic mile. She couldn't escape the fact that she belonged, heart and soul, to Rory Prescott. When Trevor touched her, she found herself longing for the feel of rough palms. When he kissed her, she yearned to be devoured by a familiar passion. Those truths held her prisoner in the past. That's why she was traveling to South Dakota. To see Rory. To break the hold he had upon her emotions. There could be no future for her and

Jacob until she was free of Rory. She had to divorce her feelings before she could divorce the man.

Mile after mile, she told herself she and Jacob deserved a life with Trevor Samuels. She liked what she had built for herself in Baltimore. Thanks to Cole Denby's shrewd investments, she would never want for money again. Her former partner had embarrassingly large sums deposited in her account every month without fail and there it grew, making her one of the most wealthy residents on Bolton Hill. She had everything money could buy, everything but happiness, and that she pretended not to need. Then she met Trevor at a Progressive fund-raiser and began to believe she could start her life over again. She had nothing in the Dakotas, just the lonely whisper of promises unkept and an unreasonable desire for a man she couldn't live with. She'd taken a chance on those things. For four years she'd tried. It hadn't worked. It was time to admit to failure and move on. She owed that to Jacob. And to herself.

Trevor had trusted her enough to let her go. She promised she would return with an answer to his question; and, after days of choking on smoke and cinders and shattered dreams, Norah was sure of her decision.

Until she saw the Bar K.

A sprawling grassland kingdom rooted in rich blue Gamma and prime Dakota beef. Its original boundaries stretched from horizon to horizon, as far-reaching as Garth Kincaid's limitless ambition. The old man was now resting under his beloved ground and the fence line had been adjusted to fit leaner times. But it was no less spectacular, no less an accomplishment. And Norah felt an overwhelming pride in what her husband had managed to resurrect from long-ago ashes.

He'd finished the house.

For a timeless moment, Norah sat in the carriage just staring at it. The big bay windows, the wraparound porch, the octagonal cupola perched three stories above the yard. Everything was perfect: The tracery trim, hung like delicate frost patterns; the attached gazebo; the diamond-shaped panes of leaded glass. Her castle, Rory had called it humorlessly. She'd never spent a night beneath its slated roof, yet its unfinished walls had echoed back words too harsh to ignore or forgive. For some reason, she'd expected him to tear it down with his bare hands after she was gone. But he hadn't. He'd finished it and it was everything she'd dreamed it could be. Only it wasn't hers. Not anymore.

"Miss Norah? Land-of-mercy, it is you!"

She smiled at the woman who'd come out onto the porch. "Hello, Ruth. I'm glad to see you're still here."

"Where else would I be?" Where, indeed. Ruth had been Garth Kincaid's housekeeper. She'd helped raise a young Scott Prescott and an adolescent Rory. The Bar K had been her home for over thirty years and she looked as natural there as the Herefords grazing in the distance and the cowhands lounging by the corrals. And Norah was suddenly very glad that her husband hadn't been alone in this big house her vanity had demanded.

"Who's that you got there with you? That can't be Jacob all grown up." The big, still-handsome woman moved to the edge of the carriage to see for herself, beaming down at the sleepy boy as he uncurled from his mother's side. He blinked owlishly through the lenses of his wire-rimmed glasses at the strange face confronting him. "What a fine looking boy! Can't say he favors his daddy, though."

"Where is he, Ruth? Inside?"

The care-worn features lifted, a study of somber lines. "He's over at the Lone Star. Hasn't been home for a meal or a change of clothes or a night's sleep since Mr. Prescott took to his bed."

"How is Ethan?"

"Still hasn't come 'round. I guess that's a bad sign. Taking it hard, all of them. Especially Rory. You know how close he is to his family."

"Yes," Norah answered faintly.

"He'll be mighty glad to see you, Miss Norah. Just the thing to bring him 'round. Less you want to rest up some, I'd be happy to see to the boy and your things while you go on over to bring him home."

Bring him home. How quickly Ruth assumed she was here to take up where she'd left off almost three years ago, as mistress of the Bar K and wife to Rory Prescott. She'd have to set the housekeeper straight on that, but first she wanted to see how her father-in-law fared. And she wanted to see Rory.

"Thank you, Ruth. I won't be long."

After stilling Jacob's apprehensions and waiting for two burly ranch hands to unload her trunks, Norah turned the buggy toward Ethan Prescott's Lone Star Ranch and was forced to deal with apprehensions of her own.

What if Rory weren't glad to see her?

What if Aurora Prescott stopped her at the door with the business end of her husband's Sharps rifle? Was she wrong to intrude upon them in this time of grief? Her determination almost faltered. But then, she'd never quailed before Aurora's intimidation. And if Rory were displeased by her presence, that would make what she'd come to do all the easier. She snapped the reins to encourage a brisker pace, straightening her spine and her resolve as she went to

28

meet her estranged family.

Seeing the Lone Star was in a way worse than her first glimpse of the Bar K. Here, nothing had changed. She could still see the scorch marks on the roof where she'd beaten down the curls of fire that had singed the prairie and consumed Garth Kincaid's ranch. She could taste the choking horror of watching Rory's little paint, Chance, dragging him broken and bleeding up to the door. She could feel the enveloping warmth of family as they said their vows before the huge stone fireplace and could see the glorious burst of pride in her husband's grin as he was handed their newborn son. She was crazy if she thought she could withstand the full brunt of memories this place and these people held for her. She was dizzy with them. But it was too late to turn back for a slender figure came flying toward her off the porch, uttering a cry of recognition.

Gena Prescott's hug was one of unabashed welcome. The fragile blonde was weeping and laughing all at once, and Norah found her own tears dangerously close to spilling.

"Oh, Norah, I'm so glad you've come home."

Again that presumption. But Gena gave her no time to make corrections. She stood back, clinging to her friend's hands. "You look wonderful. Is Jacob with you? I can't wait to see him."

"How's Ethan?"

Much of her sister-in-law's animation faded. "Nothing's changed. Is that why you've come? How did you know?"

"I saw Scott back East. I was with him when he got his mother's telegram."

"Scott. Oh, how is he? Is he well? Is he with you? When will he be here?"

"Gena, please. Give me time to answer."

With obvious difficulty, she held in her questions, biting on her lip as she begged silently for news.

"Scott's—fine." Norah refrained from a wry smile. She couldn't hold her cynicism as Gena Prescott gave a heart-felt sigh of relief. "He misses you terribly but he wasn't able to leave. At least not right away. I'm sure he'll be here as soon as he can." *The bastard.*

Swallowing down what must have been a crushing disappointment, Gena pasted on a smile and looped her arm through Norah's. "I'm sure he will. Come inside. Did you just get in? You must be exhausted."

The feeling of welcome was what was exhausted the moment the two women entered the log house. The words that greeted her were almost as effective as a blast buckshot.

"What are you doing in my house?"

"Hello, Aurora."

Rory's mother was still a striking woman, aristocratic of bearing with a disposition as fiery as her hair—hair Norah was stunned to discover liberally streaked with silver. After fighting Indians and even her own powerful father to keep her family together, Aurora Kincaid Prescott wasn't willing to offer hospitality to the woman who'd broken her son's heart and stolen her only grandson away.

"How dare you come here!" she seethed. Dragged to the end of endurance by fright and fatigue, she was in no mood to mince words.

"It wasn't my intention to cause any trouble."

"Then leave."

Fortified by her own considerable temper, Norah held her ground like a stubborn steer. "I won't stay. I just came to pay my respects and to take Rory back to the Bar K."

"You're not taking my son anywhere. If you think you can just waltz in here and—"

"Aurora," Gena interjected with a quieting authority. "Please. This isn't the time. Norah's come a long way." And with that, all objections were overcome. She gave Norah a compelling tug. "Rory's with his father." Her voice lowered as they crossed the room. "We haven't been able to get him to budge for days. He's not himself," she warned softly. "He hasn't put anything in his stomach but whiskey and coffee." *Prepare yourself*, was what she didn't say. At the threshold, Gena stopped her with a gentle hand on her arm and a firm word of advice. "He needs you, Norah. Please be kind to him."

Unable to speak, Norah smiled her promise and stepped into the darkened bedroom alone. The scent of liquor was like a slap to the senses and she drew up, waiting for her sight to adjust to the dimness. Rory was at his father's bedside. He had forsaken or fallen out of the room's single chair and was on his knees with his bright head buried in the loop of his arms. He was either asleep or unconscious. Norah was spared from seeing his face right away. She had time to pick her way around the sprawl of his feet and the discarded bottles and bend down over Ethan Prescott's still form.

Dark auburn hair, the same color as her son's, was all but hidden by a swaddling of fresh bandages. Aside from that and a sickroom pallor, Ethan looked as robust as ever. It was hard to think of him as close to death. Not a man like him who'd breathed in the outdoors and exhaled energy all his life. Very carefully, she laid her palm alongside one bearded cheek.

"Don't do this to them, Ethan," she whispered fervently. "Don't leave them yet."

There was a low mutter as Rory slowly roused to awareness. Norah stepped back into shadow,

31

abruptly afraid of confronting him face to face. She held her breath, suspended as she watched him slowly straighten and roll those broad shoulders she remembered so well. He gave a heavy sigh and scrubbed his drowsiness away with his palms.

"Sorry, Daddy," he murmured in a raspy voice. "Musta drifted off for a minute. How ya doing?" He took up a big slack hand, rubbing it gently between his. Hearing that rough, drawling accent so laced with misery and remorse hamstrung all of Norah's resolve with one crippling stroke. "You hang on now, you hear? Hang on, Daddy. Don't you go a-dying. I can't go saying good-bye. I done lost too many that I loved already."

Her trembling fingers brushed his shoulder. He was slow to register the touch, then finally turned to see who was with him. He looked terrible, wasted by drink and weariness, but at the same time so wonderful Norah couldn't keep her gaze from hungrily detailing every familiar line. The face of the man who'd haunted her soul for three long, lonely years. His chin was unshaven, his red hair untidy. His clothes were a rumpled disaster. The dark eyes that lifted to hers were swollen and almost dulled beyond comprehension. There was no spark of surprise at seeing her, just an anguish so heavy, so heart-sore it encompassed every other emotion.

"He can't die, Norah. He just can't."

And as his features crumpled and sought out the smooth satin of her skirt, she came down to him. The instant her arms encircled the slump of his shoulders, she was lost. She couldn't harden her feelings toward him anymore than she could ignore the tears of her own child. She held him tight, part of her greedily absorbing the strong textures of his body while the rest tried to cling to a shred of objective thought. It

32

was only natural for her to want to comfort him. He'd been a part of her life, a piece of her heart. She'd never stopped caring about him, despite the words, despite the anger and the hurt. There was nothing wrong in sharing his sorrow or in wanting to ease his pain. As long as her other emotions stayed under control. And she could feel them slipping dangerously. To haul herself up from the wont to wail with him, she made her will strengthen and her voice crisp.

"He's not going to. I can vouch for the hardness of a Prescott head." She could feel the ghost of a smile as her fingertips grazed his stubbly cheek. Not much, but a start. "Do you think you're doing him any good like this? He'd be the first one to tell you to go home." At the frantic shaking of his head, she held him tighter, gently stroking the confusion of his hair to offset her brusque command. "You're dead on your feet, you're drunk as a skunk, and you smell worse than a mule skinner. I'm taking you to the Bar K. You're going to bathe and sleep and eat a good breakfast; and in the morning, we'll ride back over together. All right?"

There was a long silence, then the slightest nod.

"Come on, cowboy. On your feet."

She rose with him, staggering under the weight of his dependence. As always, she was unprepared for the towering size of him. Rory Prescott was a big man, a powerful man, and—right now—an almost helpless one. As she maneuvered him around, she encountered Gena and a scowling Aurora in the doorway.

"I'll see you in the morning, Mama," Rory slurred with a groggy smile. "Norah's come to fetch me home."

Aurora said nothing. Her golden eyes fixed Norah

33

like a pronged fork through a prime cut. Norah returned the challenging glare and prodded Rory forward. He took a wobbling step and banked sharply to the right, nearly carrying them both to the floor.

"I'll help you with him," Gena offered; and with her tenacious shoulders beneath his other arm, they managed to cart him to the buggy, where he clamored awkwardly up onto the seat. For Norah, there was another quick hug from her sister-in-law and a whisper of, "I'm so glad you've come home." And again, the time didn't seem right to correct her.

It was a long drive back to the Bar K. Norah handled the reins with one hand and had the other clenched firmly in the back of Rory's shirt to keep him from toppling out of the buggy. He was bent double, head hanging between his knees, bobbing loosely with every bump. Beside him, Norah refused to think of anything beyond getting him home. She was too unsettled to sort through the mix of emotions. Too fragile inside to ruminate on how good it had felt to hold him. She could argue that she was just being sympathetic, touched by his vulnerable despair. Or she could respond that compassion in no way described the explosive longing sending brutal shock waves through her even now. She should never have underestimated his appeal or her own weakness to it. She'd have to be stronger if she were going to survive this visit to the Dakotas with her heart intact. And she was a strong woman. It had taken every scrap of will she possessed to walk away the first time, but she had. It would be easier this time because of what she had waiting. Still, she had to be careful not to let herself be sucked into the illusion of family here on these vast acres of green.

It was dark by the time the buggy rolled to a stop

before the broad porch of the Bar K. Ruth must have been watching for them for she was quick to separate from the shadows of the house to help her hoist the insensible ranch owner down. Over the slack nod of his head, she murmured, "The little boy was exhausted. I fed him and saw him to bed for you. Was out like a light, the dear. I've got a hot bath poured for the Mister."

Bless her for her competence. "Thank you, Ruth."

Between them, they wrestled the uncooperative cowboy up the grand sweep of the stairs and into the big bathroom where steam rose invitingly from the tub. Wishing the hot water were waiting for her, Norah let Rory drop into a convenient chair. Wicker groaned under his weight. Out like a light described father as well as son. Sighing, she straightened to survey the situation.

"Is there anything else you need, Miss Norah?"

I need my head examined for ever coming back here. What could she have been thinking? She wasn't ready for this. She wasn't emotionally prepared to play nursemaid to Rory Prescott. She didn't want to be alone with him, not afraid of him as much as of her own reaction to him. Instead, she knelt and began tugging off her husband's boots.

"No. Goodnight, Ruth."

"Welcome home, Miss Norah."

But I'm not—

Ruth was already gone. For a moment, Norah wanted to collapse on the elegantly tiled floor and cry. She wasn't home. This wasn't her home. So why did it feel like it? Why did it seem so natural to be yanking off this man's boots? Why had it been so easy to step back into the life she'd run from three years ago? It wasn't supposed to feel so—right.

Taking another fortifying breath, she shook off

her panic and tackled the ready problem of how to get Rory cleaned up and to bed. She would think of it like tending Jacob. Rory was little more than a big, overgrown kid, anyway. But the minute she started down the buttons of his shirt, she was pointedly aware that she was not dealing with her son. Especially when her fingertips stretched out to experience the hard swell of his shoulders. Magnificent. As hard and wide and formidable as the far Hills. Becoming lost in that rugged terrain, Norah pulled back abruptly. Good heavens, it wasn't as though she'd never seen a man's chest before! It wasn't as though she wasn't intimately familiar with every angular inch and hard plain of Rory Prescott. She'd had years to chart out the territory. Angry with herself for yearning to explore it all over again, she jerked off his shirt and flung it aside. Damn the man for being as desirable as the day she'd met him on a sidewalk in Deadwood. Here it was almost eight years later and they'd ridden enough miles in each others arms to cover the western states twice over. And still, she marveled at him. At the big, tough build that hadn't softened with the years. At the big, rough hands she knew capable of incredible tenderness. She shivered at the thought.

Get a hold of yourself, Norah, she chided sternly. *It's your own fault. You should have bedded down with Trevor. You should have grabbed up the train conductor, the man at the livery, anyone who could ease the ache of wanting before you came to him. It's been too long since you've known a man's touch, that's all.* Whom was she fooling? It wasn't any man's touch she wanted. It was this man's.

Aggravated with her lusty thoughts, she hauled Rory to his feet, stiffening as his arms draped over her shoulders. *Don't give in,* she chastened fiercely as she

36

worked his jeans down over the temptation of lean hips and long legs. *If you let yourself hold him, you'll be melting down him like hot wax on a candle.*

"Step out," she ordered gruffly, slapping at the muscular calf of his leg. He obeyed, swaying on one foot, then the other. As she tossed the denims aside, Norah was confronted by the bold contours of him clad in a soft flannel. She closed her eyes, swallowing hard. *Give me strength*, she prayed fervently and scrambled to her feet. Standing eye level with his broad chest was not nearly as dangerous. She placed her hands determinedly upon either side of his middle, readying to strip him of his drawers. Thank goodness his eyes were shut or he might have taken great amusement in her fiery cheeks. "Now you're going to have to help me get you into the tub."

He made an obliging sound and, before she could stop him, he stepped over the rolled edge and sank, long underwear and all, into the water. Norah gestured helplessly, then resigned.

"Oh, well. They could stand a good washing, too."

As she reached around for the cloth and soap, Rory slid bonelessly down the curved side and beneath the surface with scarcely a ripple. When no bubbles appeared, Norah plunged her hands under the water to catch him and drag him up. He gave a sputtering cough as his head lolled back, clunking the rim of the tub. Muttering her irritation, Norah anchored his arms over the edge. Obviously, he was not going to wash himself, which left her to the much-needed task. The front of her stylish gown was already blotched with wetness and drenched up to the elbows. If she were to wrangle him like a helpless calf, she'd need more freedom of movement. She shrugged out of her snug travel jacket, then, after a second's hesitation, peeled right down to her thin

37

chemise and petticoat.

Just like soaping a horse, she told herself as she worked a lather between her palms. Don't think about it, just do it. Start at the top and let gravity take its course. Fortunately, he never moved as she scrubbed his hair and face and moved down to the enticing spread of shoulders. There, her movements slowed, shifting subtly in purpose. Lord, he felt good: warm, hard, and sleek. The lingering circles drifted down his chest, pausing briefly as fingers brushed over the ridge of a scar curving along his ribs. When had he done that? She frowned in concern, suffering an unconscious pang of guilt because she hadn't been there to tend him.

Oh, Rory, can't you take care of yourself any better than that?

Sighing softly, she leaned further over the edge of the tub, moving to the light furring of his abdomen. She paused there, unable to go on. Her breath was coming too fast, her heart beating too strong. *Damn you, Rory,* she moaned silently as the heat of wanting quivered through her. *I must have been crazy to think I could resist you.* She threw the soapy cloth into the filmy water and began to straighten, only to find her gaze caught up by his dark, simmering stare. He was smiling, a lazy, lethal smile.

"You missed a spot there, Norah-honey," he drawled in a husky rumble. The simmer became a smolder, touching off the wick of passion in her soul. "And there ain't no way I'm gonna let you get away without seeing to it proper."

Chapter Three

His hand cupped behind the back of her head, drawing her toward him. It wasn't until she felt the warm brush of his lips upon her own that Norah's entrancement snapped. She reared back, pushing against the force of his palm, levering with her hands upon his wet chest for a saving distance. So close. She'd come so close to forgetting—everything.

"You can tend to it yourself, Rory Prescott."

He leaned against the rim of the tub, smiling loosely. "But you seemed to be enjoying yourself so much I didn't have the heart to interrupt."

She mumbled a curse at her own folly and struggled to her feet. He continued to grin. She wasn't aware that the dampness had molded her bodice to her with a revealing transparency. She wouldn't have been amused by his appreciation. Finally, his eyes slid shut and he was content to soak in the filmy water. Grasping for composure, Norah cast about for some bit of impersonal busy work. Her chest was hurting from the vigorous pounding of her heart. She was wondering about his kiss, wondering if it could still melt the soul with a single, sensuous stroke. His kiss had been her undoing in the first place. She'd never found a way to recover from its devastation—and didn't want to test to see if that were still true.

"Here. Make yourself a little more presentable."

He slit open one brown eye and then took the toothbrush from her. After a few minutes of purposeful scouring, he scooped up water from the tub to swish around in his mouth, then spat with deadly accuracy for the sink. His tongue rimmed the even line of his teeth experimentally and he nodded. "Least I don't taste like I swallowed my socks no more." He put out his hand. "Help me out, honey. This water's damned cold and I'm shriveling up to nothing."

What a liar! She knew the truth explicitly the moment he stood and she saw how the dampness coaxed his long johns to hug about his man parts. She would have retreated immediately but he had her by the shoulders, needing her steady figure to balance out his own lack of equilibrium as he stepped down from the tub. He tottered, leaning into her with a suspect amount of helplessness that let his cheek rub against her hair and his arms constrict to tuck her closer to the wet planes of his body. And for a moment, she allowed it. But not for long enough.

Norah wiggled away, tossing him a towel without risking another eyeball-scorching look. "Here. Get out of those wet things and get to ged."

"Yes, ma'am."

She should have been wary of his quick compliance but she was too eager to escape the suddenly steamy confines of the bath. The hall was cooler and she was able to suck a decent breath. Oh, my. This was not going well at all. She was as dizzy as the first time she'd ever seen him in a state of undress. How could she still be giddy after eight years? Maybe because for three of them she'd been dreaming about the sight that had just filled her eyes.

Calm down, Norah. So what if he's possessed of the most fabulous form you've ever seen—and you want him so bad your mind has gone to mush! She had to distract herself from those basic facts.

She hurried across the hall to the room which should be, if she remembered the floor plans rightly, the master bedroom. She'd just turn down the quilt, then go to look in on Jacob. That was her plan; but the moment she stepped inside, an ache of wistfulness overcame her. This was where she and Rory were to have spent their wedded nights. It was huge and airy, just as she'd pictured it would be. But instead of bearing Rory's stark masculine stamp, the furnishings were of a lighter wood and the wallpapering soft, more to her taste than his. He'd decorated it for her. Somehow that was even more devastating than the knowledge that he'd finished the house. He had to have somewhere to live but he didn't have to live amid her memory.

Scattered about the room with a comfortable sense of belonging were the things she'd brought from Baltimore. Ruth had mistakenly placed them in among her husband's. It made an intimate scene, a very wrong scene, forcing the panic she'd felt when crossing onto Kincaid ground to crest in mighty objection. Were Scott and Aurora Prescott the only ones who realized three years had passed? Were they the only ones who didn't blindly accept her presence back among them? Even Rory, who had practically thrown her out of his life, was acting as though it was commonplace to look up and see her standing there. How was she supposed to keep her distance from all of them when they behaved as though she'd never left?

Norah started to turn, needing to flee this secluded

41

paradise fashioned for a man and wife. And she ran smack into an unyielding barrier. Rory's hands spanned her trim waist, partly to steady her, partly to secure her flush against him. It was then she felt him pressing hard and large into her belly. He wasn't wearing the sodden long johns. Or the towel. Or anything else. Her eyes flew up, fastening wildly on his.

"You tole me to shuck out of them wet drawers," he explained with a sultry patience. "Ain't this better?"

"No." That frantic 'No' encompassed everything; her answer to his question, her denial of her own weakening will, her refusal to step right back into his arms after all that had passed between them. How could he think she would? Angered and more than a little afraid of the effect his closeness had on her entire system, she shoved at him. It was like trying to topple a Badlands butte.

"Norah."

That low, crooning whisper rippled along her raw nerve endings like liquid fire. She trembled in body and mind. Those tremors grew to quakes of soul-shattering intensity as his head dipped down, his eyes sliding closed, his lips parting. With the last ounce of her resolve, she twisted her face away, moaning, "Rory, no." But she couldn't break away, not physically, not emotionally.

He didn't kiss her. Norah was dazed by the surprise of it. And more deeply, she was disappointed. He nudged his head up against the side of hers and simply stood, the breath easing from him in a great, heaving sigh.

"Jus' let me hang onto you for a minute, Norah. I ain't had nobody to hold to in a long time."

There was such desperate loneliness, such elo-

42

quent despair in his voice that she found herself unable to resist being gathered tight into his strong embrace. She could feel his breaking heart banging within the wall of his chest, a hard pulse of anguish beneath a stretch of warm, moist skin. And she could feel her will softening. Like hot wax.

"I need you, Norah," he whispered low into the stylish twist of her sable-colored hair. "I'm so tired an' scared an' my head's scrambled in a dozen directions. I jus' been a-sitting there, waiting for my daddy to die, not being able to do nothing about it." He took a ragged breath and then it was Norah, holding to him. "I need you, Norah 'cause you doan need no words to tell you how I'm feeling. I got no words left. I got nothing left inside but hurtin'. Doan leave me alone. I been alone for so long."

Norah leaned away, just far enough to see his face so she could watch the way his dark eyes rolled and drifted shut as her palm soothed over the rough plain of his cheek. With a sound that was half-sob, half-sigh, she lifted up for his mouth. For a moment, he let her kiss him, not doing much to respond, just savoring the softness and the seeking hunger of her lips on his. Then, his began to move. A brush of breath over the inviting dampness of her mouth followed by the light trace of his tongue and finally, when she was quivering and clinging to him in expectation, a masterful conquest of each willing curve and the surrendering sweetness beyond.

"Oh . . , Rory," she breathed rapturously, lost and loving it. Her arms had come up to encircle his neck and her body arched against his, wanting what the taste of his kiss promised. A taste that was fresh with just a husky hint of whiskey and a liberal dose of desire for a chaser. And she drank it down greedily, having thirsted for three years.

"Lay down with me, Norah."

It wasn't really a request, that throaty growl that sent anticipation spiking through her pulse points. And he didn't wait for a reply. Keeping her occupied with his plunging kisses, he carried her to the edge of his bed—their bed—and slowly fell with her atop its welcoming softness. Norah began to twist and slide. It wasn't an attempt to escape him. Her arms clasped him tight as she shifted toward the center of the big bed, dragging him with her until they'd reached a comfortable spot to continue the seduction of their senses. And there, he continued his kisses, drugging her with passion, delighting her with his consummate skill. When she would tear at his back and shoulders with restless hands, he caught them both, enmeshing their fingers and pressing them deep into the downy folds of the comforter.

"Let me make love to you, Norah. I want to be inside you. I want to reach all the way up to your soul."

"Yes," she heard herself say in an impatient, panting, little voice. She wanted it, too, wanted his loving, wanted him so badly her body cried out with spasming shocks of pleasure wherever he moved against her. He'd stripped her raw of all but sensations, and she wanted to experience them beyond the limits of control.

He lowered his head to nuzzle between her breasts, tonguing her nipples through the damp veil of cotton until she was whimpering almost mindlessly. He caught at the tiny ribbon-ties with his teeth, tugging with a determined leisure to separate the closing of her chemise. Then he drove her to the point of distraction with the flirtatious attention he paid each pouting peak. He'd been moving above her, rucking up her petticoat with a rocking friction

44

until she could feel him, hot and huge at the junction of her thighs. And when he murmured, low and sultry sweet, "Open up for me, honey," she was quick to invite him in with the spread of her knees and arch of her hips. And as he sank and settled deep and full, no satisfaction could be mightier, no pleasure stronger.

"God, you feel good," he sighed, moving slightly to make her fingers convulse about his. He lifted up to look down upon her through eyes so dark and drenched with a wondering contentment she simply dissolved beneath him.

"Rory," she whispered thickly. She pulled her hands free so she could bury her fingers in the thatch of damp red hair, so she could draw him down to meet the needy insistence of her lips, so she could weep in total abandon alongside his ear, "It's been too long. Oh, Rory, I've missed you so much. I love you so much."

Then it was impossible to speak, to frame words or even simple thoughts as the exquisite heat of him began its push and pull. Building slowly, strongly until she had to bite down on his shoulder to contain her completing cries. Wonderful, shattering bursts of fulfillment too-long denied. And then she pressed her face into the hot cove of his throat while the same spectacular end shook through him.

The sound of their mingled breathing, hoarse and quick, was followed by replete murmurings and finally silenced by Rory's long, tender kiss. He shifted, ending the most perfect union of man and wife to ease over onto his back with a heartfelt moan of relief. Norah followed, rolling up to lean upon him, kissing his lips, his face, his neck, his chest, returning to where his mouth had relaxed into a sleepy bend of pleasure. He looked up at her, gaze lambent and consuming, and he smiled as his eyes sagged in a surrender to weariness.

"I knew you'd come back. I knew you'd come home to me."

And with that quiet confidence, he was asleep.

Was it that simple? A needy embrace, a mind-numbing kiss, a bout of soul-shaking loving? Was that all it took to erase three years of heartache and loneliness? Could they wake up together as if all the problems were pushed aside by a vow of love? She'd told him she loved him. And it was true. So true it scared her half to death with the force of its deep, relentless power. But then she'd never stopped loving him, even as the angry words were battered back and forth, even as she drove away from the home he'd promised to make for her and their son. Loving him and making love with him hadn't been the problem. Loving him hadn't made a difference. As much as she'd wanted to believe it could, it hadn't. And it wouldn't now.

Norah watched as slumber eased the lines of tension and fatigue from the features of the man beside her until he was once again the handsome, carefree young cowboy she'd rescued from a darkened boardwalk so many years ago. Simple? Nothing was ever simple where Rory Prescott was concerned. He could be as playful and lovable as a pup one second and as coldly dangerous as a snarling timberwolf guarding territory the next. She'd fallen head over heels for his sassy smile, his smoldery eyes, his tight Levis, and his heart-snatching kiss. It had taken all of one evening for love to wind around her soul—but a little longer for her head to admit it. She'd seen a deep, abiding goodness in him that made her believe anything possible. Even the forgiveness of her past. Even the doubts of a wary heart. He had promised her a love that would last a lifetime. And he was right. She couldn't imagine ever getting over the way her pulse raced at the sight of him. He'd made other promises, too. That they'd be happy together, that she'd never regret trusting him, that he'd never hurt her. And maybe he could have kept them had things been different. If they hadn't had to start over with nothing. If she hadn't discovered she was pregnant even before their vows were spoken. If he hadn't knelt beside his grandfather's ashes and made a promise that overshadowed all others. She'd never wanted anything as much in her whole life as this Dakota cowboy, and leaving him had been the hardest thing she'd ever done.

It didn't matter now if she'd been right to leave him when she had. What mattered was his failure to come after her. Another broken vow. He'd stayed between his broad green horizons, breeding his cattle, rebuilding his grandfather's empire. And even though he'd made a place for her on his rolling prairie, he'd never invited her to join him there.

And he hadn't told her he still loved her.

Sure, he'd greeted her with arms open and kisses eager. Because he was afraid and lonely and willing for the moment to depend upon her strength. But needing her and wanting to exhaust himself inside her wasn't the same as loving her. And it didn't mean he'd be willing to change one fraction of his stubborn Kincaid mind when he awoke tomorrow. All it meant was that he'd waited for her to come back and was willing to let her stay. And that wasn't saying nearly enough.

With a very gentle hand, Norah brushed the strands of drying red hair from his troublefree brow. She couldn't resist the need to feel the strong angles of his face beneath the trace of her fingertips. Her thumb rubbed over the swell of his lower lip and he smiled faintly in his sleep. *Oh, Rory, you were all I wanted. Why was that too much to ask?*

It shouldn't have been, a colder logic answered. He should have been thinking of his wife and his son instead of his promise to a greedy old man who'd died in a hell of his own making. But he hadn't then, and she should have waited to find out if that had changed before falling back into his arms and into his bed. She'd left him because of principles that wouldn't allow her to stay. If he woke up in the morning to find her snuggled into his side, how could she ever convince him that those same principles still mattered? What would keep him from believing that she'd come crawling back to him without a scrap of pride? And if he rolled up over her in the morning and filled her with that same burning passion, could she deny it was true? She had very little shame where his loving was concerned.

Even now, when she still throbbed warmly from his possession, Norah wanted him. The temptation to wake him, to beg for his fantastic loving, to curl up in his arms for a blissful slumber was almost impossible to overcome. Rory Prescott was too dangerous at close and personal quarters. If she couldn't resist the temptation, she would have to remove herself from it.

She stretched up, touching her lips to the soft cushion of his mouth, fighting not to lose herself again to that taste of paradise. "I love you, Rory Prescott," she whispered with a gritty softness. "I want to live with you as your wife. Please make it possible. Please."

He was smiling even as he awoke. Before his eyes

48

had a chance to open, he was reaching out across the sheets beside him, fingers stretching, heart swelling, body stirring. Until he came to the edge without encountering a single soft obstruction. What . . .? Norah?

He started to say her name out loud, and it was then Rory realized she wasn't there. Had never been there. Never on any of the three years of mornings he'd woken up alone from dreams so real he was sure he'd find her. He should have been used to the disappointment; but somehow, this morning, it was worse than most.

Oh, Rory, I miss you so much . . . I love you so much. Words he'd give anything he owned and everything he was to hear her say again. He lay there for the longest time struggling to find the motivating push that would get him up and moving. The Bar K. That usually coaxed him. But not today. Hell, the Bar K could get by without him this one time. If he closed his eyes fast enough and thought hard enough, maybe the threads of the dream would return and he could pretend, for a little while, that things were good again. He was just about to drift off when the fragments of his thinking fit together. Daddy.

He sat up quick, too quick, and dropped right back down with an awful moan. His head was clamoring something fierce inside like something mean was in there trying to kick its way out.

"Oooh . . . I ain't never, ever gonna drink another drop of whiskey as long as I live," he swore with the fervency of a temperance convert. How had he ever gotten home—let alone out of his clothes and clean? What he could remember was vague, a blur through too many tears and too many drinks at Ethan Prescott's bedside. Where he should be now. God, what if something had happened while he wasn't there!

Lord love Ruth for draping a clean set of clothes out over the back of his chair and lining his boots up in front of it. Norah used to do it that way. He swallowed hard, surprised by the thick achiness in his throat. He was worn down. That's what it was. That's why he was thinking of Norah and feeling low enough to start in bawling like a lost calf. Coffee. That would cut through the maudlin turn of thoughts. Coffee and good crisp Dakota air.

He dragged himself out of bed and promptly jammed his toe against a box he couldn't remember leaving out. Gone a couple of days and already he was forgetting where to put his feet in his own room. What he needed was a couple more nights like the last one with hours of undisturbed rest. And he needed to see his daddy up and around again. He got dressed in a haphazard fashion, then felt the raspiness of his chin. Before he tackled shaving maybe it would be wise to doctor up his coffee some, lest he end up cutting his own throat with the shakiness of his hands. He thought about breakfast. Someone had been nagging on him about eating breakfast. He'd grab something at the Lone Star if he'd managed to tame the rebellion in his belly by then. Food, once a priority in his minute-to-minute concerns, had lost its charm. Not even his mama's biscuits could provoke a fraction of his former appetite. Too many things to think on to be concentrating on moving around eating utensils and chewing. Whiskey and worry dulled the edge of hunger.

Bathe, sleep, and eat a good breakfast.

He frowned and found himself listening for the sound of that voice in his memory. Then he shook his head, dismissing it as fancy. But maybe he would get himself something fortifying before saddling up.

It was quiet in the big house. It was always too quiet for his liking. As if nobody lived within its walls. Ruth had a room of her own back by the kitchen, and at the mid-morning hour everything was silent as a tomb. His Cuban heels made an unnatural clatter on the steps, and he hated that he should feel like tiptoeing in his own house.

He ambled by the parlor then drew up and backtraced his steps. There, seated nearly as stiff as his starched collar on one of the uncomfortable sofas, was a strange little boy in a prissy suit. They exchanged a long curious look, the boy through steel-rimmed spectacles and Rory through the fog of several days excess.

"Howdy," Rory mumbled at last. Who'd he know that had a boy? His mind was too slow to snag on an answer.

"Hello, sir." He was on his feet as if propelled by a taut spring.

"Well, hell. Ain't you the proper one. Look like you're fixing to salute."

"Aren't."

Rory blinked. "What?"

"Aren't not ain't. My mother says bad grammar is a sign of ignorance."

"That right," the big cowboy drawled out with less than his usual humor. He eyeballed the boy, just a skinny little fella in those sissy clothes with one heck of a large chip of arrogance on his narrow shoulder. "And who might your mama be? Does she know you're running loose a-sassin' your elders?"

The boy never so much as twitched. Rory'd seen hanging judges with a more personable look about them. Then he looked, really looked, at the boy.

51

Looked beyond the stuffy velvet and lace. Behind the somber spectacles. At hair that was a deep burnished auburn, at eyes that were clear and cool and grey. The spitting image of . . . his mama's.

"Oh . . . God."

His knees felt dangerously close to collapse. He needed to sit and sit fast but he couldn't uproot himself from the spot, from staring at the unfamiliar seven—going—on—eight—year old. Because he was stunned right down to the bootheels with the knowledge that if the boy were here in his house, so was—

Her voice sounded from behind him, the low, husky tones blasting a hole through his heart the way his daddy's Sharps would at close range.

"I see you've met Jacob."

Rory turned slowly. No way was he prepared for the sight of her standing on the bottom of the stairs. It slapped the wind out of him like a fall from a good bucking horse. He stood for a long moment trying to suck air, trying to overcome the massive shock. Trying to comprehend in the numb confusion of his mind that the someday he'd been longing for was today.

Danged if she didn't look as good to him as she had to a dumb, awe-struck cowboy when he was a green twenty years old. He remembered gazing up from an undignified position in the muddy middle of a Deadwood street. His heart had been snatched from him with one look into the crystal-clear eyes of the most beautiful woman he'd ever seen. And he'd never gotten it back. She hadn't changed. She was still his cool, sophisticated Norah, dressed to the height of style in her complicated Eastern clothes. Inapproachable, untouchable, and yet so damned desirable. Dreams and time-faded memory couldn't touch on the soul-numbing loveliness of Norah Denby Prescott. They couldn't capture the dew-kissed glow of her skin that excited sensations of touch and taste he was half-mad to experience again. They couldn't recreate the illuminating sheen of sunlight upon the thick waves of sable hair that had his fingers itching to sink themselves in it. Nor could they in any way knock him breathless and speechless and mindless all at once until all he was dizzily aware of was her. She'd come home to him.

"Hello, Rory."

The whiskey-warm ripple of her voice woke him from his stupor of surprise. He grabbed for a quick breath to clear the spinning in his head. Norah. She'd come back. He'd known she would. He'd just never expected. . . . Tremendous waves of gladness won over those of disbelief. All he could think of was cinching her up in his arms and squeezing her tight. Of kissing her until the sweet shock of the moment gave way to the reality of knowing her luscious lips again. He took an anxious step forward. And she took one back.

That's when true reality struck him. He saw the distancing chill of her stare, the unsmiling line of her lips. And it knocked him back on his heels like a cruel slap. If she'd come home to him, why wasn't she wrapped around him in welcome? Uncertainty checked him and pride provoked the harsh memory of their parting. He sure as hell wasn't going to crumple all to pieces before he knew the meaning behind her reserve. Reining in his emotions, he stood stock-still and regarded the woman who'd left him three years ago. And he spoke to her softly, with words underlaid in steel.

"Why you here, Norah? Come to check on your investment?"

Chapter Four

The first words out of his mouth and they cut like a Blue Norther. Nothing had changed. She was crazy to have thought it might. To him, everything was still in terms of the Bar K. As if she'd come halfway across the country just to invade his precious grassland. All his sweet words of the night before were conveniently forgotten. She'd poured out heart and soul, and it hadn't mattered in the least. Just for a second, she'd seen everything she'd longed for in his eyes—the loving, the wanting, the needing—and she'd been ready to launch herself into his arms to beg for a new beginning. Then that damned Kincaid pride had pushed everything else aside and shut her out tight. And she could never let him see how much that hurt her.

Cool grey eyes narrowed, and Rory could see the frost of temper forming. When she spoke, her words were deceivingly civil.

"I have no interest in this land or in anything on it."

Including me, he summed up grimly. God, what a fool he was. If she'd cared, she wouldn't have left in the first place. And here he'd been hoping . . .

"Why'd you come back?" That was an unfriendly growl.

"Because I heard about your father."

"Oh." Rory backed down, prickliness punctured by the soft concern in her reply. There was no way to cap the sudden well of feeling, the anguish that would drop him to his knees if she made the slightest move toward him. But she held to her distance, offering sympathy, not comfort.

"I'm sorry, Rory. Maybe I shouldn't have come. If you want me to go—"

"No." That came out like a shot, and the intensity startled them both. He took a stabilizing breath and said, "No, it's all right. You got a right to be here. Daddy'd be glad to see you." He finger-combed his untidy hair, agitated and unable to express himself. Resolutely, he tucked in the ragged shirttails of his emotions. He couldn't have them flapping around like yesterday's wash in the face of Norah's collected calm. She hadn't come to ease the burden of his pain. She hadn't come for him at all. Shattered by that truth, he turned away, striding for his study.

Norah followed more slowly, finding him behind his big desk tossing back a bracing shot of rye. Wordlessly, he refilled his glass and poured another for her. No gentleman in Baltimore would think to offer a lady straight whiskey or any form of spirits before noon, but then Rory Prescott had known her long before she was a lady. She crossed to the desktop, reaching for the glass just as Rory was reaching up with his gaze. For a moment, they were both lost in one another. Then Norah grabbed up her glass and recklessly drained it. The burn of the liquor gave back the breath Rory's simmering stare stole from her.

"How'd you hear about Daddy?" he asked at last. When Norah repeated what she'd told Gena he looked just as disappointed. "Scotty's not coming home?" He swore softly and swiveled his chair toward the wide vista of mullioned glass behind him. "I need him here."

Norah closed the space between them, hovering behind his chair, wanting to ease his desolation with the gentle claim of, *I'm here.* But she didn't. Instead, she asked quietly, "What happened to Ethan?"

She watched the disparaging rise and fall of the broad shoulders.

"I been trying to break in a maverick for Dawn. You ain't never seen a bronc so danged hard-jawed. Ornery as the day's long and just plain cussed mean, but she wouldn't have another. Tore his leg up kicking through the stall door and Daddy come over to fix it up. Nicked him in the forehead with one of his hooves. Laid him out cold and he ain't never come 'round. The doc that come out to look at him said the longer he was out, the less chance of him waking up again. It's been a week." He pulled a long breath and let it out savagely. "I knew that horse was trouble. I shoulda shot the sonuvabitch instead of trying to impress Dawn by trying to tame it. If it weren't for me being so danged stubborn—"

"No," Norah told him fiercely. "It's not your fault. It's not." She followed that convincing fact with the stroke of her palm along one rigid cheek. Before she could withdraw, he caught her hand, squeezing it tight, scraping his rough jaw in its smooth concave. Then simply holding it, brushing his lips across the ridge of her knuckles in a way that weakened her knees.

"Rory . . ."

"Mama?"

The brittle little voice from the doorway drew them both around. Jacob stood there, his gaze shifting between them uneasily.

"When are we leaving?"

"Leavin'?" Rory echoed with a touch of panic. His dark eyes flew up to Norah's. "You ain't going nowheres. Are you?"

Norah thought of the big bed upstairs and mumbled hastily, "Maybe it would be better if we stayed in town."

"You ain't staying in no hotel. You'n the boy take the upstairs rooms. I'll bunk out with the hands."

"I don't know—"

"'Fraid of what folks'll think? We're still married, Norah. What can they say?"

She wasn't afraid of anyone but Rory Prescott and of her own inability to remain immune to him.

Seeing she still hesitated, he drawled icily, "It's your house, Norah. It's only right that if anyone should leave, it'd be me."

Her reply was equally cool. "Fine. We'll stay."

"Mama!" Jacob was clearly distressed by her decision, but he came stiffly to Norah's side when she extended her hand.

"This way," she explained softly as she rumpled the thick wavy hair, "you and your father will get a chance to know each other better."

That idea plainly didn't please the little boy. From the safe cove of his mother's arm, he eyed the big, redheaded stranger with a remote curiosity, the way he'd examine some new species of life he feared might be dangerous. He took in the rough clothes, the crude manner of speech, the harsh scent of drink and recoiled uneasily. Only his mother's firm embrace anchored him in place.

"Doan you remember me, son?" Rory flinched when the boy shook his head slightly. "C'mere so's I can get a better look at you."

It took Norah's compelling push to nudge him around the corner of the desk to stand before his father. A fact not lost on Rory. His son. This was the boy he'd wondered over and missed the way he'd miss a part severed from his own body. He was scared by what he saw because it was so unfamiliar. Pale, fragile-looking, coolly reserved. This was what Norah had made of his son. He'd dreamed long and longingly of having the opportunity to crush his boy close, but hugging the somber child before him seemed somehow inappropriate. Instead, he put out his hand.

"Welcome to the Bar K, Jacob."

The small hand slipped into his for a civil clasp then quickly withdrew.

"Rory! Rory!"

The jubilant shouts where accompanied by the thunder of hoofbeats up to the porch steps. A female voice. Norah stiffened before she recognized the childlike quality in it. Rory surged up out of his chair, sending Jacob scurrying back to the safety of her skirts when suddenly confronted by six-foot-plus inches towering over him. Rory strode from the room and Norah hurried after, stepping out into the bright morning light just in time to see a lithe figure launch directly from the saddle into his arms. She caught the flash of a fiery braid and realized that this was Dawn, Scott's daughter, wrapped around Rory with exuberant glee.

"Rory, it's Grampa. He's up and asking for you."

"What? When? Oh, God! Oh, thank God!" Then he bussed a quick kiss on the girl's cheek and tossed her back up into the saddle. "You go on down to the barn and have one of the boys hitch up the buggy. And you tell your mama to have a big breakfast waiting." His palm slapped against the rump of her horse and it bolted toward the corrals with a kick of dust. He turned toward Norah, grin blinding, eyes shiny, and she was instantly lost in his embrace. He spun her around and around with a loud "Whooee," both of them laughing until the circles slowed and awareness stirred.

Dear God, she felt good against him, all soft in the right places and sweetly clinging. The intoxicating scent of her hair, the joy of the moment, the curl of her arms about his neck conspired into a gladsome warmth of heart. And when the revolutions stopped and he held her to his chest, her toes dangling free of the ground and her eyes lifting to his, it was perfect. Her hand touched the back of his head, fingers teasing gently through the shaggy nap and trailing along his throat to where his pulse beat hard and fast. And she smiled very softly.

"You can put me down now, Rory."

"I doan want to."

"We don't want to keep your family waiting."

That 'we' and the press of her palms on his chest had the desired affect. He eased her to the ground and let her slip away from the light span of his hands about her waist. By then, one of the Bar K crew had delivered up the buggy, doffing his hat and declaring, "Howdy, Miz Norah. Mighty nice to have you back, ma'am," as he hopped down.

"Thank you, Sammy." She put out her hand and let him assist her up. "Come on, Jacob."

When the boy hesitated, Rory whisked him off the porch and deposited him beside his wife before climbing up to take the reins. With his family wedged, stiff and silent, on the single bench seat, he headed the horse toward the Lone Star.

*   *   *

"If that doan beat all," came a leisurely drawl from the doorway. "Whatcha doing lolligagging in that there bed with the womenfolk fussin' over you when you gots work outside that needs doing? I ain't doing it. Nossir. So you best be figurin' on how fast you can get to it yourself 'cause you look too dang healthy to get me feeling sorry for you."

Ethan Prescott grinned up at his son from the bolster of bed pillows. "Jus' waiting for you to come rescue me from the good intentions of these here ladies. Rory, you tell your mama to leave off her pestering afore she pampers me into turning up my toes."

Rory sauntered up to where his mother perched weepy-eyed on the bedside and soothed his big hands over her shoulders. "Let him breathe, Mama. He ain't going nowheres." When she stood, he absorbed the tearful aftershocks of her relief within the circle of a hug. "How 'bout some of your biscuits, Mama? I could smell 'em baking all the way over at the Bar K."

Aurora leaned back, drawing energy and control from the calm spread of her son's smile. His attitude told her without words that things were fine and it was time to get on with their lives. She touched his cheek briefly. "Don't let him try anything foolish, Rory. He's not getting out of that bed. For a doctor, you haven't a lick of sense, Ethan Prescott."

"I'll see he behaves, Mama." He grinned at his father and assumed Aurora's spot on the edge of the mattress while she lingered, holding to his hand. "How you feelin', Daddy?"

"Like a horse kicked me. To hear her tell it, I should be dragging dirt in over me. Why a man'd want to ruin a perfectly good life by marrying a nagging woman I'll never—" He broke off as Rory's dark eyes canted down uncomfortably. Before he could apologize for his clumsiness, his son's grin was back, wide and warm and wickedly pleased with some secret knowledge. And looking up at him, Ethan wondered what had put the spark back into his boy's soul.

"You deserve it, Daddy, scaring us all outta ten prime years of life like you done."

"You ain't planning to harp on me, too, are you? Iffen you are, you can just follow your mama out that door."

"Nossir. I'll leave the scolding to Mama. I brung you a surprise." His eyes danced with a long absent deviltry that got his father even more curious. "Look who's here to see you."

Ethan was expecting to see Scott, but never in a hundred years did he plan on the appearance of the sleek sophisticate his rowdy son had roped and wed. And lost. As soon as the shock wore off, he offered up a big Texas welcome.

"Howdy there, Norah. You're sure a sight worth waking up to."

Her uneasiness at being in the Prescott's home fled. Norah skirted her mother-in-law and bent to place a fond kiss just below the bandage. "Hello, Ethan. If I didn't know better, I'd think you were playing possum just to bring me all the way out here from Baltimore."

His bearded cheeks jerked with a smile. "Wish I'd thought of it sooner." Then he was looking toward the doorway. Hopeful. "You didn't come all the way on your lonesome, did you?"

"No." She patted his shoulder gently and stood, calling, "Jacob."

There was a sharp intake of breath from both grandparents as the boy answered his mother's summons. Wringing Rory's hand, Aurora glanced from grandson to son in askance. Rory smiled and gave a slight nod. She was across the room in a swirl of petticoats and on her knees to envelop the child, unashamedly weeping.

"Ora, don't drown the boy before I get a good look at him."

Norah stayed back out of the way, giving them the moment with her son. She didn't want to interfere in the tender reunion, yet couldn't help but feel the pang of exclusion. Then Rory's hand settled against the curve of her spine, gently bracing, lightly supporting. And without a thought, she stepped closer into his side as they watched the fawning grandparents with the child they'd made between them. Jacob cast an uncertain appeal toward Norah; and when she smiled encouragingly, he went to sink into his grandfather's embrace.

"Well," Rory declared a bit gruffly. "Looks like if I want to get any breakfast 'round here, I'm going to have to do for myself. C'mon, honey, I'll stand you to some coffee." Keeping his hand snug against the silk of her waist, he steered Norah out into the big outer room. "He'll be all right," he told her softly when her gaze lingered behind.

"I know."

"Thank you, Norah."

He said it with a heart-clutching simplicity, then left her, heading for the kitchen.

"Oh, Rory, isn't it wonderful?"

With that, Gena supplied a happy hug and a full cup of coffee. He received both gratefully, then dropped down into one of the kitchen chairs. It took a second or two for everything to settle in upon him. First the cup in his hand began to shake, then his shoulders. Then Gena was kneeling, holding him as the flood of relief broke loose.

And from the doorway, Norah stood silent and watched. Excluded.

They spent the day at the Lone Star. Despite his claim stating otherwise, Rory saw to the neglected duties around the ranch while Norah pitched in to help Gena with the household chores. If Aurora wasn't pleased by the situation, she said nothing, willing to make that compromise for the chance to visit with her grandson. Instead of helping her mother, Dawn dogged Rory's heels like a pup.

"She thinks the world of him," Gena said, seeing the direction of Norah's gaze. "With Scott gone so often, she's a regular little shadow. They keep each other company."

Norah made no comment. Gena wasn't chiding her for her own absence anymore than she was faulting her husband for his. She was just stating fact. And fact woke a peculiar pain as she watched the two bright heads bend over a horse's hoof. That was the way it should be with father and son and never would be with Rory and Jacob. She thought of the welling pride in her husband's dark eyes as his parents embraced his son. A father's pride long denied him. And soon to be denied again. She forced away a swell of remorse and almost angrily grabbed up the pile of wash remaining. And as she stalked out to hang it on the line, she didn't see Gena smiling after her.

It was nearly nightfall before the last of the supper dishes were stacked away and Ethan left to a restful sleep. The buggy was hitched, and Aurora was faced with the difficulty of turning her grandson over to his mother. With her hands on either narrow shoulder, she confronted the cool gaze of her daughter-in-law and forced the necessary words.

"Thank you for allowing us to spend time with Jacob."

How that must have killed her, Norah thought wryly. "Did you think I wouldn't?"

When Rory angled up behind his wife to band her shoulders with the curl of his arm, Aurora wisely refrained from her answer. Instead, she said diplomatically, "I hope you'll let him come visit again."

As Jacob came to her and she claimed him with a motherly embrace, Norah replied, "He can come over as often as he likes as long as we're here."

As long as we're here.

Those five words hit Rory like a pattern of buckshot. He was still trying to recover when Dawn burst in to announce, "I've saddled your horse for you, Rory."

His horse? How had he gotten back to the Bar K last night without his horse? His mind was finally clear enough to let those questions in, but the time wasn't right to ask them. With his worries over his father and the Lone Star at an ease, he was ready and anxious to see to those closer to home.

"Let's go, honey," he murmured soft and low, moving his hand along the curve of Norah's back as he spoke. He could feel the rejecting tension beneath that touch. Though she didn't step away from him, she didn't permit him the illusion that things were fine between them. She left no doubt that when they left the Lone Star, the image they made as family rallying at Ethan Prescott's bedside would quickly evaporate. And though he wanted to cling to it, to the freedom that allowed him to touch her and hold her when in the presence of others, Rory knew he couldn't.

Stoically, he handed his wife and son up into the

buggy and went around to untether his horse. Aurora was standing on the bottom step, her arms wrapped close about her as she watched the three of them readying to leave. When Rory approached, she was quick to hug him tight.

"Don't let her hurt you," she whispered with a mother's protective fury. She was surprised by the rumbling feel of his laugh beneath her cheek.

"Now just how the hell am I going keep that from happenin'?" He moved back, smiling with a bitter-sweet amusement. "Good night, Mama. I—we'll stop on by tomorrow."

They were silent, those miles between the two ranches. Norah didn't shift her eyes from the vee between the horse's ears, but she was very aware of Rory riding escort beside the buggy. And she was just as aware that the truce between them would not last much longer. The intensity mounted like a summer storm, hot and dangerous. Maybe she should have stayed in Crowe Creek. At the Bar K, there was just Ruth and Jacob. And Rory. Too late for doubts now as they pulled up before the vague silhouette of the house. Lights burned in the interior, casting the porch in shadow. It seemed—isolated.

Jacob's weight was heavy against her. He'd fallen asleep on the rocking journey overland. Rory reached up for him, carrying him easily, cradling the boy's head upon his shoulder: and, for a moment, she could see his expression, so etched with poignant emotion it rendered her helpless. With his free hand, he assisted her down and left his fingers resting gently upon the contour of her waist. The scene felt so right. Husband-father. Wife-mother. Norah walked beside him, panic quivering inside, up onto the porch and into the house, door banging softly be-hind them.

65

Jacob woke with a start and immediately resisted the unfamiliar embrace. As much as Rory wanted to hold to him longer, he let him down and watched the boy move to a safe distance. A disoriented gaze sought the figure of his mother. Rory's voice was rough-edged in its quiet command.

"Go on upstairs and get yourself ready for bed, son. I'll send your mama up in a little bit to tuck you in."

Jacob waited for his mother's nod before muttering, "Yes, sir."

"You don't need to be calling me sir. I'm your daddy."

The cool grey eyes lifted with a hint of stubborn challenge. "Yes, sir," he repeated, then fled up the steps without a backward glance or a word of good night.

"He doan like me much." That was a sad statement of fact.

"Give him time."

"How much time you givin' me, Norah?"

He walked away before she could answer, into the darkness of his study where there was a clink of glass on glass. Norah followed cautiously. Her gaze detailed the big shadow he made against the moon-washed window. He stood looking out, his back to her. Not a threatening pose, but she was still wary. She knew his moods were like the Dakota sky in which a tempest could blow up without a cloud of warning.

"How long?" he repeated softly.

"You didn't use the time you had with him, Rory."

"He was just a baby, and now he's half-growed. My own son and I doan even know him!" There was a snap of his arm as he took his drink down in a gulp.

"And whose fault is that?"

He turned then and skewered her with a dark, angry

66

glare that said it plain. Hers. She took him; she ran with him; she stole three years from him.

"No," Norah fired back with a thunderous force of calm. "Don't you dare blame that on me. Where were you when we were here waiting all alone? You couldn't spare one day, one hour, one minute for us. It's a little late to go crying about it now."

"I was building up our home."

"No." Her cry was a shout of outrage. "No. It wasn't for us. None of this was for us. It was for him. You did it for Garth Kincaid. You spent more time honoring a vow to a dead man than you spent with your wife and child."

"How can you say that?"

"I said it then and I still mean it now."

"Then why are you here? Why'd you come back?" Before she could speak, he cut in sharply. "And doan bother telling me it was because of my daddy. I know that ain't the all of it."

"It was because of you," she told him flatly, in such a way he couldn't take any satisfaction from it. "I wanted to give you and Jacob time together. I felt I owed it . . . to both of you. Please don't spoil it. Give him the chance to know you. But I'm warning you, Rory: You make it difficult for me, and I'll take him back to Baltimore and you won't see him again."

"Difficult." He mused over that word for a moment then chuckled. It was a soft sound but not necessarily a pleasant one. "Is that what I'm being? Difficult? I thought I was being down right charitable. Seems like we're always at odds in opinion now don't it, Norah-honey?"

"I don't want to fight with you."

"Hell, that ain't what I want either. I didn't spend the last three years planning on how I was gonna argue with you when you came home. No, ma'am.

67

Fighting ain't what I had in mind, a-tall."

He didn't move. He didn't attempt to close the space between them but suddenly it seemed to shrink down to nothing. His dark-eyed stare intensified into a whole new meaning of the word difficult. Norah countered the rise in heat with an increased chill of civility.

"Then we're agreed. For Jacob."

"For Jacob." He smiled ever so slightly.

"And you won't be—"

"Difficult? No, ma'am. I'll be as obliging as I know how to be." He was still smiling, and she didn't trust him one bit.

"Now that that's settled, I think I'll check on Jacob and turn in. You don't mind my taking your room?"

"It's your room, Norah. Always was. Make yourself at home."

"Thank you."

"Thank you . . . for what you did today. That was right nice of you to help out like you did. Reckon it's been a while since you had to do any of them things for yourself."

"I didn't mind."

You minded doing them for me. He didn't say it, and he had to turn away before she could read it in his moody stare. He didn't want to rock the tenuous truce they'd set between them. At least not with unpleasantness. Gazing back toward the unyielding figure of his wife, he asked unexpectedly, "Norah, how'd I get home last night?"

She was surprised and showed it. "I—I brought you."

"I don't remember it."

"None of it?" she questioned cautiously. Could it be he'd never heard her passionate declarations? Was that why his greeting had been so remote?

"Norah-honey, you don't mean to tell me that you tucked me in last night."

"Someone had to," she replied indignantly. "You were too stinking drunk to take care of yourself. Why, you would have drowned in the tub if I hadn't—"

His brows soared. She clamped her mouth shut. Color rose unbidden to her cheeks and Rory received a stunning shock of insight. Had it been a dream . . . or a memory? Did they . . . Had they . . . How the hell could he ask her such a thing? *Excuse me, Norah-honey, but I seem a bit blurry on the details. Did we make love last night? After waiting for it to happen for three long years, I just can't seem to recall.* If the answer were yes, she'd never get over the insult. If it were no, he'd never recover from the embarrassment. He settled for a tactful—if frustrating, middle-ground.

"I appreciate you seeing to me, Norah."

"I didn't mind," she answered, equally neutral. She took advantage of the moment to make an awkward retreat. "Well, good night then. I'll see you in the morning." That should clarify any wondering he might have had over where he was to spend the night. And she was a little confused over how easily he gave in.

"Say good night to Jacob for me."

She hesitated, at odds with her sudden reluctance to leave him. Finally, she turned and started for the stairs, only to be doubly surprised by the soft call of her name. She turned back and he was there, standing so close they were toe-to-toe. As her gaze flew upward, her heart gave a matching jump. She found herself quaking to the soul as he raised his hand slowly to brush gentle fingertips along her temple.

"Good night, Norah."

He said it low, like the sultry whisper of a hot

summer breeze. Her eyes slid shut as he leaned down and she was stretching up, anticipating the feel of his mouth. But not where he placed it, in a light press upon her brow. Her breath expelled in hasty confusion. Her eyes flew open to see the mocking heat in his. He took a step back and she nearly suffered sensory collapse.

"Sweet dreams, honey."

Then she remembered the image: The sleek cougar crouching on a branch, waiting for just the right time to spring. Patient. Watching. Dangerous. He'd flustered her into dropping her guard. She was going to have to be very careful because, when he decided to make his move, she didn't want to be caught unaware.

She warned him with the narrowing of her gaze that she wasn't fooled by his deceivingly quiet manner and her coldness set him back another step. Then he smiled again, a slow spreading smile of supreme male invitation.

"If you should have any trouble sleepin', I'll be right down here."

Her stare would have put ice atop boiling coffee. "Thank you, but I'm sure I will sleep just fine."

With that, she turned and began to climb the stairs, feeling the intensity of his stare following her up every step. Her retreat may have been one of majestic indifference; but inside, she was plagued by the truth.

What an incredible liar you are!

Chapter Five

Damn her!

Difficult.

What did she know about difficult?

Rory paced his study, whiskey warming in his hands with the same kind of friction heating his temper. Who'd she think she was coming back here to dictate conditions for him seeing his son? Who'd she think she was fooling claiming she'd come back because of Jacob when she all but begged for him to kiss her in the hall? Damned difficult woman, anyway!

But she was here. In his house and sleeping this very minute in the bed he'd be sharing with her before too long. Neither of them had the kind of pride that could best passion forever. They'd already learned that lesson once. What would it take for her to forget her fury and put her arms around him? How was he going to manage until she did?

Norah. God, he loved her. The sight of her, the feel of her, the aggravating strength of her. It wouldn't be easy pretending patience.

It was funny. Just knowing the two of them were upstairs filled this big unfriendly house. No way was he going to let them leave it. His wife. His son. Whatever it took. He'd made that vow to her once; and this time, he'd make good on it. Whatever she wanted right down to the stripping away of his pride. Right after she admitted she loved him. He'd hold out that long. If she owed him the time to know Jacob, she owed him the truth of why she'd returned. And the reason for why she'd run away. He could be patient when he had to be. But if she didn't give, if he had to press, he knew all there was to know about being difficult. And he'd show her no mercy.

He poured himself another drink and settled behind the mahogany desk. It was like the one his grandfather used to own. The Major'd be proud of all the work he'd done to save the Bar K since it had been ravaged by fire and debt. Hell, the debt part was still there. That was part of ranching these days. It was staying one step ahead of it that was tricky. There were always those eager to chip away an acre at a time from the grazing lands he'd managed to hang onto. It wasn't the Indians anymore or even the nesters, it was those danged Eastern developers who pushed the expansionist dream right along with railroad steel. They were the ones cutting up ranch lands in a useless checkerboard dotted with farmers. He took another drink and studied the papers spread out before him. They held offers from a big Eastern outfit hungering for his land. Not bad offers, but what they couldn't understand—tucked away in their lightless, airless buildings—was that it wasn't about money. He wouldn't sell at any price. Not as long as he had the means to graze and grain a single head of cattle.

He wasn't much for ornamentation, just a basic cowboy with a cowboy's disdain for pretty clutter. He had no use for art or fancy thingamabobs tacked up on the walls. The only beauty he needed to look upon was outside the window by the rolling mile and curled upstairs asleep. There were only two exceptions, and both were rather strange decorations. On the corner of his desk was a twist of barbed wire, crisped and blackened by fire. Beside it was a charred picture frame standing empty of all but ghosts. He didn't keep them for the sake of sentiment. They were there as harsh reminders that a man could lose everything in an instant unless he had the grit to hang on tight. From Ethan Prescott, he'd inherited his deep, quiet strength; but Garth Kincaid had taught him hard ambition. The kind that pushed a man relentlessly from dawn to dusk and had kept him sane these last three years. His daddy gave him peace of spirit, the Major toughness of mind. There was no right or left, just a straight line toward what he wanted. And that goal was very clear to him. His land, his lady, his son. And nobody, nothing, was going to take them from him.

Slowly, Rory spread his fingers out across the buy-out offers; and, just as slowly, he drew them in, balling up the sheets of paper into a wad. Nobody. Nothing. And if any of his family had gotten a look at him as he stared at that twist of wire and charred frame, they would have been chilled to the soul. Because they would have seen the embodiment of Garth Kincaid sitting in that big chair, making that ruthless vow.

How could he be comfortable like that? Observing the figure of his father, Jacob wondered if he should wake him. A six-foot-three-inch frame just wasn't meant for a sofa, yet Rory was sprawled out on the one in his study, torso twisted at an awkward angle, one leg dragging on the floor and the other propped up so that the rowel of his spurs creased the dark red-leather arm. He was snoring gently. Jacob wondered uneasily if his oblivion had to do with the empty bottle upended next to the dangle of one slack hand. But he was afraid of what had been in that bottle and of the bark of his father's voice should he be disturbed, so he kept his distance and his silence.

He hadn't told the entire truth. While he didn't actually remember the face and form of the big man draped along the sofa, he remembered lots of other things. Impressions more than images. He remembered a loud, boisterous laugh and the vibrations of a huskier chuckle. He remembered the sound of his mother's mixed in with it. He recalled the enveloping warmth of his father's arms about him and the soothing, rumbling baritone singing him to sleep. He could hear shouting, angry and ugly sounds, and then worse, the anguish of his mother's weeping. She never cried in Baltimore. But then she never really laughed, either. What he remembered most of all was the calming sense of security suddenly torn away.

A miserable groan heralded the first movements from the figure on the couch. Jacob's impulse to flee the room came a second too late as bleary eyes opened and he was greeted by a rusty mumble of, "'Morning."

Rory moaned and grumbled with each stretch of cramped muscle. The thundering in his head was no surprise, but the presence of the boy was. His son's somber gaze made him feel like something that had crawled out from under the porch. As he scrubbed his palms over his face, he heard the boy ask with a tentative concern, "Are you ill, sir?"

I'm hung over, he wanted to growl irritably. But that he couldn't say to a seven-year-old.

"My mother says only the slothful and inebriates

74

can't find their way to their own beds at night." His candid stare asked which applied to him. Since Rory didn't know the meaning of either word, he had no reply.

"Your mama tends to talk a might too much these days. I ain't sick and I ain't them other things neither." To prove it, he hauled himself into a seated position and squinted hard to keep the room steady.

"You're not."

"That's what I said."

"No, you said you ain't. Ain't is not a word."

"'Tis too."

"Not one used by gentlemen."

"Says your mama, I suppose. Afore you go spoutin' off what else your mama's tole you, hie your rump on into the kitchen and tell Ruth I need coffee in a bad way. Go on." He listened to the clatter of stiff shoe leather with eyes closed and shoulders slumped. It sure wasn't going to be easy getting to know the boy, not when he wasn't certain he could even get to liking him.

"Here's your coffee, sir."

Rory slit his eyes open and reached for the cup. He smiled slightly at the anxious boy. What wasn't to like? The boy was his blood, his only child. It wasn't his fault his mama raised him on fool notions. He opened his eyes a bit wider to study the solemn child. Where exactly had she raised him? He hadn't thought to ask her.

"Where's your mama this morning?"

"Still sleeping when I looked in on her. She usually doesn't get up until almost lunch time."

Well, that had changed about her. Probably not much call to get up early in the city. Especially if she stayed out late doing . . . what? He didn't know a thing about what his family did.

"Sit yourself down, Jacob, and let's you and me talk a spell. C'mon. I ain't gonna bite you."

"You're not," he corrected.

"That's what I said. Sit."

The boy perched next to him on the sofa, and for a minute they sat like two strangers.

"How long have you lived in Baltimore?" Rory asked at last, making his inquiry casual as he could.

"About a year now. We have a townhouse, and it's by a park."

"And before that?"

"We moved around a lot. I like Baltimore. I go to school there."

"Like school, do you?"

"Yes, sir."

"Your mama take good care of you?" He shouldn't have to ask that, knowing Norah as he did, but he had to make sure they hadn't been struggling. She hadn't taken anything with her except Jacob—no money, no belongings—and the thought that they might have gone without haunted him.

"Oh, yes, sir. Uncle Cole makes sure we have plenty."

"Uncle Cole." Rory's jaw clenched. Cole Denby. He should have known Norah would seek out her former partner if she ran low on funds. "How's good old Uncle Cole?" Now there was a man he wouldn't mind stringing up in a fit of western justice.

"I've never met him. Mother talks about him sometimes. She said he puts money in the bank for us."

Kincaid money, Rory thought bitterly. The life's blood of the Bar K he'd stolen when he'd run, covering his tracks in fire. How nice to know Norah had no qualms about living off him when she refused to live with him. He paused in that thinking, putting it aside for now.

"Whatcha do in Baltimore besides go to school?"

"Sail boats and fly kites in the park. Did you ever do that?" He looked up shyly.

"Can't say I have. Me and your Uncle Scotty used to do us a lot a fishing. You like to fish?"

"I don't know. I've never tried it. I like to read." His gaze brightened hopefully.

"Don't have time for it now, but I used to sneak them dime novels late at night after Daddy thought I was sleeping. I'd read about Bill Cody and Texas Rangers and the like. You read westerns, do you?"

"Mother doesn't like me reading about cowboys and Indians. She says none of it's true and I'd be better off making heroes out of real people."

"That so?"

Grey eyes grew huge behind the magnifying lenses. "Have you killed lots of Indians?"

"No." That was said tersely; and, sensing he'd made a mistake in asking, Jacob looked quickly to the toes of his shoes. Rory's voice softened with a tang of humor. "My brother don't let me kill no Injuns. Wouldn't even when we was little an' just pretending. I'm a rancher. I see that there's food to put on your fancy china back East. Your mama see something wrong in eating good Dakota beef?"

"No, sir."

"Good thing," he drawled. "So's that all you do back there?"

"We go to the zoo and to amusement parks and plays, sometimes."

"You and your mama?"

Jacob hesitated, wondering if he should say something about Mr. Samuels. He decided against it, thinking it better to ask his mother about it first. "Yes, sir."

"Do you know how to ride?"

"A horse? Oh, yes, sir. Mama taught me."

"She's got a fine seat, your mama." Yessir, especially in those revealingly tight britches. "Tell you what, son. When we go over to the Lone Star, I'll let you pick out a horse from Daddy's stock."

"For me?"

"Sure. Boy's got to have a horse. Can't have no son a mine going a-ground. You like that?"

"Oh, yes!" He even forgot to add sir. Slowly, his excitement dimmed. "But I don't think it's a very good idea."

"Why's that?"

"Because I won't be able to take it home with me."

"Jacob, this is your home. Wouldn't you like to stay here?"

Jacob's look was too guarded for a boy his age. He thought too much, just like his mama. Just like his Uncle Scott. "I don't think I can."

"Why not?" Rory prompted gently.

"Because all my friends and Mama's friends are in Baltimore."

"You can make new friends."

"I guess," he said slowly, not sounding totally convinced.

"Your mama got a lot of friends back East, does she?"

Even though he was only seven and naive about the nature of man and woman, Jacob caught the hint of something unsettling in his father's tone. He answered carefully. "Some."

"Any real good friends?"

"Not really." He hopped off the couch, nervous about telling a lie, and went to the window. "When can we see the horses?"

"After your mama gets up and around." Rory

78

frowned. What was the boy hiding from him? What kind of friends was his wife entertaining back in Baltimore? Ugly suspicions growled through him. Three years was a long time, and Norah was a passionate women. *Damn her!*

"You got anything 'sides them city clothes?" he asked gruffly as he put his empty cup aside and crossed to his desk.

"No, sir."

Rory viewed the corduroy knickerbockers and stockings with a jaundiced eye. "We'll swing on into Crowe Creek and outfit you with some proper duds."

"I'll have to ask Mama."

"Your mama don't know squat about dressing a man." Well, that wasn't quite true, but she obviously didn't know the first thing about turning a boy out in something that wasn't laughable.

"Doesn't know," Jacob corrected.

"Whatever." That was said with less annoyance. Could be he was getting used to the boy. "Let's head on down to the barn an' see if we can fit you to a saddle."

Jacob smiled up at him for the first time and Rory felt the brunt of it hit like a two-by-four, smacking the wind out of him. When he thought of how he'd missed the thrill of that small smile, he went a little bit crazy inside. It was a struggle not to snatch the boy up then and there. But he'd made a vow of patience, and he would be patient. His own smile was thin and strained.

A couple of horsehandlers lingered at the corral, the rest of the crew having headed for the range at daybreak. Right in the middle of them, looking every inch the slender ranch hand, was Dawn Prescott. At eight-years-old she could out-cuss, out-spit, and out-ride any boy her age and was proud of it . . . as long as she was out of her mother's earshot. Gena Prescott couldn't see what use a young lady would have for fluent profanity or accurate expectoration, and Dawn wisely heeded her uncle's advice that she not practice them at home. But at the Bar K, in Rory's shadow, she swaggered and swore with pure Prescott arrogance, delighting in her reckless role model. At his call of, "Heya, Sweet Thing," she turned with a grin. There was no doubt she was going to be a dazzler when she shed her buckskins and took to wearing petticoats. She had her father's golden skin and chiseled features, her grandmother's flaming hair and stubbornness, her mother's big blue eyes and delicate stature, and her uncle's hellraising spirit.

"Hey, Rory! I looked in on you a little bit ago, but you was still raising the rafters." She slid gracefully off the fence to hug him tight around the neck, planting a big kiss on his cheek.

"Careful there, darlin'. I'm 'bout as bristly as a cactus this morning."

Dawn laughed, unconcerned, and bussed him again to prove she didn't care. Then her gaze shifted to Jacob, and her expression altered into a stoic mask that would have done her father proud. For an instant, the blue of her eyes was as cold as a gun metal finish. Then she was squeezing her uncle with a bubbling affection.

"I come down to see if Ghost was healed up yet."

"Better'n your granddaddy. I ain't shot him yet."

Dawn made an impatient face at him. "He's my horse. You wouldn't dare."

"Honey, that four-legged keg a dynamite ain't nobody's horse."

80

"Until you ride him." Her big blue eyes cajoled sweetly, and Rory gave a snort of disgust. "Please, Rory. Pleeese. Or isn't your—pride healed up from the last ride?"

"Doan get sassy with me, girl. What are you grinning at?" he growled at the indolent hands. "Slap a saddle on that sonuvabitch and let's see iffen I can run him to ground."

"Yessir, Rory." They scattered quickly to see it done.

"Thank you, Rory."

He ducked away from her kisses, grinning and grumbling, "Stop your slobbering on me now. Doan go thinking you sweet-talked me into it. Me an' him's got a score to settle." He deposited Dawn back on the rails and ducked between them, ambling across the dusty corral. Forgotten, Jacob hung back, wondering glumly why the affection between his father and his girl cousin pricked such a painful degree.

Ghost was Dawn's name for the tall silver-grey maverick they'd pulled in off the range. The stallion had been raiding the Lone Star cavvies, stealing away with some of Ethan Prescott's finest brood mares. The animal led them one helluva chase before Rory had gotten a rope on him. Ethan knew horseflesh, and he proclaimed the wild thing would never take to a saddle. But when it came down to destroying the brute, Dawn's teary pleas had bested her uncle's resolve. He had a soft heart when it came to strays and renegades and was even a softer touch when it came to his niece. And then the outlaw had almost killed him and his father.

"Hold him," Rory ordered as he approached the restless stallion. The animal's black eyes rolled. They both knew from experience what was coming, and neither was too happy about it. Rory fit his boot into

81

the stirrup iron and paused. "Cyril, what's inebriate mean?"

"What's *what* mean?"

"Never mind." He gathered up the reins in a slow, easy loop. "If the Son of Satan tries to two-step on me, put a bullet in him."

"Yessir, boss."

From the porch, Norah watched her husband climb into the saddle. Her breath seized up in her throat the way it always did when he was bronc riding. There was something so primitive, so wildly beautiful about man and horse fighting for mastery. And there was something so indescribably exciting about Rory Prescott on the back of an untamed horse. Her heart was racing just as the animal's must be as it felt his weight in the stirrups. She trembled the same way the mustang did when confronted with a danger it didn't understand. And when the black Stetson nodded toward the men at the reins, her muscles bunched with the same tension exploding through the stallion as it plunged in stiff-legged fury to rid itself of the threat of man.

It wasn't a long ride, but it was a rough one. Daylight shone between saddle leather and denim, and Norah gripped the porch rail as Rory went sailing to the dirt. Only when he began to roll up onto his feet did she let go of a shaky sigh and started down toward the corral. She was halfway there when she heard Dawn's voice raise in a fury directed at her son. Before she could increase her stride, the girl let go of a solid punch and Jacob went sprawling.

Rory heard the wail of surprise and pain over the ringing in his ears. He looked back toward the fence to see Jacob flat on his back, his glasses askew, and his nose pumping blood. Something mighty and inexplicable grabbed hold of his chest in that second and he went running, dodging between the rails in a paternal panic. It took both arms to pull a flailing Dawn off his downed son.

"Cut it out! Cut it out, Dawn. What the hell's got into you?"

When he set her on her feet, she was still spitting mad and seething through clenched teeth. "He said you was a fool for getting on that horse."

"Looks like he was right, now, don't it? C'mon now, girl, back it down." He knelt beside the sobbing boy, conscious of an awful pinch of hurt around his own heart. He scooped the boy's shoulders up with one hand and drew out a bandana with the other. "Stop your howling now. You ain't gonna die." He tipped the boy's head back and pressed the cloth hard to stem the flow of bleeding. Jacob was nearly hysterical by then, frightened by the spill of crimson and the sharp crack of Rory's voice. But his father's hands were gentle, very gentle. "Now, quit your yelling," Rory commanded gruffly. He was more shaken than he could readily admit to. "You're jus' making it worse. I ain't gonna claim no son who can't take a wallop from a girl."

Then Norah was kneeling down in the dust beside them, and Jacob was fast in her arms. Her stare leveled fiercely over the wavy auburn hair. "How could you say such a thing to him?" she hissed at a stunned Rory. He rocked back on his heels to regard mother and child with a frown.

"Norah, you ain't doing the boy no good by spoiling him. He's gonna get hit a lot harder than that in his lifetime, and you ain't gonna always be there to dry his eyes."

"We don't hit in Baltimore," she snapped back, and just then Jacob's thin voice rose plaintively.

"I wanna go home. I hate it here! I wanna go home!"

Norah's attention turned back to the boy with a soft whisper of, "Hush now, honey. It's all right."

Rory jerked upright and stalked back into the corral to snatch up his hat, smacking it against his thigh to send dust clouds flying. And he tensed as the mournful echo cut through him.

"I wanna go home!"

"How are things at the Bar K?"

Rory leaned back against the porch rail and gave a heaving sigh. There wasn't much his daddy missed, and on this cool late October evening he was glad of it. But the swaddling of white wrapped about his father's brow kept him from blurting out his miseries. He forced a smile and said, "Coming along."

Ethan Prescott rocked back in his chair and tapped the shavings from the piece of wood he was whittling. "That so? I noticed Norah and Jacob didn't come along with you this evening." He watched his son flounder for a way to make the truth palatable and come up empty-handed. His bright head ducked, and he mumbled, "Nossir, they didn't."

"Want to tell me about Norah? Now I don't want you to think I'm prying into what's none of my business. You don't have to say nothing. But your mama's chewing glass over it and she's not gonna give me a minute's peace, so I'm asking."

"Sorry, Daddy. Suspected she would be. I doan rightly know what to tell you. Hell, I ain't figured it out yet myself."

"They staying?"

"I mean to do everything I can to see to it."

"Still love her?"

His reply was very soft. "Yessir."

"She love you?"

Softer still, "Doan know."

"Have you asked her?"

"What? You mean come right on out and asked?"

"That's usually how you find things out."

He gave a quiet laugh. "I'm plum scared right down to my socks that she'd tell me the truth."

"You don't think she does?"

"I doan know, Daddy. Sometimes things are so— so right between us, just like before, then they twist up all wrong. How can you know somebody so well and there still be a part of them that's a mystery?"

Ethan chuckled. "The nature of the gender. I been married to your mama for nigh on thirty years, and there's times I get the feeling I don't know the slightest thing about her. Jus' what she wants to tell me. 'Course fellas like us, we're so wide open with what we're thinking and feeling, no mystery there a-tall. No reason for them to wonder what's on our mind."

Rory had the grace to look shamefaced. "Got your point, Daddy."

"Now when I look at you, I see this young handsome fella, looks a lot like his daddy, good-hearted, right-headed, God-fearing, salt of the earth kind of man, kind a woman'd be lucky to get a hold of. He works hard, plays hard, and loves his family, got no terrible vices to speak of. Sounds like a good sort a fella don't he?" Rory smiled. "Now this fella, he gets himself a good woman, has a fine boy, and he wants to provide for them best he can. How's he do that? Does he ask his wife and his son what they want? Heck no, 'cause he's a man and he knows what's best for his family. So he does what he believes is best; and one day, he looks up and they're gone and this good, decent, hard-working fella, he ain't got a clue as to why. Now, seems to me that if this here fella was to get a second chance, he'd want to make danged sure he didn't make all the same mistakes he made the first time."

"But Daddy I don't know what they were."

"Then you best be quick about asking. Me, I like Norah. She's a smart woman—tough, too. I always figured she'd make you a good wife. She's a lot like your mama which is why they get along about as well as two cats tied over a clothesline. I don't know what happened between the two of you, don't need to know. If you let her go, there ain't gonna be nothing you can do in your life to make up for the loss of her. Now quit wasting your time a-jawing with me, and go home to your family."

"Yessir, Daddy."

After he'd gone, Gena came out onto the porch and leaned down to wrap her arm around her father-in-law's shoulders.

"She love him, you think?" Ethan asked as he stared out into the darkness toward the Bar K.

"Crazy about him," Gena assured him with a gentle hug.

"They'll work it out then. The good Lord tends to be merciful toward fools and lovers."

Chapter Six

Norah could hear the creak and ebb of the porch swing. She was drawn outside by the sound and by the man slowly rocking.

"Mind if I join you?"

"Suit yourself."

She settled on the swing beside him and let the flex of his knees move them to and fro in a gentle rhythm.

"Nice night, ain't—isn't it?"

Norah breathed in the crisp tangy air. Air didn't taste like this in the East. Here, it was pure, almost intoxicating. "Yes. I'd forgotten how beautiful it is. So black. So many stars. As if you looked to the left and you could see yesterday and to the right, tomorrow."

"I was jus' kinda enjoying lookin' at today."

She waited for him to say more, but his mood was oddly quiet. It was a good time to speak her mind. "Rory, I'm sorry about this morning. I overreacted. I had no reason to get angry at you."

"That's all right. He's your boy. My mama still does her share of growlin' over me."

"I'll say," Norah muttered, and she knew he was smiling.

"How's the boy?"

"Embarrassed that his father would scold him for letting a girl make him cry."

"She packs one helluva punch." His humor faded, leaving his voice a low rumble. "Guess I messed up. I ain't much good at playing Daddy."

"It takes practice."

"Am I gonna get a chance at it, Norah?"

"Do you want one?"

He was silent, and she angled on the seat to study his rugged profile. It was as strong as the outline of the far Hills. She longed to reach out to him, to brush back the playful strands of red hair that strayed over his ear, to turn him toward her so she could see what moved in the expressive darkness of his gaze. She wanted to read his answer there as he spoke it. But she found herself unable to move. His reply was hushed, as straightforward as the man.

"I been lovin' you too long to stop now." As the power of that simple claim wound about her heart, his eyes canted in her direction. "How 'bout you?"

"I'm here."

Rory shifted, letting his arm play out gradually along the back of the swing behind her until his fingertips grazed the line of her shoulder. She was wearing her nightclothes. silk over silk, and the heat of his hand scorched with promise. She knew where this slow seduction was heading and she gave no outward sign of the inner collapse of her will. If he wanted her, all he had to do was reach out, to come and get her. That's all she'd been waiting for, that chance to surrender—if he asked the right way. His thumb stroked lazily up and down the column of her bared throat and a fierce trembling began inside her.

"How you been, Norah?" A small question that made a huge demand. And she was cautious.

"I've been doing well. And so have you from the looks of things."

He cast his gaze along the horizon, and she could see the pride in that sweeping look. Her middle tensed. "Yeah, I have," he claimed. "The range is full. It's just the house that's so damned empty." He looked to her then, his eyes intense, burning darkly. "I missed you."

"Really?" She couldn't help that. There was too much bitterness to just brush it away as if it had never existed. That hurt had never eased, just as her loneliness had never eased. "I'm surprised you noticed we were gone."

"That's not fair, Norah."

"No, it wasn't." That was not an apology.

To ease the spark of flint and fire from her words, his hand strayed lower, rubbing along the upper curve of her breast, shifting silk over skin. Her response was instinctive, slight but significant. The pattern of her breathing altered. She straightened on the swing, bringing her shoulders back, lifting her ribcage, filling his palm with that swell of silk. His touch was maddeningly light, just a whisper of sensation.

"This is nice, ain't—isn't it, sitting out here like this, jus' the two of us."

"Yes," she agreed shakily.

"Night's like this, I come out an' sit a spell, soakin' up the quiet, just a-rocking and a-thinking, remembering. I remember a night like this, me jus' minding my own business when this here lovely looking lady strolled out and commenced to provoking me something fierce by pretending not to care. 'Member what she said to me, Norah-honey?"

Norah arched away from the back of the swing, pushing, rubbing against his palm more insistently.

She leaned into the circle of his arm, her head resting on his shoulder, her breath pulsing rapidly against his neck. Her voice was hoarse.

"I want you."

He slipped his hand inside the web of silk to caress the generous softness of her breast. "Yep, as I recall that's just what she said."

A low moan and a hard tremor answered. Then she said again, "I want you, Rory." Her body moved against him in a helpless abandon, her fingers gathering in the fabric of his shirt, tangling in the hair at the back of his head.

"Sounds like you almost mean that, Norah-honey," came his low drawl. His free hand cupped around the curve of her jaw, lifting her head away from his shoulder, tipped it up so he could plunder her stare. Her eyes were glazed, as bright as the stars above. "Do you?"

"Don't tease me, Rory. Not now. Not when I need so much for you to kiss—"

And he was. Deeply, drainingly. Norah dissolved beneath the searing pressure.

"Like that?" he taunted softly.

"Yes."

He kissed her again, mouth slanting recklessly this way and that along the urgent part of hers. "And that?"

"Yes."

"And this?" He settled in with a wide open temptation, tongue tangling, thrusting hard against hers. She rose up, straddling his thighs, putting all of her considerable passion into the return of that kiss until they had to break apart to breathe. Then, she let him cuddle her close to his chest as he rocked them gently to and fro. "Yep. There surely is something to be said for nights like this one." She rode out his sigh

90

of contentment. And it was perfect.

After several minutes of rocking and listening to the night sounds, he began to stroke her hair, slowly, with a sensual leisure. His knuckles brushed the slope of her cheek and trailed along the length of her arm where it curved loosely about his neck. Then he was bemused as she caught his hand, not to push it away but to turn it over in hers so she could chart the swell of each and every callus like a fortune teller searching his palm in hopes of revealing the future.

"I love your hands," she told him quietly, tracing along the lines of life and happiness with her fingertips. He didn't wear a gold band. It hadn't been the fashion when they'd wed; and, handling reins and ropes as he did all day, a ring could prove hazardous to the finger that wore it. He'd said he didn't need a wedding band to remind himself he was married. Norah wondered if that were still true. "I've always loved the feel of them. I've missed them."

He curled his fingers, balling hers up inside a gentle fist. Squeezing the way the fist of emotion did about her heart.

"I love you, Norah."

There was a fierce tremor of response but no returning vow. Not knowing what else to do or say, Rory held her, letting the hard pulse of his blood do the talking.

Such beautiful words. Words she'd come hundreds of miles hoping to hear him say. Now all she needed to learn was what he meant by them.

He was watching her closely, studying her face, her eyes, the supple bend of her lips. And when he said, "I love you," a second time, even softer, stronger than the first, she pressed those lips to his to taste the sweetness of his claim upon them.

"Rory! Hey, Rory!"

91

The gruff intruding voice pulled them apart. Without looking away from the promise in her eyes, Rory called, "Whatcha need, Frank?"

"Need you to come on down to the bunkhouse and settle something for the boys. Why, 'evening, ma'am. Didn't see you."

"What's the problem?" He canted a quick glance toward the cowboy.

"Some kinda ugly talk brewing. Thought you'd best step in before it blew up into a ruckus."

"No," Norah said softly.

Rory looked to her in surprise, then back at his ranch hand.

"Only take a minute," the man assured him.

"Don't go." That wasn't an impassioned plea. It was something a helluva lot stronger. "Let them take care of it, Rory. You don't have to do it."

Confused by her intensity, Rory looked back at the impatient cowhand and to the lights of the bunkhouse beyond, from where the sounds of trouble were escalating. "I better—"

She seized his face between her hands. "No. Rory, please."

Very gently, he captured her wrists and drew her hands away. "I'll be just a second, honey." He leaned in to kiss her but her lips were unyielding and cool. His big hands circled her waist, lifting her off his lap and settling her on the seat of the swing. When he stood, his attention was already torn away from her. "I'll see to this first and be back. Only take a minute."

"First things first," she murmured dryly.

Rory smiled and frowned and smiled again, perplexed by her unexplained moodiness. He brushed his fingertips over her cheek in a light caress. "Be right back."

She didn't move.

"Rory? You coming?"

"Yeah." He clomped down the steps and strode across the yard beside his ranch hand. Norah watched him go, blinking back the hot sting of moisture in her eyes. Nothing had changed. Nothing at all. And by the time he looked back up toward the house, the swing was moving, empty.

Rory was grateful for the scuffle of sound at the door to his study. It gave him an excuse to lift his tired gaze from row after row of blurry figures. He'd been working the accounts since dawn and his eyes felt raw from the strain of it. He massaged them gingerly even as he smiled and called out, "'Morning," to the bashful boy hovering at the threshold.

"Good morning, sir. I-I didn't mean to bother you."

"You ain't b— You're not botherin' me. I was jus' fixing to take a break."

"Do you want me to bring you some coffee?"

The boy's eagerness made him smile. "Sure. That'd be right nice."

In his absence, Rory closed his eyes to ease the tension behind them. A matter of minutes passed, then he heard the rattle of china and smelled Ruth's rich, hot brew. As Jacob slid the saucer across the desktop, the boy's interest was caught by the twist of wire and blistered frame. He reached for the empty picture holder and froze at the crack of his father's voice.

"Doan touch that."

Swallowing spasmodically, the boy jerked his hand back. Seeing his alarm, Rory's mood softened.

"I didn't mean to snap at you, son. Them things is special to me. They're all I have left of what was here

93

before. Everything else I had to build up from scratch. When they're yours, you can handle 'em all you like."

"Mine?"

"Jus' like everything here. This is all for you, Jacob."

Big eyes blinked behind wire-framed spectacles and turned with an appreciating awe to the two items on the desk top. His.

"Somethin' on your mind?"

Jacob shot him a quick look and colored up to the roots of his hair. "I-I was just wondering if we could go see the horses this morning."

"Not this morning."

"Oh." He was crestfallen. "Maybe sometime when you're not mad at me."

"I ain't mad at you. Why'd I be mad?"

"Because of what I said yesterday," he muttered, face as fiery as his father's hair.

"Oh, that business about me being a fool?" He gauged the boy's discomfort, then smiled. "Seems you were right about that. It was a dumb thing to do. But I jus' can't help showin' off for a pretty girl. Ask your mama."

Jacob risked a glance and was encouraged by his father's grin. He straightened and even tried a small smile of his own. He felt bad about what he'd said. He'd only blurted it out because he was so jealous of his tomboy cousin's importance in his father's eyes. But it seemed the big redhead was willing to be tolerant, so he pressed his luck. "Can we go see the horses now?"

Rory's grin fell crooked. "Ain't nothing I'd like better, but I gots this whole shi—shoot-load of figuring to do today."

"I could help. I know my numbers real good."

"That so." He assayed the boy then motioned to him. "C'mon on over here and have a look-see."

Jacob came around the big desk and, without hesitation, climbed up on Rory's knee so he could view the open ledger. Cautiously, heart in his throat, Rory eased his arm around the slight figure to support him.

"That should be a seven."

Rory squinted down where a stubby finger pointed. He frowned. "It is. That's the way I make my sevens." Then when the boy turned his attention to the next column, he discreetly added a top bar to the one he'd written.

"And I suppose this is supposed to be a five."

"Yeah, sure. What's it look like?"

"A nine," the boy chided.

Rory took a closer look. "A nine? Well, now, I don't rightly know what it was supposed to be. Tell you what, pard, I'm makin' you my new book-keeper." He lifted his black Stetson off the back of the chair and clapped it down on the boy's head. "Jus' as soon as you grow into that."

Jacob adjusted the brim so it didn't fall over his eyes and grinned up at his father. "Can I get a hat like this—that fits me, I mean? Could we go into town today like you promised?"

"Your father hasn't got time for that sort of thing."

From her rigid stance in the doorway, Norah's stare clashed with her husband's as it lifted over their son's head. The sight of them together had dealt her a nasty shock. It was one thing for Rory Prescott to lead her on with his careless grin and idle promises, but she wouldn't have him doing the same to their innocent child. To a boy who wouldn't understand that promises made by some couldn't be trusted.

"Get down from there, Jacob, and let your father

get back to work."

"But Mama, I was helping—"

"Do as you're told."

"Yes, ma'am." He slipped down obediently, but Rory's arm circled his shoulders before he could step away. That camaradic embrace emboldened him. "We were going to look at horses—"

Norah cut in crisply. "Your father has more important things to do."

"No, I don't." The ledger book snapped shut. Rory looked between wife and son and repeated, "No, I don't. There ain't nothing I got to do here that's more important than getting my boy a hat and a horse." As Jacob beamed excitedly, he looked back at Norah. The apology in his gaze was eloquent. Norah's stony expression didn't falter. "You're welcome to come along."

"Please come, Mama."

Mama? She blinked at that, off-balance. "I-I'll just get my hat."

"Whooee! C'mon, boy, I'll show you how to harness up a team."

Norah stood at the window watching the two of them head for the barn, Jacob's short little legs pumping to keep up with his father's ambling gait. Her hands clutched into fists at her sides.

Don't hurt him, Rory. He's only a little boy.

With his new parcel of clothes tucked under his arm and a black Stetson that was a scaled-down version of his father's perched on his head, Jacob Prescott felt ten-feet-tall. His heart was chugging with anticipation as he thought of picking out his own horse. It was all he could do to keep from tugging on his parents' hands to hurry them toward the buggy. But like most adults, they had an aggravating habit of dragging their feet and feeling obligated to stop and talk to everyone they passed. They'd probably forgotten how time seemed to move in agonizing seconds when they were young and looking forward to something so bad they were alive with fidgets.

Not that it hadn't been fun. His father had a rollicking sense of humor that sneaked in under his mother's dour mood to coax an unbidden laugh. And then he'd look at her and his smile would go all funny and she'd glance away quickly, pretending she wasn't enjoying herself. They were acting pretty silly for two grown-up people He took a great deal of amusement from watching them, able to smile himself because the air wasn't charged with the threat of erupting tempers. It was almost like they were a family.

Finally, he was able to beg his mother into letting him run ahead with the promise that he wouldn't stray off the walk. He bolted with the energy of a young colt, racing down the uneven boards at a reckless speed. He didn't hear his father's marveling comment of, "Danged if he doan remind me of me."

Jacob had no intention of disobeying his mother's command. But lingering at the buggy soon lost its appeal. He paced up and down the boardwalk, counting the planks and wondering if he should choose a black horse to go with his new hat. The sound of boys laughing together was a pleasant distraction.

A group of them had gathered in an alley between two buildings. They were hunkered down in the dirt playing mumblety-peg with a rusty-bladed knife. It looked intriguing and Jacob eased up behind the circle of them to watch. After a few failed attempts to get the blade to stick in the hard-packed ground, a burly youngster glared up and growled, "Yer in my light, four-eyes."

Jacob took a hasty step back, but not before the others noticed him, too. And suddenly, teasing a bespectacled stranger looked a lot more entertaining than flipping the knife. They rose up off their haunches like a pack of mangy dogs circling for tasty scraps. Jacob glanced toward the buggy and abruptly stumbled as a rough hand gave him a shove.

"Whatsa matter, four-eyes? Can't see where yer going?"

They laughed and took turns pushing. Having never made a fist in his entire life, Jacob was petrified by the cruel taunts and sneering faces of the older boys. A hard punch to the shoulder sent him reeling back, falling hard onto his rump. He clenched his teeth, vowing not to cry.

"Leave him alone."

The low threatening snarl brought the boys around. They chuckled their amusement at the sight of a spindly girl in a frilly dress. And stopped when they saw the knife pass deftly from hand to hand in front of her. There was something coldly dangerous in the glint of her eyes.

"We're jus' havin' some fun," the oldest bully rumbled. "Get lost, little girl."

She moved so fast the bully never had a chance to blink. He found his legs kicked out from under him and a thin forearm braced against his Adam's apple with a choking pressure. And he felt the sharp prick of a knifepoint beneath one ear.

"Mind if I play, too?"

The boy began to whimper.

"Any of the rest of you want to play some more?"

They backed away from the girl's glittering stare. She smiled, a quick flash of bared teeth. "See, my granddaddy was a Lakota warrior. I could peel your hair afore you could draw your next breath. You remember that the next time you want to push around someone in my family." She kicked the boy loose, and he went scrambling on hands and knees until he could manage a run. The others fled after him. Grinning, Dawn Prescott weighed the crude knife in her palm and gave it a toss. It embedded deep in the dirt.

As impressed by the display as the others had been, Jacob was nonetheless provoked to ask, "Why did you do that? After yesterday, I'd have thought you'd want to get in the first punch."

She smiled at him impishly, looking soft and pretty all at once. "Just because *I* hit you doesn't mean I'm gonna let strangers do it. We're both Prescotts, after all, and that's what counts."

Jacob stared after her as she skipped across the wide street to catch up to her mother. And he was astounded by the magnitude of what it meant to have family.

"How 'bout that one there?"

"No."

"How 'bout the paint? The little black an' white feller?"

Jacob sighed and shook his head.

"Boy, you're as fussy as a female looking for a new hair-ribbon."

Jacob flushed and mumbled, "Any of them would be all right, I guess."

Rory laughed and jostled him with an elbow. "Nossir. A man's horse is as personal as the fit of his boots. You take your time. If you doan see nothing here, we'll ride on out to the north pasture tomorrow. Daddy's got a nice little cavvy grazing out there."

"How come you ride a pink horse?"

Rory glanced down at him, then over at the reddish mare that went by the ignominious name of Rosebud. "Think I outta be tricked out on something a little more manly, do you?"

Jacob ducked his eyes. "I didn't mean that."

His father's laugh was deep and good-natured. "Son, Bud an' me, we go back a long way. That there little lady has got more heart, more grit, an' more speed than any of them fancy studs in there. I'd trust that critter with my life—got to out here. That's why you got to take your time. Wait until you find an animal that's right for you. You pick out a saddle horse more carefully than you'd choose a wife 'cause you got to depend on 'em more."

"Now isn't that a wonderful sentiment to be sharing with a young boy."

Rory grinned at his wife as she came up on the other side of Jacob and settled her forearms on the rail. "Now, Norah-honey, doan go getting your feathers up. We was jus' having a little man talk about horses."

"So I heard."

"Jacob, why doan you run on up to the house and tell your granddaddy you think he's breeding a bunch of broomtails?" As the boy raced away, Rory turned to lean his elbows on the rail behind him, still smiling. "Somethin' on your mind, Norah? I can smell smoke."

"I do not care to have my son turned into some arrogant, narrow-thinking posturing fool who thinks four-legged animals are more important than human beings."

"You think he'd be better off back in Baltimore becoming one of them sissy idiots who think acting rude makes 'em superior to other folks?"

"Jacob is a fine, intelligent boy who has a wonderful future ahead of him. I will not allow him to believe that tobacco-chewing, profanity-spouting, horse-loving cowboys are something to be glamorized as heroes."

"So he tells me." His drawl was low and lethal.

"I want you to stop it. I want you to quit filling his head with nonsense. I'm not going to let you get him believing in all your big promises. I am not going to let you make him think that for one minute you put either of us above the running of your ranch."

"He's my son, Norah."

"And I'm your wife. And I will not have you telling my boy that his mother ranks below a good horse in his father's eyes." She pushed off the fence and started for the house with a brisk, angry stride.

"At least I can trust my horse not to up and leave me stranded."

She jerked up at that and whirled back in a magnificent fury. She would have chosen a better place for all her anger to reach flash point, but his goading was too much. If he wanted to go at it head-on in his folks' front yard, so be it. "If you'd treated me as well as you did your horse, maybe I wouldn't have left."

He came off the rail then and started toward her with a move that was slow, graceful, and as dangerous as a stalking mountain cat. She held her ground, waiting for him to come toe-to-toe, throwing her head back to glare up at him defiantly.

"You got complaints, Norah?" he asked in a soft, chilling purr. "Didn't I grain you good and give you shelter? Didn't I see you rubbed down regular and groomed all sleek and sassy? You think my horse could claim it got as much pleasure as you from me riding it hard?"

101

He caught the hand she sent streaking toward his face, controlling it in his firm grasp, refusing to let her pull back. Slowly, he brought it to him, grazing the whitened knuckles with his lips. When her fingers hooked into sharp talons, he bent her palm back holding her harmless while he pressed a hot, hard kiss to the corded tendons in her wrist.

"Rory, Norah, I hear we just missed you in town."

The tension washed immediately away from him as Rory turned toward Gena and Dawn as their wagon came to a stop. He supplied a quick, easy smile as if he hadn't a worry in the world. "Well, here we are. Got nothing better to do than spend the rest of the day visitin'."

Norah struggled to bring her feelings in check. Her face was blotched with fiery upset, and her eyes glimmered traitorously. Try as she would, she couldn't put on a smile and pretend nothing had been interrupted. The more she fought for control, the more her emotions betrayed her. The last thing she wanted was to make lengthy and difficult explanations for her tears and trembling.

Oddly, it was Rory, the cause of her turmoil, who helped her gain back her composure. His arm was an instant bolster about the shake of her shoulders, turning her into his chest and away from the scrutiny of his family to protect her pride. Her fingers clenched in the stiff chambray of his shirt.

"Easy, honey. Easy now," he whispered against her brow, warming the skin with the brush of his words.

She made a small, choky sound, and his embrace cinched up tight.

"C'mon, Norah. Show me some grit. I didn't mean to make you mad enough to pop your corset. Don't go to pieces on me."

With Jacob from one direction and Dawn from the other converging upon them, Rory saw their privacy about to end. His hand scooped under her chin, pushing it up so he could secure her vulnerable lips in a quick kiss. She gave a start of surprise, an abrupt weakening of response, then began to wrestle away, smacking her elbow smartly into his ribs. He let her go and stepped back, grinning as Dawn launched herself up into his arms.

"Rory! Rory, guess what!"

"What, darlin'?" It took a second for him to wrest his dark gaze away from Norah to concentrate on the girl's excitement flushed face.

"Daddy's coming home."

"Scotty? When?"

"He should be here by the end of the week."

"Why that's great news."

Wonderful, Norah thought grimly. As if things weren't bad enough already.

Chapter Seven

"So what's in Baltimore that keeps you so busy?"

Norah and Gena were sitting in the warm afternoon sunlight on one of Aurora's hand-stitched quilts. A sketch pad was propped on Gena's bent knees. She was using charcoal to capture Rory, Dawn, and Jacob fishing in the swift waters of the creek beyond.

"Parties, causes, fund-raisers. And, of course, there's Jacob's school. There's always something to do in the city. Don't you miss it sometimes?"

Gena smiled up at her gently. "Never. This is my home, the only real one I've ever known. I wouldn't trade my worst day out here for all the comforts and conveniences of Baltimore." She laughed softly at Norah's disbelieving look. "You probably think I'm crazy, but I was never one for rabid socializing. I've got everything I want right here: family, a roof over my head, a beautiful daughter, and a husband I'm embarrassingly in love with." She leaned her arms along the top of her sketchbook and gazed down at the stand of cottonwoods. From the dewiness of that look, Norah guessed she was thinking of Scott's return. An ache of wistfulness welled within her own breast. Loneliness was something she understood so personally.

"How do you do it, Gena? How do you let him go? How do you survive while he's gone? Don't you ever want to just grab on and tell him, 'No, no more!'"

She blushed and admitted quietly, "Yes, but I don't."

"Why? Do you think it's fair of him to ride off and leave you for months at a time, letting you worry over him and what he's doing? He could have a safe, well-paying job in Washington, and you could lead normal lives together. How could he deny you and your daughter that kind of security?"

Gena thought for a moment about how to answer. Her lovely features were serene yet underlaid with the tensile strength of steel. "He wouldn't. If I asked him, he'd give up his work with the Lakota; he'd put on a fine suit of clothes and tight shoes, move to the city, go to an office every morning, and come home to dinner on time; and he would never complain about doing it for me. And then I'd have to watch the spirit die in him day by day. It would be like yoking something meant to be free. I couldn't do that to him. This," she gestured to the sky, the prairie and the mysterious Hills beyond, "is what Scott is. It was my choice. I knew what it would mean being married to a man like him. And for a long time, he tried his best to talk me out of it. But I love him, Norah. It's easier for me to share him than to humble him. I would live in skins under the sky to be with him."

"I hope for your sake that he never asks you to."

Gena chuckled at her friend's wry observation.

"What's so funny?"

"You pretending you don't know exactly what I'm talking about."

"I'm sure I don't," Norah drawled with a cool disdain.

"Then why did you come back?" Silence. "He still takes your breath away, doesn't he?"

Norah looked uncomfortably toward the stream, letting her gaze linger over the face and form of Rory Prescott. So handsome. Her big, redheaded cowboy with the mile-wide grin and provoking dark eyes. He was standing behind Jacob, guiding the cast of his line into the creek. Her son had changed into his western garb, a miniature of his father in blue denim and chambray and a black John B. They were both laughing, trying to keep the slick soles of their boots from pitching them into the water from where they stood on the damp bank. Father and son, an intimate portrait that clogged her chest solid with pride.

"How could you have left him, Norah?" There was no censure in her friend's tone, just a need to understand why two people she loved were no longer together. Gena waited, but Norah was broodingly silent. And she had to ask, "Is there someone else in Baltimore?"

Norah gave a laugh edged in bitter irony. "Oh, Gena, how could you of all people ask that?" She watched Rory's big hands fold over Jacob's, knowing well the warmth, the tenderness of his touch. She drew a dry-throated breath. "How could there ever be anyone else?"

"He loves you."

"I know." Her vision blurred as she watched Rory hoist Dawn up on his shoulders so she could untangle Jacob's fish line from a branch. Gena followed her gaze, and she chuckled softly.

"I haven't seen him this happy in a long time."

"Was it very hard for him . . . after I left?" She tensed, not wanting to learn of the pain she'd caused him but needing to know that her sacrifice hadn't been for nothing. She didn't want to hear that he hadn't cared enough to mourn her.

"I don't really know, Norah. He wouldn't let any of us within an arm's length of him for the longest time. He worked too hard, drank too much, and spent nearly all of his time in town."

"Upstairs over some saloon?" Why did that hurt so terribly?

Gena blushed, unable to answer. Or unwilling to answer. "Is that why you left him? He never said."

"No. If Rory had a mistress, she was measured in acres, not inches."

"Mama! Mama, come quick!"

Jacob's shrill cry startled Norah to her feet and had her running as fast she she could in the tight hobble of her skirt. When she drew close to the trio on the creekbed, Jacob turned toward her, displaying a shimmering trout flapping on the end of his line. She slowed her frantic pace only to have the wind knocked from her again. Jacob was grinning broadly, his eyes alight with pride. And in the youthful sweetness of his face, she saw Rory Prescott so clearly it staggered her senses. In the years spent in Baltimore, she'd tried so hard never to see the resemblance. She'd tried to crush out similarities too painful to view. But here, under the clear Dakota sky, beneath the shade of his Stetson brim, Jacob was every inch his father's son.

How on earth was she going to take him away?

"Mama, look what I caught! All by myself!"

Smiling thinly, Norah made a great show of examining the silvery prize. "My, that is a beauty. I can almost taste him all golden for breakfast."

"Really?" he sounded amazed. "Can I keep him? Can we have him for breakfast, Father?"

Rory was hunkered down behind him, looking as

smug as if the accomplishment had been his. His dark gaze lifted to hers and the dancing lights of enjoyment settled to a flickering simmer. "When you work hard going after something you want, you hang onto it tight. Catchin's the easy part. There's a lot of work goes into it before you gets to sit down to the savoring. But it's worth the trouble. Believe you me, it's worth the trouble."

Then he broke from Norah's riveted stare, and she was able to breathe again. Somewhat shakily.

"First, you got to get that hook out. Grab 'em there behind the gills. Reach on in there—he ain't gonna bite you. Give it a little bit of a twist, and pull slow. Slow, I said."

"Owww!" Jacob's hand jerked back, hook embedded in his thumb. Before Rory could catch it, he'd yanked hard, snapping the fragile shank.

"Lemme see. Jacob, lemme see it!"

His eyes huge and damp with fright and hurt, Jacob extended the injured hand, biting back a whimper as his father prodded the ball of his thumb.

"That's down there pretty deep," Rory murmured. "No reason to make a big hoo-ha. Scotty used to cut 'em out of me right regular. It's gonna hurt some. Awright?"

Jacob nodded bravely.

"Attaboy. Here, Norah-honey. Hang onto this, will you."

Norah made a grimace of distaste as Rory jammed the trout's open gills over her fingertips.

Rory had the boy's hand anchored tight; and, though he was plainly scared, Jacob mustered up a trusting smile. He winced when Rory pressed the tiny wound between his teeth and bit down hard. But almost immediately, the barb was spit out and a fresh well of blood pinched up.

"There you go. That weren't so bad, was it?"

"No, sir."

About that time, the trout decided to make a bid for freedom with a massive flop. Norah made a noise of surprise and grabbed for the slippery girth.

"Mama! My fish!"

"Doan let it get away!" Rory called.

The trout shot from Norah's hands like a compressed pat of butter. It landed on the mossy bank and started cartwheeling crazily. Both she and Rory dove for it at the same instant, he snagging it by the lip and she snagging him by the band of his Levis as her feet skidded on wet grass. As he caught her up, the fish managed to flip down into the wrapped surplus of her bodice, eliciting a shrill squeal of protest.

"I got it. I got it," Rory declared confidently as his hand plunged down the front of her dress. What he got was the hard crack of her elbow beneath his jaw. Unbalanced, his bootheels scrabbled for purchase and over he went, dragging a shrieking Norah with him.

The water was cold! A great shower of it was displaced by the long length of cowboy as he went in rump first, Norah riding on top of him. His shout of surprise was swallowed up beneath the icy surface, then he struggled with a flail of arms and tangle of feet in her long skirt. It wasn't deep, or he probably would have drowned, the way she was angled, awkwardly upended, to pin him down. Sputtering and coughing, he wedged his elbows into the soft bottom of the creekbed and levered up to find Norah nose to nose with him.

"Have you got my fish?" Jacob was wailing.

"He's in there somewheres," Rory hollered back. He could feel it squirming between the press of their bodies. "Hang on, pard. Stop your wiggling, Norah,

109

or he's gonna get away."

About that time, the shock of water gave way to an awareness of the hard form beneath her. Norah stopped fighting. She was panting slightly, trapped by the sodden wrap of her dress and the unnatural tilt of their position. And for a moment, she forgot all about the fish writhing inside her bodice and the group gathered on the shore. She was mesmerized by the feel of wet denim over manly physique.

"Norah-honey, if you're groping around for that there trout, you best be trying a little higher up."

The husky amusement in his tone was a colder dash than the water. With an indignant growl, she rose up, pushing off his chest and shoving him under in the process. He bobbed up, spitting and laughing as she wrestled with the weight of her sodden clothes and started for the bank.

"Whoa! Norah, wait. Your dress. I got my spurs caught in it."

She took another angry stride only to have the material yank and bind, tripping her. She stumbled and capsized into the shallows, kicking furiously as he reached to free her. Then his hand closed around her ankle, effectively stilling her leg, effectively stilling her breath. His fingers massaged the curve of her calf even as he worked the fabric from the rowel of his spurs. Sensation rippled up from that firm ply, seducing, suggestive. Rory grinned as he flipped her hem free. And abruptly, her foot was planted upon his shoulder, shoving hard to topple him onto his back pockets. He was laughing as she dragged herself up the bank, sodden and shivering.

Trying to hold back her own amusement, Gena was quick to wrap the quilt about her friend's drenched figure. Norah scowled at her severely, but it didn't help. A repressed giggle escaped the pinch of

110

her lips. Norah fumbled about in the shapeless sag of her gown and withdrew one troublesome trout, extending it to her son.

"Nice bit of anglin' there, Norah-honey."

She glared back at the grinning cowboy and, with all the dignity she could manage, declared, "I am going home to get out of these wet things. Come along, Jacob."

"But, Mama, I want to show Grampa my fish!"

"I'll bring him with me," Rory told her with another aggravating grin. He felt like smiling all over. Home. Lord above, he liked the way she said that! And as she marched away with the quilt dragging in her wake like a queenly mantle, Rory sat out in the chilly rush of water, grinning foolishly while his thoughts smoldered.

Soaking in water as hot as she could stand it, Norah sipped wine and scowled fiercely at her bare toes.

What was she going to do about Rory Prescott?

He aggravated her. He enraged her. She wanted to strangle him for holding such one-sided, narrow-minded opinions and for flaunting himself before her as if he were God's gift to the female form. The fact that she thought he probably was didn't settle her mood any. He was everything that annoyed and enchanted her in a man. Brash, teasing, gentle, strong, virile, boyish, vulnerable, determined—an endless list of contradictions. He was a constant chafe of irritation she couldn't reach with a soothing scratch.

How very nice for Gena that she'd found contentment waiting in the shadow of her Prescott man. How fortunate that she could serenely sit idle while

111

he saw selfishly to his own goals. Skins and sky, indeed. Not her. That was not the life she wanted for herself or for her son. She'd known fourteen years of abandoned desolation while her father had pursued his dreams. She wouldn't wish that same heartache upon Jacob. Nor would she endure that kind of neglect, herself. She wanted to be more than a creature comfort like a hot cup of coffee, a warm bedroll, and a good horse—things appreciated for the moment as needed, then left behind without a thought. That's what she'd been compared to the Bar K. The ranch was Rory's life; she was a convenience. She'd taken all she could of his coming in late—if he came at all—smelling of the range, too tired to talk to her, too busy to share with her—wanting nothing more than to crawl in bed beside her, to spend his passions on her the way he might with a two-dollar whore before falling asleep without a word. And in the morning, he was gone. Seven days a week, three hundred and sixty-five days a year, he'd been gone.

It wasn't that she didn't understand. It wasn't that she didn't love and respect him for what he was trying to do. She had. She did. She'd watched him work himself to the point of dropping and cried over him after he'd fallen into an exhausted sleep, loving him so much she'd lain awake just to hold him. She knew what was driving him so mercilessly—that relentlessly approaching deadline when the note on the ranch was due. But she could have made it easier for him. She tried to make it easier for him. And damn his Prescott pride, he wouldn't let her.

Norah sipped her wine and blinked back the bitter memory of those years. Why had she come back? He hadn't changed. He still had to do it all himself. He still wouldn't rely on her for anything more serious than the ease of his desires. And that wasn't enough.

Why couldn't he understand that it wasn't enough? Prideful man. Arrogant, stubborn, thick-headed, prideful Prescott man.

And in spite of it all, she loved him. Or because of it.

What was she going to do about Rory Prescott?

Dispirited because she was no closer to finding an answer than when she'd left Baltimore, Norah climbed from the bath. As she dried off, she glanced toward the window. It was almost dark. Why hadn't she heard Jacob return? Or Ruth, for the housekeeper hadn't been home when she arrived? Father and son were probably at the Lone Star being shamelessly spoilt by Aurora Prescott. She frowned at that image. Fine. Let them enjoy themselves. She wouldn't wait up. She'd grab something cold from the kitchen and the rest of the bottle of wine and sulk in her room for the rest of the evening. That would teach them. But, of course it wouldn't, so she might as well dress and wait for them downstairs with a proper impatience.

There was a rattling in the dining room and the faint acrid scent of something burning. Norah swept into the room, at first surprised by its dimness. Rory was leaning across the big oak table lighting a branch of candles. Hearing her, he turned, and Norah realized the tapers weren't the only things burning. There was a definite fire in Rory Prescott's eyes.

"'Evening," came the rumbling caress of his voice. A slow appreciative dip in his gaze took in her gown of primrose faille with its proper white-satin collar and cuffs and lacy ascot, scorching all the way down to her shoes and back up. "You look mighty fine, Miss Norah."

Miss Norah? She eyed him warily. What game was he playing now? He had changed into a crisp white

113

shirt, as stark in color as the brilliance of his smile. Against it, his skin was dark and weather-warmed right up to the pale strip of his brow that was ever-shaded by his John B. He let that smile play out lazily, then lit the remaining candles. The table was set for two.

"Where's Jacob?" she questioned with a mounting suspicion.

"He decided to bunk over at the Lone Star for the night. Hope you doan mind dishing up for yourself. Ruth's helping out at a friend's who's laying in and feeling poorly. Looks like it's just you and me."

"And the rest of the Bar K hands."

He met her wry observation with another slow smile. "Doan think we have to worry over them. Made it right clear that I'd shoot any man jack who puts a boot on the porch steps tonight."

"Oh." How much more obvious could he be? There was nothing remotely subtle in his lingering grin. He was planning to seduce her and didn't want any interruptions. Norah was at once angry and anticipating. How dare he assume she'd fall right in with his plans. Oh, Lord, how good it would feel to be in his arms! She drew a cautious breath and advanced into the room, very aware of how his gaze followed her. Hot and hungry.

"This will be a fine time for us to talk, won't it?"

"Talk?" He was studying her gown as if trying to decide how best to go about taking it off her. "That what you want to do? Make talk?"

"About Jacob," she clarified crisply.

"Jacob. We could do that. If you want."

"Unless there was something else you had in mind?" Her stare skewered him, but he just grinned.

"No, ma'am. Talk's fine."

Dangerous. Oh, he was dangerous. More so now

than when she'd met him. Then, he'd been little more than a handsome boy, full of swaggering charm and child-like wonder. That boy was gone, honed by years of hardship and heartache into a man as hard-packed as the Dakota plains. He'd toughened in body and in mind, become lean of muscle and spare of expression. Time had weathered him, shaping him in its passing—not into long, comfortable lines like his father, but into harsh unyielding angles, like Garth Kincaid. However, even as she mourned the loss of his boyish innocence, Norah was drawn by the commanding presence of the man he'd become. A man to be reckoned with. A man used to getting what he wanted. And tonight, he wanted her.

She should have run for her room and turned the lock on the door, but her pride demanded she stand her ground. After all, she was more than a match for this one simple cowboy. She had complete control of the situation. She could keep her wayward wants in check and Rory Prescott at arm's length. But more deeply, where her heart was untouched by cool reasoning, came the whisper, *Let go. Let him love you. Isn't that why you came all this way?*

"Jacob tells me you have him lined up to work your books." Coffee. She needed coffee to keep herself on edge and wary. To reach it, she had to pass between Rory and the big sideboard. A tight fit considering he refused to give even a fraction of an inch. As she sidled by, his head dipped slightly. She could feel his face brushing against the nape of her neck where tendrils of hair clung in damp wisps from the bath.

"You smell good," he murmured huskily.

She scooted away from him to assume a defensive pose. "About Jacob," she prompted tersely.

Rory smiled. "He's a smart kid. Couple more years and I could really use him."

115

Use him. Norah hung onto that telling phrase to fire her determination. "He tells me he's going to own the Bar K someday."

"Well, now, I doan plan on stepping down any time soon; but someday, it'll be his."

"What if he doesn't want it?"

Rory's smile grew mystified. "Not want it?" He clearly couldn't comprehend such a thing. "A course he'll want it. I'm building it up for him, for his future."

"Are you? Then maybe you'd better ask him if he has any desire to be a rancher."

He studied her, intense in thought, eyes darkening to a flat black. "What are you saying, Norah? That what I am isn't good enough for my son?"

"I'm asking that you consider Jacob and what he might want for himself. What if he decides he'd rather take on a career in the East?"

He gave an arrogant snort of disbelief. "Why'd he want to do that? Scotty, he was all full of Eastern schoolin', and he still came back home."

"We're not talking about Scott. And we're not talking about you. I want what's best for Jacob."

"Speak it out plain, Norah. You doan want him working for what he gets. You want to hand it to him so's he never has to get his hands dirty. You doan want him to be an ignorant, good-for-nothing-but-cows cowboy like his daddy. It weren't good enough for you, and it ain't good enough for him."

"That's not what I said."

"I thought you said it pretty loud and clear three years ago." He stalked from the room, his spurs hissing like rattlesnakes stirred up into a striking anger. He was pouring Scotch whiskey into a tumbler when he heard her come up behind him. The light touch of her hand upon the small of his

116

back brought a rigid snap of objection. "I ain't got nothing here that either of you want. You might's well go back to Baltimore." He bolted down a good portion of his drink and glared out over the acres darkening into the indigos and deep purples of twilight.

"Rory, I thought we were going to talk, not fight."

"Well, it doan look like that's possible, now does it? You an' me, we ain't never gonna see eye to eye on nothing."

She'd struck him a crippling blow and he was reeling, wanting to cover his wounds as best he could and protect against further hurt. She'd knocked the pride of accomplishment out from under him, making him think that everything he'd struggled for, everything he loved, had no value. That wasn't what she'd intended. Not at all. And suddenly it was very important that he know that.

"Rory, we don't have to agree on everything. I just want to have a voice in things."

"Seems you got yourself a mighty loud one lately."

"But are you listening?"

"What have you got to say that I want to hear?"

"Maybe nothing, but I want you to listen anyway. Will you?"

He was silent for a moment, studying the contents of his glass. "Awright. Talk."

"You're wrong."

He gave a bitter laugh. "That's news."

"You're wrong about my not wanting what's here," she explained softly, strongly. Her palms moved in slow circles along the tense line of his back. "You've got everything I want. Everything. You always have, Rory."

"Well, hell, that makes perfect sense." He turned to curve an arm about her, drawing her up to his

117

chest. "To everyone but me. Am I jus' too dumb to figure it out?"

"Too stubborn, maybe." With her head resting over the hard thunder of his heart, Norah closed her eyes and sighed.

"I love you, Norah, you an' the boy. An' I want you to be happy. I want you to be happy here with me."

"Do you know what would make me happy right now?"

"What? Name it."

"Dinner." She felt his start of surprise and gave him a squeeze. "I'm starved. Let's go see what Ruth left us."

"Sounds good." He lifted his glass to drain it then paused, frowning. "Norah, what's inebriate mean?"

"A drunkard. Why?"

Slowly, he set the glass down untouched. "Jus' asking." Then he hooked his arm tightly about her waist and escorted her to dinner.

Chapter Eight

"Everything looks wonderful."

Rory detailed the elegant curve of Norah's back as she bent over one of the platters Ruth had arranged on the sideboard. He wet his lips, and his voice came in a low rumble. "It surely does."

The husky insinuation made Norah pause, then she began to fill her plate. She was nervous. She was fluttering inside like a girl in short skirts with her first beau. That was ridiculous, of course. Her relationship with Rory Prescott had been very, very physical. It wasn't apprehension or the unknown that had her hands atremble; it was the anticipation.

She heaped slice after slice of cold beef on her plate, following with potatoes and vegetables and bread. As long as they were eating, the situation would be stable. They could sit down at the table with each other for a quiet meal, pretending that they weren't alone in the house, that their thoughts weren't fixed on the big bed upstairs and what they'd do when they got there. Norah wasn't fooling herself. She knew that's where they were headed. It was inevitable. It was what they both wanted. Unless they got on some flammable topic that caused tempers to flare hotter than passions, they would be making love tonight. Their long separation only made the tension keener, the wanting stronger. Awareness was thick and almost palpable between them.

Slow down. Don't rush it. Make him wait. She told herself over and over as she felt him behind her like heat rising from a well-stoked fire. As soon as they came together, things would change. She would lose her tenuous control. She would be allowing him rule over part of her; and, though she wanted it, she knew it wasn't the wisest thing to do. She couldn't let Rory consume her. She couldn't become lost in him again. Not until the lines were more clearly drawn. There were concessions she had to have, assurances he needed to give. So she loaded down her plate, thinking of every extra morsel as a second gained toward forestalling what was bound to come.

Rory watched her with a bemused smile. "After you stow all that away, you planning on finding a hole somewheres to put up for the winter?"

She looked at the embarrassingly large amount of food and said testily, "I'm hungry."

"I guess so. Where you meaning to put all of it inside that there tight corset?"

"I'll just have to take my time. I enjoy savoring a good meal. You're not in any big hurry, are you?"

"No, ma'am. You know me. I likes taking my time." And he grinned, wide and provocatively.

Oh, yes. How well she knew. His dark eyes gave hers a caressing gaze before sliding lower to linger on the fragile quiver of her lips, lower still to the agitated movement of silk over her bosom. Hang him for looking so comfortably smug! Norah was clinging to her composure by the fingernails, and he was easy as you please, the way he might be in a familiar saddle. He was showing no signs of the anxious tension gnawing away at her will. How could he be so relaxed? Angrily, she added another helping of peas to her already over-laden dish.

"Got everything you need there, Norah?"

She looked down at her plate, wondering how she was going to stuff even a portion of it into a stomach shrunk tight by anxiety. "For now."

"Guess I might as well take what I want then."

He'd watched her build that dish of dinner up the way she'd erect a good-sized wall. Rory figured she'd be chewing on the last of it come spring. And he couldn't wait anywhere near that long to satisfy his gnawing hunger. That's not what he'd envisioned when he'd planned this night for them together. He didn't want to push her. He'd hoped she'd meet him halfway. He'd hoped he could melt her will like butter if given the chance, but she wasn't warming to him in the least. With want wadding up inside him, he tried to dredge up more patience. He really tried.

Was she still mad about the words? he wondered as he stabbed a piece of Prescott beef. She could hold to her vexation longer than any human he'd ever known. Weeks would go by and, suddenly, she'd be throwing something up at him that he'd clean forgotten. And then she'd be twice as angry because he had. That never made sense to a man who enjoyed a good fight but never carried a grudge. Maybe that was the problem. Maybe Norah had too much time on her hands to just sit back and stew. He'd have to find some way to distract her.

"What are you grinning at?" There was a cautious edge to her question.

"Nothin'." But he grinned wider and came to join her at the table. Before taking his seat, he withdrew a bottle that had been chilling in a bucket and extended it for her examination. "Whatcha think?"

She read the label and her brows soared. "My!"

"Scotty sent it to me. Me, I doan know nothing 'bout grapes, jus' grain, but I trust his call when it comes to such things."

"That's a very good year."

He looked at it, unimpressed. "They say things get better with age. Think they're right about that, Norah-honey?"

"Some things do," she replied in a tone as dry as the vintage he held. "Take grapes. If you take care to preserve them the right way, you have a fine wine. If you don't, they wither and rot on the vine."

He chuckled, a low, throaty sound of appreciation. He loved it when she was like this, all prickly and provoking. Her wit kept him on his toes, like hot-footing it through a nest of rattlers. The stings were sharp, but—damn!—a man never got bored. And he'd been so bored with nothing but his own company. He remembered excruciatingly well how much he enjoyed making love to her, but he'd forgotten the simple joy of just talking with her. He'd forgotten how much he liked Norah Prescott.

Before she could stop him, he jabbed his tableknife into the cork and began to twist, finally wrestling it free. Then he filled two glasses, passing her one of the slender stems.

"What do you say, Norah? A toast?"

She was wary but warming slightly. "All right. What shall we drink to?"

"To keeping good things from spoiling on the vine." He lifted his glass and waited for her to do the same. Smiling somewhat wryly, she did.

Rory took a big gulp and froze. Godalmighty what kind of poison had Scotty sent him? Had it gone to vinegar in the bottle? He held it in his mouth, not wanting to swallow the sour stuff and not able to spit it out. Across from him, Norah took a sip, swished it genteelly, then she sighed. Dang, was it supposed to taste so vile? Manfully, he forced it down his throat, feeling as though he'd just inhaled a mouthful of corral dust.

"What a surprising bouquet."

He answered her praise with a drawl of, "Ain't that the truth," then discreetly pushed his glass aside. Smiling, he hoisted the bottle. "Let me top that off for you, honey."

And so they dined, Norah tackling her mountain of food and bottomless glass of wine and Rory leaning back in his chair with a lazy ease, watching her through eyes that were anything but.

Finally, Norah had to concede. If she put one more forkful beyond her palate, she was going to pop. But the minute she stopped, Rory Prescott, who was lounging back like a big, dangerous cougar on a branch, would spring without mercy. There had to be some way to keep him at a safe distance without compromising her corset stays.

"So, Rory, tell me what improvements you've made to the Bar K."

He looked at her blankly, then with a steeping suspicion. He knew how Norah felt about the ranch. But her prompting smile undercut his hesitation, and he found himself going on and on about his favorite topic of conversation, absolutely thrilled to have her as an audience.

She did listen, listened with her teeth gritted and her resentment simmering. The Bar K. He might as well have been bragging about how many whores he'd lustily bedded in her absence. He loved the pastures and the prairie. It was all too obvious from the softening of his voice and the pride in his expression. He didn't talk about his son that way. He didn't refer to his marriage with equal reverence. It was the land, that hallowed Kincaid ground, that controlled the big cowboy's heart and head. It was the land that had stolen him out of her bed each morning and returned him drained of life. It sapped his strength and, like a greedy lover, was never satisfied. How could she compete with that?

Because the land was so dear to him, she could resent it, but she couldn't hate it. As Gena had said, it was part of what he was. A part of what she loved. He'd worked hard and long because that was the nature of man he was. He'd toiled with his own hands because he wanted to know the pride of accomplishment personally. And he'd kept those things he cherished selfishly to himself. He never shared the frustrations, the worries, or the fears, yet she'd always known when one or all lurked behind his disguising smile. If she asked, he'd evade. If she demanded, he'd deny. It wasn't until he'd worked through the worst of it on his own that he'd tell her with that matter-of-fact modesty of what he'd overcome. He refused her counsel and her comfort. And he would have sold everything he owned right down to his spurs and black John B. before he'd have mentioned the fact that they were in financial trouble. He would have hocked his saddle and mortgaged his soul before he'd have bent to take one cent from her. Because he was a Prescott and a Kincaid. and they humbled themselves before no man. Or woman.

"You 'bout finished with that, or was you planning to get a second helping?"

Norah glanced down at her plate and refrained from groaning.

Rory's smile grew silky with insinuation. "Well, if you're done eating and I'm done talking—"

"Maybe I will have dessert," she blurted out recklessly.

"Ruth left an apple pie in the kitchen. How 'bout a nice fat slice topped off with some cream?" He grinned wickedly when she swallowed hard.

"Maybe I'll pass on the dessert." His eyes at once flared up like lanterns with the wicks turned high, so she added defensively, "But there are some things I think we should discuss before we—while we have the time."

"Like?"

"Jacob."

"We already talked about him. And we talked about the ranch, and we talked about how my daddy was doing and about everything including the weather. I ain't done so much talking since I had to explain to my mama how her best Sunday stockings ended up stretched between my slingshot. I can't think of a single thing that needs saying except that I think it's time you and me stopped talking and started—"

"You and me. We need to talk about us, Rory."

"What about us?" He stared her down from across the table, his dark gaze impatient, his frown moody.

"I think before we—before we get on to other things, we should clear the air."

"Do you?" His eyes narrowed unpromisingly. He wasn't easy now. His big frame was still in a relaxed posture, but he was as tense as a fence line. "And after we finish up making talk, then we can—get on to other things?"

She gave a stiff nod.

"Then talk."

Norah drew a deep breath. This was what she'd been waiting for, but now she was suddenly scared. What if nothing were resolved in words? What if nothing could be resolved? Then, she would be forced into a decision, one she was far from ready to make. The coming back had been too easy. She'd found a husband who still loved her, a family who was ready for the most part to embrace her back into the fold, and a situation not at all as dire as the one she'd fled. Part of her wanted to slip back into the pattern of living on the Dakota prairie and into the arms of the man she loved. The other rebelled against such a softening of spirit. If she were to stay, it would have to be without reservations; and, at this point, she had plenty. And now was the time to air them.

"Will you let Jacob take his schooling in the East?"

"If that's what he wants."

"And if he wants to stay there to find work?"

"I gots lots of problem with that." Rory shoved away from the table and stalked to the windows. His fingertips drummed aggressively against his thighs.

If he thought he was going to stuff the Bar K down his son's throat, Norah would fight him to the last breath. She was preparing to tell him so when his growling words surprised her.

"But if he wants to, I guess that'll be his choice."

Norah blinked. That sounded like Ethan Prescott instead of Garth Kincaid. She began to silently hope. Still, she was cautious.

"And if I decide I'd like to live in town for a while?"

"We tried that before." The tapping stopped, and his fingers made a fist. "I live here. It'd be inconvenient, doan you think?"

"Not as inconvenient as Baltimore."

"What you're saying is you doan want to live with me as my wife."

"No, that's not—"

"Well, with you there an' me here, it makes it kinda hard for me to be a good husband to you regular-like."

"You weren't when I lived here." The words came out of the blue. She hadn't meant to say them. He took them like a slap. His head snapped back; his eyes blinked, then grew hard.

"You mind spellin' that out?"

"I'll write it down if it will make you understand it better. We've been over this before."

He sucked in a breath, and she knew he was going to get difficult.

"Well, hell, Norah, I'm just an ignorant ole cowhand. What did you expect? Me to catch on first time? It's purely amazing that a smart female like you would marry up with a man who's harder to train than a deaf hound."

"Stop it."

"Stop what?"

"That poor stupid-me business. You're not stupid, Rory Prescott. You've got too much of your grandfather in you. If you don't catch on, it's because you don't want to learn."

"What you trying to teach me, Norah-honey. Good manners? Proper grammar? Sophistication? Who the hell have I got to impress out here in the middle of a field of cows? What do I need to be them things for? Why should whether I say ain't or isn't matter a hill of navy beans?"

"It doesn't."

"Then why we fightin'?" he shouted back at her.

"I don't know." Norah broke off. Her breath was coming in quick, hard gasps. A frustrating wetness stung her eyes. Why couldn't she concentrate when they were together? Things that were so clear to her tangled up in confusion the minute their voices

127

escalated. She fought to separate emotion from reason. This one time, she had to make her thoughts known without feelings getting in the way.

"Was that why you left? Because of the fighting?" he asked in an abruptly deadened tone.

"No. It wasn't the arguing. It was the loving."

He stared at her, wildly bewildered. "What?"

"When did you stop caring, Rory? The day we buried your grandfather?"

His confusion grew. "I never—"

"That's right. You never. You were never there for me. You were never there when I woke up in the morning. You were never there when I needed you."

"Never there? You ain't making the least bit of sense. I ain't never been anywhere else. You was the one who left."

"You left a long time before I did. You used to be so considerate, so kind. I loved that about you more than anything else."

Loved. Past tense. As in "used to but no more." Rory went cold inside.

"Kind? I ain't never been nothing but kind to you! Have I ever laid a mean hand on you? Have I ever forced you to anything against your will? Have I ever done anything but my damnedest to make things easy for you? Norah, have I ever hurt you or made you cry?"

"Yes," she cried to that last question. "Yes." And then she was crying, a whole river of bitter tears.

"Don't do that," he growled, horrified by the intensity of her weeping. He could hold his own against the harshest words, but the faintest glimmer of tears undid him. A sobbing female always put him in a helpless panic. "Norah, don't." But she continued to wail, not in dignified little sniffles but in great, gulping sobs that reddened her nose and turned her eyes to silver. "I'm sorry, honey. Don't cry. Awww . . . hell."

He framed her damp face in the cradle of his hands and crushed her mouth beneath his. She gave a muffled sound of protest, but he wouldn't relent. Her hands pushed against his shoulders, but he wouldn't yield. Not until he felt her will buckle and her lips part.

"Norah-honey," he whispered against those desire-slackened lips, "I never meant to hurt you. I won't never do it again. I'll be kind to you. I'll be so damned good to you. But right now, I want to love you. Let me love you."

That was his answer to their every conflict. If he couldn't best her with words, he would crush her with the strength of her own passions. Not this time, she swore.

"Rory, no."

"No? What do you mean, no?" And he was kissing her again, deeply, druggingly.

Struggling, she wrenched her face away. "Stop it."

He'd come down on his knees beside her chair so his stare could burn into hers, dark and full of hot promise. "Stop? You want me to stop?"

"Ye—"

His mouth opened wide over hers, spreading the way for the plunge of his tongue. It stroked hers, tempting it into a return play of pleasure. And when she was lost to that sensuous dueling, he drew back, leaving her panting and wanting more. Her neck arched as his kisses scorched down from jaw to collarline and her hands fluttered up to mesh tight in his fiery hair.

"You want me to stop, Norah?" he taunted huskily. "You want me to stop kissing you and touching you? Would you rather spend the rest of the

129

night arguing or upstairs making love with me?"

What kind of choice was that when he was sucking at the pulse point of her neck to provoke a hurried rhythm of response? Her body was already traitorously answering, moving with his roving caresses. Even if she said no to him, there wasn't the slightest chance that she'd have another coherent thought all evening. She wanted what he had to give too desperately.

"Upstairs," she whispered.

Rory rocked back on his heels to appraise the flush of readiness on her lovely features. His fingertips gently brushed away the last hint of her tears. Gruffly, he rumbled, "Hot damn."

His palms grazed the slope of her shoulders, and Norah gave a gasp as the bodice of her gown dropped away. Even as she reached to catch it, his head lowered so his mouth might ride the pale white swell of each breast in turn. By then, she'd forgotten the dress and was holding to him instead. His hands moved restlessly along the hard shell of her corset, wanting to feel the soft woman trapped inside.

"Why do you wear so danged many clothes?" he grumbled as he fumbled for the fastenings of her quilted corset cover. The bit of cotton and lace went sailing, and he turned grimly to the hard cage constricting her ribs and already-tiny waist. Where the hell had she put all that food?

Norah's forearms rested on his shoulders. Her fingers laced behind his bowed head, and her thumbs massaged his neck lightly. Trembling with anticipation, she studied the curve of his lashes where they lay in surprising thick crescents along the weather-tanned cheeks. She watched his big hands work the tiny eyelets with a Herculean patience, and she felt as though the corset suddenly shrank two sizes. Then he

130

was peeling that away, too, and only the thin cotton of her chemise remained. Her breath caught, her sensitivity heightened to an unbearable degree as she awaited the tender roughness of his touch. But instead of easing the achy yearning, he bent further and began to unlace her shoes.

The delay was making her crazy. Her hands were restless, kneading in agitated circles along his shoulders and back, frenzied by the hard feel of him. He sent one shoe flying. Then his hands were warm upon one slender leg, sliding up to find the top of her stocking. Norah closed her eyes and tried to quiet the agony of need when his touch didn't reach high enough. Her hips twitched, scooting toward the edge of the seat as her free leg rubbed his back and began to curl around him.

He tried to concentrate on the other shoe, but the back of her leg was stroking along his shoulder blades. There was only so much a man could stand, and he'd reached his limit. The second shoe followed the first, landing with a resounding crash. Rory's arm hooked about Norah's waist; and he jerked her forward, centering himself between her wide-flung thighs, and kissed her to near delirium. With one hand, he began pulling the pins from her hair. The other burrowed beneath her petticoat. She gave a muffled cry into his mouth as the heel of his hand pressed against her. He could tell by the damp heat through the cotton bloomers and by the trembling along her limbs that she was more than ready. She was almost there.

His kiss deepened as he set up the tempo her body craved. She moved with him and against him, making soft sounds. Within seconds, the noises became low, throaty moans. She broke from his kiss, burying her hot face against his neck while the breath panted from her in irregular shudders. Her fingers clawed at his shirt until, finally, her body jerked rigid and collapsed into a series of dissolving tremors.

When, after several minutes, she hadn't moved so much as an eyelash, Rory nuzzled against the spill of her hair and whispered, "You all right, darlin'? It'd be damned inconvenient of you to expire just now."

Norah gave a gusty chuckle and her lips moved upon his ear, nibbling, tracing wickedly with the tip on her tongue. "Ummmm. Better than all right. You know it always is. You've always done your best bragging about how well you satisfy me."

"I never brag." His arms cinched up tighter, squishing her to his chest. "Was that night you came for me at the Lone Star anything to brag on? We did make love, didn't we?"

"Yes." She paused just long enough to provoke his suspense. "And you may brag."

"Cain't brag if I cain't remember."

"Let's go upstairs, and I'll go over the high points with you."

"Yes, ma'am."

He eased back onto his heels and let her stand. Her crumpled gown dropped about one bared, one stockinged foot. Her arms curled about his neck, so that when he stood, he lifted her right off the floor. Her knees bent, and her ankles locked behind him.

"Make love to me, Rory Prescott. Ride me hard."

"Yes, ma'am."

He strode through the dining room with her wrapped burr-like around him. With her body wriggling and her kisses sketching the angles of his face, he was lathered into a state of confusion by the time he reached the hall. Her hips were rocking, inviting an arousal that pained for release. Her breasts rubbed and pushed against him until he was feverish with need. He stopped at the foot of the stairs, and Norah chose that moment to kiss him. She twisted like a hungry cat around him, her tongue slick and searching in the far reaches of his mouth. A guttural sound tore up from his throat as he cupped her impudent buttocks and ground her hard against his groin. When she dragged her lips across his cheek, the last of his restraint caved in completely.

"I can't make it all the way up them stairs. I can't wait that long."

"Don't wait," she urged, breathlessly.

He dropped her down right there on the hall runner, shucking off her drawers, kicking out of his boots, and rucking off his shirt and jeans. Then his weight was heavy upon her and his heat was pressed against her. Norah shot a frantic look toward the front door.

"Rory, what if someone comes in?" It was a faint protest, for he was already yanking her knees up on either side of him.

"That'll teach 'em to knock first."

Then he drove inside her, so hard and deep she cried out from the shock of it. Immediately, her legs clasped about him as he pounded into her at a merciless pace. The force of his thrusts shoved her along the rough nap of the carpet, chafing her backside just as he was abrading her insides. It was a maddening friction. Her hands tore at his shoulders then flung wide to seek out some grasp on reality. She caught at the fine-turned leg of one of the wall-hugging tables and hung on for dear life. All the show pieces set atop it began to shiver and clatter and finally to topple as he rammed into her with one last plunge. He rasped out her name as his life-giving strength pumped hot and full inside her. Her answering cry was swallowed up by his kiss.

It was a long moment before either of them could move. Norah could feel laughter vibrating through the broad chest that crushed her to the floor.

"Now that was something to brag on."

She should have chided him for his monumental conceit, but all she could do was whisper back contentedly, "Yes, indeed it was."

Chapter Nine

The soft give of the bed was infinitely better suited to making love than the scratchy wool carpet on the hall floor. They spent the remaining hours of the evening in it—touching gently, laughing softly, kissing deeply.

This was the homecoming she'd wished for. Differences were washed away in that initial riptide of passion, and now what remained was the quiet pull and ebb of emotions. How could she hold out against him when he was once again the sweet-voiced charmer who'd courted her so determinedly so many years ago? He made love to her with a rollicking playfulness that was both delightful and devilish. She was shaken by gales of laughter and lusty groans. He teased her mercilessly about the rug-burns on her rump and about how quickly her appetite had turned from Ruth's cooking to his kissing. And right in the middle of some rambunctious fondling, he'd go suddenly still, looking down on her through a gaze so tender it shook her all to pieces. And he'd smile, that slow, sassy smile that never failed to whip up her heartbeats in a hurry. Dear God, if it were possible, she'd swear she was falling in love with him for the very first time.

She had no idea what time it was when she finally fell asleep curled up against him and around him. It was the most satisfying sleep she'd known in a long, long while, deep and surprisingly dreamless. The sun was high when she stirred at last, stretching with a languid pleasure beneath warm covers then going rigid as soon as her eyes opened. To empty sheets.

After all his sweet loving, he'd left without waking her!

Devastated, Norah rolled over, straight into the smooth tanned flesh of Rory Prescott's shoulder. He was sleeping with his back to her, perched on the very edge of the bed. Weak with relief, she cast her arms around him for a reckless hug. He jerked, startled from his slumber by the hard squeeze and soft press of her. But with awareness came a long, contented sigh. He cuddled her arms to him in no particular hurry to move.

"'Morning," Norah purred. Her lips brushed over the untidy red hair where it curved behind his ear.

"Ummmmhmmmm."

"I didn't expect to find you here." She continued that soft caress along the hard line of his shoulder.

"Where else'd I be? This is our bed."

Our. It sounded nice. "I thought you'd be out with the boys riding herd already."

"I done my ridin' last night. I was plannin' on sleepin' in a few more hours this mornin'," came his groggy grumble.

"Don't let me bother you."

"I won't."

And with that, he flopped onto his back, sidling down deeper into the comfortable embrace of his bed without opening his eyes.

Norah lifted up on her elbow and let her gaze

linger upon the relaxed angles of his face. As a cool, calm, clear-thinking woman, she should have been using the time to speculate on how best to benefit from this shift in their relationship. Instead, she was following the swell of his biceps with the admiring graze of her fingertips and her mind was fully occupied with heated remembrance of the night before. It had been too long since she'd felt this lazy, sated happiness. And she realized that here was the only place she'd find it, here with this man. That should have disturbed her, but oddly, it brought a strange sense of satisfaction.

"I love you, Rory Prescott."

"Hmmm? What? You say somethin', honey?"

"No. Go back to sleep."

He nodded and appeared to do just that.

I love you, Rory Prescott.

She settled her head upon his shoulder and closed her eyes. But sleep hadn't the same charm as all those naked inches of solid man right beneath her fingertips.

Rory's state of sleepy bliss was easing into one of arousal. He let it happen, relishing the slow, heated threads of pleasure twining through him. He did nothing to hurry the condition. Norah was seeing to that. And, damn, it was glorious. He kept his eyes closed, savoring her nearness through all his other senses. Her touch was light, just a whispering caress. It moved along the top of his skin, skimming like wind blowing soft across the plains. Over the swell of his shoulders, down the hard-packed plain of his chest to the flatlands of his belly. And once it slipped beyond, it was danged hard for him to pretend he was relaxed. He held his breath as her hand stroked down his thigh and let it out in a rush when she paused on the return.

"Am I bothering you?" she asked sweetly.

"No, ma'am. You jus' go on with what you was doing. I'll let you know if it gets bothersome."

"You do that."

If the provocation of her clever fingers wasn't bad enough, her lips began to follow along that same heart-shaking trail. She lingered at the scar on his ribs, licking along it until he nearly forgot how to breathe, then continued wetly down the jerk and quiver of his abdomen. Lower. His legs began to shift restlessly upon the bedcovers, then his heels shoved down deep as a jolt of unexpected sensation rocked him. Lordamercy, where had she learned such a thing? Even the well-versed doves of Crowe Creek hadn't pleasured him in such a fashion during his early run-loose days. He'd never experienced passion quite so wild and raw. It shocked him, amazed him.

Moments later he grabbed her head, nearly dragging her up by the hair so he could savage her with his kiss. Her mouth was bruised by it, but she was smiling when he clutched her close to the harsh laboring of his chest. His fingers raked through the tumble of her sable-colored curls.

"Honey, you oughta give a man some warnin' when you're gonna do something like that. You danged near stopped my heart."

"You might be surprised how creative I can be in the mornings if you stayed around long enough to find out."

His hand cupped under her chin, lifting her gaze to his. His eyes held a deep, lambent glow that warmed her through to the soul. "Darlin', I aim to become the laziest ranch boss this side of the Missouri."

Norah searched his dark stare. Did he mean that? She wanted to believe he did, but she'd trusted before and been hurt by disappointment. Her smile was small and skeptical as she rubbed her thumb across his moist lower lip.

"You talk a good line, Rory Prescott, but seeing is believing."

"Guess you'll just have to wait around and prove it to yourself then, won't you?"

"Maybe I will."

His expression grew very quiet. "I love you, Norah."

"I know you do."

That wasn't quite what he wanted to hear, nor was the assurance that she'd stay quite as certain as he'd hoped it would be. But for now, it satisfied him. The way she satisfied him. He coaxed her down for a slow, sizzling kiss.

"I suppose I should head on over to the Lone Star to fetch Jacob," he murmured with a notable lack of motivation.

"I'm sure he's just fine where he is. He's probably having trout for breakfast."

He chuckled, and his smile played out into a tantalizing grin. "Well now, if we're in no hurry, why doan we finish up on what you started?"

"I suppose we could, since you haven't got any other plans for the morning."

"Not a one." He clapped his big hands down on her buttocks and lifted her effortlessly until she was astride him. "You forget how to ride after all them years in the city?"

Her smile was full of saucy smugness. "It's not something you forget. It's like driving a car."

"That ain't very reassuring since the last time I drove we ended up smackin' into a tree."

"Then leave the driving to me."

He put his hands, palms up, on either side of his head. "It's all yours."

"All mine," she echoed with a look that was both thoughtful and full of deviltry. She shifted atop him, wiggling with a naughty temptation. When he reached for her hips to position them where he would have them, she slapped at his hands. "No, you don't! I'm driving. Keep your hands to yourself."

"Yes, ma'am." He grinned and laced his fingers behind his head. That smile faltered when she leaned low to brush kisses along his jaw. Her breasts were hard passion points grazing his chest, and he fought the need to sample their supple allure. He turned his head to try for a kiss, but she sat back out of reach. She was driving, all right. She was driving him plum crazy.

About that time, she figured she'd teased him enough. The smolder of anticipation in his dark eyes ignited her own. She eased back, lifting slightly. Then she came down upon him, sheathing him so hot and tight his hands flew down involuntarily to grip at her knees. When she moved, it was in imitation of his strong, sure thrusts. His fingers bit deep, leaving individual imprints on her pale thighs that would last every bit as long as the undignified scrapes on her bottom. Brands of how intent, how intense their loving was.

Rory reached up for her, grasping her shoulders to pull her down to him. His kiss was wide and wet. His voice was ragged.

"Oh, God, I love you, Norah. Doan ever leave me. Doan ever stop loving me."

At first, she thought the loud banging was from her heart crashing into her ribs. Then she realized the sound came from below, an insistent knocking upon the front door. Rory heard it, too, for his features tensed in extreme annoyance.

"I'm gonna have somebody's butt for breakfast,"

he growled menacingly.

Norah turned his face back toward her and teased him with the thrust of her tongue into his mouth. "Why don't you finish what you have on your plate, first?" was her sultry suggestion.

He gripped her hips, jerking her down as he arched up and she gasped as pleasure expanded inside her. Her head fell back as she felt the wild ride run away with her. Even as the pace slowed to a gallop, she heard the thunderous echoes of the door knocker.

"Maybe—maybe you'd better see—who it is?" she panted faintly.

"I'll be in a much better mood to be obliging in just a second," he rasped in reply. Using his hands upon her hips to control her movement over him, with several fast and furious plunges, he was shuddering his relief.

There was little rest for them. Another volley of knocks sounded, provoking a rumble of resentment from the big cowboy.

"I'm gonna kill whoever's makin' that racket." He plucked Norah off him and rolled out of bed, casting about in frustration. "Where the hell are my clothes?"

Norah eased over onto her belly and grinned up at him. "I'd look downstairs, if I were you."

"Oh, yeah." He grinned back and bent to kiss her hard and quick. He grabbed out a fresh pair of long johns and donned them hurriedly. Then he glanced to where she lay sleek and naked in the midst of his rumpled covers. And he groaned. "Doan you move. I ain't finished with you yet."

Norah watched him stomp out of the room in his socks and listened to his heavy tread on the stairs. She sighed happily and let her head rest on her folded arms. Oh my, what a man! How had she existed for three years without this, without him?

Then she heard voices, below, a man's mixing with Rory's low rumble. And she sat bolt upright, stunned, crying out in dismay.

"Oh, no! Trevor!"

"Awright! Just a minute, goddammit!"

Rory wrestled up his jeans and was securing them as he jerked open the door. The dire expression on his face would have sent any of his men scrambling for cover. But it wasn't one of his men. Or any of his family. He looked the slicked-back dude up and down in mystification. And he tried to be civil.

"Who the hell are you and what do you want?"

Trevor Samuels was not a man to be easily intimidated. But confronted by this giant redhead whose voice roared like a cannon volley, he knew a moment of caution. He'd obviously dragged the man out of bed. "I do apologize if my arrival has been inopportune. I'm looking for Norah Prescott. They told me in town that I might find her here."

The big man's eyes narrowed. "Why you lookin' for her?"

"My name is Trevor Samuels. I'm her fian—I'm a friend of hers from Baltimore."

"That so," he replied in a deceivingly soft drawl. "I'm her husband."

Surely not! Trevor had met Scott Prescott in Baltimore. Norah's brother-in-law was sleek, dark, and refined. Nothing at all like this huge, half-dressed, gruff-voiced fellow with his rugged, weather-chiseled handsomeness and fiery hair. Brothers? It seemed unlikely. A husband to Norah? Even harder to believe. He couldn't picture her cool sophistication beside this man's rough edges. But apparently it was so.

"Norah's upstairs in our room. We wasn't expecting no visitors this morning. It ain't like us to sleep in so late. I'd offer you something, but the kitchen's cold."

"That's all right. Really."

"You might's well come in. It'll take her a while to get up and dressed." With that growly invitation, Rory turned his back and strode to the stairs, hollering up them, "Norah-honey, we got us a guest." Then, he dropped down on the steps and began tugging on his boots.

Trevor advanced slowly into the sun-washed hall. Norah had told him very little about her husband's ranch in the Dakotas except that it was vast and that she would never live there again. He'd prepared for a rude cabin not this elegant house. Nor was he prepared for the scene that greeted him in the entry-hall. It looked like a cyclone had torn down the center of it. The expensive runner was bunched up and twisted into an 'S' pattern. Picture frames grouped on a gateleg table were knocked face down and a Tiffany-shaded lamp overturned as if struck by an earth tremor. It was then he noticed a woman's silk stocking dangling from one of the gaslights. Rory, who was in the middle of buttoning the cuffs on the shirt he'd picked up off the floor, followed his bemused gaze. Without comment, he reached up to tug the ribbon of silk down.

"Trevor. My, this is a surprise."

Norah appeared on the landing, immaculately groomed and garbed. She snatched her petticoat off the newelpost and gave it a toss behind her, then gracefully descended the stairs. She looked between the two men awaiting her at the bottom and, for an instant, her poise failed her. A stark expression crossed her features before the bland surface-charm was restored. That brief insight told both men everything.

She's been in his bed.

He's more than a friend.

"Good morning, Norah. You're looking lovely, as always."

Lovely. As always. Rory's teeth grated. Why hadn't he been the first one to tell her that? Who was this dandy with the brass to stand in his house paying compliments to his wife? A city boy, all spit and polish, while he—Rory—was stuffed into yesterday's clothes, looking like a stampede had run over him. He raked a tidying hand through his hair. And Norah, she was stiff as a statue, a brilliantly false smile pasted on her face. False for whom? The man who'd come all the way from Baltimore to wish her a good morning or to the man who'd spent a good part of the nighttime hours between her knees? He wondered, and he hated not knowing.

"You didn't tell me we were gonna have company, honey."

Not fooled by his quiet tone, Norah cast a frantic glance at her hard-eyed husband. Panic left her mind paralyzed. Instead of grabbing for him, pleading with him not to believe the worst, all she could think to say was a brittle murmur of, "I wasn't aware we were until just now."

He was staring at her, staring through her with eyes so impossibly cold and distant she felt frost-bitten. "Well now, here he is, come all the way from Baltimore just to say howdy. Ain't that nice? Why doan you make our guest feel to home while I ride over and fetch our boy?"

"Rory—"

But he turned from her and smiled with a chilled

144

politeness at Trevor Samuels. "You'll excuse me, won't you? I'll be right back. Why doan you go on into the dining room, and Norah'll fix you up some coffee." Then he was walking to the door, snatching up his Stetson without breaking the long, angry strides.

"Rory."

He didn't turn or pause. The door banged behind him.

Norah wished she had the luxury of crumpling upon the stairs to give vent to anguished weeping, but there was Trevor to think of and he was heading into the . . . dining room. Good Lord!

She was up and running, darting around him in hopes of preventing the worst. But he was standing stock still in the doorway, staring at the leftovers of last night's passion. Oh, it was dreadfully obvious, she resigned with a groan.

Their plates were still on the table. One of her shoes stood in the middle of her cold potatoes. One of her stockings veiled Rory's half-emptied glass of wine. She moved to pick them up as if the damage could be undone, but it just got worse. She grabbed her corset off the sideboard in passing and found her other shoe in the remnants of a shattered vase. By the time she'd gathered up all her hastily discarded clothing, she was close to dying of embarrassment. Trevor hadn't moved. His expression was as somber as stone. She stared at him through a haze of miserable tears.

"I-I'll go put on some coffee."

She fled to the kitchen with her collection of guilt, depositing it in a heap the moment the door swung shut behind her. Oh, God, how much worse could it be?

"Norah." His hands capped her shoulders with a

gentle strength. "Please don't."

She spun toward him, her uplifted gaze aglitter with distress. "Oh, Trevor, I—we—" She gestured toward the dining room with a helpless flutter of one hand.

"It's not necessary for you to explain." He smiled with a sad understanding. "I know how in love you were. I know how confused you must be coming back to all these memories. You needn't apologize. And please don't think that I'd condemn you for being human."

She did crumple then, right into his caring embrace. And she found the needed comfort in his silent support. She'd forgotten in the short span that they'd been apart how good he was at calming a troubled spirit. Rory couldn't. She could only find ease with him after her emotions were stirred and stretched to the brink of exhaustion. There was nothing calm about what she and Rory had. Which was why it was so easy to cling to Trevor Samuels in relief. She was exhausted in body, in heart, in mind, and she needed his restful presence.

"Norah, I'd ask two things of you. Would you answer truthfully?"

She nodded slightly.

"Are you still in love with him?"

Her reply was faint and forlorn. "Yes."

He was silent for a moment, then he asked, "Does that mean you've resolved your differences and you and Jacob will be staying here with him?"

"No. I mean, I don't know." She struggled for the words to express her turmoil. "The things that were good in our marriage are still good. I need time to know if that outweighs the problems. It's so—so hard to walk away, Trevor. Because I do love him. I don't say that to hurt you."

"I know."

"Rory's been a piece of my life for a long time. He's just getting to know his own son. I don't know if I'm ready to leave that behind."

His hand was gentle as it stroked her hair. "I'm not pushing you to decide. I want you to be very sure, and I'm willing to wait until you are. I think you already know in your mind that you'll leave with me. Your heart just hasn't accepted it yet. I won't rush you, Norah. I care for you too much to risk hurting you."

Her sigh was eloquent. "Thank you, Trevor. You've no idea how much your understanding means to me."

He pressed a light kiss to her brow and held her a moment longer. Then, she was pushing away, in control once more.

"I think we could both use some coffee. Would you wait in the front room while I—tidy things up a bit?"

He pinched her chin tenderly. "Take all the time you need."

"Ready to go, pard?"

Rory bent to scoop Jacob up. The boy came to him without reservation, hugging him tight, then chattering excitedly.

"We had my fish for breakfast. Well, that is, I did. Grandma fried him up for me."

"How was he?"

"Full of bones, but good."

"Things always taste better when you catch 'em yourself. My daddy taught me that." He squeezed the boy to him until Jacob squirmed in protest, then let him down. He glanced up at Aurora. "He been behaving himself for you, Mama?"

"A sweetheart." She rumpled the boy's hair fondly.

"Jacob, run on down to the barn and say goodbye to your grampa." When the child raced off, she straightened and looked her son in the eye until he was squirming.

"Somethin' wrong, Mama?"

"I don't know. Is there?"

"No." His gaze broke from hers and slid downward, so she knew he was lying.

"What's she done?"

He bristled up at her flat accusation. "Nothin'. You jus' been a-waiting for something to go wrong, haven't you? It's jus' killin' you, isn't it? Why is it so hard for you to believe she'd come back to me?"

"Because I know what she was and know what she is."

Rory's eyes thinned out dangerously. "What she was and what she is is my wife. Doan forget that, Mama. You keep on bad-mouthing her to me, and I ain't gonna be coming 'round no more. Think on it." He stomped to the door and let it slam behind him.

She was still standing in the same spot when Ethan arrived some minutes later. He took one look at her teary gaze and swept her up tight against him. When she relayed the harsh words that had passed between them, Ethan was gentle but firm.

"You ain't doing nobody no good, Ora. Let him go. He's a man full growed and he knows his mind."

"But—"

"Let him go."

Aurora gave a savage sigh. "She's going to break his heart all over again."

"If she does, he'll put the pieces back together. If you want to help him, stay out of it now. You listening, Ora?"

"He doesn't deserve this, Ethan." Her expression

148

grew fierce. "She doesn't deserve him."

If Ethan Prescott agreed, he didn't say so.

"We got us a visitor at the Bar K."

"Oh? Who is it?" Jacob asked from where he bounced on the saddle skirt behind his father.

"A friend a your mama's. Trevor Samuels. He one of them good friends you was talking about?"

"Those."

"Huh?"

"Never mind."

"You know him, this Samuels feller?"

"Sure. He's real nice. He helped me build my kite. A real highflyer, too. He called it an aeronautical cutter. I call it my hornet because it fights with its tail. He talked Mama into letting me use glass set in wax for the knives on the tail. He can talk Mama into just about anything."

"That so?" Rory stewed on that for a moment. "You see a lot of him, do you?"

"He comes over all the time. He takes me to the park and lets me go with them when he takes Mama to the theater. Well, sometimes. If there's a lot of singing or a lot of kissing in the shows, I'd rather stay home anyway."

"Sounds like a real pal to have around."

"He's a lot of fun."

"He a special friend of your mama's?"

"Guess so. He's at the house an awful lot."

Rory didn't quite dare ask the boy if those frequent visits were overnight.

That, he'd hear from Norah.

Chapter Ten

"Hi, Trevor!"

Jacob clomped across the parlor in his new boots and launched himself into the Easterner's arms. The sight stopped Rory dead in the doorway. That and the fact that Norah was seated beside her guest on the sofa. It made a cozy scene, the three of them together.

"Hello, Jacob. Why you look like a regular cowboy."

"Like my father. He taught me how to fish. I caught this great big trout. It was this long." He placed his hands at an impossible distance. "I ate him up for breakfast. Do you know how to fish?"

"My father taught me when I was your age and, as I recall, I liked it very much. That's something fathers and sons should do together."

Danged if Rory didn't like the man for saying that. Somehow, that made him all the angrier as he stood there like an outsider.

"Are you staying here with us?" Jacob asked Trevor in innocent eagerness.

"No. I've got a nice room at the hotel in town. The Grand." He made a face, and Jacob laughed. He slid a significant glance toward Norah. "I thought maybe you and your mother would want to stay there, too, so I wouldn't be lonely."

Sonuvabitch!

Rory took a quick step forward. It wasn't Norah's sudden pallor that reined him in. It was Jacob's candid reply.

"Thank you, but I want to stay here. This ranch is going to be mine someday. My father told me so. You can come out here and visit us every day, if you like. We can go fishing."

"That's a fine offer, Jacob. We'll have to make time to do that before we go."

Before we go.

"I've got some work to tend to, so if y'all would excuse me."

"Rory, can't you join us for a cup of coffee?"

He gave his wife a flat, black stare. "Another time. I'm sure you gots lots to talk about. You doan need me in the way."

Hang you, Rory Prescott! Norah muttered to herself as the big cowboy continued down the hall. Why did he have to be so—difficult! Forcing the tension from her jaw, she managed to smile serenely and ask, "Care for another cup, Trevor?"

The anger she'd held to all through Trevor's visit burst like a thundercloud the minute Norah stepped into her husband's study. Part of that anger stemmed from fear, a fear that all the good things they'd started between them last night—and this morning—would never have a chance to expand. She was afraid because she didn't know how Rory was going to react. Things were still so tentative, so testy, not a great time to drop a bombshell like Trevor into his lap. She could hope he would be open-minded. She could

151

hope, but then he was a Kincaid and that narrowed the possibility right down to practically nothing. The signs so far weren't encouraging. The best she could do was bluster and pray he wasn't in the mood for reading between the lines. If she acted the indignant wife perhaps he'd respond like a repentant husband.

"That was very rude."

Rory looked up briefly from his ledgers. "Your— friend gone already?"

"Would it have killed you to be polite?"

"Possibly. Norah-honey, he didn't come all this way to see me, now did he?"

"He's here on business for his father."

"That so? Good of him to take the time to look you up."

His snippety attitude made her ignore the warning signs of a blowup to come. Why couldn't he be nice? Why couldn't he back down long enough for her to explain? But she knew it was too late for that. She should have explained about Trevor Samuels right after she arrived. But she hadn't. She'd been afraid if he knew he wouldn't have let a night like last night happen. And now he was acting as if it didn't make the slightest difference. Her tone chilled to the impersonal cool she knew rankled him. "Why wouldn't he? He's been very kind to me and Jacob."

"So Jacob's told me."

"What else has he told you?"

He gave her a long gauging look. "Is there something I shouldn't know about?"

"Don't be ridiculous."

"Jus' asking."

"Trevor is interested in politics. We belong to a lot of the same organizations. It's only natural that we should know one another. I've helped him with some

152

of his speeches. He's escorted me to the theater. You'd like him."

"I'm sure we'd be bosom pals. Look how much we got in common."

"Meaning?"

The sharp crack of her tone had no effect on him. His stare remained fixed, his expression bland. "Nothin'. Just making talk."

"Rory . . ." She broke off, sighing with frustration. She'd known he was going to be this way about it. Actually, she'd expected worse.

"Honey, I gots a lot a work to do here. Was there something else?" He managed to look both impatient and indifferent, and she was ready to fling something at him.

"No. Yes. Trevor invited me to dinner in town tonight."

No change in expression. "You going?"

Her head lifted a notch. "Yes. He asked you to join us, too."

He smiled then, a slow, close-lipped smile. "I don't think I can make it. Convey my apologies."

"I will," she returned icily.

"You want me to get a driver for you?"

"I haven't forgotten how to drive, thank-you."

"Suit yourself."

"I will." She started huffily from the room, then turned back to him. "You'll see to Jacob, won't you?"

He glared at her. "Doan worry about him. You jus' have yourself a good ole time."

A good ole time. That was quite impossible, but she did try.

Trevor was pleasant company, as always. He warmed her with sincere flattery and did his best to make her believe they were once again back in Baltimore where Rory Prescott wasn't even a shadow

153

in her thoughts. She tried, but she couldn't pretend that was true. In Baltimore, she was the wealthy Norah Prescott of independent means. No one questioned where she went or what she did. But here, in South Dakota, in the little town of Crowe Creek, she was Mrs. Rory Prescott; and nearly everyone they passed on the walk to the restaurant knew her husband and his family. And they wondered why his wife was walking on the arm of some city dandy. And all she could think of was him at home stewing.

"'Evening, Miz Prescott. Nice to see you again. Remember me to the Mister, won't you?"

"Hello, Mrs. Jamison. Yes, I will."

She clutched Trevor's arm tighter without meaning to. He patted her hand and smiled to ease her discomfort.

When they entered the restaurant, for the first time she could recall, Norah was actually glad to see Trevor's aide, Carter Clemens. She had an instinctive dislike for the spindly little man. It was nothing he'd done. He was always courteous and more than a little self-effacing, Maybe that was it. All his scraping and bowing didn't quite ring true. But Trevor swore by his counsel, so she said nothing. She dragged up a smile when he hurriedly offered her a chair.

"How good to see you again, Carter."

"Thank you, Mrs. Prescott. Actually, I loathe traveling, but there's always the chance that Mr. Samuels might need my services."

"Oh, Carter, stop," Trevor laughed. "You know you're invaluable to me and my father."

"You said you were here on business," she prompted. It seemed a much safer topic than the one they'd discussed that morning.

"Yes. Ironically, I'm here to meet with your brother-in-law."

"Scott?"

"I'm sure you're aware of the lobbying he's done in Washington. I'm here to evaluate the situation firsthand. We're so far away from the actual problems and needs of these people, I thought it would be advantageous to see for myself if any of his claims have merit. After all, he is part of your family."

"Oh, Trevor, how kind of you. I'm sure you'll be unbiased in your opinions. Be warned, though. Scott Prescott will be a bit different out here from the man you met in Baltimore."

"How so?"

She smiled, not wanting to spoil his surprise when the savage side of Rory's brother emerged. "You'll see soon enough. He's supposed to be here in a few days. Scott can be very narrowminded when it comes to the welfare of the Indians. He's shrewd and he's brilliant, but he won't give an inch. He's a hard man to reason with."

"He struck me as quite different from your husband."

Norah smiled again because that was said with all the diplomacy of a politician. Her response was wry. "They're more alike than you'd guess."

"But not in looks."

"That's because they favor their fathers. Their mother's first husband was a Lakota warrior. He fathered Scott. After he died, she married Ethan Prescott. Rory's their son."

She saw no need to elaborate on the colorful story. If Trevor remained in Crowe Creek long enough, he was sure to hear it. The older residents still regaled newcomers with the tale of how Garth Kincaid's innocent young daughter had been captured by renegade Sioux. She was something of a celebrity

155

with them, having survived her ordeal in the brutal Hills, giving birth to her half-breed son and saving her Texas husband-to-be from a warrior's arrow and her father's noose. She was a living reminder of the state's wild past when the name Lakota was feared and cursed and good men were glad to wake up with their hair. Few would believe her Harvard-educated son carried on that barbarous heritage. But then they didn't know him like she did. They didn't know that once, many years ago, brother had fought brother over the land rights of the Sioux. Or that Rory had shot his half-brother to keep him from murdering their grandfather in cold blood. Few would believe that of the articulate Scott Prescott, but she would never be fooled by his smooth facade.

"I can handle Prescott," Carter said with an uncharacteristic certainty. For a moment, there was a gleam of toughness in his eyes, then it faded to familiar timidity. But Norah had seen it and she was puzzled.

"Don't be too sure. Scott is a dangerous man."

"You sound serious," Trevor challenged lightly. She met his gaze with a sober stare.

"Oh, I am. Be careful of him. Watch your hair."

Trevor burst out with a hearty laugh. "You had me going there for a minute. Watch my hair, indeed."

Norah's smile was thin. He'd learn soon enough.

"Mrs. Prescott! It is you. I'd heard you were back. How are you, my dear?"

Norah's soul shrank on the spot. "Why, Reverend Fowler, what a pleasure to see you." She introduced the lanky pastor to her dinner companions and tried not to wither up in her seat.

"We all heard about Ethan. His recovery was an answer to prayer."

"Yes," she agreed faintly.

The clergyman bent down to press her hand; the hand that wore Rory Prescott's gold band. "Now, you tell that husband of yours that I'll be looking for him on Sunday. He has an unfortunate habit of forgetting the days of the week."

Ready to die of shame, she murmured, "I'll tell him."

"Good to have you home, my dear."

Norah couldn't face Trevor. She knew her features flamed with guilt, and she didn't want to place any of the blame on him. She didn't have to look up. With his usual sensitivity, he guessed her dismay.

"I'm sorry, Norah. I should have known this would be uncomfortable for you, here amongst all your old acquaintances."

Uncomfortable? It was pure hell!

"Oh, Trevor, don't be absurd. What do I care what they say about me? What kind of wine shall we order?"

"How was dinner?"

His voice rolled out of the open study doors, as dark in tone as the room was within. Norah paused. She could see him silhouetted against the window. He'd been drinking. Her nostrils flared wide. She could smell it. For a moment, Norah suffered unusual cowardice. She wanted to flee for the stairs and the safety above. But she held firm, telling herself she had nothing to fear from Rory Prescott. Still, she cringed inwardly when he turned.

"Well?"

"It was very nice. You should have been there."

He laughed. It was a low, vicious sound interrupted by the lifting of his glass. "Now wouldn't that have been a sight? Me, my wife and her lover all sitting together real civilized-like. Is that how they do things back East, honey?"

"My what?"

"Want me to write it down so's you can understand it better? Is there another word you'd like to use to explain him?"

Now she was afraid. Afraid of him in this strange, dark mood rallied by drink. Afraid of telling him the truth, of hurting him, of angering him, of forever cutting her ties to all she had here. And because she was afraid, she struck out defensively.

"How dare you—"

"No!" he roared, smacking the empty glass down on the desktop. She jumped. "How dare you! How dare you bring him here to my house! How dare you ask me to be polite to him! How dare you cozy up to him right in front of my boy!"

"Rory, you've no reason—"

"No reason? What other reasons do I need? How'd you like it if I brought home some fancy whore and shoved her right up in your face and asked you to sit down to tea with her? I oughta have shot the sonuvabitch right outta his patent leathers whilst he was sitting there with you on my sofa!"

"Trevor Samuels is not my lover."

He gave a hoot of harsh laughter. "Why sure, honey. I believes you."

"I'm not going to argue this with you, Rory. I'm going to bed."

Before she could complete her turn, he'd crossed the room and had hold of her arm. His grip was painless but inescapable just the same. "No, you're not. Not until we have us a talk."

"Let me go," she said coldly, pulling against his hand. "You're drunk."

"Yessir, an honest-to-God inebriate."

158

"Let go of me."

"Not until you tell me who the hell he is and what he means to you. I want to know why he's here and why he feels he can make free with my wife under my very nose in my own house. Answer me, Norah. And doan tell me he's a friend. I know the look of a man in love, and he's mooning all over you." His fingers tightened, suddenly hurtful, as he hauled her up against him so close she could hear the hiss of his breath through gritted teeth. "Have you been letting him in your bed?"

Anger plucked at all the strings of her emotions. Her voice shook with it. "If you cared whom I took into my bed you would have spent more time in it yourself."

"Are you sleeping with him?"

"No!" she shouted back.

"Liar!"

"He asked me to marry him!"

There was a long, tense silence. Then came the quiet growl of Rory's voice.

"Now that'd be right difficult, wouldn't it, seeing's how you already got yourself a husband?"

"He wants me to divorce you."

Rory made a low, guttural sound, the kind a man would make if he'd been smacked in the gut with the head of a shovel. He released her arm and took a quick step back. He was reeling. He'd never, not once, thought of their separation as permanent. Even as the weeks, the months, the years went by, he'd told himself she'd be back. He'd built the house for her. He'd slaved over the ranch for her. He'd kept himself for her. He'd managed the day to day loneliness by thinking ahead to the time when she'd return, stuffing his days so full of exhausting work that the nights went by quick and, for the most part, painlessly. But to lose her forever, to have no hope of a future. . . . He couldn't begin to comprehend it.

"Is that what you want, Norah?" he asked slowly, disbelieving.

"That's what I came back to decide."

"So all this time . . . last night . . . you were just biding your time, waitin' for the chance to spring this on me? That what you been doing?"

"Rory, I—"

With a roaring curse, he hurled his empty glass against the book-lined wall, shattering it the way everything was breaking apart inside him. Norah flinched and trembled but didn't move. Muttering hoarse obscenities, Rory tottered back to his desk, leaning on it when his knees would give way, wobbling more from shock than whiskey. The hurt was terrible. He fought for a way to endure, at least for a little while longer.

From where she was rooted by the doorway, Norah watched his strength buckle and his broad shoulders sag. All at once the felt the intense need to tell him she hadn't meant it, that she wouldn't leave him; but the words dammned up tight. Instead, she offered wretchedly, "I didn't come back here to hurt you, Rory."

His shoulders started to shake. A deep rumbling laugh issued from him, broken by the bitterness in his voice. "That right? You didn't think it was gonna bother me a-tall you coming here to tell me you was fixing to take up with another man?" Another rough laugh rose into a raw bellow of rage. He seized the picture frame off his desktop and smashed it face down again and again and again with increasing force until the glass was everywhere in glittering splinters and his knuckles were bleeding. Fury spent, he hung his head and moaned like something

160

wounded deep. "Doan you love me no more? Doan you love me, Norah?"

Fighting the fierce burn in her eyes, Norah couldn't answer. She couldn't tell him the truth. If she did, he would never understand. He would never let her go. By saying nothing, she was protecting them both from more hurt than they could stand. By saying nothing, she was proving how much she cared.

He was silent for a time, panting hard and fast, his heartbeat racing as frantically as a wild thing trapped and lost to panic. Then, slowly, he quieted.

"Do you love him?"

Surprised by the point-blank question, Norah took a second to gather a response. She made her tone gentle. "He's good with Jacob. They're already very fond of one another. Trevor will see that he's well provided for. He'll make sure he gets the best education. He'll be loved and cared for." Then her words snagged on a soft sob. "Rory, please try to understand."

Oh, he did. That was the worst of it. He did understand. He understood why his Norah would prefer a smooth, educated man and an exciting big-city life to what he could give her here, where his own best had never been quite good enough. He could see why she'd want her son exposed to culture and chances he'd never find on the range. But while he could understand that, he couldn't accept it. Unless she answered him. He turned to her and asked again.

"Do you love him, Norah? If you do, if you really do, I'll let go. I won't make things—difficult, and I won't hold nothing against you. If you tell me that you love him and that you want to spend your every day and night with him instead of me, I won't fight you. Tell me, Norah."

"Rory—I—" She sucked a ragged breath and lowered her head.

"No." That was a firm command. His hand fit under her chin, prying it up. "No. You look at me when you say it. You look me in the eye so's I can believe it when you tell me he's the man you want, not me."

She jerked away from his controlling grasp and cried out in anguish, "I can't."

Rory let his head drop back. He squeezed his eyes shut and mouthed the words, "Thank you, God. Thank you. Thank you." Then he looked back down at the weeping woman before him, his heart swelling up with a tender determination.

"I ain't letting you go."

"It's not that simple," Norah argued.

"Sure it is."

"I can't live with you, Rory."

"I'll make you want to stay."

"You can't."

"Sure I can."

Before she could react with an objection, he was kissing her. The sensuous slide of his mouth over hers was will-sapping. By the time he was finished, she was hanging in his arms, dazed beyond thought or reason.

"Now you gonna tell me, Norah-honey, that there's a man alive that can do what I do for you? You gonna tell me that you could walk away from this, from what we are to each other? You're never gonna stop wanting me. Not ever."

Because that was true, she trembled. She held to just enough presence of mind to murmur, "It's not enough."

"It's everything. I can't live without you, Norah. You're mine. You got my boy; you got my name; you got my heart and soul. I ain't letting you go. I won't let you go."

That last was said with forceful Kincaid authority. And it was that tone and that hard look in his eyes that brought Norah back from near-swooning resignation. She straightened. She pushed away from him, her own pride blazing forth in an equally determined glare. Rebelling against his arrogant claim, she said staunchly, "It's not your choice to make."

He faltered then, the stoniness of his stare melting down into a soul-snatching plea.

"I love you, Norah. You can't leave me."

Her emotions came apart. It was either fall into his arms or run like hell.

She ran.

She was halfway up the steps when she heard his deafening roar of pain and fury. Stumbling, sobbing, she scrambled the rest of the way as the explosive sounds of glass breaking echoed up the stairwell. Then the house was silent.

Afraid he would come after her, afraid she wouldn't resist if he did, Norah fled to the safe shadows of Jacob's room. Just seeing his small outline mounding the blankets had a quieting effect on her frayed emotions. She leaned against the closed door, hands over her mouth to stifle the sounds of her irregular breathing. From below, she heard the sound of the front door banging. Slipping to the window, she parted the curtains to watch her husband stomp in bowlegged fury across the yard, down to where the lights still glowed in the bunkhouse. He'd be safe there. That was a strange thought to have, but it reassured her.

Sighing softly, Norah moved to the edge of the bed to look down upon her son. Rory's son. Very gently so as not to disturb him, she brushed her fingertips across his sleep-warmed cheek, pausing when she came to a thin trail of wetness from the corner of his closed eye. He'd heard them.

"Jacob?"

There was no response to her quiet call.

Reflexively, she tucked the covers in around him and bent to touch a kiss to the top of his head. When she straightened, unknown to her, a fresh shimmer of tears rolled over those that had nearly dried.

Chapter Eleven

It was a miserable walk from the barn to the front porch. Sunlight bounced up off the hard-packed ground to sear through his eyeballs all the way to the back of his head. His knee ached as it was prone to when the weather was about to take a sudden change. The slashes on his knuckles stung. His heart was hanging so heavy it was like he was dragging the watering trough up behind him. He'd been up most of the night playing poker and shooting back shots of rye. Then he'd risen before dawn to inspect a problem with a windmill in one of the northern pastures. He was bone-weary and spirit-broken.

The sight of Jacob sitting on the front steps fleetingly lifted his doldrums. Until he saw the boy was wearing his Eastern sissy suit and he felt the cool bore of his stare.

"'Morning, pard," he called with a brave attempt at a smile.

"Good morning, sir."

Sir, again? Rory frowned slightly. "Thought we might ride on over to the Lone Star to see if we could find you that special horse."

"No, thank you, sir. My mother and I are taking

Mr. Samuels over to the Indian reservation this morning."

"Oh." He tried not to sound too disheartened as he sank awkwardly down on the steps beside his son. The boy was rigid as a post. Absently, he rubbed at his knee. "We can do it later. I didn't know your mama had plans."

"I don't think I'll be needing a horse, anyway."

"Why's that?" he asked, pretending not to know. Pretending his heart hadn't dropped right into his boots.

But Jacob wouldn't answer. He was trying very hard not to cry. He didn't want to talk about the horse he would never have. Or think about the father that would never be his. Hoping for both things left a great hollow of disappointment in his heart. It was better to pretend neither mattered. After all, the big, rough-talking cowboy at his side wasn't going to stop his mother from taking him away again. Wouldn't he stop her if he cared? He swallowed hard and looked toward the gates of the Bar K almost gratefully.

Uncomfortable with the silent little stranger his son had become, Rory followed Jacob's gaze to see Dawn racing up full tilt.

"Heya, Rory, Jacob!" She kicked out of the saddle and slid down with the grace of a sleek otter.

"Heya, fireball. Whoa, careful there."

She settled beside her uncle, noting his grimace. She was at once full of youthful concern. "Knee paining you again? Maybe you oughta have Grampa look at it."

"Mind your own business, now, girl."

Ignoring his growl, she leaned across him to confide to Jacob, "Rory took a bullet and tore the hell outta his knee to save my daddy's life."

166

"Dawn!" Rory scowled at her, aware of the way his son's eyes went wide and wondering. "Watch your language. And where'd you hear such a lie?"

"It ain't a lie. Mama told me, and she doan tell fibs." Her stare challenged him to say that wasn't so, knowing well he couldn't. "And there ain't nothing wrong with the way I talk."

"Yeah, well you try telling that to your daddy. You doan think he's gonna know where you picked up them words? I doan want him over here a beatin' on me 'cause you let your mouth run away with you."

"He won't. I'll just tell him I learned 'em from Grandpa."

"Sassy, ain't you?" But Rory grinned at her. "You ain't over here to pester me into riding that back-breaker, are you?" As he said that, he caught sight of Trevor Samuels in a hired rig crossing under the Bar K arch.

"Naw. Daddy'll be home soon. He'll gentle Ghost for me. He's the best there is with horses."

"I said I'd do it for you, and I'll do it!" Dawn was staring at him in open-mouthed surprise as he surged up in a commanding anger. "Ain't my word good enough for anybody 'round here anymore?" That said, he hobbled with a stiff dignity down to the corral.

Dawn blinked. "What's got him all riled this morning?"

"He and my mother had a fight," Jacob told her glumly.

"Oh." She glanced at her cousin and saw the moisture welling up in his eyes. "Well, hell, Grandma and Grampa fight all the time, 'an they been married thirty years! It doan mean nothing."

The boy sniffed hopefully, and Dawn socked him in the arm.

"C'mon. Let's go watch the ride."

As the two of them raced down to the fence, Norah came out onto the porch. She had a quick smile for Trevor, but her eyes were on Rory.

"Good morning, Norah. This is very kind of you to show me around the Cheyenne Reservation. If I know what I'm talking about, maybe your brother-in-law won't have such an advantage."

"It's no trouble, Trevor." She mouthed the words as she watched the hands wrestle out the big silver stallion. The animal jerked and twisted at the end of its lead, rearing up, slashing at the air with its hoofs. Rory approached confidently, favoring his knee, and she knew he was hurting in both body and soul. Not a good time to be taking on a four-legged demon like Dawn Prescott's Ghost. It was a struggle to remain on the porch making polite conversation as he swung up into the saddle and looped the reins about one hand.

Noting her distraction, Trevor glanced toward the corral, then stood beside her in silent amazement as Rory Prescott took his wild ride. The powerful maverick surged about the enclosure in sharp, stiff-legged hops, then wriggled as fiercely as Jacob's trout on a line. Even as rider was pitched from saddle, Norah was off the porch, skirts held high to dash across the yard. She could hear Rory bawling angrily as she grew near.

"Grab him up, boys. I ain't takin' no more of his sass."

He was aboard again and signaling his men away by the time she reached the rails. Ghost exploded, rearing then plunging into a series of spine-crunching bucks.

"'Morning, Miz Norah," one of the cowhands called respectfully.

"Hello, Cyril. He's not going to get himself killed, is he?" She said it lightly, as if it wasn't a real concern.

"That one's a bad'un. The boss has been a-fighting him for a good part a the summer. Rammed Rory into the rails this July. Stoved in half his ribs. Took close to twenty stitches to close him back up. Had to fix the fence, too." He flashed a tobacco-stained grin at her. "Got to be kinda personal with him after that."

The scar. Norah hugged the rail apprehensively and tried not to look as scared as she suddenly felt inside.

A snap to the left and one to the right. A wicked jerk and a downward pitch. A fish-tailing jump and Rory was flung clear. He hit hard, rolling twice, then he lay in the dirt, balled up and unmoving. Several of the hands raced after the bucking stallion while the others ran to their downed boss.

"Git away from me! I'm all right!"

But he wasn't. That much was obvious when Rory tried to stand. His knee gave way, dropping him back to the dust where he curled around it, features gray and harsh with pain. Dawn ducked beneath the rail and ran to him.

"Doan fret, honey. I'll get him this time. Jus' give me a second."

"No. Forget him, Rory. I doan want him. He's not fit for riding. Grampa was right. Jus' forget him."

"I ain't forgetting nothing," Rory growled. He used her youthful shoulder for balance as he dragged himself upright. His glare followed the animal as it paced the perimeter of the corral, snorting fiercely, wheeling about to evade the cowboys trying to corner it.

"Rory, please." She tugged at his hand. Her

169

uplifted gaze was glistening.

He smiled down at her reassuringly. "Honey, I ain't gonna let that broomtail get the best a me."

"Please. I won't have you getting all busted up because of me. I don't want him. I won't ride him. And I won't forgive you if you climb back on and break your neck!"

He grinned at her, unimpressed by the mulish expression or stubborn set of hands on hips. "Yes you will, darlin'. Now get on outta here. I got work to finish." He gave her a push and she bolted with an angry sob, dodging through the rail and running for the barn.

It took three men to subdue the fearsome stallion. They held him against the far rails, staying clear of his flailing hoofs and shifting hindquarters. When Rory started toward him, his limp more pronounced than ever, Norah couldn't keep silent. He turned when she called to him. And frowned when he saw her standing there with Trevor Samuels.

"Rory, don't," she said in firm entreatment.

He gave her a crooked smile and told her, "Be the best thing for everybody if I broke my fool neck, now wouldn't it, honey?" He tipped the brim of his John B. to Trevor and walked away from his wife's stricken look.

"You shore you want to get back on, boss?" one of the men muttered nervously as Rory fit his boot into the stirrup iron. "'Pears he'd like to bury you."

"Did I ask your opinion?" the redhead snapped. "Keep it to yourself. Now, hold him."

He swung up, and the minute he touched to saddle leather, Ghost leaped forward, dragging the men at his bridle off their feet.

"Get clear! I got him. I'm gonna show him who's boss."

Ghost wasn't interested in being shown anything by the man in the saddle. When he realized he couldn't toss the clinging weight from his back, he got it into his head to scrape it off. He charged the fence, crashing against it. Having seen it coming, Rory was able to jerk his leg clear as the top rail splintered from impact; and, for a moment, he hung dangerously off to one side. As Rory fished for the stirrup, Ghost lunged around the circle again, then headed straight for the broken fence. With a powerful surge, he sprang over the rail. His hindlegs cracked against it when he cleared, but he landed without breaking stride and was off and running. Rory made no attempt to haul in. Instead, he spurred the animal on.

"He's gonna try to run him to ground," Cyril cried out, and the men scrambled to saddle up.

Dawn, who'd been watching sulkily from the barn, sprinted across the yard and flung herself up on her horse. She reined up next to Jacob and thrust down her hand. "C'mon." He took it and stepped into the stirrup she'd cleared for him, then the two of them headed after the runaway.

Trapped in her society clothes, Norah stood helpless while the Bar K riders took out in pursuit.

"Hang on, you crazy fool," she whispered fervently. "And don't you dare break anything!"

It probably wasn't the smartest thing, heading out across rough prairie on the back of an unbroken maverick. Rory knew if he lost his seat, he'd be on his own, so he stuck tight. Each time the animal slowed to gather its bucking legs underneath, he jammed back with his heels, goading it to run. As long as the pace was all out, the horse wouldn't be thinking on how to throw him. Once he'd driven the animal to exhaustion, the question of mastery would be solved. Then, there'd just be the question of how to get back home.

It was a reckless race across uneven ground and well-suited to the frustrations of man and animal. Both were furious and out of control, pushing hard and to the limit. Miles whipped by as they fought each other over every inch in between.

And then Ghost shot up over a rise and into the gully below. Rory saw what lay in their path, glittering sharp and wicked in the bright Dakota daylight. He hauled back with all his strength, sawing at the bit. Instead of slowing, the animal plunged ahead wildly. The wire barrier was struck at a dead run, tearing the vicious strands from both posts, the release of tension snapping them in a lethal coil about horse and rider. Both went down in a tangle.

The fall slapped the sense from him, but it took Rory only a moment to realize his real danger. As the terrified animal thrashed beside him in its struggle to get free, the twists of wire tightened about him, piercing denim and tearing exposed flesh. He couldn't move. His arms were pinned against his ribs by the prickly band; and, with unfortunate insight, he realized that if the horse gained its feet, he'd be dragged to a very ragged death in a matter of minutes.

"Whoa. Whoa, son," he muttered softly as he tried to work out from under the encircling steel. The horse kicked and rolled, and he cried out harshly as the barbs stung the backs of his legs and ripped through his shirtsleeve. The Devil's Hatband. That's what they called it when they strung the first fences across the wide spaces. He'd hated it then for cutting up the freedom of the plains. He hated working with it and around it. And he hated being caught up in it.

"Rory, are you all right?"

"Dawn-honey, be careful. Doan go spooking the horse."

The two youngsters slid down the bank to where he and the stallion were trussed up like holiday birds. Ghost gave a snort of fright and started fighting to get up again. All Rory could do was try to protect his face and yell out, "Keep him down. Doan let him get up."

Without thinking, Dawn threw herself down on the horse's lathered neck, levering with her slight weight to keep the animal still. It wasn't enough.

"Jacob, help me." When there was no response to her command, she looked at her cousin. He was standing at a distance, his eyes magnified behind the glasses into great circles of alarm. "Jacob!"

He couldn't move. Every functioning part of him just shut down. There was blood seeping through the rents in his father's clothes. It glistened wetly on the silver-gray hide of the straining stallion. Those bright splatters filled his whole field of vision into a sea of red. He was going to be sick.

"Jacob! Come here! Help me! I can't do it by myself."

The horse was making terrible sounds. Its legs were kicking out frantically, each movement jerking the wire taut. Rory shouted out when one of the strands snapped up just beneath his eye. He managed to block it with his hand, tearing open the ridge of his knuckles. Jacob's stomach seized up, but he couldn't look away. Ghost was scrambling, groaning and wheezing with terror. He gave an awkward surge and stood, pulling Rory several agonizing feet. Dawn hung around the animal's neck, as useless as the dangling reins. But the wire proved an effective hobble, bringing the stallion down again.

"Over here!" It was Cyril's voice from the top of the ridge. "Sammy, got your cutters with you?"

As the Bar K hands slid down toward them, Ghost writhed, shaking Dawn like a saddle blanket and yanking Rory about.

"Shoot him! Shoot the sonuvabitch!" Rory ordered as the barbs made a painful pattern along his back.

"Whoa, there. Whoa."

Two of the men assisted Dawn, leaning on the panicked animal while another knelt beside Rory with his wire cutters in hand.

"Stand clear."

It was a slow process, the careful clipping and peeling back of each twist of wire. Once free, Rory staggered up and went straight to Cyril to snatch out his sidearm. When he pivoted, his face set into hard angles, his men leaped from the downed stallion. Even Dawn backed away without protest. It was then Jacob realized what his father intended to do. He looked down at the helpless animal, seeing the heaving sides, the twitching hide, the wild glaze in its rolling eyes; and his heart broke.

"No! Daddy, no!"

Surprised by the arms twining about his, Rory hesitated. His voice was an impatient growl. "Son, that horse ain't good for nothing but coyote feed. He ain't worth fixing up."

But Jacob was adamant. "Daddy, please. I'll take care of him. Don't shoot him."

Daddy, please. I'll take care of him. He'll be my horse. I can make him into something. Please, Daddy. Give me the chance.

Rory could hear his own father answering the pleas of a teary-eyed fifteen-year-old. *Rory, what'd*

174

you want with this scrawny ole bag a bones? He's full of screw-worm, son. It ain't worth fifteen cents to save him.

He needs me, Daddy. Please. I'll make him into a good horse. You'll see. Give him a chance. You'll see.

Slowly, he lowered the gun and put a gentle hand atop his son's head. "Cut him loose, boys. And doan let him tear himself up. We got enough work to do as it is."

Norah let her breath out in a shaky gush as the riders returned through the Bar K's gate. Jacob was behind Cyril, and Rory was doubling with Dawn. Behind them limped a sad-looking silver stallion. Appearing equally worse for wear, Rory slid down and hobbled toward the barn, leading the spiritless animal. Jacob chased after him, then drew up to look back at his cousin.

"Aren't you coming? He's your horse."

Dawn sneered down at him with a haughty contempt. "I doan waste my time on worthless animals or on boys who freeze up like frightened rabbits, *Istamaza.*" She jerked on the reins of her horse and sent it racing toward the Lone Star. Head hanging, Jacob scuffled to the barn.

Norah started from the porch, but Trevor stayed her with a firm hand on her arm. She looked up at him, puzzled and slightly annoyed. Rory was hurt.

"They're all right, Norah. They don't need you."

Though kindly spoken, his words had a cruel cut. No, she supposed they didn't. She couldn't imagine Rory accepting her offer of help. Not after last night. He'd never needed her.

"If you're ready to go, I'll get my parasol."

175

Trevor nodded. "I'll see if Jacob wants to come with us."

It wasn't Jacob but rather Rory Prescott he came face to face with at the barn door. The bedraggled cowboy gave him a severing glare made all the more menacing because he was dripping blood from the gash beneath his eye.

"What do you want?" Sharp as a snap of taut barbed wire.

"I came to ask Jacob if he were going to the reservation with his mother and me."

"He's got things to tend to here. Now, git outta my way."

"Mr. Prescott."

Rory jerked up short as the man took a hold of his arm. He went rigid.

Trevor's voice was steeped in soft sincerity. "I am not trying to steal your wife and son from you. It's their choice to make. If they don't want to stay here, I'd be crazy to turn them away. Norah's a wonderful woman, and Jacob's a fine boy. Any man would be lucky to have them. If that man is not you, it's going to be me."

"You finished?" Rory growled dangerously.

"For the moment." Trevor released him, and Rory took a quick step back. They eyed each other for a long, tense moment.

"I ain't gonna let you have 'em."

Trevor nodded with a civil understanding. "Norah told me to watch out for my hair when I was around your brother. Should I watch my back when I walk away from you?"

Rory's grin was sudden and wide. "Might not be a bad idea."

*　　　*　　　*

"Whoa, son. Easy now."

Rory's voice held a soothing cadence as he smeared ointment into the lacerated hide. Ghost stood quiet, shivering and blowing hard where he was cross-tied in the stall.

"Is he going to be all right?" Jacob asked faintly.

"Should be. Those cuts on his legs are the worst. Doan reckon there's much chance of getting my daddy over here to tend 'em. I'll bind 'em up good and keep a close watch. If he ain't running hot by morning, should be fine. How you doin', pard?"

When there was silence, Rory glanced behind him. Jacob was hunched down against the wall of the stall, head ducked between his knees. His narrow shoulders gave a telltale shake.

"Jacob?"

"I didn't do anything," he mumbled thickly. "I couldn't get my feet to move. I didn't do anything to help you."

Rory wiped the goo off his hands and came to hunker down awkwardly before the boy. "Jacob . . . son, look at me."

His head lifted slowly. His grey eyes shimmered with a wash of guilty tears behind the magnifying glasses.

"Son, out here a man's gotta act quick without a lot of thought. There ain't time to be scared. Doan reckon you have to face things like that in Baltimore, do you?" A slight negating shake. "Sometimes, you gotta make yourself do things that ain't easy. Jus' pull in a breath and close your eyes and get 'em done. There ain't nothing wrong with being scared. You jus' can't let it get in the way of what you've got to do. That make any sense to you?" A braver nod. "Now git on over here and help me with this cayuse."

Sniffing forlornly, Jacob clamored up and went to

stand at Ghost's head. He was too miserable to be afraid when he reached up to stroke the damp muzzle. The horse snorted, then lowered its head. Jacob pet him, rubbing the twitching ears.

"I'm gonna put some of this stuff on his hindlegs. You talk real nice to him and keep him quiet. I doan want him kicking what few brains I got through that knothole."

At first, Rory was too preoccupied with the restless hoofs to pay much mind to his son. Then he found himself listening to the soft murmur of Jacob's voice as he crooned to the horse. He smiled to himself.

As Jacob rubbed under the animal's jaw, he mused aloud, "Dawn's awful mad. I don't think she'll want to be my friend anymore."

Rory didn't sound too concerned. "Son, Dawn's as tough as that there barbed wire but she's a lot more forgiving. She'll come around. Doan you worry."

"She doesn't like me."

"Doan matter. You're family."

"She thinks I'm a sissy."

"What do you think?"

Silence.

Rory rose up stiffly from his crouch and turned to the solemn boy. His big, battered hand curved beneath the child's chin, lifting up his head to a proud angle. "Jacob, you're a Prescott and a Kincaid and your mother's son. I ain't worried about you a-tall. You'll be fine as long as you remember who you are."

In a flash, the boy's arms were wrapped around his neck tighter than the fence line. Rory held him easily.

"Don't let Mama take me away."

"I won't. I promise."

Jacob hung on fiercely for another few seconds, then he asked, "Can Ghost be my horse?"

Why wasn't he surprised? "We'll see, son. If he cleans up good and has learned himself some manners, you might have a right good saddle horse. You want him, you work for it. Get your hands dirty."

"Yessir!"

Late afternoon sunlight slanted into the stall, filling the air with floating dust motes and casting father and son in a golden glow.

Norah stood at the gate for long moments, looking down at them. Jacob was curled up in the fresh straw, sound asleep. Where he was propped up next to him, Rory's head was nodding in a doze. Ghost stood quiet, eyes closed, ears flicking lazily. The big cowboy gave a sudden jerk, and his unfocused gaze lifted, sharpening quickly on her tender expression.

"How's the horse?"

"Lemme take a look." He dragged himself up and took a minute for some thorough checking. "Seems fine."

"How are you?"

He didn't sound as optimistic there. "I'll mend." He was taking in her pretty gown and stylishly twisted hair, thinking how beautiful she was but, at the same time, so out of place in his smelly barn. "How'd things go at the Cheyenne?" *How was your outing with Samuels?*

"Fine. I think he can help Scott do some good in Washington. We spoke to George White Cloud and some of the others. I believe they were impressed with Trevor's honesty."

Rory had no comment. He was suddenly feeling very sore and very tired. He stifled a huge yawn and glanced down at Jacob. His features softened. "Guess

179

what horse he wants?"

"Oh, dear. Rory, is that safe?"

"I'll make sure of it. Can't always reason why a horse takes to some and not others. I think they'll be fine. Heart doan always pick wise, but it knows what it wants."

"Yes," she echoed softly. "Come here."

Warily, he crossed to the gate. Norah wet her handkerchief and gently dabbed at the gash below his eye, washing the dried blood from his cheek. He endured it for a moment then flinched away. "I best get cleaned up before supper. Shall we let him sleep?"

"Not out here. I'll get him."

"No. That's all right. I got him."

Bundling the boy up to his broad chest, Rory angled out of the stall as Norah held the door open, then hobbled up to the house.

He felt better after a long, hot soak. It eased the swelling in his knee and the aches from the rest of him. With a towel slung about his hips, he limped from the bath to the bedroom and drew up short. Norah was there. Her eyes did a quick, involuntary survey of all the towel didn't cover, then lingered immodestly over what it did conceal. When she spoke, her words were rather strained.

"Ruth gave me this for those cuts. Put it on."

"They ain't nothing but scratches. They'll heal up fine."

"Right up until they poison your blood. Don't argue."

He scowled sourly. "Wouldn't do no good." He took the salve and sniffed at it. "I'd rather have the blood poisoning." At her stern glare, he sighed. "Awright." She didn't move. "Do you mind? I need to get dressed."

"Oh." Norah flushed awkwardly. "Of course. Excuse me."

As she started for the door, Rory called, "What about the places I cain't reach? Seems kinda silly to worry over one side and let the other go to chance."

Norah halted. After a moment of internal discussion, she looked back to him, her features grim. "Stretch out on the bed. I'll see to them."

His expression was carefully unchanged, and he didn't argue. Once he'd draped his long form across the coverlet, Norah settled gingerly beside him. When she touched the greasy ointment to the first tear on his back, he cleared the bedspread by a good four inches, yelping like a whipped pup.

"Golldarnit, why doan you just' use hot coals!"

"Stop whining."

"Well, it hurts!"

"I thought cowboys were supposed to be tough," she chided, smearing more of the noxious stuff on the crisscrossing pattern of holes in his flesh.

"Not when it comes to having our hide burned off. I suppose you're enjoying this."

"I'd enjoy it a lot more if you didn't bellow quite so loudly."

He made a disgruntled noise and tensed in sulky silence.

She was enjoying it. Not the twitch of pain but the feel of man. As she doctored the small tears, she began a massage of his shoulders with her free hand, easing the knot of muscles and her own restless want to touch him. Finishing with his back, she shifted down to his legs where the wire had punctured the backs of his thighs.

"This is going to sting."

"What do you call what it was doing before?" he grumbled sullenly before sucking a sharp breath.

"You look like a pincushion."

"Jus' get on with it."

When she reached for the towel, he gave a shout of protest.

"Norah!"

"What? I've seen your backside before so quit your yelling."

"Well—well, that was different. You weren't torturing me at the time."

"Hush!" She flipped up the towel and was forced to remind herself that she was supposed to be concentrating on the tiny wounds, not on the firm contour of his seat. "This is going to hurt me more than you."

"I'll jus' bet—Owww!"

"Sorry. I'm almost done."

Contrarily, she took her time, mesmerized by the powerful bunching of muscle with every jerk and tense of his flanks. Her voice was thick when she finally murmured, "All done."

"'Bout time," he mumbled, expelling his breath in gusty relief.

"Roll over."

"Unuh. No way. I'll do it myself."

"Rory, stop your—"

He rolled just as she leaned, and she found herself stretched out over him and eyeball to eyeball.

"Rory . . ."

His kiss was slow and sweet and nearly as torturous to her heart as the ointment to his raw flesh. She shifted slightly, her arms coming up to fit over his shoulders, settling in atop the hard lines of his body. And from downstairs came an interrupting call.

"Mama?"

She tore herself from Rory's kiss with difficulty. "Just a minute, sweetheart." Then she leaned back down for his lips.

Rory's head turned away. "You best see what he wants," he suggested quietly.

With a reluctant sigh, Norah eased off the tempting terrain and shook the wrinkles from her gown. She didn't dare look at him, stretched out naked and desirable. By the time she returned to the shadow-laden room, Rory was flopped over on his belly, sound asleep. She pulled the sheet over him. And when she came up to tell him supper was ready, he was gone.

Chapter Twelve

He didn't need this now. It wasn't like he didn't have enough upheaval to occupy his mind.

Rory glared down at the mail he'd opened. Bills. No end to them. Expenses multiplying by the minute. And there, all fat and tempting, the buy-out offer from the East. He wished he could just shove them all together, dump them in a drawer, and let them work out their differences in the dark. But they wouldn't. Sighing, he started to prioritize, stacking debts into piles of "Got To," "Don't Want To But Got To," and "Ignore It and Hope it Goes Away." He could take out another loan, but he knew he was stretching dangerously thin with the bank. He could hint for a handout from his father, but his pride still held out against worry. He could sell off some acreage. But that was like trying to decide which one of his appendages he could do without. Dang, there had to be something he wasn't seeing.

"Hello. Bad time?"

He looked up from his desk and smiled with a genuine welcome. "No. Great time. C'mon in, honey."

Gena advanced into the room and found herself

staring at the glass-fronted bookcases behind the big desk. "What happened there?"

Rory leaned back in his chair and drawled casually, "I slipped, and my fist went through the glass."

"Through all four of them?"

"It was a mighty hard fall."

"I see."

No, she didn't. His smile pulled at the corners, wanting to collapse. "Sit yourself down. What's on your mind?"

Gena pulled up a chair so that they faced one another with a familiar closeness, then sat, carefully arranging her skirts. "I just wanted to see how you were doing."

"Mama send you over?"

"No."

"'Cause if she did, you can go right on back and tell her if she's so danged curious, she can make the trip herself. It wouldn't kill her."

"She didn't ask me to come," Gena restated gently. "As a matter of fact, she's as touchy about the whole matter as you are. And you both should be ashamed of yourselves."

Rory made an uncompromising noise, but he didn't disagree.

"How are . . . things?"

"Things in general or is there something specific you're jus' dying to get to?"

"How are things with you and Norah?"

"Gena, that ain't none—"

"Don't you dare growl at me, Rory Prescott. I won't tolerate it."

He shut his mouth and blinked as if he were a yapping dog that had been dealt a stinging blow on the snout.

"Now then, if you want to talk, I'll listen. If you want me to go away, say so in a civil manner."

"Go away."

"No."

He threw up his hands. "Lord above. To think once I was thrilled to no end to have relatives living so close by. Awright, Gena. What do you want to hear? What personal little details would you like to poke and prod at? Go on. Take your best shot."

"Rory, what's happened?" She asked that softly, with an intuitive concern.

"Norah wants to divorce me."

"What?" Gena sat bolt upright. "No! You must be mistaken."

"Well, I ain't making it up!"

She slumped back in her chair, trying to regiment this news with what Norah had said at the stream. She shook her head. "I can't believe that. She loves you."

"She hasn't told me that. Some fancy feller she's been sparking with in the East shows up at the door all ready to pull her and Jacob right out from under me. What am I gonna do, Gena? I can't let her go."

"No, of course not." And to her, it was that simple. People didn't get divorced. She couldn't conceive of it. They stayed together for better or worse. How well she knew that. Hadn't her own parents been prime examples? One took what they had and made do the best they could. And there wasn't a day that went by that she didn't thank God for what she had. She looked at Rory Prescott and couldn't imagine why Norah would be crazy enough to leave. He was a good, dependable man who worshipped her completely. He was kind; he was fun; he was handsome. He was home.

"What?" he demanded, frowning because of her pensive expression.

"Oh . . . nothing. I was just thinking." She reached for Rory's hand and held to it tightly. "She can't do it, Rory. She can't leave you. I don't believe it for a minute. Just as surely as I know I couldn't leave Scott."

"But, Gena, Norah ain't like you." He sighed in frustration. "I wish she was. Sometimes, I wish she was. You understand me. You doan try to change me. You're easy on a man, Gena. Scotty's awful damn lucky."

"Remind him of that when he gets home. He may have forgotten." And suddenly her eyes were full of wetness.

"Oh, honey, I doubt that." Hating the sight of her tears, he got all mushy inside. "Doan do that, Gena."

"I'm sorry," she sniffed miserably. "It's just that he's been gone for such a long time and I get to missing him so much I think I must be going crazy."

"I know, honey. I know." His touch was gentle upon her damp cheek, comforting in its strength. She leaned into his palm, accepting his care with a desperately lonely heart. His kiss was warm against her temple, then soft upon her lips. Sweet. Loving without being passionate. Nice. So she allowed herself to draw from it the same way she gathered encouragement from his words. And when he pulled back, she let her breath out with a quiet, "Oh my, you do that well."

"I *must* be crazy. I didn't mean nothing by that."

"Yes, you did. And thank you for it." She put her hand to his warm cheek.

"Maybe I should have aimed better all them years ago and married you myself."

She laughed warmly, teasing him with her eyes.

"Why, Rory Prescott, what a nearly incestuous thought!"

He grinned at her. "Why, Sis, doan tell me you never once thought . . ."

She took in his sassy smile and arrogant good looks and smiled back. "Thought, maybe. But want to change what I have, no. And Norah would be crazy if she does." She stood up, then leaned down to hug him quickly. "I've got to go. You be patient with Norah, and don't do anything—crazy. All right?"

"Awright. An' maybe I'll beat some sense into that brother of mine when he gets home."

"Maybe I'll let you." She brushed a fond kiss along his cheek.

"Is Dawn still stewing, or is she ready to come on over and bury the hatchet with Jacob yet?"

"She's in the barn seeing to it now. Were you and Scott that bad when you were children?"

"'Bout the same," he admitted with a grin. "'Cept Dawn packs a meaner wallop than Scotty ever did."

"She'd be proud to hear you say that. So, please don't."

"Yes, ma'am."

Norah watched Gena Prescott climb aboard her buggy. She whirled away from the upstairs window and began to pace in a frenzied agitation. Rory and Gena. No! Calmer logic defied it; what she'd seen in the study stated it plain. He'd taken a lover in her absence—how convenient that he keep it in the family! The words she'd overheard raked across her heart. The embrace she'd seen shattered it into tiny hurtful pieces.

Norah ain't like you. I wish she was. God, what a fool she'd been! Meek, maternal Gena Prescott, her friend, the woman to whom she'd confided her pain. The woman who confessed such undying love for her own husband was lost in his brother's embrace. She couldn't believe what her own eyes told her. Not of Gena. Her one true friend.

A furious growl of anger rumbled deep inside. Her steps quickened as her thoughts ran away with her. Rory and Gena. Close. Close as brother and sister. Alone and lonely. Left to an isolation where innocent friendship could ripen into intimate involvement. *Urrrr!* She'd murder them both, the two-faced, scheming, liars! She'd do it with Scott Prescott's big scalping knife. Maybe he'd help!

Trembling with the force of her rage, Norah paused in the center of the room, panting hard. Closing her eyes, she could see them, touching, kissing; but, try as she would, she couldn't force the picture beyond to the things she and Rory did together. That calmed her somewhat but didn't lessen the pain in her chest that swelled up to an intolerable degree. With quieter thought came the truth that really frightened her. She understood sex. She knew why a man and woman came together in uncontrollable need. What scared her was the way Rory responded to Gena's care. The way he poured out his heart, the way he broke down so trustingly as he had upon his father's recovery. He hadn't turned to her; he'd looked to Gena for comfort.

You understand me. You doan try to change me. Norah's not like you. I wish she was.

I wish she was.

A soft sob escaped her.

He'd told her—hadn't he?—long before they married. He wanted a woman like Gena Prescott. He wanted a woman like the one his brother married. He wanted a wife and mother for his children who would be there uncomplainingly. A woman who was good and decent and, above all, a lady. And try as she would to pretend, Norah was no lady. She wasn't good and she hadn't been decent and Rory could never forgive her for that. It didn't matter that he loved her. It didn't matter that he wanted her. He just plain couldn't forget what she'd been. That's why he wouldn't trust her. That's why he wouldn't depend upon her.

That's why he'd turned to Gena.

And that's why she and her son would return to Baltimore with Trevor Samuels.

"How's he doing?"

Jacob looked up in surprise to see his tomboy cousin leaning on the top of Ghost's stall beside him. Her golden features were stoic, her tone neutral. He looked away glumly.

"He's fine. Daddy says he'll heal up good as new. I suppose you're wanting him back, now."

"No. When my daddy gets back, he'll pick out a good horse for me. No one knows horses better'n a Lakota."

Jacob sniffed at that and said nothing. She'd sure changed her tune. Fickle female.

"How come you wear those funny glasses?" she asked abruptly.

"So's I can see the nose in front of my face. Our President wears glasses just like these."

"My daddy's met the President."

"Well, Mr. Roosevelt's been to our house in Baltimore for dinner."

Dawn clapped her mouth shut. She couldn't beat that. So she changed the subject. "I know where there's a real Indian burial ground."

Jacob tried not to look impressed by her bragging. "So?"

"My great granddaddy's buried there. If you look around real good, you can find old arrowheads and stuff."

Now he was interested. Arrowheads. Wouldn't they make a humdinger of a kite tail! "Where is this place?"

"Up in the Hills. It takes a couple of hours to get there on horseback. It's a rough trip even for a good rider. You'd never make it."

"Would too." No way was he going to let this skinny girl best him again.

"C'mon then."

"I'll have to go ask—tell Mama I'm going."

"Ask Rory. He won't say no," was her sage advice.

Knowing she was probably right about that, Jacob raced up to the house from the barn. He was about to hop up onto the porch when the sound of raised voices reached him. Angry voices: His mother's, his father's. He stopped, choking up inside. Then, after a moment's hesitation, he turned and ran back to the barn to lose himself in his cousin's adventure.

She stormed downstairs determined to announce her decision. She was leaving. There was no use pretending things could work between them. She would say it fast and get it done. And now she didn't have to worry over whether or not Rory would survive it. He would. With Gena's support. Wounded pride shoving her forward at an impetuous pace, Norah pushed open the door to his study, ready to launch into her prepared speech. And no sound came.

He was sitting at his desk, rubbing at his eyes. It

191

was a tired gesture, a familiar one. Norah paused at the doorway, for a moment too overwhelmed with conflicting emotion to move. She'd wanted to hold to her anger, to her outrage; but something in that weary movement, in the way his shoulders rose and fell so heavily, distracted her from it. Pride trembled and fell before stronger tender feeling. Oh, how she wanted to be there for him, to be the one who eased his aches, his pains, his fears. That's all she'd ever wanted. She wanted to be more than a lover. She wanted to be a wife. She wanted the chance to prove she could be. And if she left now, if she ran from this fight for his affection, she never would. Here was everything she wanted, not in Baltimore with Trevor. She wasn't ready to let go yet. Consciously, she pushed her hasty resolution aside. She wasn't prepared to excuse him, but she wanted the chance to forgive him. And to be forgiven by him.

At the touch of her hands, Rory gave a jerk. Then he sighed and relaxed into the kneading pressure. He made a contented noise and let his head loll loosely.

"Oh, honey, that feels good," he murmured.

Norah's hands stilled. Her thumbs were riding the virile pulse of his neck, her fingers dipping down in a vee toward his strong throat. *Maybe I ought to just strangle him and get it over with* came the furious growl of her jealousy. But then he heaved another of those consuming sighs and let his head roll back upon the cradle of her forearms. His eyes were closed. He looked so trustingly vulnerable. Her hostility melted in an instant.

He gave another start of surprise at the touch of her lips on his. He didn't move. He let her take what she wanted from the hard slanting kiss, then opened his eyes when she slid on the pivot point of her arms about his neck to settle on his lap.

"What was that for? Not that I'm complaining."

"I love you, Rory."

He grabbed for a hasty breath. "What?" he whispered.

"I said I love you."

He exhaled shakily. His stare was dark, intense in its study of hers. "You sure pick the dangedest times to come out with things."

Then his hands were on her face, cupping it between them, pulling her down to meet the eager part of his mouth. It was a hot, hungry, tongue-stabbing kiss. He arched away from the back of the chair, pressing against her, passion flaming through his body as if it were made of a good hardwood. She succumbed to it, wanting the ravening taste of his desire, wanting it to bruise her, to claim her. To make her forget. And she almost did until the kiss broke and her cheek rubbed his. And the tangy scent of lemon verbena stung her nose.

Gena's scent.

She pushed off his lap, leaving him to stare up at her in a stir of confusion. He looked so surprised and uncertain. She wanted to strike out at him, to slap him silly, to collapse upon his chest in a flood of anguished tears, to demand to know why he couldn't care for her with a trusting tenderness. She wanted to believe in the deep longing she saw steeping in his dark eyes and carved upon the angles of his face. She wanted to believe she was the only one who meant anything to him.

But she knew that wasn't true.

But could it be?

Could she walk away from him without giving him one last chance to instill hope within her broken heart? Time to see if anything at all had changed or could change. *Let me in, Rory. Please.*

"How's your knee?"

"Aches like a bad tooth," he answered with unusual candor. He was watching her, expression carefully veiled. Wary.

"Did I hear Gena earlier?" She forced that out with a calm she didn't feel.

"She stopped over to say howdy."

Norah's gaze narrowed. Her fingers curled into her palms, nails slicing in sharp crescents of pain. She struggled to get beyond that gorge of hurt. She was gaging the future of their marriage, not its failings.

"What were you working on when I came in?"

"Just some business." Subtly, he scooped all the loose papers into one protected pile, huddling over them like a dog with a meaty bone.

"Anything I should know about?"

"Naw. Just business."

"Bar K business?"

"Ummmm."

"Then it concerns me. Let me see."

She reached for the top sheet, but his palm had flattened out upon it. She tried tugging, but the pressure of his hand intensified.

"It ain't nothing for you to worry over," he stated firmly in that none-of-your-business-so-stay-out-of-it tone.

"I only worry about things that are being kept from me." Those words cut with double meaning. "Are we in financial trouble?"

"I said I'm taking care of it." More aggressive, more defensive. It must be bad.

"That's not what I asked. Rory, I'm not a simpleton. I'm not some fluffy female who's going to shriek and fall into vapors. I want to help you. I can't unless you talk to me."

"Like I said, I'm handling it. You doan need to fret

about a roof over your head. I ain't gonna let you starve. I ain't gonna let you lose the clothes on your back."

"I've survived all those things, Rory. I've survived worse than you can imagine. You can't protect me from a life I've already lived."

His features tightened down the way they always did when she spoke of her past. She couldn't read what was behind them. Distress? Distrust? Distaste? She didn't know.

"You won't have to go back to it, if that's what you're worrying over. I tole you I'd take care of you, and I will. Whatever it takes. You and Jacob ain't never gonna lack for nothing."

"Even if it kills you."

His jaw spasmed and clamped down.

"Even if it tears our marriage apart."

He said nothing, pride giving him lockjaw.

"You simple, stubborn, mule-headed man! Why can't you ever answer me? Why do you have to hoard everything that has to do with this ranch like it was your own precious pot of gold? Are you too proud to admit to needing help? Are you too vain to take it from me? What?"

"You'd like to see me fail, wouldn't you? You'd like to have me crawling to you a-begging to be rescued. Well, it won't happen. I made me a promise to the Major that I'd keep the Bar K going strong. And I have. I will."

"And just where do you rank the promises you made to me? Somewhere near the bottom? Somewhere unimportant?"

Rory's expression softened. He could see where things were headed, and he wanted desperately to rein in before all control was lost. "Norah, you know you mean everything to me."

195

"Do I?" She had the bit in her teeth, and she was running. "If that's true, let me see those papers."

Slowly, deliberately, he opened the top drawer of his desk and raked the papers into it. Then he pushed it shut. And locked it. The key went into his shirtpocket. "No." Flat, unyielding.

"Will you tell me how much we owe?"

"No."

"Will you take my money to pay our debts?"

"No."

She drew a long, determined breath. "Then I guess we have nothing to talk about, do we?"

Rory watched her sweep from the room, her head held high, her back stiff as a fencepost, beautiful and, as ever, elegant in her anger. He wanted to call to her. He wanted to fall on his knees to do the required begging. But he was a Prescott and a Kincaid, and they didn't go a-crawling. Even when they were wrong.

He leaned back and let his eyes close. God, what was he going to do? Go to her and confess that he was going to lose the land out from under them? That he'd tried and tried and it still hadn't been good enough? Didn't she know how desperately scared he was of appearing a failure in her eyes? Did she think he'd forgotten the promises he'd made her? How could he when they were a daily weight upon his heart? *I'll love you. I'll take care of you. I'll make you so happy. I'll see you never want for nothing.* He'd been so confident at twenty. So sure that if she'd only marry him, the future would take care of itself.

But he hadn't counted on the fire. He hadn't counted on Jacob coming so soon.

They'd been married less than two weeks when she told him she was pregnant. He'd made enough joyful noise to be heard four counties over. He'd been so excited by the idea. Norah round with his child. He couldn't wait. He remembered how Gena glowed when she was carrying Dawn, how Scott had strutted around like he was the first of the species to ever spawn a child. He remembered hearing that first cry of new life when he and Norah had helped Gena give birth in the back of a buckboard. He wanted those things.

He hadn't counted on Norah being the worst pregnant woman in the world.

She was sick almost from the day she announced the news, so weak and testy the whole family tiptoed around her. It wasn't easy with all seven Prescotts crowded under one roof for the winter. He was bewildered by the weepy, shrewish woman he loved so desperately. One minute she'd be chewing on his rump over some petty little thing Aurora had said to her, then she'd be wrapped around him, loving him so fierce and hard he couldn't remember where he was. He was in a constant state of uncertainty. It took one month, and battle lines were drawn between his wife and his mother with Gena in the middle. Two women at one stove, his father diagnosed somberly. What the hell did that mean?

It was easier for him to endure that winter. He was gone for sometimes twenty-hour stretches trying to dig the Bar K out from under the ashes. He had not only a wife to provide for but a baby, too. He was young, but he knew about responsibility. He had prime examples: His grandfather, his father, his brother—all willing to sacrifice for family. Norah would have what she deserved, what he'd promised her.

Jacob was born in the spring. It wasn't a miracle. It was a nightmare. Norah labored hard for two days. He wanted to be with her, supporting her, loving her;

but she flew into an unreasonable rage whenever he came into the room. Her pain was his fault, she railed at him; and though Ethan told him not to listen to the words, he heard them in his heart. She gave him a son, a tiny, noisy, incessantly collicky son. Rory smiled wryly, remembering. Lordabove, he loved that boy, but he was never quiet or content the way Dawn had been. He had to sneak down to the barn to catch a few hours' sleep, and the only time he felt at peace was atop his little red mare riding down strays.

It was the cradle that forced them to leave the Lone Star. A fancy affair of brass and porcelain came all the way from Paris when Jacob was three-months old. No card was attached, but he knew. It was from Cole Denby. The minute Norah placed Jacob in it, she gave the Prescott family an unforgiveable snub by overlooking the lovingly crafted piece of maple shaped by Ethan's hands. It had rocked Scotty, Rory, then Dawn, but wasn't good enough for Jacob. Aurora raged. Norah simmered coldly. And Rory, who deeply wished he could run like hell, grimly backed his wife instead of family. He was heartsick over it because he was secretly furious at Norah himself, but he did it. And two weeks later, he packed up wife and son and drove them over to their new home.

He could still see the look on her face. Stark and stricken. It wasn't much. What had she expected? More soddy than house, but it was theirs. She just looked at it; and he wanted to break down and bawl like a baby, feeling awful and humbled for the first time in his life. But he didn't. He spent the first three days inside with her, making love to her until neither of them could move. She was better after that; and he went back to the range, more determined than ever to get her everything she wanted. He'd wake up early and see her sleeping beside him, his beautiful Norah; and he'd fill up inside until he couldn't breathe. That would push him out on the days he'd yearn to linger, driving him with that memory of her curled trustingly at his side.

Then the snake came calling. He came home to find Norah nearly hysterical, brandishing the poor flattened hide of the miserable little creature that had slithered in for warmth and had the bad luck to nail a crawling Jacob on one chubby hand. She'd had enough, she announced and began to pack. He'd tried to console her, to take her in his arms, but she'd have none of it. She was pregnant again. She and Jacob were moving into town. If she were going to be wretched, she'd be wretched in comfort, not in some dirty soddy. Hurt to the quick, he'd swallowed back his arguments and had driven her into Crowe Creek. The ride back alone had been the longest and loneliest of his life, and the months that followed went by in an exhausted daze. All day on the range, the long ride into town for a few hours sleep, then up before three to head back to the Bar K. He was nearly worn through when Norah lost the baby. Behind her tears, he thought he saw a whisper of relief; and then came the unforgiveable question creeping into his thoughts, fleeting but never really forgotten: Had she done something to get rid of it? Ridden by a horrible shame at conceiving of such a thought, he took his grieving to the lonesome plains where only the cows could hear him wailing. He never betrayed his heartbreak in front of Norah lest she think he blamed her. She couldn't have any more children.

She came back to the Bar K with him, a quiet, shadowy companion. She didn't complain about anything and, slowly, he was able to warm her with his loving.

199

They lived in the soddy for almost two years. He worked until he dropped. He'd smear tobacco juice under his eyelids so the sting would keep him awake. He scrimped and saved every penny. Norah dreamed of a house. He put up a barn. She looked through catalogs of new clothes. He bought fencing and feed. He dragged himself out early, and she lay awake listening to the incessant moan of the Dakota wind.

Then he'd ridden in after a particularly grueling day to have her fly into his arms with welcoming kisses. She'd gotten a letter from Cole Denby. His investments had paid off big. They were rich. The news stopped Rory cold. After all the work he'd done, it was a letter from her thieving ex-partner that brought her into his arms with smiles. No. He refused to touch a penny of it. They fought. For four weeks. Then a long tense silence settled in. She shut him out of her conversation, out of her field of vision. The only place she allowed him was in their shared bed. She was never cold to him there.

When the first thaw of her mood came, he should have suspected, but he was so happy to see her smile, he never once thought she was planning something. Until the house arrived. Crate after pre-cut and labeled crate. Windows, shingles, mill-turned porch-posts. Everything. He stared at the expansive blue-print the way she'd done his lowly soddy. And he walked away without a word. She hired men from Crowe Creek to work on it. He wouldn't pull any of his hands in to lift a hammer nor would he. That big skeleton rising outside his front door was a beacon to the world that he couldn't provide for his family.

And after that, things had gone straight to hell.

He revolved in his chair, angling it to look out over the neatly arranged corrals and outbuildings and knew, galled, that he'd have none of it if it hadn't been for her money. If she hadn't bailed him out when the five-year loan came due. He'd torn the paid-in-full notice to pieces and had thrown them in her face. He'd said things in a craze of hurt and anger that three years and a thousand miles couldn't heal. And even now, even at this desperate point he'd come to, he couldn't make himself take a word of it back.

A knocking on the front door roused him from his grim daydreams. He went to answer it, mood plummeting at the sight of Trevor Samuels in his shiny suit and slicked-back hair. Representing all the things Norah wanted that he could never be. He had no fight left to do more than mutter, "Grab yourself a seat. I'll tell her you're here." When he turned, Samuels called to him.

"Mr. Prescott?"

He gave the other man a flat black stare.

"I'll take very good care of them."

He didn't react. Inside, his gut took a nose-dive into his boots. He made himself walk away, up the turn in the stairs, to the room he and Norah had shared so briefly.

And there she was, her luggage opened upon the bed, her clothes neatly folded and ready to pack away.

Chapter Thirteen

"Goin' somewheres?"

Norah paused only briefly in her arranging of garments. "Into Crowe Creek. I'm going to take a room at the hotel."

"How convenient," he drawled to cover his panic. "You takin' the boy or would he jus' be in your way?"

She gave him her full attention then. Her glare nearly cut him in two. "Jacob has never been in my way. How could you say such a thing to me, Rory?"

He backtracked quickly and mumbled, "I'm sorry, Norah. I didn't mean that."

"No one, not even your sainted mother, could ever accuse me of not being a good parent to my child!"

"I know." He hung his head with a satisfactory repentance, then glanced up at her through the fringe of his lashes. She had to look away. He made her heart quiver when he did that. It made her want to drop everything, to hug him close as if he were little more than a soulful-eyed child in need of tender loving care. Well, not this time. She stuffed her stockings in with a careless disregard.

"That as far as you're goin'? To Crowe Creek?"

"As soon as I can get Jacob ready," was her curt reply.

"Can I come visit him there?"

"If you like."

"Can I come visit you there?"

A pause. "If you like."

"Can I bring a change of clothes?"

"No."

She crammed in her corsets and her petticoats, taking out her aggression with the vigorous mashing and mooshing. She dropped the lid and yanked the straps through.

"Your ride's downstairs."

She gave him a blank look. "Trevor? Good. That will save on the return of the buggy." She leaned on the closed trunk, fighting to still her inner trembling. She had to leave fast. It was too dangerous to linger near him. Her will was much too fragile. "Can you carry this down for me or shall I have Trevor do it?"

"I'll bring it. I don't want him up here."

"Fine. I guess I have everything."

"You didn't leave anything long enough for it to go getting lost."

Norah fought the thickness gathering in her throat. She wouldn't cry. This was just the first step she was taking. First Crowe Creek, then Baltimore. She was a bit surprised that Rory was taking it so well. Then, he decided to get difficult.

"Doan go."

"Rory . . ."

"Please."

"Rory . . ."

He didn't try to touch her or come any closer, but the look in his eyes reached deeper than any caress to snatch desperately at her emotions. It was such a temptation to put her arms around him, to soothe

203

that anxious look. But he'd already been in someone else's arms and he didn't come to her for the soothing for his soul. When he saw that she was holding firm against him, he let his pride down a notch lower.

"Norah, doan go. Once you leave here, I know you ain't never comin' back. Please doan do this. Please give me a chance."

"To what? Give you a chance to what? Change? Are you ever going to do that? Can you take back any of the things you said downstairs?"

Silence, then a very quiet, "No." His honesty was crushing, but she couldn't help respecting him for it.

"Then why stay?"

"Did you change your mind already about what you said?"

"What did I say?"

"You said you love me."

Her sigh was massive, full of aggravation and anguish. "That has nothing to do with this, Rory. Nothing!"

"I doan—"

"No. And you never will. Ever. I love you, Rory. I just can't be your wife anymore."

As she hurried from the room, the full impact of that struck. *I just can't be your wife anymore.* She'd decided. She was going for good, Jacob with her. The sense of helplessness was paralyzing. What could he give that he hadn't already given? Except his pride and his land, she had everything else. If love weren't enough to hold her, what else was there?

Help me out, Lord. I'm outta miracles, and I need one. He closed his eyes, praying with all the fervency in his soul. When he opened them, he still had no answers. Just Norah's big suitcase packed and ready for him to tote below. He grabbed onto the handle and heaved it up. One nice toss and he could send it sailing right through the window and straight down to Samuels's buggy below. *That fast enough for you, Norah-honey? I thought you was in a big hurry to get out from under me.*

He smiled at that image. The only thing that could improve upon it would be Samuels standing below to catch it. Right on top of his spit-polished head.

Rory was musing, staring out the window, when his eyes came into focus and he frowned. Forgetting all about the suitcase, he bounded down the steps, past the startled couple in the hall to push out onto the front porch. He stared down at the corral where the stock was milling in anxious circles. He could feel the short hairs rise up along his arms. What the hell?

"Rory?"

Norah came to the door. She watched him scent the breeze like a hound, lifting his face toward the clear Dakota sky. A brisk wind ruffled through his red hair and plucked at the lightweight wool of his shirt, molding it to one side in sculpting detail.

"Rory, what is it? What's wrong?" She stepped outside, feeling the breeze snap against her. It was surprisingly cold compared to the balmy autumnal Dog Days they'd enjoyed. "Rory?" She touched the back of his arm, feeling its tension. "What?"

"Doan know." He scanned beyond the perimeters of the ranch, across plains lit with an intense blue light. Then he turned and froze up. "There she is. Norther's coming."

Norah followed his gaze and felt cold right to her bones. It was a fearsome sight, that blast of frigid snow gathering above the Hills. The horizon was almost solid black as storm clouds mounded, ready to tear open in a fury as they caught on the jagged peaks.

"Where's Jacob?"

Rory's low-pitched question had her instantly alarmed. "He was in the barn with that horse last I knew."

"Heya, Sammy? You seen the boy?" Rory hollared against the strengthening wind.

"Rode on out with Dawn couple hours back."

"Probably over at the Lone Star," he mused aloud, then gave Norah a tight smile. "Nothing to worry over."

"Nothing?" She gave him a chiding glare.

"What's going on?" Trevor asked from the other side of the screen door.

"Storm coming in. 'Less you want to winter here for a spell, you might think on headin' back to town real quick like."

He frowned and looked up at the endless blue of the sky. "I hardly think—"

"You doan know what to think, mister. Them clouds are goin' blow up and over us so fast you ain't gonna have time to button your coat. That buggy of yours could be belly deep in snow in a matter of minutes. So you'd best git and git fast."

"Surely you don't expect me to believe—"

"Trevor, he isn't exaggerating." Norah watched the sky, her expression growing pinched. Her fingers tightened on her husband's arm. "Rory, would you please send someone over to the Lone Star for Jacob? I want him home. Now."

Home. "I'll go myself."

"I'll stay with Norah, if you don't mind."

"Suit yourself." He yelled down to the barn, "Sammy, gear up Bud for me."

"Sure thing, boss."

He was about to turn back to the house when he saw a buckboard careen through the Bar K gates.

206

Gena. He came down off the porch to meet her, grabbing at the reins to haul in her winded team.

"Is Dawn here? Ethan says there's a big blow coming."

Norah strode forward, hugging her arms about herself. "She's with Jacob. They're not at the Lone Star?"

"Haven't seen them."

Just then Sammy came trotting up from the barn leading Rosebud. "Rory, Crawford says he heard the younguns talking about hunting up arrowheads and such around some burial site."

"Damn," Rory muttered fiercely, his eyes turning toward the bank of black clouds. "They're in the Hills."

"Oh, no," Gena gasped. Her hands flew up to cover her mouth, her eyes rounding above them.

"Now, Gena-honey, doan get all riled. C'mon down here." Rory put up his arms and she slid down into them, her own locking tightly around his neck. Norah turned away, teeth clenched.

"If they get caught up there—"

"They ain't gonna get caught, Gena. You calm down. Dawn, she's a smart girl. She knows how to read signs. They're probably on their way home already. Think I'll jus' ride on out and meet up with 'em halfway."

"Thank you," she said weakly, hugging to him.

"I want you to stay here. I'll send one of the fellers over to the Lone Star to tell Mama and Daddy you're gonna shore up with us."

"But Scott . . . what if he gets in tonight?"

"Scotty knows his way over, and he ain't afraid of a little snow." He set her down. "Norah'll take care of you whilst I'm gone. You don't got nothing to fret about. Norah-honey, you see Ruth puts some coffee on."

"Of course," she said flatly.

Rory gave her a quizzing stare. She was in an odd mood. His suddenly soured. Of course, she hadn't wanted to stay at all. She was hoping they'd be halfway to Crowe Creek by now. Well, too bad if she had to play hostess at his home a while longer. Angrily, he stomped up the steps and went inside to fetch his heavy coat and gloves. He turned to find Norah right behind him, looking pale as death.

"Rory, you find him and bring him home safe. Please. He's all I have."

Very gently, he took up her hand in both of his, drawing it up to his lips. They caressed warm and wonderfully over the tight ridge of her knuckles. And suddenly, she was clinging. "No he ain't, honey. You still got me."

"Rory," Gena called, coming in to interrupt the tenuous moment between them. "Dawn wasn't wearing a coat. I don't think she was even carrying a bedroll with her."

"I'll take some extra blankets." He moved away from Norah to take up his sidearms and check the loads in his Winchester. Gena hovered close, agitated and in need of reassurance. Norah couldn't find it in herself to supply it. As Rory shrugged into his bulky outerwear, the fragile blonde woman caught at him again. She hooked an arm about his neck, drawing him down so she could plant a kiss on his tanned cheek.

"Be careful, Rory."

"Doan worry over me, Sis," he blustered with a big grin. Then he started for the door.

Norah stood frozen. She hadn't grabbed him up and kissed him and told him to be careful. She'd been full of fright over Jacob. Only Gena had sent him off with a word of caution for his own sake. And now it was too late to amend it.

He'd reached the door and was clapping his hat down on his head when, suddenly, he turned back to her. In four great strides, he was before her, clamping her face between his big hands, his mouth crushing down over the top of hers. She had time to make a soft, wondering sound before he pulled back and started away again. As he opened the door, her daze of passion broke.

"Rory?"

He paused.

"Come back safe. All of you."

He gave the brim of his hat a smart tip. "Yes, ma'am."

He had a long ride ahead. Rory notched out his mare into a swifter pace. She was eager to run, sensing his mood and the threat of weather, and he had to hold her in. He kept his eye on the horizon and tried to keep his heart out of his throat. He hadn't let on to the women, but there wasn't a chance in hell of his getting Jacob and Dawn back to the Bar K before the sky tore open. He'd be lucky if he could even find them. He was riding into the Hills because he'd go crazy waiting at the ranch doing nothing. Better to be out here skimming across the eerily lit plain with the thunder of hoofbeats echoing those of his heart.

He tried not to do much thinking. His brother had taught Dawn well. Ordinarily, he wouldn't worry. But Jacob was out there, too, and it was a new, purely visceral anxiousness gnawing through him.

"Dawn-honey, you take care a him for me, you hear," he whispered into the whip of Rosebud's mane. "Hang on till I get there."

The flakes started filtering down when he reached

209

the foothills. It was cold. He shivered and hunched down inside his sheepskin coat. It was agony thinking of the two children in their shirtsleeves. He urged the mare to climb, and he started looking for signs. He was no tracker, not like Scott, but he did know a thing or two about hunting up a trail. As it was, he stumbled on it by accident.

Dawn's horse went tearing by him, riderless, scrambling downhill with a recklessness born of fear. He didn't waste time in pursuit. He could double both children on Bud if he had to. He was more concerned with where the horse had been then in where it was headed in such a hurry. He goaded Rosebud upward, keeping a tight rein on his own alarm.

"Jacob! Dawn!"

The wind shoved their names back down his throat. Then faint, almost like the moan of the pines, came the call of "Over here."

He turned the mare toward the sound—or to where he thought the sound came from; it was hard to tell with the way the wind bandied about. Rosebud picked her way daintily along the outcroppings while Rory scanned the tree line. He shouted again and waited, trying to quiet his heavy heartbeat to hear. There it was. He nudged with his heels; and, as horse and rider crested a rise, he spotted them. Nothing had ever looked as good as those two little figures huddled together out of the force of the wind.

"You two holding up down there for the winter or are you lookin' to get home for supper? I know a two rumps that're gonna get chewed ragged by a couple a real outta sort mamas."

"Daddy!"

Jacob shot up with that squeal of relief and was wrapped around Rory so tight he couldn't breathe

the second he stepped down off Rosebud. Which was fine by him.

"You younguns all right? Bet you're 'bout froze. What the Sam Hill you doin' a sitting up here like it was a picnic? Saw Dawn's horse a ways back heading for hay and a warm barn. Doan see yours, either, pard. Mind telling me how you was planning on getting home?"

"We were looking for arrowheads when Dawn—"

"It was Jacob's fault. He was supposed to be holding the horses and—"

"She fell and hurt her ankle, and I couldn't just leave her."

"Climb on down, son." Rory set the boy on his feet and went to kneel beside Dawn. She was pinch-faced with pain and not in a good humor. Her eyes glittered moistly as Rory reached for her boot. "Lemme take a look-see," he crooned in a bracing voice. As he eased the boot off, he heard her breath suck in sharply, but she made no other sound, even as he gently prodded. "Looks to be a good twist. Must hurt like a son-of-a-gun."

"I didn't cry," she told him with a soberness so reminiscent of his brother that he had to smile.

"Your daddy'd be right proud to hear that. Me, I'd be hollaring my head off. Lemme bind this up tight, and we'd best be thinking on what we're gonna do."

She never so much as whimpered when Rory bound the bulge in her ankle with his bandana or when he fixed her boot back on. Now that his worries were relieved, he could afford a little gruff scolding.

"Doan recall any too-big-for-their-britches kids asking permission to ride up here. Or am I just getting deaf an' forgetful in my ole age?"

"That was my fault, sir," came Jacob's quiet mumble.

211

"That right? It your idea to ride up here with a storm a brewing? Making both your mamas plum crazy with fretting?"

Dawn's bravado gave a notch at that. She hated to think of causing her mother's upset. "It just blew up real sudden, Rory. We were on our way back. We would have made it—if Jacob hadn't let loose of the horses. Then, the big sissy, he wouldn't go looking for 'em. *Istamaza.*" She hissed at the shamefaced boy, and he shrank beneath the scorn if not at the unknown meaning.

"Now, you hush that kinda talk up, girl."

"She's right, Daddy. I was supposed to be holding the horses. Only she fell and yelled out. I only dropped the reins for a second to see if she was all right, and they ran off."

Rory frowned slightly. The two horses were well-trained range animals. When their reins were down and their riders aground, they should have stood like statues. Something must have spooked them. Maybe the storm.

Jacob straightened his narrow shoulders into a mock-manly pose. "Daddy, I couldn't just go off and leave her by herself. Not hurt and all."

Rory laughed. "Son, I pity the critter that thinks to dangle with your cousin. But you did right. Doan worry on it. Dawn's jus' biting at you 'cause she's hurting and too much like her daddy to let on." He slipped out of his coat and draped it close about the girl's shivering figure. "Jacob, I got your jacket and some blankets tied behind the saddle. Fetch 'em for me."

"Yessir."

Dawn was looking up at him through solemn eyes, and he knew there was no avoiding her question.

"We can't get back before the storm hits, can we?"

"No." He put a hand on her head, brushing fingers through the bright hair. "I'd hate to get caught down there on the plain when all hell starts howling. Figure we'd head for Daddy's cabin. It's not too far apiece. Bud'll carry us."

"I'm sorry, Uncle Rory. I should have known better." Tears glistened. Pain wouldn't make her cry, but pride would.

"Doan you go a-wailing on me, honey. It'll freeze on your face. You think your daddy an' me never did nothing stupid? Why, it's purely amazing that we lived long enough to hollar at you for doing the exact same things." His thumb stroked across her blue eyes, erasing the shimmer of weeping. "Enough making talk. We best be getting 'fore we're snowed in tight."

Rory hoisted her up in his arms and carried her to Rosebud, settling her in the saddle. Then he turned to Jacob.

"You bundled up good an' tight, pard?" He pulled the edges of the coat closer to the boy's wind-flushed cheeks.

"Was Mama real scared?" His eyes misted in distress.

"Jacob, your mama's tough as bootheels 'neath them fancy city clothes. Takes a lot more an' a little blow to put a scare into her. She'll be mighty glad to see you, though."

"Rory, my hat," Dawn cried, pointing to the spot where they'd been.

Rosebud began to snort and dance nervously.

"Whatsa matter, girl? Easy now. Here, Jacob, hang onto these for a second." Rory pressed the reins into the boy's hand and gave Rosebud's neck a reassuring pat. "Doan you go kicking up a fuss over a little wind, you fool horse. You leave me aground and I'll

213

have you stuffed and put a set a rockers under you."

The mare whinnied soft and pushed at him with her nose. But she was still fidgeting. He frowned.

"Hang on tight, Jacob. I'll be right back."

Rory started walking back for Dawn's hat. Rosebud's agitation had him puzzled. She was basically a calm mount. Probably the storm, he thought as he bent down for the Stetson. A snuffling sound in front of him lifted his gaze and the spit dried in his mouth.

"Oh, sonuvabitch."

As he rose up to his full six-three, the grizzly he was nose to nose with did the same, topping eight feet, easy. The animal roared, muzzle opening wide to display an aggressive set of teeth and a lot of savage slobber. As Rory lunged backward, something with the force of a fifteen-pound maul struck the side of his head. His hat went sailing, followed by a crimson spray.

Chapter Fourteen

Snow whipped across the prairie like a freight train, piling up on the front porch of the Bar K until it blocked the view out of the windows. Outside, temperatures plunged. Inside, the fires were banked to a cheery heat that failed to warm the two women who waited.

Ruth set out a hot lunch that only Trevor touched. Gena sat nursing a cup of tea in the parlor. Norah prowled the halls.

"I'm sure they're all right," Trevor said softly, placing his hand upon the small of Norah's back. She tensed all over and stared at him through eyes both blank and wild. She looked at him as though she had no idea who he was or why he'd dare try to console her. He quietly retreated to the dining room and a bottle of surprisingly good chablis, wondering whom she worried over: Son or husband.

The wind quieted to a persistent gale force around two o'clock, and a weak sunlight teased over the drifts at the windows. By four, hope of their returning had dwindled down to a restless frenzy. In less than three hours, it would be completely dark. And they'd be in the Hills for the night, alone and unprotected. Unless they'd been caught out on the plains. Unless . . . the possibilities were endlessly gruesome. Better not to dwell on them. Except there was little else to do as the minutes ticked by and the Dakota wind wailed.

Norah found herself in Rory's study, picking up the shards of glass he'd left on the bookshelf ledge. Some of them were discolored. How badly she'd hurt him. Would she have the chance to tell him she was sorry? She brushed the broken slivers into the wastebasket and dropped bonelessly into his big chair. With her cheek pressed into the sleek leather and her arms wrapped around its high back, she closed her eyes, conjuring the sight of him from the familiar scent. Leather, tobacco, more faintly horse and outdoors. Did he know how much she truly loved him? How hard she'd really tried to be the wife he'd needed?

At first, she thought she imagined it—bootsteps on the front porch. She eased out of the big chair, almost afraid to let her hopes lift. When she reached the hall, there was a bitter blast of cold as the door pushed inward and a snow-covered figure turned in and wrestled it closed again. She caught sight of the black Stetson and with a soft cry, raced the length of the hall.

"Oh thank God! Thank God you're safe."

He turned as she flung herself upon him, her lips smashing over his chilled mouth in a grateful passion . . . for all of two seconds. Then, her eyes flew open to stare up into a pure golden gaze, and she lunged back in a confused dismay.

"Well, hello Norah. Quite a greeting."

At the sound of his voice, a shriek sounded from the parlor.

"Scott! Oh, Scott!"

Scott Prescott caught his wife up to him, hugging her tight before kissing her with enough blistering desire to melt the prairie snows bone dry. Norah retreated a few uncertain steps, her dazed stare fixed on the Stetson; Rory's, she was sure of it. She'd thought . . . she'd hoped. . . . She swallowed hard to dislodge the disappointment.

"Oh, Scott, I'm so glad to see you," Gena was sobbing as she scattered kisses over his bronzed features.

"I'm all wet."

"I don't care!"

"Here, just a second. Let me get out of these things."

Gena backed up just far enough for him to have room to shrug out of the damp coat. When he reached for the hat, he noticed Norah's glazed attention.

"It's one of Rory's old ones. I didn't have a hat, and it's colder than a bitch out there. I take it they aren't back yet."

"Something's happened," Gena moaned. "I know it. Oh, Scott, Dawn's out there—"

"Shhh." He touched his fingertips to her quivering lips, and her panic stilled. "Quiet, *mitawicu*. Tell me how long they've been gone."

Norah, who was calmer, told him, "Rory left around ten this morning. The storm hit about noon. Do you think they're all right?" Her fingers clutched in her skirt to hide the way they were shaking. She might not like Scott Prescott, but she had a deep respect for his instincts. And she was grateful to have him here. He would take over the burden of charge and know what to do.

"Rory wouldn't have started back knowing the snow was coming. My guess is, they've holed up in the Hills to wait it out."

217

"They should have been here by now," she said with an ominous quiet.

Scott gave her a thin, close-lipped smile. "Knowing Rory, he's probably got them lost. He couldn't find his butt with both hands. I'll go up after them."

"Wait. I'm going, too."

He blinked, then shook his head. "No."

"You forget whom you're talking to, Scott Prescott. My son and my husband are out there, and I'll be damned if I'm going to just sit here another second. You stand right there until I change my clothes, or you'll be joining your ancestors here in this hallway."

She didn't wait for his response. She was racing up the steps, her fashionable skirt dragged up out of the way. It was then Scott caught sight of Trevor Samuels snoring in wine-soaked oblivion in the dining room. What the hell was going on here? Someone sure had some fancy explaining to do for him to make sense of this scene. But as intriguing as it was, it would have to wait.

In the few minutes it took for him to hold his wife and soothe her fears, Norah reappeared ready to ride. She was wearing a pair of tan britches and a heavy flannel shirt. One of Rory's coats swung around her knees and sagged off the determined square of her shoulders.

"Let's go."

Scott stood firm, looking her up and down with a coldly critical eye. "You know what you're up against?"

"Don't worry about me. I can hold my own on a horse. I won't slow you down."

He gave her a stare that said very plainly, *You do and I'll leave you behind and never look back.*

"Do you know where to look?" she thought to ask

218

as she secured a scarf over her tightly braided hair.

"I know where I'd be, and that's where Dawn would head. You don't need to go." *What are you trying to prove?*

"I'll meet you at the barn." *Don't get in my way.* And she headed out.

"Scott, be careful."

"I will, Gena. If we're not back tonight, don't panic. You stay put. Have breakfast ready and, when we get home, have the covers pulled down. It's been a damned long four months, and I'm not interested in wasting too much time between now," he kissed her hard, "and then."

She rebuttoned his coat for him and brushed the fabric smooth across his shoulders. "Bring them home, and I'm all yours."

"I'm going to kick their butts for dragging me away from here."

"Find them first, then kick them. And Scott, take care of Norah. I don't want Rory sending you to your ancestors just now, either."

Norah waded through the drifts, using her anger to propel her. It was a safer, more constructive emotion to rely on. Better than her fear. Now that she had a definite goal, her thoughts moved ahead with a crisp logic. When Scott came down to the barn, she was lashing a bundle behind the saddle of her horse.

"What have you got there?"

"Some first aid equipment, feed for the horses, foodstuffs for the five of us, coffee, whiskey, and extra shells for my carbine." She lifted a questioning brow, waiting for his comment.

"Fine."

Smart woman, he thought begrudgingly. Might

219

not be so bad taking her along. Rory wouldn't have planned it out so carefully. On second thought, neither would he.

"Daylight's wasting."

Kill him to say something nice, Norah grumbled to herself as she swung up onto a big bay. At least he knew how to track. The snow wouldn't slow him down, nor could it cover anything he was intent on finding. He was Lakota. That's all that mattered.

It was a soft purple dusk by the time they reached the Hills. They'd plowed through drifts that brushed their horses's bellies without a word between them. Neither felt much like conversation. The snow wasn't as deep on the sheltered slopes, and Scott was able to find plenty of signs. Rory was about as subtle in passing as a Conestoga wagon. When they reached a small rise, Scott reined in and studied the lay of the land.

"Wait here," came his brusque economy of words as he swung down.

Norah sat, working the reins impatiently. "What is it?"

He squatted down, brushing at the snow. "They were here. The three of them."

"Thank God. Rory found them." The stiffness went out of her in a rush. She could have hugged Scott Prescott for giving her that news.

Scott continued to detail the shallow gully, features taut and stoic. Then he rose and waded down to where patches of bare ground appeared between the in-blown drifts. He drew up, pausing for a long minute before dropping down to one knee. He touched the crumpled grass and the stains upon them, getting a very descriptive picture from what he saw.

"Norah, he's not the only one who found them."

The still of his voice shook through her like a blast of sub-zero air. "Scott, what did you find?"

"A grizzly, probably about a ton worth." His tone grew even more remote. "And Norah, there's a lot of blood."

She swayed in the saddle, clinging to its horn for a desperate balance. The word came out, hoarse with dread.

"Whose?"

She saw him pick something up off the ground and crush it to his chest, hunching over it for a long, silent moment. She couldn't stand the terrible suspense.

"Scott, whose?"

He rose and turned at the same instant and climbed back up to where she sat in a rigid column of anxiety. He looked up, his expression grave, his eyes glittering like newly minted gold pieces. And he handed her a hat. A black Stetson with its side brim ripped to ribbons.

Rory's hat.

"No. No!"

First a whisper, then a wail. Norah hugged the cold wool felt to her. A shaking started inside her that wouldn't still. Rory. Oh, God, Rory. Then a sudden shaft of reasoning thought.

"Where is he? Where are they? Scott, tell me where they are!"

His hand was resting on her knee, his fingers squeezing with an unconscious intensity. He turned his gaze toward the trees, and she saw in him a sudden stark reluctance to discover what lay ahead. Finally, he drew a shallow breath and dropped his hand.

"Let's go find out."

*　　　*　　　*

The first blow must have killed him.

Jacob watched, stunned. His father fell and lay unmoving as the snarling bulk of the bear crowded over him, slapping and tearing with huge mauling paws. A scream surged up into the boy's throat, lodging, swelling with a silent horror. In a vague distance, he could hear high, girlish shrieks but they made no impression upon his numbed mind. Terror completely blanked it until Rosebud reared up and the jerk on the reins lifted him off his feet. *Hang onto the horse. Hang on, Jake.*

Rosebud snorted and sidestepped while Jacob dragged down on the reins. The scent of bear and blood filled her nostrils, bringing a wildness to the normally docile mount. She went up on her hindlegs again, swinging Jacob like a pendulum as Dawn went tumbling from the saddle.

"Whoa! Whoa, Bud. Please, whoa," he cried in a panic. *Hang onto the horse, Jacob.* He wanted to look around; he wanted to see what was happening in the shallow gully, but the mare fought and pulled, dragging him until he was able to snag onto a tree with his foot and whip the reins about it. He made the best knot he could with hands shaking, then scrambled back to where Dawn had crumpled to the ground. She was sobbing uncontrollably, trying to stand on the twisted ankle, knife clenched in her hand. She was planning to throw herself upon that big old bear with a puny blade.

She was going to get herself killed.

Like his daddy.

And his family was never going to forgive him if he let it happen.

He grabbed her wrist and fell atop her, wrestling for possession of the blade. He finally tossed it free and managed to pin the lithe, bucking figure down.

She was screaming Sioux obscenities in his face.

"Hush! Shut up! Dawn, shut up." He clamped his hand over her mouth, and her eyes rolled fiercely above it. "Do you want it to come after us, too? Then who'd take care of Daddy?"

That brutal logic reached her. She went limp beneath him, wetness rushing down her face. For a moment, they were both still—panting, frightened, just children. He eased off so she could roll over, then the two of them huddled down on the cold ground, quaking with stifled sobs and hanging onto one another to combat the shock as they looked below. Wanting to hide, to run away, but needing to see. The grizzly was still there.

"What's it doing?" Jacob whispered as a grim puzzlement overcame his horror. The bear had Rory by the foot, and it was dragging him away. One hand trailed behind, palm up, fingers slackly curled. Jacob couldn't take his eyes off it, remembering the gentleness of the hands that held him.

Dawn choked on her tears and muttered with a devastated candor, "Bear's bury their kill . . . for later."

Later. What did that mean?

Slowly, a terrible understanding came and, right behind it, a hot surge of objection.

No!

No bear was going to scratch dirt over his father and make a meal of him later! His mama wouldn't stand for it. She'd want him buried proper with a stone they could pray over.

"Jacob!" Dawn hissed furiously as he raced back to Rosebud. When he returned with Rory's Winchester, she stared, for once impressed beyond words.

"How do you use this?" he demanded with a taut urgency.

Quickly, she explained the rudiments of firing a rifle. He took it all in with a gripped-jaw determination. No mangy sonuvabitch was going to make a dinner of his daddy! He pushed up his glasses and swiped at the blurriness in his eyes with the back of his hand. Swallowing hard, he stood and looked down into the now-empty gully. Swirling snow was rapidly filling over the blood-soaked ground. The wind cut through him with a bracing vigor. *Pull a breath, close your eyes, and get it done.* Yessir, Daddy.

Toting the rifle that was nearly bigger than he was, Jacob slid down the snowy incline and started after the bear. It wasn't a trail that was hard to follow. Bright splotches marked it clear. He clenched his teeth to keep them from chattering and clung to the memory of his father's patient voice. *Nothing wrong with being scared; just no time for it now.* He started forward, stepping in the same track the grizzly had made. His boot didn't reach from front to back of the impression.

And then he came up behind it. It was as big as one of the Bar K steers and twice as broad. Fear making his chest chug like fireplace bellows, he brought the rifle up to his shoulder. Then, incredibly, he saw his father's fingers move. Jacob blinked, sure it was a trick; then, as he readied to pull another bead, Rory's eyes flickered open in a face unrecognizable from all the blood. Catching movement, they focused on the boy and the gun, and his mouth began to work, silently at first, then with one gusty rattle of sound.

"No! Jacob, no. Run. Get clear. Run, Jacob."

The grizzly had let Rory's foot drop and was lumbering around, scenting the boy. Its small eyes fixed on him and, with a rumbling growl, it started forward. Rory kicked out with his good leg, bootheel

224

smacking the animal in the face to distract it from his son. It gave a roar of surprise and fury.

"Jacob, run!"

A hard slap from a massive front paw sent Rory tumbling to skid face down several yards away. He was still.

"Daddy!"

With a loud drooling snarl, the bear bunched and began to rise up. Jacob jerked up the Winchester and fired. The recoil shattered through his shoulder with a force he was sure broke his arm. His glasses went flying. And the bear charged him.

Jacob brought the rifle up again, ignoring the numbness in his arm. He squeezed at the trigger. Nothing. It jammed. Useless. With a terrified cry, he stumbled backward, catching his heels on a tree root to drop down hard on his rump. The bear lunged. He squeezed his eyes shut, breath forced from his lungs in one frightened sob. And he heard an earth-shaking thud.

He fumbled for his spectacles, finding them hanging by the wire earpiece. He affixed them on his nose and stared in amazement. There, with its muzzle inches from his boots, the burly creature sighed its last breath, blowing up snow to powder his pant legs. Jacob let out a tremulous sound, his head falling atop his knees while beset with a shaking so bad he couldn't move.

"Jacob!"

Dawn burst through the brush astride Rosebud. She hauled in the nervous mare and stared down at the mammoth corpse in slack-jawed awe. "You did it! Jacob, you killed it!"

But Jacob didn't hear her crowing words of praise. He was staggering up to his feet, picking his way around the bear, running on weak legs to where his father lay motionless.

"Daddy?" He was sobbing freely, great gulping sounds he hadn't dared release before. "Daddy?" He stretched out across the broad frame of shoulders, hugging tight, wailing for all he was worth as the wind whipped up to an equal howl.

White. Everything was white and cold.

Rory blinked slowly as the wet flakes stung his eyelids and burnt along his cheeks. He tried to move but couldn't. He rolled his head slightly to evade the blinding snow; and instantly, a small warm palm pressed to his cheek.

"It's all right. Don't try to get up."

"Jacob?" he rasped out softly.

"Right here."

"Bear . . ."

"Shot him dead."

The corners of his mouth twitched upward. "That right? Good boy." He rested for a minute. His eyes were so heavy it was a struggle to hold them open. "Dawn?"

"She's here."

"Bud?"

"I hung on, just like you told me."

"Good boy."

He started drifting. Something wasn't right. He didn't feel any pain. He should be hurting . . . plenty! He lifted his right arm, unsteady hand rising for the side of his head. His sleeve was slashed into threads and soaked with blood. He stared at it stupidly for a long moment, then continued to bring his hand up. Jacob caught it, firmly, gently, and eased it back down.

"It's all right."

What was wrong? Were his brains gooshing out or something? He lacked the strength to check. It was then he noticed the horizontal movement of the snow. The norther. Right on top of them. No time to seek a comfortable shelter. And if they didn't batten for it, they'd be frozen solid.

"Jacob, help me sit up."

"No, you can't. You've got to stay still."

"I doan want to be as still as we're gonna be in a matter a minutes. Do what I tell you."

He saw more than felt the boy lift his other arm and lever his narrow shoulders under it. He pulled and Jacob hauled and finally he was upright. The dizziness was overpowering. He didn't feel the slice of the wind cutting through the wool of his shirt. He had to hang on. He had to think of the children. Then he could give way to the sucking weariness that pulled on him.

"Bud. . . . Bring her here."

"Here." The reins were pressed into his hand. "Are we going to ride out?"

"No. Get her down." He dragged on the reins. "Come on, Bud; get down. Jacob, kick her back legs. Hard. Do it. C'mon, Bud. Down. Attagirl. Attagirl, Bud." The animal's knees buckled, and she collapsed beside him. "Get all them blankets, Dawn-honey. Hurry now."

For the first time, Rory noticed the tight banding around his left calf just above where his boot had been torn off. He could see his foot, a bloody mess. He bent forward to give the binding a closer look. A strip of cloth had been wrapped twice about his leg and a stick thrust through and turned tight.

"What's this?"

"A tourniquet," Jacob explained in a tight little voice. "You were bleeding something awful, and I couldn't get it to slow with pressure. I learned the knots from my *American Boys' Handy Book*. I learned how to make kites from it, too."

Rory gave an amazed snort. "Boy, you're full a surprises."

"Here are the blankets, Uncle Rory."

"Thanks, darlin'." He dragged himself over to his downed horse and lay down across her neck. "Easy, girl. Doan fight me. Attagirl, Bud. Dawn, Jacob, c'mon down here. Curl in close. Real tight. Get them blankets over the top and anchor 'em down good. Doan want the wind to snatch 'em off."

Both shivering children nestled into his body like pups, Rory draped his sound arm over them and held on tight. There was a quiet little whimper, he couldn't tell from which one.

"Hush, now. We'll be fine. Alls we got to do is hang on an' wait for it to blow over. Then Scotty'll be coming for us. Scotty'll be coming."

And with the wind tugging at the blankets tented over them and the warmth of horseflesh beneath him, Rory's let his eyelids sag shut.

Doan let me down, Scotty.

Norah joined Scott in the gully. She surveyed the patch of ground with wide, anguished eyes.

"What happened? Where are they? The damned thing couldn't have swallowed boots, bones, gunbelt, and all." Her tone was hard and angry. She was rattling inside, every muscle pulled taut to contain the tremors. She wanted to scream, to run in hysterical circles just shrieking madly. But Scott would probably slap her silly, and she didn't want to afford him the pleasure. She struggled to regulate her breathing, keeping it slow and deep to calm her panic.

And then Scott found something else.

His moaning sound brought her around. "Scott? What? What have you got?" Something terrible. She flew at him, trying to pry it away. "What? Give it to me! Give it to me! Is it Rory's? Let me see!"

She wrenched it out of his arms, then just stared, aghast and sickened to the soul. Rory's boot—leather ripped and chewed to pieces, dark with dried blood. She clapped one hand over her mouth, struggling to hold the surge of bile and the crazy screams. She couldn't stand it. She couldn't stand finding him one piece at a time. With a desperate sound, Norah began to run, clutching at the boot and the battered hat, running along the trail the bear must have taken, her tears blinding her.

"Norah!"

She didn't stop. Not until she saw the still shape on the ground, indistinguishable beneath the snow. She whirled away, starting back, colliding with Scott, clinging to him. When he saw what she had, he went rigid.

"Oh, God, Scott. I can't look. You do it. Tell me it's not Rory. Please tell me it's not Rory."

He pried her away, and she could hear the shush of his boots in the snow. Then there was a long silence.

"Scott?" Her voice quavered. Her heart bobbed up to lodge painfully in her throat. "Is it—"

"It's going to make one hell of a rug."

Confused, she turned and saw him crouching over the huge shaggy mass of the silver-tip grizzly he'd uncovered. He looked up, features inscrutable.

"Come on. Get your horse. I know where they are."

Quiet.

That was the first thing he noticed. The wind had

229

died down to a gentle moan. He must have been drifting or maybe lost consciousness altogether. There was a burning, tingling sensation in his leg. Pain roared through his head with the slightest movement. His backside was numb and stiff with cold, but where the children burrowed against him, there was a lifegiving warmth. Blood had frozen on his face and skin. It itched and crackled when he moved.

"Jacob? Dawn?"

At the sound of his voice, Rosebud stirred, kicking out restlessly to disturb the mountain of snow piled over them.

"Whoa, girl. Easy."

Jacob crept out from beneath his arm to toss back the blanket. The cold fell in on them, so intensely bitter it froze the breath in their lungs.

"Is it over now? Can we go home now, Daddy?"

He sounded so exhausted, so miserably in need of his mother, Rory hated to tell him no. "Sorry, son. We'd never make it afore dark."

"Oh." Rory saw his lower lip tremble as the boy struggled not to cry. Dawn was sitting up beside him, burrowed down inside his big coat, looking close to weepy-eyed herself. They were freezing. He was in desperate straights. Nighttime was fast approaching and, with it, a killing cold. They'd never survive it.

"We gotta move. Daddy's cabin should be just over yonder. Think you can find it, Dawn?"

She nodded solemnly, and he blessed her for being Scott's daughter. She'd find it.

"Truth is," he panted softly, finding it more and more difficult to pull a satisfying breath, "I'm in a bad way and feeling poorly. I doan know if I can hang on till we get there. You two, you do what you have to, but you get there and you get yourselves warm and out of the weather. If that means leaving me behind, you leave me. Understand?"

"But Rory—"

"No, argument, Dawn. Now, this ain't no game. You do what I tell you."

"I'm not leaving you," Jacob insisted.

"Jacob—"

"No!"

He shook his head in exasperation. He had no strength to argue with his son nor could he force him to obey. "Danged cussedly stubborn little—hell, guess you come by it naturally enough. All right. Let's get the three of us in front of a warm fire."

Rory instructed the children to scoot back, then he dragged his injured leg over Rosebud's saddle. It was like moving a chunk of wood. Hanging onto the horn with both hands, he gave a nudge and a "Get up, Bud."

The mare scrambled and pawed and finally got to her feet with Rory already in the saddle. He put down his good hand to Dawn hauling her up in front of him, then freed a stirrup so Jacob could clamor up behind. Then, all he had to do was keep from falling off as Dawn picked up the reins to guide them.

That, and stay alive.

Chapter Fifteen

Wood smoke. She could smell wood smoke!

Norah stood in the stirrups, her eyes straining through the gray of twilight. There, just ahead, nestled at the edge of a man-made clearing, was the outline of a cabin. Plumes rose in a dark curl from its stone chimney.

She was off the galloping horse before it reached the door, plunging the rest of the way on foot.

"Jacob!"

She shoved the door open and dropped to her knees as the little figure hurled into her arms. She crushed him to her, weeping insensibly until she heard him murmur, "I'm all right, Mama. Don't cry."

She rocked back on her heels, holding him by the shoulders until her hurried gaze proved that to her satisfaction. His glasses were bent and his cheeks windburned. Fatigue pulled at the corners of his eyes, but his smile was huge and so like his father's.

Rory.

Her head flew up. She took in the room with a single sweep: Crude table and chairs; big throated stone fireplace with a hearty blaze burning, Dawn crouched before it; a rope bed in the corner; red hair.

"Mama, there was a bear," Jacob began.

"I know, honey," she soothed distractedly. She was rising up, crossing the room almost apprehensively, seeing again all that blood, the tattered hat, the gnawed boot. She sank down on the edge of the bed, mind dazed, eyes overflowing, heart banging against her ribs. "Rory. Oh, God. Oh, Rory, you promised me you'd be all right. Why couldn't you have kept just this one?"

"Daddy!"

She heard Dawn's excited cry and turned to see Scott lift up his daughter, kissing her, murmuring soft things in the Lakota tongue. The relief etched into his bronze features almost warmed her toward him. Then he came to stand behind her.

"Is he alive?" came his flat query.

All she could do was nod.

"Let me see."

Setting Dawn aside, he bent down, crowding Norah out of the way with an impatient shoulder. She wouldn't fight him. Not now. Instead, she turned to her son and demanded to know all that had happened. While he relayed the gist of it, with Dawn putting in her random comments, Scott saw to the extent of his brother's injuries.

It was bad.

His Stetson had absorbed some of the abuse from that first blow to the head, but not all. Furrows raked along his scalp, not deep but causing profuse bleeding the way head wounds always did. His hair was matted with that darker crimson and his face covered with it. There were superficial scratches along his neck and chest and some nasty lacerations just above his right elbow. But it was his left foot that gave Scott pause. There, the puncture wounds sank deep all around his ankle where the bear had worried his boot off and had latched on hard to drag him. Cold and the restriction of blood left the skin pale and hard to the touch. Life-threatening. He didn't need his daddy's education in doctoring to know that.

"Rory?" His fingertips eased along the unscathed side of his brother's face. Dark lashes fluttered faintly, then parted.

"Heya, Scotty." He licked his lips slowly and tried to smile. "I'm a hell of a mess, ain't I?"

"I'll get you home in the morning, and Mama and Daddy'll put you back together."

"Okay. Scotty . . . Damn, I'm glad to see you." His good arm made a loop about his brother's neck, pulling him down for a surprisingly strong embrace. When it eased, he asked, "Kids all right?"

"Yes."

"Bud?"

"I'll take care of her for you. You rest up. I'll see to things here."

"Be obliged if you did." His eyes closed, flickered once, twice, and stayed shut.

Scott straightened, feeling Norah's somber stare upon him. He scrubbed his hands over his face as if to erase any emotions that might have lingered there. And he stood away.

"He should be cleaned up, the wounds dressed and bound, kept warm."

"I know that." Her reply was testy.

"Probably suffering from blood loss, exposure, frostbite."

"I know that, too."

"I'll let you see to it then." And he turned away, dismissing her in favor of her son. "Jacob, I'm your Uncle Scott." He put out his hand solemnly, and the boy reached for it. They looked each other over with a

234

proper caution, then Scott knelt down. Without hesitation, Jacob was in his arms, hugging tight.

"Think you're up to coming outside with me for a minute?"

"Scott," Norah warned. "It's almost dark. He's been through enough already."

"I'm not asking you. I'm asking Rory's son. What do think, Jacob?"

"I'm fine, sir. Let me get my coat."

Norah ground her teeth until the two of them were out the door. Then she flung out of her bulky coat, muttering under her breath, and saw to unloading the supplies she'd brought. She scooped a big kettleful of snow and set it to melting over the fire, gave a suspiciously quiet Dawn a handful of jerky, and sat back on the edge of the bed to tend her husband. Carefully, she wiped away the gore and applied a whiskey-soaked pad to the jagged tissues. Rory jerked and moved restlessly, but he didn't come around. For that, she was thankful.

She cleaned and wrapped his arm and cautiously released Jacob's tourniquet. There was no fresh bleeding. The cold had effectively stemmed it. When the water warming over the fire had reached a comfortable temperature, she wet towels and wrapped them carefully about his mangled foot to restore circulation. It was then she heard Dawn's soft whimpering.

"Dawn?"

"It's my fault."

"What is, honey?"

"Everything," she sniveled wretchedly. "I should have known better. I let my pride get in the way instead of using good judgment."

Norah smiled softly. "I think that's a family trait, so you're not to blame for that."

"If Rory dies—"

Norah's heart seized up. Her reply was unintentionally sharp. "He won't." Then, seeing the child's distress, she went to kneel down beside her, taking her into a reassuring embrace. "Rory's going to be fine. Just fine. We all love him too much to let anything happen to him. Now, no more talk about this being your fault, all right?"

The bright head nodded against her shoulder, and it was then that Scott and Jacob returned. Scott dumped something bulky onto the floor.

"Rory'll want that in front of his fireplace."

It was the bear's head and hide.

"Here's dinner, Mama." Jacob thrust two large slabs of raw meat at her. "The sonuvabitch wasn't expecting us to have *him* for supper." How unexpectedly savage that sounded coming from her young son.

"Jacob Prescott!"

There was a sudden rumbling sound, and Norah realized it was Scott. She couldn't remember the last time she'd heard him laugh, if ever. It was a nice sound.

They dined on bear steaks, Jacob with particular relish; and afterwards, Norah made coffee. Scott laced his liberally with whiskey and did the same for hers. Rory slept. The room was warm and isolated from the howl of the wind outside. The mood was strangely companionable.

Scott checked his daughter's ankle, smiling when she told him she hadn't cried, then he told both children it was time for them to get to sleep. Jacob kissed his mother, then climbed in next to Rory; in a matter of minutes, Dawn was nudging between them. They settled in without argument, and Scott drew a blanket over the three of them. After touching his brother's brow to feel for fever and checking the color of his foot for improvement, he gave a weary sigh and fixed a pallet for himself in front of the fire. He took off his boots, leaned back against the rocks his stepfather had laid, sipped his coffee, and watched Norah pace.

She moved like a caged thing, this woman his brother had wed. He could see her exhaustion, her worry. She was hugging herself as if chilled though the room was pleasantly heated. And her eyes never left Rory even though she'd left him years ago without looking back. Scott puzzled over her. And finally, his mood softened.

"Norah, come over here and sit down. You're wearing out the floor."

"Sorry. I didn't mean to annoy you." Her tone was brittle, but she came over anyway and sank down beside him. She huddled there, with her arms wrapped about her knees and her somber stare on the bed. "What is this place?" she asked finally.

"I was born here. Ethan used to run his trap lines out of it. He found my mother on the trail on a day much like this one, close to giving birth. He brought her here, made her strong, and delivered her first son. I was rocked in front of this fire in the cradle he made out of love."

Her shoulders stiffened at his mention of the cradle.

Scott considered her tense posture for a long minute, then placed the flat of his hand between her shoulder blades in a neutral gesture.

"He'll be all right."

Norah made a small noise in the back of her throat, like something frightened and in pain. She turned to him, pushing her face into his shirt front, curving her arm about his neck with a need that made her indifferent to all other feelings. At the moment, it didn't matter where the source of comfort came from.

Scott sat unmoving for a long second, breath suspended, muscles taut. Then, slowly, he made himself relax. This was Rory's wife, the mother of his brother's son, and it didn't seem important that they had differences—only that they had so much in common. He held her loosely, letting her shiver with silent weeping. His hand stroked over her braided hair, finding it soft, like Gena's. He closed his eyes, thinking of his wife, thanking his mother's God and every god of his father's whom he could call by name that he was bringing their daughter home safe to her.

When Norah's arm dropped limply, he eased her down to a more comfortable rest upon his lap. He sat for a long while, listening to the wind, wondering over this woman he didn't like and couldn't trust but whom he suspected loved his brother with a protective fierceness that rivaled his own.

"Scotty?"

He came awake with a jerk, momentarily confused by Norah's sleeping weight across his knees. Carefully, Scott eased out from under her and padded in his stockinged feet to the bed where his brother was shifting restlessly. It was still dark out. The fire had died down to a soft glow, its glimmer highlighting the beads of perspiration on Rory's face. Scott put his hand to his brother's cheek and swore.

"Scotty?"

"Right here. Shhh. The children are asleep. How you feeling?"

"Not so good."

"I know."

"My foot, it hurts somethin' awful."

238

"You rest easy. Let me take a look. All right?"

Rory nodded jerkily. He shut his eyes; and when they reopened, they were dull and vague. He seemed to have forgotten Scott was there.

Moving carefully, Scott peeled off the wrappings to lay bare the wound. The area was swollen and red, hot to the touch. Dark fingers of infection reached up the calf of his leg. He didn't have to see any more.

"Rory? You think you could travel? We've got to get you home."

"Sure, I can ride." But when he was taken by a hard, shaking chill, Scott had his doubts. He kept them to himself.

"I'll have Norah get the children ready."

"Norah." Rory's attention sharpened. His brow crowded with a different kind of pain. "Norah's gone to Crowe Creek. She ain't coming back. She's leaving me, Scotty. She's divorcing me."

"That's crazy talk, Rory. Norah's right here. She wouldn't stay behind."

But he didn't hear. His shifting grew more irregular, more agitated. "Oh, God, Scotty, what am I gonna do? She doan want me no more. I ain't got nothing to go back to. She's taking the boy. . . . What's a man supposed to do without his only son? What's a man to do?"

Scott kept his hand resting easy on his brother's shoulder; but inside, he was knotting up in a powerful hatred for Norah Prescott. He made his voice soft, calming. "Rory, no one's taking Jacob from you. He's here, right here. So is Norah. They're not going to leave you. That's just fever playing with your mind."

"Norah's here?" All his energies channeled into that one hope; and to himself, Scott cursed the woman in every language he knew. But outwardly he smiled.

"I'll get her for you."

The dark eyes followed him as he stood, gaze anxious and desperately eager. Scott smiled again, a tight, muscle-crunching smile. Then he went to Norah.

"Wake up."

She stirred, disoriented. Why that sounded like . . . Scott Prescott? Norah stretched on the hard bed of blankets, thoughts groggy and impossible. She seemed to recall falling asleep with Rory's brother's arms around her. Rory. . . . Things sharpened quickly.

"Scott, what is it?"

As she dragged herself upright into a sitting position, he rocked back on his heels to stare at her dispassionately. "We're leaving. I'm going to get the horses ready."

"It's still dark."

"You want to wait until the sun's good and high so we can see real well to bury my brother?"

She took a shallow breath. "He's worse?"

Scott's features hardened. His golden eyes glittered with a dangerous animosity. "Sit with him until I get back. Keep him quiet. Tell him whatever he wants to hear to keep him calm, even if it's a lie. You shouldn't have any problem with that."

He stood in one fluid movement and went for his coat. Where was the man who'd consoled her last night? Surely not somewhere behind that frigid stare.

Forgetting about Scott, Norah hurried to Rory's bedside, kneeling down so she was within his field of vision. His head turned toward her with a restless toss; and his quick, panting breath stopped.

"Norah? Oh, God, you *are* here."

He seized the hand she put to his hot cheek, crushing it with his own, needing to feel flesh and bone to reassure himself that she was there. He pressed frenzied kisses to her knuckles, her palm, her wrist, then held the back of it to his face. With a heavy sigh, he was quiet. His eyes closed; his rapid breathing eased, and his words cut through her heart.

"I thought you'd left me again." He gave a hushed laugh and rubbed against her hand.

"I love you, Rory," she told him simply. "I won't ever leave you." And from behind her, Norah heard the sound of Scott slamming out of the cabin. "I'm here. We're going home. Back to the Bar K. You, me, and Jacob."

It was a chill silver dawn when Scott helped his brother out to the horses. A travois would have been easier on him but horseback was faster. Rory growled adamantly that he wouldn't be towed behind no horse like a broken cart. He'd sit in his saddle. Norah would have argued, but Scott's curt nod overruled her. With his foot rewrapped and the hat and coat his brother and wife had borrowed set in place, Rory hauled himself up on Rosebud and sat weaving like a drunk.

"Going to make it?" Scott asked him soberly.

"Dang right." He patted the bundle lashed on behind his saddle. "I aim to see this big ugly cuss all tanned and stretched out on my floor so's I can walk over him every day."

Scott smiled thinly. "Grab on to the horn." When Rory complied, his brother lashed his hands to it. "There. Now we won't have to stop every few feet to pick you up."

"Your confidence is truly heartwarming."

Scott clamped his hand down over Rory's for a hard squeeze, then he went back to secure the cabin as Norah and Jacob got up on her horse. She'd given her coat to Rory and was huddled down inside a doubled blanket with her arms curled about Jacob to warm and protect him from the biting wind. She managed a ghost of a smile when Rory looked her way. His grin was weak but wide.

Scott hoisted Dawn up into his saddle. She scooted forward to give him room then looked down in question. His words were soft-spoken and dear to her.

"Tanyan ecanun yelo." Simple praise. *You did well.*

She accepted with equal gravity. *"Pilamayan ate."*

He swung up easily behind her and gathered the reins. "Let's make some tracks."

It wasn't snowing, but the air was heavy with its crystals. Scott lead with a pace as rapid as the drifts would allow, sometimes cantering, sometimes forced to a trudging walk. Norah brought up the rear, clenching her teeth as she watched Rory begin to bob slackly after the first fifteen minutes. In a half-hour, he was lying along his mare's neck. Her reins were loose, but Rosebud was a range horse. She followed without direction. Scott never looked back.

Angrily, she nudged her mount up to the front. Scott spared her a stoic glance. "He's not going to make it. We need to stop so he can rest."

"He makes it or he's dead. We're not stopping."

Only the presence of the children kept her from letting her fury fly. Muttering dire threats under her breath, Norah reined in until she was abreast of the roan-colored mare. Rory lifted up slightly and gave her a lopsided smile.

242

"Doan mind, Scotty, honey. He's jus' mad 'cause he'd rather be all bundled down in bed waiting for Gena to bring 'im breakfast. I'm fine. Jus' restin' up."

But he wasn't fine. She could tell by looking at him. His color was terrible. An increasing stain of blood was beginning to show on the sleeve of his coat. The ride was killing him, and he wouldn't complain. Damn, Scott Prescott, anyway!

Nothing had ever looked so good as the outline of the Bar K set against stark Dakota snows. Gena was out on the porch in her dress sleeves, bouncing anxiously to ward off the cold as they came to a stop. Then she jumped heedlessly into the knee-high snow to reach up for Dawn with one arm and Scott's hand with the other. Trevor was there, Norah observed with some surprise. She'd forgotten all about him. Had she even said goodbye before riding out? She couldn't remember. He waded out to take Jacob from the saddle, but she didn't wait for assistance. She jumped down and was quickly at Rory's side.

He was hanging off the saddle by the thong securing his wrists. When Scott slashed through it with his knife, Rory spilled down into his arms. He was able to drape his forearms over Scott's shoulders, but he lacked the power to hold on. His knees buckled, and he started to slide down.

"Let me," Trevor said.

Scott's glare flashed up, molten and full of deadly warning. "I've got him," he hissed at his sister-in-law's lover, but he was clearly struggling beneath the sagging weight.

"Don't be a fool. Let him help." That was from Norah. She'd had more than enough of Rory's brother. As Trevor slipped beneath one of Rory's arms, she yelled down at the hands lingering anxiously at the barn, "Sammy, you get over to the Lone Star and fetch Ethan. Tell him to bring everything he's got." The cowboy started running for the corral. "And Sammy. . . . You'd better tell Rory's mother she should be here, too."

"Yes, ma'am," he called back grimly.

Norah ran ahead as the two men lugged her husband up the stairs. She threw back the bedcovers just in time to receive him upon the fresh bottom sheet.

"Get him out of those things," she instructed sternly, all business and control in her own element. While Rory groaned and grabbed for breath, Scott stripped him of coat, shirt and remaining boot before signalling Trevor to ease him down. When his foot came up, he gave a wail of pain, twisting helplessly to find relief. Norah bent down, and he snatched for her hand, clinging hard and fast.

It was then that Scott saw the suitcase, packed and ready to go. His gaze lifted slowly to affix Norah's. There was no way to describe the contempt of that long look.

Trevor saw the case, too. He saw it as the means to delicately suggest it was time Norah detached herself from the Prescotts. They were clearly a straining influence upon her. He'd noticed the difference right from the moment he arrived. In Baltimore, she'd been composed and sweetly attentive. Here, she seemed forever poised on the edge of frenzy. How unlike his phlegmatic Norah to go rushing off into the face of a blizzard without a word of goodbye. And then there were the scandalous trousers she was wearing. Of course, he could understand her mother's instinct. But that didn't explain the way she held to this man from whom she was considering divorce. Obligation to an old love should extend only so far.

"Norah, would you like me to carry that downstairs for you? We should be able to get through to Crowe Creek in the buggy."

Just then, Rory's eyes opened, blurred but fastening upon her face with a concentrated effort. "Norah? Norah-honey, are we home?"

"Yes, shhh." Distractedly, she stroked his cheek. "Yes, we're home."

"Oh, thank you, Lord. I didn't want to worry you none, but I didn't think I was gonna make it."

Tears sprang unbidden to blind her. She blinked them back and looked up at Trevor Samuels. "I'm sorry to have put you through all this, Trevor. But I can't leave now. You go."

"I-I think I'd rather stay. Perhaps I can be of some help."

She ran a weary hand through strands of limp hair. "Yes. Could you stay with Jacob, keep him downstairs? I don't want him too upset with all that's happening."

"Yes, of course." He leaned forward, ignoring the maiming scowl on Scott Prescott's face to lightly kiss her brow. "And if there's anything I can do for you, don't hesitate to ask."

Norah nodded and smiled, thankful. The moment he was gone, Scott prodded her trunk with his toe.

"Going somewhere?" There was a lethal purr to his voice. "And here I was beginning to believe in your undying devotion."

"Stop it, Scott," she snapped at him irritably. "I don't need this from you right now."

He gave a conceding nod. "The minute he's better, I'll give you a ride to town, myself. As a matter of fact,

245

I'll drive you all the way to Baltimore." *And good riddance.*

"How kind of you," she drawled icily.

"The least I could do."

"I'm sure it is. Let me have your knife." At his sharply raised brow, she sighed. "Don't worry. I have no designs upon your hair." *Yet,* she muttered to herself.

He drew the knife—a wicked thing it was. With a seemingly careless flip, he caught it by the blade to extend the handle to her. Wordlessly, she began to slit the bottom of Rory's pant leg from tattered hem to mid-thigh.

"How is he?"

Norah looked up at Gena over the tip of the glittering blade. Her eyes held the same cold sheen. "We'll know when Ethan gets here. You're in my light."

"Is he awake?"

Without waiting for her answer, Gena slipped around Norah and knelt down at Rory's shoulder. Her hand curved around his cheek. "Rory?"

He blinked slowly and gave a wobbly smile. "Heya, Sis. I brung 'em back, like I tole you. 'Course it took Scotty here to get it done proper."

"I thought you said you'd be careful," she chided gently.

"Oh, hell, Gena-honey, you know me. I'm always falling into the thick a things." His teeth suddenly gritted up, and his eyes squeezed shut. Then he relaxed and was smiling at her again. "Sorry to be pulling Scotty out on his first night back."

"I wouldn't have made the sacrifice for anyone else, you know." She brushed a kiss across his cheek and pressed hers against him. "Thank you for keeping them safe."

"Think it was the other way around."

She gave him another quick kiss then straightened, looking to Norah with shamelessly sincere eyes. "Is there something I can do?"

Norah bit back her initial response. She counted to a slow ten, then trusted herself to speak. "You can stay close to Dawn. She shouldn't be by herself right now."

"All right," Gena replied, not sure she understood but intuiting the importance of what Norah said. She headed for the door, bumping Scott on the way so she had an excuse to lean into him. He caught her head to his chest, kissing the top of it before letting her continue on. Then he and Norah exchanged hostile looks.

"Am I in your way?"

"You have the hospitality of the Bar K at your disposal." *For now*, her chill smile concluded. Then, after a glance down at Rory, she amended softly, "Thank you, Scott."

His eyes narrowed. He looked uncomfortable with her candid appeal. Then he nodded. "There's nothing I would not do for my brother." And his flat tone told her she was mistaken if she thought he'd done it for any other reason.

They stayed with Rory in an awkward truce until Ethan and Aurora arrived. Norah had to leap back to keep from being bowled over by his mother.

"Doan fuss," was the first thing he said to her.

"Rory Prescott, I swear I've put more stitches into your reckless hide than I do in most shirts." She leaned over him, hugging carefully, kissing him gently. And when she straightened, her eyes shimmered like liquid gold. But she didn't fuss.

"Doan know if your fancy stitchin'll turn the trick this time, Mama." He was smiling, but there was

247

a somberness to his gaze. As if he knew he was already beyond the healing powers of needle and thread.

"Well, let's see what we can do to get this boy put back together. Ora, move on out of there."

"Heya, Daddy."

"You look terrible."

"Knew I could count on you to put it plain."

"Hurtin' bad?"

The redhead nodded jerkily. There was no point in lying.

"I'll give you something for it as soon as I take a look-see. You hang on for me, pard?"

"Sure, Daddy."

Ethan held Rory's head steady to check the size and response of his swollen pupils, then tapped into both wrist and throat to time a heartbeat. His calming bedside manner didn't stem his son's restlessness.

"Did you see Jacob's bear? One shot right through—"

"Hush!" Ethan started his count over until satisfied. "The taste a you was probably what killed it. Look up at me. Rory, look up. Follow my finger. Good. How many do you see?"

"On which hand?"

Ethan smiled. "Either."

"Two."

"Good. Anything rattled loose in that stubborn head a yours?" He threaded his fingers back through the encrusted red hair, examining the tears in his scalp. "Seeing double, hearing anything funny like ringing?"

"Nossir." His breathing quickened into shallow pants. His shifting grew more pronounced.

"You're doing fine. Just rest easy." Very carefully, he felt along the sides of Rory's neck and moved his

248

head. "Boy, you got a skull like your mama's cast iron skillet."

"Take after you."

"Good thing." He gave a cursory look at the scratches on his chest, pausing at the pattern of holes. "This bear truss you up in wire, did he?"

"That there horse a Dawn's tossed me into it."

"And you ain't shot him yet?"

"Breakin' him in for Jacob."

"Thought you liked the boy. Easy. Easy. Ora, these'll keep you busy. Might want to run him through that Singer a yours." He felt on down from the slices in his arm to Rory's fingers, checking color and movement and peeking under the bandaging over his knuckles. "That ole grizzly throw you through a window, too? You've had one helluva week, haven't you? Feel like anything's busted up inside?" He pressed here and there as Rory shook his head. "Okay. So far, so good. Nothing some rest and a little more common sense won't cure. Lemme take a look at that foot."

"No!" He came up on his elbows, his chest laboring, his eyes swimming. "Leave it, Daddy. Please. It hurts so bad I can't stand for you to be touching it. It'll be awright if you just' leave it be."

Ethan eased him back down, brushing a reassuring hand across his wet brow. "Thought you were going to tough it out for me."

"I can't, Daddy."

"All right. You done the best you could."

Rory sagged in relief as his father moved back. His eyes closed, then snapped back open at Ethan's soft-spoken command.

"Scotty, hold your brother down. Keep him from moving as best you can."

"No! Daddy, doan—"

"Ora, find him something to bite on." He reached for his medical bag, ignoring his son's thrashings. "Norah, you prone to keeling over? Good. Bring that light over here. Who put the tourniquet on him?"

"Jacob," Norah answered quietly as she knelt at the foot of the bed. She was watching Ethan's face as he snipped away the dressing.

"Smart boy. Probably saved his daddy's life." Then he eased back the noxious wrappings and all the muscles in his face stiffened up. His lips moved in a silent oath as his eyes squeezed shut. Norah felt a terrible chill as Ethan's features spasmed and hardened once more. Then he opened his eyes and turned his attention to the mangled foot. "Scotty, you got hold of him?"

"Yessir."

"Grab on tight." And he started examining the horrible wounds. When it was over and Rory's muffled screams had stopped, he motioned Scott aside and went to sit with his younger son. He took the darkly flushed face between his hands and spoke softly, firmly. "Rory, can you hear me? I need you to listen to me now. Rory?" A brief nod and the dark eyes focused. "Rory, I . . ." He looked away, unable to continue.

"Daddy," Rory entreated. "Put it plain."

"Son, I'm going to have to take your foot."

Chapter Sixteen

Rory blinked. "What?" Take his foot? He didn't understand.

"Son, I've seen it hundreds of times in the war. Sometimes worse, sometimes not as bad, but always leading to the same thing. If there was another way . . ."

"You want to cut off my foot," he murmured in a dull sort of disbelief.

"It's bad, Rory. There was a lot of bleeding. When Jacob put on the tourniquet, he kept you from bleeding to death; but it cut off the blood supply to your foot. The cold got it clotting, but frostbite stopped the circulation even further. Then there was the shock from traveling. You should have been kept still, but Scotty did the right thing hurrying you here. There's a heap of infection and I don't know how much tissue damage. I ain't never seen such a bad set of circumstances. All I know is when gangrene sets in, it'll kill you in less than two days and there ain't no uglier way to die. I'll make it clean and quick. You're tough as an ole longhorn. You'll be healed up in no time."

"You want to cut off my foot." He repeated it,

dazed. And then he read the grim finality in his father's face. "No. Daddy, no." A great sob caught in his throat.

Ethan looked around impatiently. "Get on outta here, all of you. Ora, you too. Now. Now!" When he and his son were alone, he stroked the fevered brow and smiled. "Rory, it's the best deal I can cut you. I want you alive."

"Ain't there somethin' one a them city doctors—"

"Son, the trip would kill you. I'm putting it plain, and I want you to listen to me."

Rory's head rolled helplessly from side to side, dark eyes frantic in their search for an option. "I surely could use a drink 'bout now."

Ethan reached for laudanum. "Take this. Packs a better punch than Red Eye." He tipped it up and Rory drank it down. He lay back on his bed of pain, twisting, panting hard, fighting the inevitable.

"Ain't there—"

"No." Firm and final. "No, Rory. This is the best way I know."

"Can't you wait a while . . . just to see?"

Ethan shook his head. "I don't want you suffering without cause. The sooner we get it done, the quicker you'll mend."

"When? When you gonna do it?" He lay back in a jerky panic, trying to keep from plunging off the deep end of hysteria. Pain pulsed up his leg in fierce beats, driving home all his father said.

"First thing in the morning. I'll need to get some things in town. That'll give your body time to gather strength and shake off some of the shock. But no later than that. You can't afford it."

Rory swallowed convulsively and asked, "Where?"

Ethan put a gentle hand just above his kneecap. "Probably here, just to be safe. We'll see how it looks in the morning."

"Oh, God." He shut his eyes. After a second, he wiped at his face and muttered, "Damn knee didn't work anyway."

Ethan had to bite down hard to keep his composure. All he could do was ruffle through his son's bright hair. After a minute, Rory's bones began to melt into the balming embrace of the laudanum, and he quieted.

"Still hurting?"

"Not so bad," he mumbled thickly, letting his eyes drag down.

"I'm going to send your mama in to stitch up your arm. Then I want you to rest, and I don't want you to think about nothing. All right?"

A slight nod. He was nearly under.

Ethan eased away from the bed and went into the hall—straight into Aurora's arms. She held him tight, hugging his big shoulders as anguish shook them.

"Ora, I never, ever wanted to look a man in the eye again to tell him I was taking off a part of him. Not my son. Not my own son."

Norah moved through the house in a numbing haze. She wanted to be alone, to curl up with the devastating news she'd received to try and find the means to cope with it. But the house was full of Prescotts and the porch laden with Rory's men. No escape. Then she saw Trevor and Jacob in Rory's study looking through a book. Jacob's head flew up, his gaze catching on her with a needy desperation she could not ignore. He looked—older. After the past few days, she wondered if he would ever be her sweet little boy again.

"Hi, Mama. I was showing Trevor a picture of my bear."

She smiled thinly and came to take the book from him. He surrendered into the intensity of her hug without complaint.

"How's Daddy? Can I go up and see him?"

"Not yet, honey. Your grandfather's still with him."

"Is he going to be all right?"

Norah smiled. "Ethan says you saved his life twice: By shooting the bear and by thinking of the tourniquet."

That made no impression on the boy. He was plainly worried, searching his mother's face for reassurance. He couldn't be placated with a smile. He'd been through too much, seen too much.

"Honey, your father was hurt very badly. It's going to take him some time to mend, and he's going to need us to be strong for him. But he's going to be all right. He's going to be all right."

The narrow shoulders slumped with relief.

"Jacob, why don't you see if you can help Ruth with lunch? Maybe she'll let you peel some potatoes."

"Okay." He bounded off, glad to have something to occupy time when there was nothing to do but wait.

Trevor saw the starkness of Norah's expression and opened his arms to her. She sank down beside him on the couch and curled into the comfort of his embrace. She felt strange to him in her mannish garb, with her usual strength in absence. He wasn't quite sure how to reassure her. She was always so vital, so in control of every situation. It was one of the qualities he admired most. It was one he relied upon.

"Is there anything I can do?" he asked softly.

"You're doing it. He's going to lose his leg, Trevor."

He made a sympathetic noise and stroked her hair.

"Norah, you need to get away from here. He has his family to care for him. You must think of Jacob."

"Jacob?" She considered that and shook her head. "Jacob is his father's son. He's stronger than he looks."

"But he's only a little boy, and his father is almost a stranger. Is it fair to place such a strain upon him? Wouldn't it be better for him to remember the man his father was?"

"Am I interrupting something here?"

Scott's drawl was slick as ice. Norah sat up, pulling out of Trevor's arms. She hated the fact that she felt guilty beneath his hard stare. Hoarding the remnants of her composure around her like a tattered cloak, she stood with a chilly "If you'll excuse me, I'll go check on Jacob in the kitchen," then swept by her brother-in-law with a dignity she was far from feeling.

"So, Mr. Prescott, since we're both here, perhaps we could talk about your lobbying efforts."

Scott turned from his study of Norah's rigid back to level his dissecting gaze upon the dapper would-be politician. His teeth ground. Did the insensitive ass think he'd want to talk business while his brother was lying upstairs staring death in the eye? He wondered how the man would look gutted and stretched out next to the bear on Rory's floorboards.

Mistaking the cool-eyed lawyer's hesitance, Trevor approached with a disarming smile. "I think you and I could do good things for your people, Mr. Prescott. I hope you won't let my relationship with Norah get in the way of that."

"I don't confuse business and personal feelings." To Scott Prescott, they were one in the same; but the

Easterner nodded with a blind naivete.

"I'm very glad to hear that."

Scott studied the man, unsure what to think. He sensed honesty and integrity; and those things were good. But he scented weakness, and that made him cautious. Trevor Samuels was one of those whose compassion went out for the many, leaving none to spare for the few. He could be a friend to the Sioux; but the man was messing with his brother's wife, which made him his enemy. However, Scott was curious and in need of something to distract his thoughts, so he would let the man talk.

"Have you come to make false promises? I've heard them all, so don't waste my time."

"I don't make promises I can't keep, Mr. Prescott."

"Let's hear them, then."

Trevor smiled, encouraged. He moved around the big desk and swiveled the chair toward him. Scott Prescott's voice slashed him like a knife blade.

"Don't sit there. That's my brother's place, and you may not take it."

"Sorry." He backed up, short hairs quivering along his neck. He remembered Norah's warning. It didn't seem amusing now.

Rory opened his eyes, blinking slowly in an effort to focus. His body was pretty much dead as a chunk of fencepost, but he struggled to keep his mind clear.

"You 'bout finished there, Mama?"

Aurora clipped her thread and smiled gently. "All done."

He had to concentrate hard on twisting his arm so he could judge her stitchery. "Nice seams," he murmured.

"You wear some of my finest work." She put a

hand to his cheek, stroking lightly. "Could you drink a little something? Ethan said you were to have plenty of liquids."

"How 'bout some a that dusty ole Scotch from down in the pantry?" he suggested to goad her.

Her reply was predictably arch. "I think water was more what he had in mind."

"Awright, if I have to." He let her lift him—he had no strength to do it himself—and swallowed obediently. The temptation to let his eyelids sink as he settled back onto the mattress was a powerful one, but he fought it. The soothing brush of his mother's fingertips along his face didn't help.

"Why don't you rest awhile, Rory? I'll sit with you if you'd like."

He shook his head. "Could you ask Norah to come up?"

Her features didn't register the slight. She merely smiled. "Whatever you want, honey."

"Thanks, Mama. An' thanks for doin' my mending."

The two women met in the hall. They eyed each other with the prickly caution of sparring cats.

"He wants to see you."

Norah started by her without comment, but Aurora seized her arm.

"He needs all of us. Don't you crumple up on him."

Norah's gaze narrowed into frosty slits. "Did you think I would? He's my husband. I'm not going to crumple."

But she almost did. When she stepped into the bedroom and saw him stretched out, swaddled in fresh bandages, a brave smile of welcome on his face and a tragic light melting in his dark eyes, she almost went to pieces. Instead, she made herself pause to draw a cleansing breath before advancing with a smile.

"You look better."

"Than what? That snake that crawled into the soddy when Jacob was little?"

Her laugh was quiet music as she settled on the edge of the bed. "I'd forgotten about that. I think he was considerably flatter than you are, with a lot less life in him."

Rory's smile tightened, and he looked away. His fingers cinched up around the hand she slipped over his, but he wouldn't look at her. "Norah . . . honey. . . . Maybe you an' Jacob oughta go on and move into town."

He wanted her to leave? How could that be? She didn't believe him for a second, not with the way he was hanging onto her hand like a lifeline. The big dumb fool was trying to spare them. She was at once furious with him and so desperately touched she had to blink back tears.

"Rory Prescott, what a thing to suggest. How could I just up and leave a whole houseful of company? Why, your mother would never let me hear the end of it."

"Norah, please." His tone was low and so gravelly with emotion the words sounded raw. "I ain't gonna be no good to you. You might as well get on with what you was planning. I doan want to tie you d—"

She drowned out the rest of his sorrow with a kiss—a long, leisurely, protest-silencing kiss that wrung the breath and heart right out of him. Then she leaned back just far enough to capture his shiny gaze in hers.

"I don't want to hear any more of that. I'm not going to leave you, not when you need me, and I'm not going to crumple up under you. I know you're scared, but even a half a Rory Prescott is more man than most can claim. You'll be able to ride and rope

258

and get around on your own and do about anything shy of a fancy two-step. It's not going to make any difference to me."

He turned away from the sincerity of her stare. "That's easy for you to say when I got ten toes staring up at you."

Norah caught his wayward cheek and brought it back around. Her voice was a sultry whisper against his lips. "Five toes more or less isn't going to matter a diddly-squat when it comes right down to what's important."

Her mouth teased over his until he surrendered with a sigh and reached his good arm around her. She eased away slowly.

"I want you to get some sleep. Think you can now?"

"Unuh. Not 'less you come down here with me."

"Rory, I—What about—"

"Let 'em take care a themselves. What are they gonna say? An old married couple decided to take a nap together in the middle a the day."

She smiled, her fingertips caressing the curve of his cheek. "I was just wondering where I could settle in where it wouldn't hurt you."

"Hell, I'm hurt all over. Drop any where."

With Norah curled into her husband's side, her arms hugged about his middle, they slept a good part of the afternoon away; and the Prescotts managed just fine on their own.

He didn't know how much she really meant to him until he saw her lying on the big bed with her arms around Prescott.

Trevor backed from the doorway, a terrible sense of impending loss strangling through him. He'd come

259

up to say goodbye and to make one last bid to take Norah into Crowe Creek with him, eager for something to take him away from all the sober-faced Prescotts below. He'd had enough of this house and these people, not that they were outwardly rude to him. It was just that they represented a part of Norah's life he was trying to separate her from. And he was failing. He should have seen it immediately.

She couldn't be in love with the man. He was gruff, uneducated, uncouth—and she so far above him that Trevor was surprised that there had ever been an attraction. It was the past that held her, the memories, the fact that he had fathered her child. And now, the pity would hold her even stronger. He had to get her away before she lost herself here in this desolate, undeserving world.

He had a much better picture in mind for Norah Prescott. His wife, his partner, his companion. It would be a brilliant match. They could weather the scandal of divorce. Despite his father's reservations, she was the woman he needed beside him. Her strength gave him confidence. Her clear-sightedness gave him goals. Her way with words helped him create speeches with the power to invoke passions of the heart and mind in those who heard them. What a waste should she remain out here in this remote cow pasture. She was a sparkling jewel in need of a proper setting. She belonged with him in Baltimore—in Washington.

Now he saw very clearly that his greatest threat was not his father's disapproval or the scandalmonger's whispers. It was the big redheaded Dakota cowboy she was lying with. Helpless with the situation, he saw no alternative but to leave. Though they didn't express it, the Prescotts were glad to see his buggy pull away from their porch. They weren't about to surrender Rory's wife to an outsider. And all the way back on the difficult journey to Crowe Creek, he wondered how he was going to overcome their hold.

"Mr. Samuels! Whatever happened to you? I was quite beside myself when the storm hit."

"I'm fine, Carter."

"If you don't mind my saying so, you don't look it."

"It's that man, that Prescott," he grumbled, throwing off his soiled coat for the little man to snatch up and shake out.

"Which one, sir?"

"Her husband. She was all set to leave him. She had her bags packed. Carter, what am I to do? I will not leave this place without her."

It was just what the wily lawyer was waiting to hear. The opportunity to get Trevor what he wanted and Martin Samuels what he needed. And himself what he deserved.

"Sir, perhaps I could be of some assistance? If you will allow me to make some discreet inquiries."

"Do it. Whatever it takes, Carter."

And Carter Clemens smiled, a thin self-serving smile.

The laudanum wore off.

It was a fierce fever of pain that woke him, jarring him awake with an agony like none he'd ever known. He was burning up, from the inside out, searing his flesh, cooking his brain. God, it hurt. Rory reached his hand down along his leg, then paused at the kneecap. His father would end his misery in the morning. His fingers clenched tight upon that part of him that would be gone tomorrow, and he moaned in wild objection.

261

No.

He'd seen a one-legged man before. When he was a boy riding herd with Garth Kincaid's drovers. The man's leg was shattered in a fall from his horse and was taken off just below the hip. Jingo, that was the feller's name; and he'd liked him well enough for his swaggering air and cowboy grit. Until he lost his leg. He'd gone from a rowdy, fun-loving hellraiser to a not-quite human thing that sat on the porch rocking in a stupor of liquor. He'd had to have someone lift him up and help carry him just so he could piss off the edge of the porch. Was that what he had to look forward to? His men toting him around like a useless piece of broken furniture? Shaking their heads somberly behind his back. *Poor ole Rory. Was a hell of a feller once. Too bad.*

Oh God!

Then he saw the suitcase standing sentinel at the bedside and felt Norah's softness tucked beside him. He squeezed his eyes closed as panic wailed through his soul. *God, you wasn't listening. I asked for a way to keep her. I didn't mean like this. Couldn't you find some other way?*

Oh, he had her all right. She wouldn't leave him. Not now. Not when he was grabbing onto her pitying heart with desperate hands. She wouldn't leave him, not a crippled husband. She'd stay and fuss over him and pretend she didn't hate doing it until resentment took over for compassion. Eventually she'd find someone to two-step with, and what would he do about it? What the hell could a one-legged man do about it?

"Rory?"

He rolled his head toward her, his face wet, his features twisted up in an agony of despair.

"Oh, honey." She whispered that with a tender

262

sweetness and gathered him close, letting him cry against the swell of her bosom until he was bone dry and aching inside. But by then, he knew what he had to do.

He lay back, breathing in gusty snatches, trying not to scream from the pain pounding up his leg. He rubbed at his knee with a restless vigor until Norah stroked his damp brow and asked if he wanted more laudanum.

"No. No more a that. I gotta think straight, not turn into a toadstool. Is Scotty still here?"

"I think so."

"I wanna talk to him."

"Rory, you really should—"

"Now! I wanna talk to him now!"

"All right," she murmured quietly. "I'll get him."

"Norah," he moaned miserably. "I'm sorry, honey. I didn't mean to holler at you." It was starting already. Him snapping in impotent surliness. Her complying with an uncharacteristic meekness. Him begging her forgiveness. What a terrible look into the future. Inside he crumpled.

"It's all right, Rory." She touched his face gently with a spirit-bruising sympathy.

"Norah." He grabbed her hand and jerked her down, kissing her with all the pent-up passions in his soul. It wasn't his best kiss, just a lot of desperate slobbering, but she yielded to it willingly enough. And when she lifted up, her eyes were swimming with unshed tears. He brushed away a lone shimmer that escaped the damp spikiness of her lashes. "You loved me, didn't you, Norah?"

"Yes," she whispered. "Oh, yes."

He let his hand drop and his head turn away. "Scotty. I need to see him."

She bent once more, her lips feathering across the

untanned strip of his brow. A low, mournful sound swelled up in his throat, but he swallowed it back and let her go.

He waited, clutching, rubbing at his knee and thigh in a restless anxiety. The sharpness was fading from his thoughts, undercut by the relentless tide of pain. He hung on as long as he could; and then Scott was there, sitting himself on the edge of the mattress, smiling in that bland, emotionless way of his. Thank God for Scotty and his tough Lakota heritage.

"You look like hell."

Rory gave a rattly laugh that trickled down into a groan. Concern clouding his expression, Scott started up.

"Maybe I'd better let you—"

Rory snatched at his hand, hanging on tight, pulling on him with all his remaining strength. "Doan go, Scotty. Give me a minute."

Scott resettled and waited, inscrutable, endlessly patient.

Finally, when he was able to conquer the excruciating throb, Rory smiled up at his brother. "Scotty, I need you to promise me something."

"Anything."

"I know you doan cotton to Norah much, but I want you to see to her and Jacob. I doan want them to lack for nothing."

"I will."

"The Bar K—"

"I'll see to it for you."

"Oh, hell, Scotty, you doan know nothing about ranching. Pick a good man to tend it and hold it for the boy. But doan let it drag on 'em. Sell it if you have to. Take care of the money for 'em. See that they get whatever they want."

"You can see to it, Rory," he said very softly.

"No." His head thrashed from side to side then stilled. "Scotty, do something for me."

"Anything."

"Lemme see that big ole toadsticker a yours."

Scott drew the blade, and Rory's hand clamped over his.

"Doan your people hold that it's bad medicine to go to your gods lessen you're in one piece?"

"Yes."

"I want to meet my Maker whole." He dragged his brother's hand over until the knife blade lined up along the base of his throat. "If you love me, Scotty, make it quick."

Scott didn't move. He didn't twitch a muscle.

"Please."

He pulled against the blade, but Scott held it immobile with a superior strength. "Rory, what you're asking—"

"I'm begging you, Scotty! Please. I can't close my eyes without thinking part a me is gonna be gone when I open 'em. I ain't gonna have no kind of life, not for a man to live. You see that, doan you? I can't go on day to day knowing Norah's staying with me outta pity instead of love. I can't stand the thought a looking out over all that green grass an' being trapped in some damn chair for the rest a my life. Scotty, for the love a God, help me. I'd do it for you. Please, Scotty."

Slowly, Scott's free hand curved around his cheek, rubbing gently before moving up to slide across his eyes, covering them, closing them. Rory let out his breath in a thankful sigh. He released Scott's other hand and waited. And waited.

"Forgive me, *mitakola*."

Another heartbeat passed.

"Scotty—"

The pressure of the blade eased. "I cannot steal your light. I'm sorry." His hand returned down the side of Rory's face, then settled on his shoulder. "Another thing. Any other thing and I will do it."

"Aw, hell," Rory sighed heavily. "Guess I'da been kinda annoyed if you'd been all that eager to cut my throat."

Scott smiled. "What can I do for you?"

"Get me outta here, Scotty. Take me somewheres where I can be close to the sky and the grass, where things doan smell like dying slow and ugly. The rest a them, they mean well but they doan understand like you do. I'd rather go to heaven on my own hindlegs then live crawling in hell."

Scott nodded, once.

"Will you stay with me?"

Scott was silent for a moment. Did he know all that he was asking? For him to defy their family, to risk their hate, their eternal damnation? For him to sit and watch the brother he loved suffer and die horribly when, by doing nothing, by refusing, he could save his life? Did Rory realize the hell of what he was asking?

Very softly, very surely, Scott answered, "I will."

Norah was waiting in the hall when Scott emerged. He paused, giving her a long, unswerving look, conveying something she couldn't quite grasp. Then he strode by and took the stairs in a hurry.

"We're going home. Get Dawn."

Gena stared at her husband in surprise. "I thought you'd want to stay here with Rory."

"Get your coat and tell Mama good-bye."

Confused by his mood but knowing him too well to argue, Gena complied. Dawn was the one who

266

balked. She wanted to stay with her uncle. So Aurora promised to bring her home when Ethan came that evening, and the two of them made a silent journey to the Lone Star. Once inside the familiar log home, Gena couldn't contain her curiosity.

"What is it, Scott? Is it Rory? I know how upsetting it is, but he'll be fine. Your father knows what he's doing."

"Gena . . ."

"The important thing is he'll recover."

"Gena, I almost—"

"Almost what?"

His stare was riveted to the floor. He wouldn't raise it.

"Scott? You almost what?"

He did look at her then, through eyes so keen with torment she flinched back in involuntary alarm. Seeing her fright moved him to embrace her, hard and close to the taut frame of his body. The feel of her against him was the perfect balm. His hand scooped under her chin, lifting so he could take her lips with an abrupt savagery. It wasn't until his kiss gentled that she put her arms around him.

"Scott—"

"I've missed you, Gena. I've wanted you. I've needed you."

But she knew whatever brought him running home wasn't the longing or the wanting. It was the needing, and she wasn't quite sure why it was suddenly so acute.

"Let me love you, Gena."

He was asking. After four months, did he think he had to ask? In the time it took to climb the stairs and shed their clothes, they were buried deep inside each other's loving; and only afterwards, when he pulled away and lay beside her, grimly silent, did Gena begin to fear again.

"Scott, talk to me."

For a moment, he was unmoving, facing her with the rigid set of his shoulders and the back of his glossy black head. Then he turned with an intensity that bore right to her soul.

"Gena, if I do something that you don't agree with, that you feel is wrong and can't understand, could you forgive me for it?"

She was very cautious, trying to read beyond the flat gold of his stare. "Is this something you feel strongly about?"

"Something I've pledged my heart and soul to do."

She touched the dark bronze of his cheek with fingertips, then with her palm. He leaned into her touch. "If it's something your conscience demands, then it's nothing you need to ask forgiveness for."

He smiled thinly. Now that was a diplomatic answer if ever he'd heard one, carefully shifting blame from her heart to his soul. How well she knew him. "There are few things I would do to risk what we have."

"But this is one of them." What? What could be that important to him? Rory. It had to be Rory. There was no one outside of his daughter that he loved to that limit. "I love you, Scott. There's nothing you could do that would change that. Nothing."

And that's what he needed to hear.

He drew her close, kissing her with a tenderness that urgency hadn't allowed earlier. He spent the time until his parents and Dawn returned exploring the depths of his devotion to her—in ways that made her wild with ecstasy.

Over dinner, he seemed himself—attentive to her, lavishing his love upon their daughter, speaking of his accomplishments in the East even as they all ignored what preyed foremost upon their minds. When they retired for the night, he made love to her again with a slow sweetness that stirred to the very boundaries of delight.

And when she awoke in the cold pre-dawn hours, he was gone.

Chapter Seventeen

She must have slept without intending to because the room was bathed in pale morning when she opened her eyes. Moving stiff muscles, Norah straightened in her chair and stared at the empty sheets.

"Rory?"

Her gaze flew to the end of the bed. His right boot was gone. So was his old hat and his coat.

"My God. Rory!"

She jerked on the tan denims and heavy shirt, racing down the steps as she worked the buttons. He wasn't in the house. Scott. Scott had taken him. That was the only explanation for that look he'd given her. Wild with panic and fury, she roused Ruth to ask that she care for Jacob and then she ran to the barn. Rosebud was there, contentedly snoozing in her stall. She snorted when Norah slapped the saddle down.

"Come on, Bud. We've got to find Rory before his damn-fool brother kills him."

Where would they go? Scott didn't think like most men she knew. She had no clue as to the workings of his mind only as to those of his heart. The Sioux.

He'd go there, or they would know where to find him.

A fresh snow was falling and by the time she reached the Cheyenne, sunlight dazzled off its untouched surface. The air was crisp, holding the plume of Rosebud's breath like steam from a locomotive, but Norah was drenched with a sweat of apprehension when she reached the small dwelling of George White Cloud. She could only pray that Scott's friend High Hawk was home.

He was. At her call, he emerged from the shack rubbing the haze of excess from his eyes. He was a handsome man, though sadly dissipated by the effects of drink. His dark eyes regarded her with a dull wariness.

"I'm looking for Scott—for Lone Wolf. Have you seen him?"

The Lakota shook his head, scowling.

"He has my husband with him. You know him. Lone Wolf's brother, Rory Prescott."

"Ah, *Pehin Luta*, Red Hair. I know him, but I have not seen them."

Ready to moan aloud in frustration, Norah struggled to stay calm. "My husband is very ill. Where would Lone Wolf take him?"

"Is it so bad that *Wasichu Wakan* has no medicine?" He frowned to think that. He liked the white brother of his friend Lone Wolf. Red Hair had ridden with them in defense of his sister's honor. He was of a good, strong spirit and very much loved by the one who walked between two worlds.

"Scott doesn't think it's powerful enough. Where would he take my husband? If you know, please, please tell me."

"If he seeks to expel demons, he would take Red Hair to a shaman who is a mightier *wakan*."

271

"Do you know of such a man?"

"*Sinte Gleska.* You would say, Spotted Tail. He has great influence with the spirits. Lone Wolf would take him there. He is in the *Paha Sapa,* Where the Tears of the Gods Flow."

Norah looked behind her, across the impossible distance. "In the Hills." She took a bracing breath. "Where?"

By pushing Rosebud mercilessly, she was on their trail by early afternoon. She could make out the signs of a travois mixed in with those of a half-dozen horses. Ethan had given his son two days at most. One of them was almost gone. She whipped the reins against the roan's wet flanks and began the climb.

Then she came up on them. Scott was astride a big buckskin, riding bareheaded, leading a string of fine stock. Behind his horse a heavy-laden sled was dragging. He must have heard her approach, but he didn't turn or show any surprise when she drew abreast of him.

"Just what the hell do you think you're doing?" She might well have been shouting into the wind. "Scott! Scott, what are you doing? Don't you want to save his life?"

He looked at her then, through eyes hard as agates. "I'm trying to."

"Then take him home. For God's sake, take him home. This is madness, what you're doing. You're killing him."

Scott had no reply to that, nor would he look at her again. He continued to use his heels, goading the horse to higher ground and goading her temper to a higher degree.

"Take him back, Scott. Let your father save his life."

"That's not the life he wants."

"How dare you decide that!"

"I didn't."

"Rory asked you? I don't believe that for a second. He doesn't believe in your hocus-pocus any more than I do. He wouldn't risk his life on the dreams of some crazy Sioux medicine man."

The golden eyes pierced through her. "Rory asked me to take his life, to end it for him."

She was too startled to respond at first. "Is that what you're doing?" Horror thickened her words.

"He's my brother. I would do anything for him but that. I'm trying to save him the only way I know how, the only way I can and still keep my vow to him. You're stealing minutes from him that he can't afford to lose. Get out of my way."

She sat stunned as he continued to climb, riding on with that stiff Sioux arrogance she had no time or patience to understand. She jerked her carbine from its sheath. She saw his shoulders stiffen when she brought it to full cock.

"Scott, take him back."

"Or what?" he called without looking around. "You'll shoot me?"

"Yes!"

"Shoot me then."

She actually went so far as to sight in on his unyielding spine before she realized what she was doing. With a sob, she released the hammer and shoved the carbine back into its boot. The strain of grief was making her crazy. She urged Rosebud up beside him and stretched out to snag his arm.

"Will you at least stop long enough for me to be sure he's all right?"

The bright wash of tears upon her face convinced him to rein in. She kicked off Rosebud and raced through the knee-deep snow, dropping down in it without a thought to the cold.

Scott had wrapped him well. Beneath the stack of blankets, he was warm and safe from the cutting wind. But external comforts had no effect on the fever of infection eating him up inside. He was unconscious, his skin wet, his breathing shallow. But he was breathing.

"I dosed him with all the laudanum he could stand to make the trip. He shouldn't come around for another hour or so. By then, we'll be there."

He'd never make it all the way back to the Bar K. He'd wake halfway there, and the constant jar of movement would kill him. Scott must have known she'd come to that conclusion for he sat in his saddle unconcerned. This trip he had planned well. And there was nothing she could do but go along.

Norah straightened after securing the blankets. She met her brother-in-law's unblinking stare with a look of deadly promise.

"If he dies, I will shoot you."

Scott nodded, accepting those terms without hesitation.

The shaman, *Sinte Gleska,* lived with his family members in a dense copse of pine. Scott didn't go directly into the circle of tipis but reined in and called in the Lakota tongue until several women appeared. He talked with them in the strange gutturals Norah couldn't understand, gesturing to the horses and to the travois. When they disappeared into the largest of the tents, Scott turned to her.

"Don't speak. Don't argue. Don't interfere. I promised Rory I would care for you. Don't make me break that vow before he's even cold."

"Will you at least explain what you're doing so I won't think you've completely lost your grip on sanity."

He gave her that thin, slightly contemptuous smile. "You would not believe."

"But I will listen."

"All right. The Lakota believe every object, artificial or natural, is inhabited by a spirit capable of helping or harming. They believe disease or illness is caused by spirits, that an offended god sends the spirit of an animal or a bird to punish. This angry spirit sends destructive foreign bodies into the man who has offended, possessing a part or the whole of his body."

"And where does your witch doctor fit into this?"

He scowled at her condescending tone. "The shaman is part-priest, part-doctor. He is *wakan*, a sacred man who is inhabited by a god who helps him cast out demons."

"And you believe this? A man of your education?"

He regarded her blandly. "It's what you wanted to know so I'm telling you."

"Your father is a doctor. How could you accept such nonsense as truth?"

"My father was a Lakota warrior, and Ethan is the first one who would tell you not to dismiss the *wakan's* wisdom."

She found it hard to picture the calm, rational Ethan Prescott taking counsel from a man who thought himself possessed of spirits instead of knowledge. But she was ready to believe in anything that would save her husband's life. Until she saw the Lakota medicine man.

He emerged from the tipi with a great dramatic flair. In spite of the cold, he wore beneath his ornamental headdress and special blanket only a

275

breechcloth, moccasins, and trailing leggings. An anatomy lesson could be given along the show of ribcage and yards of sinew and only the fervid glitter of his eyes lent a show of life to his cadaverous form. Scott immediately shimmied off his horse to pay the proper respect. Norah sat her saddle, staring in a confusion of amusement and pity until Scott shot her a withering glare, then she slid down. The shaman—he was so emaciated she couldn't tell if he were old or young—gave her a haughty glance, then began to discuss the horses that were obviously to be his fee. And from the looks of him, his dinner.

Apparently, the gift was enough, for the conjurer looked pleased until he threw back the blankets. Norah heard the word *wasicun,* which she knew to mean white man, and then a flurry of sentiments accompanied by the shaking of his head.

Scott was quick to draw the man's attention back to the fine string of horses, lifting a fetlock, stroking along glossy hide, displaying strong teeth. He gestured to Rory and then himself, striking his fist over his heart. The plea was stated eloquently in his eyes. But the medicine man was adamant. Until his shiny eyes lit on Rosebud. He ran his palm along the oddly colored coat and he nodded.

"Scott? What does he want?"

The Indian grasped Rosebud's bridle, and Norah tore it away.

"Scott?"

"Give him the horse, Norah."

"But she's Rory's horse."

"Give him the horse."

"No."

He strode over to yank the reins from her and placed them in the witch doctor's hands with a curt nod. The Indian grinned toothlessly and called to the women, who rushed out to take charge of the animals, including Rory's little mare. Norah started forward, but Scott gripped her arms to deliver a stern shake.

"How could you?" she cried up at him, furious in the face of his indifference.

"It's a horse."

"Not to Rory."

"If he's not alive, what difference does it make?"

The sharp words were like a slap, and she reeled from the truth of them. If Rory didn't live, none of it mattered. She turned away, tears bright in her eyes. "He's going to hate you for this."

"Better to welcome his hate than weep over his soul." And with that, he followed the procession of Sioux into the inner circle of tents, leading his horse with Rory dragging behind. Brushing angrily at her eyes, Norah followed.

They stopped not before the shaman's tipi but at another. Two young men came out to lift Rory from the litter and carry him inside. Scott ducked in; and when she would go with him, one of the women grabbed her arm, holding her back.

"Scott! Scott, either I go in or I take Rory out of here."

She waited impatiently, hearing voices from inside, then Scott appeared with his hand outstretched. She took it and let him lead her within. He leaned close to whisper in a harsh aside, "You do anything to interrupt, and I'll lash you over the back of my horse like yesterday's game."

The interior of the tipi was roomier than she would have supposed from the outside. There was a large central fire, and the floor was carpeted with leafy ferns and scented with other aromatic herbage. Rory was stretched out and stripped of blankets and all clothing down to his wool flannel drawers. He was starting to break from the effects of the laudanum, his head moving restlessly from side to side on the bed of furs he had been moved onto. Norah took a seat beside Scott, and he held her there with the firm cuff of his hand about her wrist. When the shaman threw off his woven cloak, she gave a soft gasp.

"Are those fingers?"

Scott looked at the grim necklace adorning his scrawny chest and nodded.

"You don't suppose that's part of his fee, do you?"

He never blinked. "If it is, I'll give him mine."

She stared, wondering if he could possibly be serious. Her attention was drawn away when the witch doctor leaned over Rory, waving his hands above him but not making contact.

"What's he doing?" Norah whispered.

"He's trying to learn the name and nature of the spirit possessing him. Then he will address it and attempt to drive it out."

"What if it decides not to leave?" she asked dryly.

"Rory dies."

She swallowed hard.

When the shaman had organized his attack upon the offending spirit, he began to dance, making a slow circle around the fire with his left hand toward the room's center. The other hand held a gourd rattle which he shook to the rhythm of his steps. One of the young Lakotas began to palm a drum and chant softly. Both the steps and the chanting intensified, building to near frenzy as the medicine man spun and began to circle Rory, placing his hand upon skin glistening with the sweat of fever. In spite of herself, Norah found she was sitting rigid, her breath suspended, her fingers somehow interlaced with

Scott's. Spotted Tail began making horrid noises, gesturing wildly toward the heavens before falling to his knees to massage Rory's ankle. Rory bucked on the sickbed, twisting in an effort to evade the sudden hurtful pressure. Scott's fingers clenched tight to hold Norah still as the shaman howled his prayers and waved sacred amulets over his brother.

By now, the gaunt figure had thrown himself into a trance under the control of his personal spirit. He blew on the injured limb through a hollow piece of bone and reached high into the air with his soul-snatcher to bring back the sick man's errant soul. Then when Norah had had almost enough of the nonsense, he placed the hollow bone tube to Rory's foot and made a great display of sucking out the offending intruder. When he spat out a great wad of bloody phelgm, she heard Scott take a quick breath of expectation.

It was then that Rory opened his eyes. His shout brought Norah up only to have Scott wrestle her back down.

The shaman concluded his incanting, then solemnly approached Scott. He spoke and gestured, and Scott's expression grew taut with anguish.

"What's he saying?"

"He says that Rory is too badly injured, that it's for the gods to decree whether he will live or die."

"Then tell him he has to return the horses."

The shaman peered at Norah through slitted eyes. Slowly, Scott translated, and he scowled his displeasure. He snapped a few words and stalked away.

"What?"

"He says he will smoke on it."

So they sat and waited while the medicine man puffed his pipe, contemplating the nature of Rory's possessing spirit. The women came in and knelt to

279

bathe Rory with cool moist moss. Scott whispered that with the drying of the moss, the evil spirit it absorbed would be released harmlessly. Before he could catch her, she slipped around the fire to crouch beside the Lakotas, dipping a handful of moss into water and soothing it along the laboring chest. Scott glanced nervously toward the medicine man, but he nodded slightly.

As she sponged him with the moss, Norah eased her hand back through the sweat-soaked red hair. She could feel the chills shaking through him and the spasms of pain jerking at his muscles. His head rolled toward her, and his eyes opened—dark, vague, scorched by fever. He didn't know her, and that frightened her more than anything else could. She bent, touching her lips briefly to his, whispering gently, "Don't be afraid. Scott and I are here with you," but he was already turning away. Biting her lower lip to contain the threat of weeping, she scooted back to her place and sat trembling.

"Don't do that again," Scott said in soft warning.

She cast him a resentful glance. "Did I disturb your witch doctor's discussion with the spirits?"

"No. He respects your devotion to your man. But don't interfere again." Then the hardness left his voice, rendering it a low whisper. "How is he?"

"Your shaman better work harder if he expects to earn his horses."

The dancing, the rattling, the chanting began again. Water was poured over hot rocks, filling the conical room with a thick, acrid fog. The shaman assembled a mixture of barks, roots, herbs, and what looked like mold and spread it upon a hot poultice. When he wrapped it about Rory's foot, the injured man groaned and thrashed in protest. Then he returned to his calumet and gourds and his exhorting of the gods.

It went on all night—the dancing, chanting, the intervals for smoking. Norah was exhausted in body and mind. Her tolerance for the shaman's tricks was sorely strained. The heavy steam made her light-headed; and she wondered if that, too, were one of the witch doctor's clever sideshow effects. Beside her, Scott sat stiff and unmoving, his expression somber, his attitude reverent. She wanted to swat him, to demand to know how a man of his intelligence could be taken in by such obvious ploys of chicanery. And on his bed of agony, Rory worsened by the minute.

Awareness that something different was happening broke through Norah's near-lethargy. The Lakota braves were hanging an effigy on a pole above Rory's pallet. She leaned against Scott, asking for an explanation.

"It is the image of the offending spirit. It will be shot with arrows; and as it falls, the spirit in the *wakan* will leap upon it and kill it."

She laughed, loudly, hysterically. "Oh, please. No more. Hasn't this farce gone far enough? Stop it, Scott." She was too tired, too drained by grief to be intimidated by his fearsome glare. For a moment, she thought he might strike her. Then, surprisingly, his arms went about her, pulling her tightly to his chest, holding her there with a controlling forcefulness.

"Norah, be strong for him. Rory trusted me with his life. I wouldn't have brought him if I didn't think there was a chance. Don't be so quick to cast away that which makes no sense to you. I have seen miracles at the hands of such men. I have prayed for one. Add your voice so it might be strong enough to bring back his soul. If you love him, don't turn from this last chance to save him. Trust me. Trust me, Norah."

Perhaps it was just the weariness of her will that made her nod her head. Or maybe it was the sheer strength of his belief. Whichever, she needed to cling to something. And all she had were the shaman's theatrics and Scott Prescott's faith.

When his embrace eased, she sat back and arranged her features in stoic lines as the shaman went through his pantomime. The drum thundered like pulse beats. The chanting vibrated the mist-laden air. And from his haze of delirium, Rory cried out hoarsely.

"Scotty!"

Scott went rigid at her side. His strict Lakota training held him in his place, but it wasn't without tremendous effort. That discipline was put to a torturous test when the panicked pleas came again.

"Scotty? Scotty, where are you? Don't leave me. Scotty, please!"

With a soft, moaning oath, Scott was up, circling the fire, kneeling down at his brother's side, Norah right beside him.

"Scotty?"

"Right here." He scooped up one of the restless hands, and Rory's fingers closed about his, clutching tight. The dark eyes opened—hot, bright, fearful.

"What is this place?" Rory shifted in agitation, movements jerky, almost convulsive. "I doan like it. I wanna go home."

"Not yet."

"No. No. Now. Wanna go now. There's things in here . . . awful things. Scotty, doan leave me. Doan let 'em take me."

"It's the fever," Norah said softly.

Scott looked up at her briefly. He said nothing, but his silence was a rebuttal. He believed in whatever demons writhed in his brother's uneasy mind.

282

"Scotty, I'm scared of this place. I wanna go." His hand squeezed plaintively. "I want Daddy to take the hurtin' away. Please, Daddy, I doan want to hurt no more."

"Oh, God," Scott whispered. "What have I done?" Helplessly, he put a hand to his brother's wet brow. "I'm sorry, Rory. I thought I was doing what you wanted." Unable to look upon the suffering he'd allowed, Scott shut his eyes and let his head hang low, trying to dredge up some measure of control. Failing. It was then he felt the clumsy brush of Rory's fingertips smearing the dampness on his face.

"Hey. Hey now, Scotty, doan be doing that. I ain't blaming you none. I ain't gonna tell nobody. I ain't gonna tell. It doan hurt that bad."

The strangeness of his voice, one that echoed of a half-score of years instead of nearly thirty, the familiar sound of the words reaching back to faint memory had Scott frowning. "Rory, I don't—"

"Doan cry, Scotty. It doan hurt none."

Then he remembered.

"It ain't so bad, Scotty," came the faltering bravado of the rough-and-tumble boy Rory Prescott had once been. The little brother Scott had left behind when he went to school in the East over twenty years ago.

"Scott, what's he talking about?"

Scott glanced at her for a distracted second and gave a weak smile. "Something from when we were little."

"What?" Norah prompted softly.

Holding Rory's hand over his heart while his brother drifted toward unconsciousness, with the drum and quiet chanting as background, his words sounded like Lakota legend rather than a piece of Prescott childhood.

"I was about nine or ten, I guess, Rory was probably seven. We told Mama we were going fishing, then snuck into Crowe Creek. We weren't supposed to go into town alone, but Rory'd been wanting to buy this deck of fancy playing cards so the ramrod at the Bar K would teach him how to play poker."

Norah couldn't help smiling. She could picture a seven-year-old Rory Prescott so vividly, full of life and sweet deviltry. She'd seen it shining through in their son. The man had never lost that part of the boy.

"Well," Scott continued quietly, "he didn't get his cards. He was a penny short. I can still see him sitting on the steps out front of Vernon's Mercantile with his face all long and his eyes all swollen up with tears, trying not to let on how disappointed he was. Hell, I couldn't stand it, so I went on in to buy them for him. Vernon's son was working the counter. He was a big bully of a kid, about fifteen, and he'd made it plain he had no use for me because of who my father was. Well, I bought the cards and before I could get to the door, he was grabbing on my arm, dragging me back to where his daddy was working the dry goods counter. He said he caught me stealing the cards. Ole Vernon blew up like a thunderhead and told me he was going to see my daddy switched me but good, but not before he taught me a lesson. I gave him a good kick in the shins and hiyed it outta there."

It didn't take much for Norah to imagine the scene. A bigotted bully taking advantage of a mixed-breed boy. Anger swelled in her heart and a certain sympathy for Scott Prescott with it. How hard it must have been for him to swallow such abuse. But he hadn't.

"We were kids, full of vinegar and pride—Prescotts, you know." Norah nodded. "We didn't take stuff off anybody. It didn't take us long to start thinking of a way to get back at ole Vernon. One of us, probably Rory, got to thinking it would be fitting for me to take the scalps off these big expensive baby dolls Vernon had shipped in from the East. It sounded good at the time. So we snuck on in, and I'd lifted the horsehair off about three of them when little Vern got curious. We lit out running. I dropped my knife and when Rory stopped to snatch it up, Ole Vernon caught hold of him."

Scott paused, feeling his pride and panic all over again. His hand moved slowly through the thatch of red hair.

"I couldn't leave him. I threw myself on Junior with my best war cry. Scared the soup out of him before he realized the whole Sioux nation wasn't out for his hair. But he was bigger and he got me around the neck so I couldn't so much as move. Then Ole Vern asked who lifted the hair off his pretty baby dolls. Rory spoke right up saying he did, and he had the knife in his hand. Guess he thought they'd go easier on him than me." Scott's features tightened and his voice became a gruff rumble. "Vernon rucked up his shirt and wailed him with a razor strop. Now our daddy had given us our fair share of whippings but he never, ever marked on us. If Rory'd started crying and carrying on like he was sorry, he might have stopped, but you know Rory. He never gave Vern the satisfaction of knowing how bad he was hurting. Damn fool pride. He let the man beat him senseless."

He would. Norah knew it. A Prescott would rather die than accept insult or defeat. Or was that a Kincaid? Or a good smattering of both? And at seven, that was already ingrained in him. Foolish, prideful man. "And then what happened?"

"They threw us out the back and warned us not to

ever come in again. Rory—he was in a bad way. I was crying, scared to take him home because it was my fault he'd gotten hurt. I was the oldest. I was supposed to know better. Then Rory, what does he do but go and say, 'It ain't that bad. It don't hurt at all. I won't tell nobody.' So we rode on home and went to sit at the table like nothing had happened. Rory was dead white, trying to fool Mama and Daddy into thinking nothing was wrong. Might have gotten away with it, too, if he hadn't fainted right out of his chair. There was nothing I could do but spill it all."

When he fell silent, Norah urged, "What did they do?"

"Mama didn't say anything. Daddy raised up Rory's shirt and saw there wasn't an inch of skin on him not raised up in a welt. He patched him up, put him to bed, and rode into town. Didn't find out till later that he paid for the damage then dry-shaved off half of Vernon's hair right in the middle of the street for daring to put a hand to one of his boys. By the time he got home, he was mad as a rattler fixing to strike. Rory got between us and started squeezing out the biggest mess of tears you've ever seen, blubbering and whining about how it was his fault and all the while pushing me behind him. Had Mama eating out of his hand."

"And Ethan?"

Scott smiled faintly. "Daddy's nobody's fool. Neither of us could ever pull anything over on him. I was feeling so bad I was hoping he'd take a switch to me. But he didn't. As soon as Rory was up and around, he marched the two of us to Vernon's and made us both apologize. Then he and Rory waited in the wagon while I worked off the price of those dolls sweeping and toting trash and doing every dirty little job he could think of. Then Daddy bought Rory his deck of cards and he took us home. Never said another word about it. And far as I know, Rory never did break the seal on that deck of cards."

He took a jagged breath. "He can't die, Norah. He just can't. He's the best friend I've ever had."

She started to reach out to him, but he shied from her touch. She didn't push, allowing him the dignity of recovering on his own. Then she told him softly, confidently, "We won't let him, Scott."

Chapter Eighteen

It was a cold, gray dawn. Norah got a glimpse of it as one of the Lakotas slipped out, silent as a passing ghost. She was stiff and almost numb with fatigue. She was ready to place her full belief in the sinewy medicine man as he worked his charms and fetishes. Rory was still alive. Scott had to be every bit as weary, but he never moved to ease sore muscles or once shifted his solemn stare from the sickbed. Occasionally, she'd see his lips move in prayer, but she never asked whom he called to.

She said nothing as the shaman produced pebbles and splinters through his bone straw. She didn't care that it was cheap magic. She had more faith in the steaming poultice the women replaced every time it cooled. Rory lay unmoving, and that was almost more disturbing than the constant thrashing. She couldn't help but wonder if the fever had burned away the strength it would take to recover.

She couldn't see at first what the shaman was doing as he leaned over the still figure. Scott's sudden tension was enough to alert her.

"What's he doing?" Silence. "Scott?"

Scott wet his lips. He looked uncertain, and that

scared her badly. His unwavering stance was what sustained her. "He's freeing the flesh of evil spirits."

"How? How is he doing it, Scott?"

"Bloodletting."

Her eyes swelled up in size. "What?"

"Norah . . ."

"My God, Scott, he's lost more blood than he can spare. This is barbarous. Worse, it's dangerous."

"It won't injure him. The scratches aren't deep. They'll be rubbed with medicines, and then he'll be purged in the stream."

The stream. She remembered the icy chill of the water from the day they'd been fishing. It would be worse now, frigid with snowy melt. In Rory's fevered state, weakened as he was . . .

"Scott, no. It'll kill him. The shock will kill him. You have to know that. You have to see that. Don't you?" He just stared at her, eyes expressionless. "This is craziness. I won't allow it."

She was up before he could stop her, charging across the tent, pushing between the shaman and her vulnerable husband. A pattern of thin gashes had already been drawn above and below his elbow on his left arm with a comb of splinters cracked from a turkey leg. She felt Scott's hands upon her shoulders and was about to fling them off when she heard him speak flatly to the Lakota.

"*Ayustan*. Stop."

"Blood alone will satisfy the spirit in your brother's body."

Norah gave a start of surprise. The man spoke English. Very well.

"He cannot spare it. His spirit is too weak to fight."

"Then you must find a mightier *wakan* for my spirit-helper is not strong enough to win back his soul from *wanagi ta canku,* the path of spirits."

"There is no time to find another."

"Then the fight is his. He must choose to come back into this body. His soul has fled in fear of the intruding spirit of the bear. It must be driven out or he will die."

"How?" Norah leaned toward him, her eyes glittered with a fever of anxiety and desperation.

"An offering for his soul from the one who loves him best."

Scott thrust out his forearm, pushing up his sleeve. His arm was marred by countless scarrings. Norah remembered him crouching in the yard at the Lone Star, slicing his flesh to bring Gena back from unconsciousness. He believed his sacrifice had captured her spirit. Perhaps it had.

Boldly, she put forth her own arm, shoving up the sleeve to expose fair, unflawed skin. The *wakan* studied her, eyes unblinking. When he took her hand, Scott stared in a confusion of anger and hurt at having his offer of sacrifice overruled. The shaman spoke softly.

"You would do this for your man?"

"I would do anything for him," she answered in a strong voice.

The shaman nodded. He had a firm grasp on her wrist, pulling her arm so it was above Rory's shallow moving chest. With the turkey bones, he raked down from elbow to wrist, once, twice, three times, then four. Norah held her breath and ground her teeth. Her arm was steady as the blood oozed up and began to trickle. Scott drew his sharp-bladed knife and made a quick hard slash across his palm. As it filled, he clamped it down over the wounds on her forearm, squeezing fiercely until their blood mingled and splashed on the bared chest below.

"Call him back, Norah."

At that moment, she believed she could. She believed she could reach into hell itself to retrieve him if that were what it took. She looked down upon his still features, cupping the side of his face with her palm. Concentrating.

"Rory. Rory, wake up. I need you. I need you to come back to me." Nothing. She felt panic begin to swell. She was losing him. "Rory. Damn you, Rory Prescott, you listen to me! Don't you dare die! Don't you dare leave me. I love you! Do you hear me?" His face was hot beneath her hand, unresponsive.

Lifting her angry eyes toward the heavens, she shouted, "Give him back to me! I curse you. I spit on you. I defy you, you weak and silly spirits, good for scaring little children and old men. Give me back my husband if you're not afraid to show me you have power over life and death. Give him to me, or I will know you for the impotent shams you are."

Silence. Scott had stopped breathing. His eyes were huge, his features drawn in shock. Even the *wakan* eased back as if he feared the ground would open to swallow her whole. But nothing happened.

Norah sagged, her fury spent, her brief hopes shattered. She sank down upon Rory's chest, clutching at him, rubbing at the warm feel of him, fearing he would soon grow cold and that there was nothing she could do to prevent it.

"Rory, I love you. Please don't go. Please don't leave me."

There was a caressing touch against her cheek, soothing, smoothing along the wet curve. Scott trying to console her. Or so she thought until she felt the rough burr of calluses.

She sat up, clinging to Rory's hand, staring up with fragile amazement at the man beside her. There

291

was nothing more beautiful than the sight of Scott Prescott's smile.

Nothing except the opening flicker of his brother's eyes.

They started back for the Bar K before noontime with Rory well-wrapped and fairly comfortable on the sled and Norah riding double behind Scott. Rory's fever had broken and his rest was deep and easy, but Scott was eager to get him home so his father could confirm that he would recover. The shaman, in his opinion, had earned his horses and Norah was of no mind to argue. Even hard as it was to ride away with Rosebud whinnying at the end of her tether, prancing restlessly as she was left behind.

It was a silent ride. Scott had said little since Rory had so briefly regained consciousness. He'd made the proper thanks to Spotted Tail and his family, he'd loaded his brother, and he'd started home. He still treated her as an afterthought. But when she began to rock with weariness, he pulled her arms tightly about his middle so she had no choice but to lean against the spread of his shoulders. She rested her head gratefully against him, smiling as she closed her eyes. *You're not so tough, Scott Prescott. I suppose we're blood brother and sister now. Bet that just kills you.*

She heard a sound behind them and looked back briefly. There, following alongside the travois with broken rope trailing, was Rosebud, stepping daintily, occasionally nosing the blankets with an almost mothering care. She smiled again and decided to say nothing to Scott lest his sense of honor provoke him into returning the horse to the shaman.

In front of her, Scott was smiling, too. He'd heard the mare's extra steps for the last mile. He affixed

Norah's arms more securely and was gladdened to the soul that his brother had so many who would follow him out of love.

She must have fallen asleep, trusting Scott to keep her from toppling. The next thing she knew, he was nudging her with a soft, "Norah, you're home."

The Prescotts were waiting.

Scott had stiffened in the saddle. Was he worrying over his reception? Without thinking, she rubbed a hand along the tense line of his shoulders. He gave a start, surprised by her show of silent support. Support from the woman who'd been ready to shoot him in the back.

"What the hell have you done?"

Ethan met them with that fearsome growl. He came off the porch in several long strides and knelt down beside the travois.

"Ethan?" Aurora called anxiously. She hadn't moved. She waited on the porch, her fingers curled over the caps of Jacob's shoulders. Her features were so pale and drawn Norah knew she hadn't seen a moment's rest since her sons had disappeared. The past few days had been a hell for all of them.

"I'll be damned," the big Texan muttered. "Scotty, help me get your brother into the house."

Scott swung his left leg over the pommel and jumped down. Then he paused and reached up for Norah, bringing her down easy so she could go up to embrace Jacob.

"Is Daddy all right?"

"He's going to be fine, honey. Just fine. Why don't you take Rosebud down to the barn and tell the boys to grain her good. We'll get your daddy settled in so you can see him."

Looking as though he'd rather linger, he took a manful breath and murmured, "Yes, ma'am," before ambling off with the little mare.

When she straightened, Norah found her gaze pinned by Aurora Prescott's golden glare.

"How dare you take such a risk with my son's life," she hissed in a low, slicing voice. "If he had died, we would have driven you off this property like a cur dog."

"Mama, it wasn't Norah." Scott's words were quiet yet powerful in their strength. "It was me. I took Rory to a shaman in the Hills. If he had died, the fault would have been mine. Would you have driven me away with stones?"

Aurora looked to her son, her features pulled taut in a turmoil of emotion. Just then, Ethan's command intruded.

"Scotty, ain't got all day. Grab his legs and be gentle about it."

Norah whisked away from Aurora without a word. She held open the door for the two men bearing her husband, then preceded them up the stairs. The rest of the Prescotts trailed behind, excluded when Norah shut the bedroom door. This was not a time to have family crowded close, not yet.

Rory was stirring as they settled him on the bed. His eyes blinked slowly with a dragging weakness, but their light was cool, aware. His hand turned outward on the counterpane, palm up, inquiring, and Scott's fingers pressed over it, squeezing firmly. Ethan unwrapped the crude bandaging about his ankle and foot. With each layer unbound, his expression grew tighter until the wounds were laid bare for his study. Sore, raw-looking wounds. Warm, healthy-looking skin. None of the dead white of frostbite or the angry red of infection or the fatal black of gangrene.

"Can you feel this?" He raked his fingernail up the

sole of Rory's foot, and it jumped in reaction.

"How's it look, Daddy?" Scott asked quietly.

"Them Sioux shaman, they put on a dandy of a show, but they got a way with nature that puts modern know-how back to the Dark Ages. Whatever he packed in that poultice sucked the infection clean out." The Texan stood for a time, fingers curled over those healthy toes, expression solemn. Then he glanced at Scott.

"You sporting any ails I should know about, son?" No need to explain the bottom line of Sioux spirit healing to him. He took the proffered hand and checked the clean cut across its palm, dusting it with antiseptic powder and rebinding it.

"Norah, let him take a look at your arm."

That did surprise him. He examined the reluctantly bared forearm with brows high and lips gripped shut. None of his business. Norah twitched as the deep scratches were cleansed and treated and glanced up as Scott took hold of her wrist to steady her arm. His gaze was veiled, but there was the faintest sketch of a smile at the corners of his mouth. She supposed that was the most acknowledgment she would ever get from him. It was enough.

"Scott," she said as she pulled her sleeve down over the snug wrapping, "let your mother in before she claws her way through the door. I haven't been much of a hostess. I'll have Ruth get dinner ready. I seem to recall that we have plenty of bear steaks on hand."

Scott grinned. His smile split wide and white, dazzling. It made him suddenly approachable, as if he'd allowed all the barriers he lived behind to abruptly fall away. His hand curved behind the back of her head, and Norah found herself propelled into a hard embrace. She felt the warmth of his cheek against her temple and heard Lakota words spoken huskily.

"Hel yaun kin he waste hanka." Then he released her with the same abruptness and walked away.

"What was that he said?"

Ethan smiled to himself. "Something about being glad you're here."

"Oh."

"And he called you his sister."

"Oh," was all she could think to say again. And she felt absurdly pleased.

"I'll go talk to Ruth," Ethan offered. "Why don't you scrub up, and I'll have Rory's mama sit with him."

She heaved a grateful sigh. Hot water, warm suds. Heaven.

Twilight, soft and silvery, settled over the rolling acres of the Bar K. A peaceful stillness wrapped around the big ranch house, the kind that came with knowing all was well. But all was far from well in the troubled soul of Scott Prescott as he stood in his shirtsleeves on the snow-dusted porch, looking toward the far Hills. He felt cold, but it was an inside chill. Like the one in his mother's eyes.

"Where's your coat? Why you don't come down with pneumonia, I'll never know," Gena scolded.

His wife's concern made him smile. Sometimes she treated him like a soft city-bred white man, but he didn't mind it. Because of the love behind her care. She amazed him with her ability to know the secrets of his heart so well, and yet she could be so blind to the obvious. He was a hard man on the outside, toughened by a harsh Dakota upbringing and by sometimes cruel Lakota training. A little cold air wasn't going to phase him. But what could cripple him with fatal consequence was one unforgiving stare. Because, on the inside, he was a white man, soft and dangerously sensitive to the world around and the will of those he loved.

"You're freezing." Gena took up his hands, noting the way they shook with the slightest of tremors. She fit them around her waist and stepped in close to press against him. "Is that better?"

He nuzzled into the silkiness of her blond hair, and he nodded.

"I can make it even better." She felt his small smile and loved the way he shifted in closer with just a subtle move. "And then we need to talk about some things."

"Can the talk wait a while? I'm too worn out for words."

She was quiet for a moment, then said, "It can wait. For a while."

She continued to hold him and he, to rely upon the warmth of that embrace even after a quiet drawl interrupted them.

"Looks to be a nice night." Ethan strolled to the rail and stared thoughtfully across the wind-swept snow. "Supper's 'bout ready. You coming in?"

"In a minute. Daddy . . ."

"Don't chew it till it gets tough. What's on your mind, boy?"

"I'm sorry I broke faith with you." Just that, no more. It said everything.

Ethan glanced over at the man he'd raised as his own son, seeing the stamp of his true father upon the bronze of his skin and the restraint of his expression. Seeing as well the tenderness and torment of his mother's half. And he sighed.

"Scotty, what you did was about the bravest thing I've ever seen. I'm right thankful you had the guts to do it."

"I meant no offense to you. It would break my heart if I thought you believed that."

"We just saw things different is all. I don't hold that against any man. But if you'd done nothing and I'd a taken off that boy's leg and you'd spent the rest of your life wondering if you could have done something, now that I wouldn't have forgiven you for. I did the best I knew how, and you had to let your own convictions prove it wasn't enough."

Scott's voice thickened. "If he had died . . . ."

"Then you would have felt the same as me if I'da chopped off his foot. Decisions like that just ain't easy to swallow down. They shouldn't be. Sometimes you just don't have a choice. And then you live with them."

He nodded, once. Then he voiced his final concern. "Mama—"

"Son, your mama is a female of the species. Don't matter how long or how far her little ones are gone from the nest. She loves you boys and one a you gets hurt, she gets kinda rabid about it. A right dangerous animal, mamas. There ain't nothing either of you could do to make her turn her back on you. Nothing. I am kinda curious as to how you got Rory to go along with seeing a shaman. That ain't exactly to his sort of thinking."

"He didn't argue." He'd been unconscious at the time.

"Now, I can smell that dinner and my stomach's growling 'bout as loud as that poor departed bear. 'Less you got something else you want to jaw on—"

"Let's eat."

It was right in the middle of passing the potatoes.

Gena took the dish from Dawn and was about to scoop a heaping on her plate when Scott leaned over to playfully pat her midriff.

"Maybe you'd better pass on those. Mama must have been feeding you good while I was gone. A few more heapings of potatoes and you'll have to let out your seams."

Gena responded to his teasing grin with a small smile and a gentle, "I was planning on it."

When Scott took the dish from her and started to fill his own plate, Ethan stared at him, frowning.

"Pard, you are dumb. Ora, we've raised ourselves a stupid child. All that education and he can't figure out a thing." Then he reached quick to catch the bowl as it fell from Scott's fingers.

"Oh my God. Oh my God!" The stunned golden eyes fell from his wife's warm blush to the gentle swell of her abdomen. "Gena, you're—After all this time trying and hoping, I just never thought . . ." Her cheeks had gone positively fiery. "What a thing to drop on a man in the middle of dinner."

"I wanted to wait until we were alone," Gena murmured. Then her smile blossomed. "But you are the dangedest man to corner."

Scott sat his chair, stunned as a pole-axed steer, until his daughter prompted him.

"Daddy, aren't you gonna kiss her?"

"Yes. Hell, yes!" Then he looked around the Bar K table at all the smug, expectant faces—Norah and Jacob were the only ones who looked as surprised as he was—and he grabbed Gena by the hand. "Somewhere a little more private." He dragged her up and out of the room, into the dimly shadowed parlor where he kissed her wildly. Then sweetly.

"Why didn't you tell me, *mitawicu?*" His hands stroked restlessly over her features, over her waist, unable to stop touching her.

"Are you pleased?"

"Why didn't you tell me, Gena?"

"It's not something a woman tells her husband by telegraph."

His voice lowered, becoming rough with emotion. "I would have come home."

"It was too soon. I-I wanted to wait."

"Wait? Why? For what?" Dread made his next words shiver. "Is there something wrong?"

"No." She rubbed his cheeks, erasing their stiffness. "Your father says everything is fine this time. But after the others—I wanted to be sure. He said after the first three months, the risk would go down. I didn't want to disappoint you again."

"Gena. *Wowastelaka.* I should have been here. I would have been here for you."

"I wasn't exactly alone."

"It's not my family's place to comfort my wife. It's mine!" Then he said it again, more to himself this time. "It's mine."

"I'm quite comfortable now," she murmured, easing her arms around him. "Dawn is looking forward to becoming a *tanke.*" Then Scott chuckled, and she had to ask, "What? That means sister, doesn't it?"

"The older sister of a boy," he corrected. "It would seem our daughter has made up her mind already."

"Perhaps she's had one of her great-grandfather's visions."

"Or maybe she just wants a brother. Brother. . . . I can't believe Rory didn't spill it. He can't keep a secret worth a hang."

"He doesn't know." She smiled against his shirt front. "I thought you'd want to tell him."

"God, I love you, Gena."

300

"Are you happy?"

"Let me take you home, and I'll show you."

The house was very quiet. The Prescotts were gone; Jacob was tucked in, and Ruth had retired to her own room. Wearily, Norah climbed the stairs. For the last three days, what little sleep she'd managed was either on a hard floor or against a hard back. She was dying to crawl beneath the downy covers of a real bed, to close her eyes. Her arm ached, her shoulders slumped with exhaustion. And then she entered the bedroom, and the first thing she saw was her packed suitcase.

She stared at it incomprehensibly. It seemed like months ago that she'd stuffed her things inside it, ready to leave the Bar K and the man she loved. So much had happened, so many tremendous rifts of emotion cramped into a few interminable days. She was drained from hosting all those feelings, but not once had she had time for thinking. About the reason she'd had for packing that bag. About what Scott had told her when she'd caught up to him on the trail. And she didn't want to think about it now. The soft bedding called to her, inviting her to rest. And the hollow just below Rory Prescott's outflung arm beckoned her to curl up close and forget. The temptation was just too great.

Kisses. Warm, moist, sweetly searching, moving with a tantalizing whisper upon her sleep-softened lips. Nothing could melt her soul the way Rory Prescott could with his kiss.

Without opening her eyes, Norah arched against him, rubbing impatiently, reaching fingers upward to thread back through his fiery hair. Her mouth parted invitingly, and that's when he drew back.

301

"Whoa there, honey. I was jus' saying good morning not giddiyup."

"'Morning," she murmured huskily, rising up on her elbows to pursue the pleasures of his kiss. She followed him over until he was flat on his back and she, almost astride him.

"Norah . . . Norah-honey . . . Norah. . . . Woman, would you let me breathe! I damn near died, and now you're trying to kill me."

"I'd send you with a smile on your face," she promised as her kisses wandered along his rough cheek and lean jaw.

"Yes, ma'am, I believe you would."

She had his face between her hands, holding him so she could look down into the simmering warmth of his stare. "You scared the hell out of me, Rory Prescott. Don't you ever do that again." Unashamed tears started up in her eyes.

"No, ma'am. I won't."

She lowered to enjoy the cushion of his mouth, just a maddening sample of what she might have done had he been strong enough to endure it. "How do you feel?"

His arms came up to hold her loosely. "Like I should be making love to my wife instead a laying here like yesterday's trail leavings."

"You're worth waiting for." She'd waited three years. What were a few weeks? She snuggled in beneath his chin and rode out his sigh of contentment. While he held her in the bend of one arm, his other stretched down, feeling along his leg until he reached his kneecap. "Everything's there," she told him softly.

"Wasn't sure. Been having such strange dreams."

"How much do you remember?"

"I reckon I survived the run-in with the grizzly

since I'm here to talk about it." He shifted uncomfortably. "Still feels like he's down there a-gnawing on me, though. Jacob and Dawn, they all right?"

"They're fine."

He made a sound of relief. "Were we at my daddy's cabin?" She nodded. "All right. That much was real. An' Scotty, he was there? Things get jumbled up after that. I keep thinking I was with Indians. Now, ain't that crazy?"

"Ummmm."

"And then you was yelling at me 'bout something, only you was so far away and I had to come back so's I could hear what you were saying."

"What was I saying?"

His voice was very soft. "That you love me." Then he laughed off the entire thing. "I musta been outta my head. Indians. Imagine. And there was them other things . . . crowding in, snatching at me. An' Scotty . . ." He trailed off and grew very still.

"What do you remember about Scott?"

"Scotty? Uhhh, nothing. Why? What did he tell you?"

His tone had changed, shifting subtly into a defensive mode. And because it did, her mood altered, too.

"You weren't even going to say goodbye to me."

When he didn't respond, Norah knew he knew exactly what she was talking about. At least he didn't try to deny it.

"Is Daddy still planning on taking off my foot this morning?" he asked with apprehension. At her look of confusion, he demanded, "What the hell day is this?"

"Rory, that was three days ago."

"Three . . . three days? Then Scotty didn't . . ."

"What? Do what you asked him to? Yes, he did.

303

You weren't expecting to wake up here, were you? Scott was supposed to drag you off so you could die with dignity out there somewhere. Thank God he loved you enough not to listen to such foolishness. He took you to the Sioux, and one of their shaman used a poultice to save your leg and the life you were ready to toss away. How dare you decide something like that all by yourself! Didn't you think I had a right to an opinion, to at least say goodbye?"

Norah drew a ragged breath, giving him time to reply, time to make some kind of apology or explanation that would make what he'd done more palatable. But being Rory Prescott, he didn't. He gripped his jaws tight and just stared up at her with that look that said *I'm a Prescott and a Kincaid and I don't humble myself to nobody.*

"Damn your pride, Rory Prescott. And you for caring more about it than me."

And she was up off the bed, storming out of the room before he could think of one single way to stop her.

Chapter Nineteen

That damned trunk.

When was she planning to unpack it?

Rory eyeballed the offending piece of luggage from his bolster of pillows. He was feeling as surly as that late departed grizzly and ready to chew on something that would bite back.

Patience and rest. His father's prescription. How much coddling was a man supposed to take before he found himself turning into stewed plums? After a week, his foot wasn't near as distressing as his boredom. He wanted to pull on his pants and stuff his feet—both of them—down into a good pair of boots. He wanted to hear his spurs jingling when he walked. He wanted to sit a saddle, rope a steer, swig rye, spit tobacco, cheat at cards—anything except spend another minute in the soft embrace of this sissy room. Idleness was rotting him faster than gangrene could have taken his foot. However, his restlessness hadn't come close to outweighing his reasons for remaining where he was—the benefit of having Norah waiting on him and the fear that the minute he could do for himself, she'd be packing out the front door with that danged trunk in hand.

There'd been a definite frost to her mood since she'd stormed out of their room spitting nails. With his family ever-present, she hadn't been able to vent any more of her spleen. She simmered. Watching her temper steep was about the only interesting thing he had to do all day. She couldn't ignore him, laid up as he was and smack dab in the middle of her bed. She brought him his meals and cared for his ails and settled in beside him every evening, all with scarcely a word. He could endure the chilly snap of her indifference during the day because it warmed so sweetly every night.

She could stomp around all she wanted, flinging his plates at him and choking on polite conversation in the company of his folks. But when it came to changing his bandages, there was nothing prickly about her touch. *Oh, Norah, you fraud,* he'd think to himself as she'd climb into bed in her chaste flannel gown, taking excruciating pains not to intrude upon his half. Because as soon as the lights were out, with every tick of the clock, she was drifting over closer, inch by cautious inch. And the second she thought he was asleep, she was wrapped up tight around him. It was a hellish delight; but since he wasn't fit for any fancy two-stepping, the lush press of her was pleasure enough.

But she wouldn't unpack that trunk.

It became a point of pride. He refused to mention it, and she stepped around it every day without a glance.

"Aw, hell!"

He swung his feet down off the bed, tensing as he tested his weight upon the left one. Not bad. A little teeth-gritting could get him past it. He wobbled upright and took a hesitant step. His teeth snapped together. One, two, three more. Not so bad.

Then he heard her brisk tread on the stairs. Afraid to let her catch him on his hindlegs bold as you please in the middle of the room, he spun and started for the bed only to crack his toes on the edge of her suitcase. He swallowed down a howl of anguish and hopped the rest of the way, dropping down on the covers just as Norah swept into the room. She paused, startled by the bright flush of pain heating his face, and was across the space in a caring heartbeat.

"Are you all right?"

With her fingertips fluttering along his cheek, for a second he forgot he was in any discomfort at all. At least, in his lowest extremities.

"What happened?" She twisted to examine the wrap on his foot, giving a very nice detailing of her breasts as her shirtwaist pulled taut.

"I-I tried to put a little weight on it. Guess I'm just not ready yet."

"Don't hurry it. These things take time to heal." Her hand settled just above his knee, rubbing gently.

Oh, no, ma'am, I ain't in no hurry a-tall.

"Do you want a pillow under it?" She fussed tenderly, and he should have been ashamed of himself for moaning with just the right martyred intonation.

"It's fine, honey. You doan need to cater to me none. It doan hurt." And he forced a pitiful grimace, then allowed for a growling complaint. "You doan need to be coming up here all the time a-checking on me. I know you're only doing it to put up a show in front a my folks."

"That's not true." She bristled up in a pretty affront. "I come up because I'm worried and—" He started to grin. She shut her mouth tight.

"That so."

Enough was enough.

With one smooth move, he caught her about the shoulders and bulldogged her down to the mattress, rolling up to pin her beneath him. He silenced her sputter of angry protest with a very healthy kiss. Her arms flailed for a helpless second then they were curled about him, hugging tight. By the time he was done kissing, she was done objecting.

"I want to make love to you."

She couldn't think of a reason not to let him. Until a cool voice sounded at the open doorway.

"Norah, your gentleman friend is coming for a visit. We passed him in town, and he said he'd like to take you up on your offer of dinner this evening."

"Thank you, Aurora," she said stiffly from her compromising position. She give Rory a shove, but he wouldn't budge.

"Now," he demanded softly. "I want you now." There was an intensity in his dark eyes that went beyond the passion of moments before. It was a controlling quiet, that low voice, that penetrating stare. And that, more than the fact that his mother was standing a few feet away and Trevor was closing upon their front steps, made her resist.

"I'd better go talk to Ruth and see about supper." She levered up sharply, dumping her would-be lover over onto his back. Where he stayed, glowering as she fixed her hair back away from her flushed face. It was then she saw Aurora wasn't alone. Gena stood with her in the hall. Her fair cheeks were rosy with embarrassment over what they'd intruded upon. "Rory, it looks like you have company, too."

He shoved his elbows under him to take a look, and the dark mood was instantly gone. "Heya, Sis. C'mon in. I'm just about starved for a little friendly conversation."

Norah was sorely tempted to swat the bottom of his

foot just to see how much he was still really suffering. She got up, snapping the crinkles from her skirt before breezing by both women. Gena looked as though she might speak, but Norah kept her attention focused elsewhere. The snub made the delicate blond blink in confusion before she went inside the bedroom to sit with Rory.

Aurora didn't follow her. Instead, she went after Norah, stopping her at the top of the stairs with a firm grip on her elbow. Norah froze up solid because it wasn't a friendly grasp. She wondered fleetingly if the older woman was considering giving her a good push down that curving staircase. But, no, Aurora was still trying to behave in a civil fashion.

"Do you think it's in good taste to invite a man to dinner when your husband is prostrate upstairs?"

"I beg your pardon?"

Between the two of them, their tones could have chilled milk in the udder.

"Why are you flaunting your faithlessness in front of my son? Have you no sense of shame or decency at all? Wasn't it bad enough to dally with the man in full view of the entire town? Now you carry on beneath your own husband's roof while he's too weak to interfere?"

"What I do in town or beneath my roof is none of your business. What's between Rory and me and Trevor and me is also none of your concern." Before the redhead could open her mouth to disagree, Norah went on icily. "I have allowed you to come and go as you please during this past week because you're Rory's family and he loves you, but make no mistake. This is my house, too. If you want to cross that front porch, you'd better leave your meddling intentions outside the door."

Aurora bristled up like a threatened she-cat. Her

golden eyes all but shot flames. Instead of backing down before that warning, she took a step closer, making her son's wife aware of her perilous balance atop that high step.

"Don't you dare draw lines for me. You may have fooled Rory and Scott and even my husband into thinking you're some kind of saint, but I'm not fooled. I know what you are. I know what moves a woman like you. You're here to strip him of everything he has, just like before, and I won't allow it. Now, let me give you a word or two of caution. Rory isn't stupid. He may love you, but he'll figure you out sooner or later. Then you'll be the one tossed off the porch. And when you go, Jacob will be staying here. Think about that, Norah Denby, and think hard before you hurt my son."

Norah stumbled when Aurora released her. Her slippered foot slid on the step; and, for a second, her balance wavered. Then, it was her mother-in-law's anchoring grasp that steadied her. As Norah stood, trembling with restrained emotion, Aurora gave her a cool disdainful stare.

"Why don't you sit with your husband? I'll go down and tell Ruth to prepare an extra plate for dinner." With that, Aurora Prescott descended the stairs with a starchy grace.

She was breathing in short, hissing snatches. For a long moment, Norah couldn't move. How dare the woman! How dare she level such threats! That was it! Visiting hours were over for the Prescott clan. And if Rory wouldn't back her, she'd hold them off on the front steps with her carbine if she had to.

Her self-righteous march down the hall was pulled up short by the soft sound of weeping from the bedroom. Gena? Not meaning to, she drew closer, quieting her step. She didn't want to intrude on something private, yet her own disturbing thoughts cajoled her into listening to the conversation.

"Gena-honey, doan carry on so." That was Rory's crooning whisper. The caressing sound of it brought a tension surging through her veins. "He loves you. He ain't gonna do nothing crazy."

"But what if he suspects this baby—"

"Gena, a man'd be crazy not to want a whole passel of kids underfoot. Scotty ain't no different. He's gonna love this baby just like he loves Dawn."

"But, Rory, if he thought for a minute—"

"Why you worrying? He ain't gonna think no such thing."

"He already has." There was a small silence. "He wants to take us to Washington."

Rory's breath drew sharp and loud. "What?"

"The Office of Indian Affairs has asked him to take a job there. They've increased their number of employees over twofold, and they want him among them. Oh, Rory, what am I going to do?"

"Well, you ain't going! Nossir. I ain't gonna let him move you all the way cross-country. He ain't gonna take everything I love away from me."

Norah reeled from the doorway. No! There had to be some other meaning to the words she'd overheard. Gena's baby. . . . No, it couldn't be. She wouldn't believe it, yet the suspicion was already there. A child created in Scott's absence. Rory's angry words echoed. *He ain't gonna take everything I love away from me.* What other interpretation could there be?

Did he want her to stay just to cover up his dangerous dalliance with his brother's wife? Was that why after three years he was still willing to let her come back into his house without conditions? Why he hadn't pried into her life in Baltimore and had allowed her to continue seeing Trevor? Because

311

it didn't matter? She knew all about using and being used. She'd been both victim and schemer in that heartless game. But Rory. . . . Wasn't that why she'd been so drawn to him—because she was so sure he'd never be less than honest with her? And hadn't he been keeping things from her since the day they'd said 'I do'? Was he just using her now for the pleasures of her body and the presence of his son? Why else would he want her, a woman who'd left him, a woman who he was sure had betrayed their vows, a woman who couldn't give him what he wanted most—unconditional love, trust, and more children? Things Gena Prescott could provide.

And in the hardened, desperately clever turns of her mind, it was so perfect this twisted plan of deception. It was the kind of thing Cole Denby might have applauded. It was the kind of thing she might have considered in her early years, before she meet a sweet, redheaded cowboy and put such schemes behind her. How incredibly cruel and fitting that fate would strike her down with such an irony.

It was the sound of Aurora's footfalls on the stairs that galvanized her into motion. Unable to face another confrontation in her state of agitation, she escaped along the quickest route, ducking into Jacob's room where he was stretched out on his belly doing his schoolwork. With a composing breath, she crossed over and sat beside him.

"How's it coming?" She touched the softness of his hair and fought the overwhelming urge to crush him close as Aurora's threat whispered through her.

"I'd rather be spending time with Ghost; but if I'm going to help Daddy with his books, I've got to work on my ciphering."

So he and the Bar K can start using you, too.

She did hug him then, leaning over to put her arms

about his narrow shoulders to clutch him tight.

"Mama! You're squishing me!"

Dear Lord, how like his father he sounded with that petulant growl of independence. How soon before he'd stop needing her? She sat back, choking on the emotion wadding up in her throat. "Do you mind if I just watch awhile—if I promise not to do any more squishing?"

He looked around and grinned that cheeky Prescott grin. "I don't mind. And I don't really mind the squishing, either."

Smiling to stem the advent of tears, she settled on her elbows and let her mood calm as he did his figuring.

Eventually, Aurora and Gena left and with them, her sense of being imprisoned. Norah issued her son a stern order to see to his hands and a change of clothes before dinner as she stepped out into the hall.

"Norah?"

She froze up solid.

"Norah. Hey!"

Inhaling slowly, she starched up her resolve and began to walk toward the stairs, moving past his door without glancing in.

"Norah? Didn't you hear me?"

Who couldn't hear him, with that impatient bellowing? She went determinedly down the steps to the sound of his string of muttered curses. Let him stew and plead and spout obscenities. Nothing was going to coax her back into that room in her present state. Not when she didn't know whether she'd rather cut out his heart or collapse in desolate tears.

Rory stared at his dinner nicely laid out on a tray delivered up by Ruth and now sitting as cold as the knot in his stomach. It looked good; it smelled good and was probably what they'd dined on below, but he couldn't force a forkful to save his life. Because there was another man downstairs sitting at the head of his table.

He scowled at that sickbed tray, getting angrier by the second, wondering what they were talking about over their fancy sour wine. Goddammit, there better not be any candles lit! Knowing Jacob was down there between them was the only thing tethering his sanity. And then he heard the boy come upstairs.

"G'night, Daddy."

"Awful early to be turning in, isn't it?" he called to his son, hopefully. "Thought you'd want to stay downstairs and keep your mama and her friend company."

"Naw. They're talking grown-up stuff, and I'd rather read than sit in the middle of that."

Rory gritted his teeth behind his smile. "What kinda stuff they talking about?"

"Oh, you know," was the maddeningly vague reply.

No, he didn't know. And he wanted to. Badly.

Jacob noticed his tray. "Aren't you hungry? You want to have Ruth send up something else?"

The boy's concern softened his mood for the moment, and his smile eased. "I'm awright. I'll just piece on it after a while. You go on to bed. I'll see you in the morning."

Jacob paused, then he came into the room to give his father a quick hug. Rory grabbed onto him with the same squeezing desperation his mother had shown earlier. A sense of alarm began to simmer inside the child. "I could keep you company for a while, if you like."

"Thanks, pard, but I ain't much in the mood for it."

"I'm not in the mood."

"What? Oh, yeah." He grinned wanly. "Get on outta here before I give you a swift kick."

"G'night."

"G'night, son."

As the silence settled once more, so did Rory's disagreeable mood. He glared at the tray. Idly, he picked up his fork and drew in his potatoes, making increasingly agitated patterns. Then the fork went sailing out into the hall, clattering against the floorboards in a rebound off the wall. It made such a satisfying sound, he followed it with his knife and his spoon and finally he sent the whole dang tray flying.

After the incredible din quieted, he waited, expecting to hear footsteps on the stairs. Nothing. Well, hell, he could have fallen out the damned window and nobody would have even bothered to check. What had them so preoccupied that they couldn't spare a second to see if he'd broken his fool neck?

It was about time he found out for himself.

"What's wrong, Norah? Please don't try to deny it. I've watched you try to keep from crying all evening long."

How good it felt to sag into the warmth of his embrace, to feel the tenderness of his care as he held her close and stroked her trembling shoulders. It had been a nightmare, trying to pretend because of Jacob. But now that need was over. Trevor would understand, and Norah wanted badly to unburden the twisting pain from her heart. Was it loyalty or shame that kept her silent?

He didn't pressure her for an answer. He let her sob quietly into his elegant shirt front as they sat side by side on the parlor sofa. Then, very gently, he asked, "When are you going to stop letting him hurt you? Norah, when are we going home?"

"Trevor, please don't . . ."

"But, my darling, how can I sit silent and watch what he's doing to you? He's changing you into someone I don't know. I cannot bear to see the pain he's put you through. I realize you still hold a place for him in your heart; but, Norah, you must face facts. The man is never going to change what he is, and he's going to make Jacob over in his image. Is that what you want? Do you want to watch him take that bright little boy's future and drag it through despair?"

"W-what are you talking about, Trevor?" Protective instincts brought her out of his arms to demand an answer.

"Is this the legacy you want for your child?"

"The Bar K is—"

"Broke. I'm sorry. There's no other way to put it. Your husband has this place drowning in debt. He's going to drag you and your son down with it."

Norah sat very still, absorbing this. "How do you know?" *She* didn't even know for sure.

Trevor squared his shoulders defiantly. "I had Carter do some checking."

"You what?"

No look of apology crossed his handsome features. "For you. I was concerned for you and Jacob."

"And what did you find?"

"Your husband holds thousands of acres he won't be able to maintain through another year. He has no credit left and no way to pay his debt. Unless he sells."

"Sells . . ."

"I didn't want to make this difficult for you. I'm

sorry to bring the truth to you this way."

"No." Norah began to rally, her spine stiffening, her jaw firming. "No, I need to hear the truth. Finally. From someone. How bad is it?"

"If something isn't done within the next few months, he'll lose everything. Even the house."

Her eyes squeezed shut. *Oh, Rory, why didn't you tell me?*

"He'll be ruined. Unless—"

"Unless what?" Norah snapped at that. Her heart swelled for the prideful cowboy. As angry as she was, she never would wish such hurt upon him.

"Because you care for him, I could use my resources. My father is looking for prime land in the Dakotas. I could arrange for him to make a very, very generous offer. It would be enough to guarantee him—and you—a comfortable life. If the man is of reasonable intelligence and wants to see his family provided for, he'll take the offer. If he waits, he'll lose it all and have nothing to start over with."

Nothing. Norah chilled. She'd had nothing before. She'd lived that life of spiritless poverty. She'd been forced out of sheer desperation into an existence of shame. She'd survived out of cunning and cold determination . . . until a young, painfully naive cowboy swept her from it and gave her dignity again.

He would never survive it. Not like she had. Rory had too much pride. And Jacob, how could she allow him to suffer needlessly? It would be needless when the solution was so clear. Sentiment was fine, but it didn't provide a roof or a meal or allow the soul esteem. Pride was fine when it didn't overshadow reality. She'd lived with harsh realities all her life, and honor had no place among them.

"I'll tell him," she said with a quiet strength.

"And if he refuses?"

Norah swallowed down that terrible fright. "If he refuses, then I have no reason to stay here."

Trevor tried not to show his delight too blatantly. Carter was a genius. He'd said it was a perfect plan. He'd assured him that a man of Prescott's monumental arrogance would not buckle. And that was what he counted on.

"And when you return to Baltimore? What then?" He'd drawn closer, his gaze searching hers, hopefully, encouragingly.

"Then I have a life to start over with my son."

"As Mrs. Trevor Samuels?"

Norah looked at him with candid speculation. And softly, she said, "Yes."

Muttering fiercely, Rory hobbled across his room to grab up a pair of denims and a shirt. Serve 'em right if he stomped down there in his longjohns, but it was somewhat lacking in dignity. He dropped back down on the edge of the bed to dress, then cast about for footgear. He couldn't go unshod. His boots were standing next to Norah's trunk. His eyes narrowed as they touched on that latched and mocking piece of luggage. Then he stuffed his foot into the right one and picked up the left. Or what was left of it. Hell, if it had been good enough for the grizzly, it was good enough for his wife's visitor. Let 'em both choke on it. He pushed his foot inside the tattered leather and nearly forgot his temper as pain exploded upward. He leaned on his knees, panting, waiting for it to simmer down to a manageable level. Time to go say a polite howdy.

Halfway down the stairs, he began to doubt the wisdom of his plan. It hurt so bad he was ready to sit himself down on the step and just wait there until someone came along to haul him back to bed. But remembering the cool snub of Norah's mood was just the stiffening he needed. He would not be ignored in his own house!

He paused in the hallway to catch his breath, then ambled as casually as he could into the dining room. To find it empty. Scowling because he had to walk farther when his whole leg felt as if it were on fire, he limped down the hall, listening for voices. Not hearing any. A light shined dimly from inside the parlor, and he headed for it with an ill-tempered frown. Not much talking going on for two people supposedly discussing grown-up things. Then his thoughts drifted further to other grown-up things that didn't require words.

The doors were almost completely closed with just a goading strip of light shining between them. He stared at that ribbon of light for a long moment, then reached for the gunbelt he kept hanging off the front coatrack, checking the loads. Didn't hurt to be prepared.

Then he shoved the door open.

Trevor's embrace was enthusiastic. His confidence shook Norah to the soul. Was she being foolish, then, to hope things could yet work out here in the Dakotas? Was she the only one who saw a chance? Trevor seemed so certain things would work in his favor, that he would have her for his wife. But he couldn't know that Rory would spurn the buy-out offer. He didn't know Rory like she did.

And then the truth settled deep. He probably knew Rory very well. Anyone with eyes to see could tell that he wouldn't give up the Bar K. She knew it. She knew in her mind even as her heart decried it. She knew she'd be leaving him for Baltimore and Trevor Samuels. There was no joy in that knowledge, just a deep sense of loss. And a deeper resentment simmered.

She pulled from Trevor's arms to regard him carefully. Was this the man she'd be wed to for the rest of her life? Would he be sharing her bed, her dreams, her son? She felt no great resistance to the idea. Trevor was a fine man, kind and generous with his affection. But was he a man who could give her the delights of marriage as well as the security of his name? She owed it to herself to find out. Could he ease the pain of what would ache forever in her heart? Could he slake her desire for the redheaded lover she'd be leaving behind?

She leaned forward; and, with just a second of hesitation, he responded with a kiss. A warm, giving kiss. Very nice, very sweet, very easy to break away from. He would have to do better than that. Norah took his face between her hands, forcing his mouth open with the aggressiveness of her own. She could feel his shock as her tongue invaded with a claiming boldness. Hadn't he ever had a real kiss before?

Suddenly, it became very important for her to prove to herself that she could respond to a man other than Rory Prescott. Prodding her, was the mental picture of Rory with the lovely Gena in his arms. If their vows meant so little to him, why should *she* keep them sacred?

Purposefully, she leaned back against the rolled arm of the sofa. Trevor followed her down, beginning to take some initiative on his own. But the more he warmed, the cooler she became. It wasn't right. It wasn't the same. His kisses inspired nothing but cold despair. And panic. She wanted to push him away, to brush the feel of him off her as if it were something

320

dirty and unpleasant. She wanted to cry out that the only man she wanted was upstairs, but the words didn't come. Because the man upstairs didn't want her as a wife, not the way Trevor did.

Determinedly, she took his hands, lifting them, positioning them just above the curve of her breasts. She would get used to his touch. She'd have to.

And then they heard a grating click.

The unmistakable greeting of a Colt .45.

"You move them hands so much as an inch, and you'll be picking up your tableware between your toes."

Chapter Twenty

"Git off my wife!"

Trevor sat up, going deathly pale at the sight of that single bore staring him between the eyes. More frightening was the dark emotionless void of Rory Prescott's glare. It was the look of a man who could easily squeeze off a killing shot.

"It's not what you—"

"No? Hell, Mister, do I look blind? I may be lame, but there ain't the slightest thing wrong with my eyesight. Git up."

Trevor scrambled to his feet shakily. Nothing like this had ever happened to him before. The threat of violence was so thick he could taste it in the back of his throat—the harsh, metallic flavor of fear. It wasn't until he heard the rustle of Norah's gown behind him that he thought of something beyond his own brutally quick demise.

"This isn't her fault—"

"No? No, a course not. Why, what would she know about seducing a man? My Norah, she's as pure a heart as an angel. Ain't that right, honey?" The sneer of his drawl sounded ugly. Its nastiness woke a gallant defense in the Easterner.

"There's no need to take such an insulting tone—"

"You shut up!"

Softly, Norah's hand touched Trevor's arm. "No, it's all right, Trevor. He has every right to speak that way." She stood, facing down her husband with a cool, unnerving gaze. And for a moment, Rory almost weakened under it. Then his eyes narrowed fiercely.

"When I allow a man to sit at my table, I ain't inviting him to help himself to anything but dinner. Git outta my house."

"Trevor is my guest," Norah challenged with a steely quiet.

Rory pulled a slow, steadying breath. Trevor was able to breathe much easier when the pistol in Rory's hand lowered and the hammer eased down. The dark, angry eyes pinned his for a long, hard minute before the rancher said again, "Git out. You can take that whore with you, if you want; but that's all you're taking." Then he turned and stalked from the room.

"Come with me," Trevor urged. "I won't leave you here with him."

His prompting broke through her haze of shock. A cold fury began to seep outward in its place. *How dare he! How dare he dismiss her so callously! As if he were through with her. As if he didn't care.*

What if that were true?

"No. You go, Trevor." She shook off his protest. "Rory would never harm me. Not ever."

"He looked pretty dangerous to me. I don't like this, Norah. Are you sure you'll be all right?"

"Yes, of course. Besides, I would never leave Jacob."

"I'll come by in the morning. Just to make sure you're all right."

She nodded distractedly, and then gave a start of

surprise when he leaned down to kiss her. She'd never felt less responsive to anything in all her life. "I'm sorry, Trevor."

"I'm not," he stated grimly. "Now maybe you'll see how hopeless this sham of your marriage is."

He withdrew with a stately dignity—after first peeking out into the hall to make sure Rory Prescott wasn't lurking there ready to make a target of him. Coat and hat in place, he climbed aboard his buggy and headed for the safety of Crowe Creek, determined that on the next day he'd be taking Norah and her son back with him.

Rory heard the buggy whir out of his yard, but he didn't halt his laborious journey down to the barn. He couldn't go back up to the house with his insides churning from smooth cream to clotted butter. He needed to think. He needed to protect against the awful urgings of manly pride that made him say such cutting things to the woman he loved. And he needed to prepare for the inevitability of her leaving.

"Hey, Bud. Whoa, girl. Mind keeping me company or are you gonna get all snappish, too?"

The little mare nickered softly and nudged against his chest in affectionate welcome. He smiled unhappily and took up a brush to groom her pinkish hide. After repeating the motion with a soothing regularity, his mood quieted.

"I doan understand her, Bud. If she doan want me, why doesn't she just go?"

"I do want you."

He didn't turn, but the brush strokes faltered, then continued with a faster rhythm.

"I've never wanted anyone but you." She moved

324

up behind him, placing a hand along the curve of his shoulder. His flesh jerked beneath it like the rejecting twitch of his mare's skin.

"Sure had me fooled." The brush strokes grew crisp and sharp. "That little scene I walked in on in the parlor, what was that?"

She didn't explain, and his anger swelled up to choke off reason. His emotions gave a hurtful jump when her palms rubbed up beneath his coat, shifting the fabric of his shirt up and down along his rigid spine.

"Rory." There was sweet temptation in the way she said his name. Soft, sweet music underscored by the seducing knead of her hands over firm, denim-clad flanks. The brush made a startling clatter as he pitched it into a bucket. Rosebud snorted, and Norah gave a shallow gasp as he turned to seize her up against him.

"Whatcha come down here for? Whatcha want from me, Norah? Is it this?" He grasped at her hips, dragging them roughly into his own. "You come chasing down here after me 'cause your fancy feller done got you all het up and then left your hanging so you figured I'd just finish for him? That what you figured?"

"Rory—"

He bumped her hard, back into the slatted boards of the stall, and pressed up against her. His expression was dark and menacing but was offset by the shimmer of anguish in his eyes. "Oh, honey, doan you worry. I'll give you what you want."

"Rory, please, don't—"

"Don't? Doan what? Shame you?" His laugh was grating. "Honey, you ain't got no shame. Never did. Not with me, not with any man who could get himself up under your skirts. How'd you get by for

325

three long years without me? Betcha did jus' fine, didn'tcha? Who you been bedding? Who you been lying to? Hmmm? None as plain-as-mud-stupid as me, I bet. None fool enough to fall in love with you."

His hand came up to tangle in her hair, twisting, yanking back to bow her neck. He let his mouth trail damply along that taut curve until she quivered and arched toward him. Then, just as abruptly, he stepped away. His fingers hooked on the neckline of her gown, jerked her out of the stall, and swung her around so that when he let go she tumbled back upon a mound of fresh straw. He stood towering over her, his dark stare raking mercilessly over the sight she made, sprawled with skirt pushed up above her knees, bosom rocking with a frantic motion, eyes silvery and wet with tears. Her upward glare was remorseless. There was no fear in her eyes nor did she make any attempt to escape him. If she'd shown just a hint, just a trace of regret or alarm, he would have backed off immediately. But her cool defiance refused tender feelings or contrition. It demanded retaliation. He reached for the band of his jeans.

"Open up for me, honey. Time you got what you came for." He kicked her knees apart and dropped between them, pushing her gown up to her belly. She didn't resist. His hand moved roughly over her sex, then stabbed inside the slick heat of her body. "This just for me or were you all ready and rearing to welcome him the same way?"

Angered further by her lack of response, he withdrew that provoking touch and caught the bodice of her gown. It came apart with one wrench of his hand, exposing the soft pale swells.

"This what you were offering him, honey? Something to brag on, that's for sure." His fingertips spread wide to encompass one generous globe. It wasn't a gentle caress, but neither did it hurt her. Even in his rage of temper, he was careful not to hurt her. His breathing seethed. Pain beat up fiercely from his foot and from the constriction of his heart. What would it take to get a reaction from her? One that was honest. One he could believe. Her composure was goading him to madness. Didn't she hurt? Didn't she care? Or was she everything he accused her of being?

"Let's see if you can think of him while I'm up inside you."

His hands scooped under her buttocks, lifting her so that when he settled in, it was deep and sure and she'd have no question of who'd come calling. At his first powerful thrust, she made an uninhibited sound of pleasure. Her long legs wrapped about his waist, pulling him deeper into that hot valley between her thighs. And he forgot everything, all his anger, all his pain. Damn but this was honest. Her hands were frantic as they tore at him, sinking into his hair, wrestling his head down so she could take his mouth aggressively. Their tongues touched, then he was groaning, kissing her wildly. His need had become a savage desperation.

And then she did the unforgiveable.

Her hungry little mouth slipped away from his, and she whispered breathlessly. "Oh, Rory, I love you so much. There's never been anyone but you."

His eyes opened. He lay on top of her, wedged inside her frantically eager body, and remembrance cut him cold. If she loved him, why had she been encouraging Trevor Samuels on his sofa? Why had she been kissing him with the same passionate abandon? She lusted for him, that much he knew. But love him?

And why hadn't she unpacked that trunk?

He drove into her hard, letting himself lose control

in a shattering burst. And then he pulled away while she lay panting in an unsatisfied frenzy. Even as she reached for him, he tottered up, grabbing onto the stall for balance. In a voice as uncharitable as the November snows, he told her, "Now, honey, you just think on all that you'll be missing," and he walked away.

Norah lay panting, the feel of him still impressed upon her and within her, branding her as his. Jerking down her skirts and gathering close her tattered emotions—as well as her bodice, she wobbled up from the bed of straw. He couldn't have found a better way to prove his point. To have beaten her would have been kinder. At least physical violence wouldn't have intruded upon the areas of their relationship she'd always been able to treasure. *You belong to me,* that rough possession claimed with a selfish arrogance. *Mine to use and abuse as I please.* And that sentiment left her shattered.

She left the sheltered warmth of the barn, glancing quickly about the snowy yard. No sign of Rory. He couldn't have gotten to the house so quickly. He must have detoured to the bunkhouse for a bolstering drink and a little rawhide companionship. Just as well. She didn't want to see him . . . not now. She floundered up through the bitter cold and seeping wetness, feeling neither. Feeling nothing beyond the incredible brunt of pain.

He'd called her a whore and he'd taken her like one.

In the eight years they'd been married, through all the sacrifices and struggles, through all the long, satisfying nights and tender kisses, he'd never gotten over what she'd been. What's done is done, he'd told her. It doesn't matter, he'd vowed. And he'd married her, never having had the time to come to terms with the truth. A truth that had simmered in the back of his mind since the day he'd discovered that she and her partner, Cole Denby, were wanted in a half-dozen states for fraud. Though she'd never plied a horizontal trade—not like her mother, she'd used sex to get what she wanted from men. She'd lied; she'd cheated; and she'd stolen, all without remorse. Because it was better than starving, because she was too smart to spend the rest of her life on her back, letting indifferent men take from her. She'd gladly put all that behind her when she met Rory Prescott.

But obviously, he hadn't been able to.

She reached the front porch and stumbled into the hall. Her first thought was to run for the stairs, to hide in her bed and weep until the anguish lessened. But colder, clearer logic told her the pain wouldn't wash away with tears. Nor was it something she could hide from—not behind a closed door, not on a train to Baltimore. It had to be faced head-on, now. And, by God, she was tired of apologizing.

Casting off her snowy coat, Norah marched straight into Rory's study, right up to his desk, to its locked drawer. She looked about impatiently then seized up the first object her gaze settled upon. Jamming the letter opener into the gap between drawer and hard wood, she broke the lock and yanked open all Rory Prescott's secrets.

"Let's see what you've been keeping from me," she muttered, dropping down into his chair.

It didn't help and it didn't last. Not the whiskey, not the good-timing company of his crew, not the self-righteous fury. Under it all were two basic facts: His leg hurt like a son of a bitch and he'd acted like one.

He tried to soothe his battered spirit among things familiar and accepting, things as uncomplicated as a straight shot of rye and a straight flush. But in the back of his mind, he kept hearing her words, whispered in a moment of exquisite passion. *I love you so much. There's never been anyone but you.* Was he a damn fool for still wanting to believe it? Even after having the proof of her infidelity crammed down his throat?

He'd been right to be angry. He'd made her his wife, and she had no right to shame him as she'd done with Trevor Samuels. But he was her husband, which meant she was deserving of his respect. He'd shown her damned little of that. And he was sorry. Sorry enough to fold a winning hand and toss down one last warming whiskey to the regret and chidings of his friends, who wished him a cheerful good night. Bracing his shoulders and gritting his teeth, he hobbled up to the house, ready to do the required humbling.

Catching sight of a light burning down the hall kept him from making a futile climb up the stairs. Why would she be in his study? Unless she'd left the light on to direct him to his sleeping quarters for the night. Glumly, he limped down that long ribbon of carpet and peered around the door. At first, he thought the room was empty, and the decanter behind his desk looked like just the thing to ease the gnawing pain in his foot. But as he rounded the edge of it, he caught sight of the opened drawer and the splintered lock and he paused, not knowing what to make of it.

"Looking for these?"

A quick, graceful turn was out of the question. He grabbed onto the edge of the desk and hopped awkwardly around. Norah was sitting on his leather sofa, her features concealed by heavy shadow. But there was enough light for him to see the ruin he'd made out of the neckline of her gown and to recognize the papers spread out across her knees.

"When were you planning to tell me? When they came to cart the furniture away?"

A quick offense was his only defense. "You had no right—"

"No right?" Her voice slashed through that feeble protest. "I have every right in the world! Did you think I wouldn't find out? Did you think I wouldn't want to know that you were hanging onto this ranch by your fingernails and a prayer? How were you going to pay these bills, Rory? How were you planning to get through the winter? On lies and stubbornness?"

"I was taking care of things." He said that very softly.

"How? You're broke. You've got nothing in the bank and nothing to get by on but pride."

"What the hell do you care? You've got your future all snug and secure. Why should you give a damn about how I'll get by?"

"You don't get it, do you? You just don't get it! This is my home, too. Not just your grandfather's ranch. Not just a promise you'd kill yourself to keep. You want me to stay? Then, by God, I mean to have a say in how this place is run."

"You want to be bossman and run the whole show, that it, Norah?" His drawl was dangerously quiet. But instead of treading gently around his prickled pride, she stomped right over it.

"No. I expect *you* to take care of it. And I expect you to be *man* enough to ask for help when you need it." She surged to her feet, sending the stack of debts cascading to the floor. "I expect you to have the decency to tell me what's going on and be smart enough to listen to my opinion. I have the money it takes to keep this ranch going. Why can't you put aside your monumental arrogance long enough to see that I want to help you? This is my future, too, mine and Jacob's; and I have a right to do what I can to salvage it. I am not going to sit back on my thumbs and watch you turn into Garth Kincaid."

"You gonna see to that, are you? You gonna put a bullet in my head like you did his?"

His words were incredible enough, but the pain behind them was crippling. Norah faltered, confused. "What are you talking about?"

A long-festering emotional wound tore open, and it was filled with more poisons than had threatened his leg. "I'm talking about you and Cole Denby. I'm talking about how the two of you stripped him of his pride and stole everything he loved out from under him. Even me." His angry voice broke and grated harshly. "I'm talking about how you left him with nothing, not even the will to go on living. You might as well have had your hand on the trigger when he blew his brains out."

"He shot himself?" she whispered in horror. "I didn't know. I thought it was the fire—"

"It was your greed! Your lies! You and Denby killed him. This is all you left behind." He grabbed up the twist of charred wire, shaking it in his fist. "You let that man suck the life out of the Bar K, and then you have the gall—the goddamn gall—to ask me to go crawling to him for the money he made off my grandfather's grave!"

Norah stood frozen. Where had all this fury come from? Where had he hidden it for eight long years while professing to love her? He blamed her. He had never forgiven her. He'd married her, believing in his heart all the ugly things he was shouting at her. How was she ever going to get over that, the knowledge that he held her responsible?

But he wasn't through. "You just can't help shoving it down my throat, can you?" That coldly furious mood fractured and he mourned softly, "I've worked and slaved to make a home for you and Jacob, but it was never good enough for you. You couldn't be happy with what I could give you. You just couldn't wait. You built this house to spite me; you paid that note to shame me, and now you want me to sell my soul to keep you. I won't. I won't, Norah."

She was shaking hard, inside and out. Though her mind was telling her there was no way to uproot the pain planted long ago between them, her heart begged her to try. It urged her with an achy fullness to do anything she could to stay close to this man she'd pinned her future to over a heap of smoldering dreams. Her eyes were swimming with tears when she told him, "Rory, please. You have to let go. You can't hold out against the world forever. Just like your grandfather couldn't. His lies killed him—and his greed. Bury him, Rory, and move on. You have me and Jacob. Let us in. Let us help you. We love you. Don't push us away. If you won't take the money, at least save us something to start over with. You can't afford to keep the Major's dream alive. Here." She thrust a paper at him, and he stared at it warily for a long moment before reaching out and taking it from her hand. He looked at Trevor Samuels's offer, and she could see her future crumbling as his features hardened into unyielding angles.

"He's offered to do that as a favor to me. Not because he wants the land, but because he cares about me and Jacob. Do you? Take it, Rory. Take it and we can start over, the three of us. We can build up together."

"And what are we gonna do when you run outta old lovers to bail us out? Or is there a chance of that ever happening?"

Her patience snapped. Desperation made her words into a fierce ultimatum. "Stop it, Rory! Is your pride more important than your family? Is hanging onto the past more important than moving on to a future? Let it go! If you love me, let it go! Either take the money or take the offer. I can't stand by and watch you ruin your life, and I won't let you take Jacob down with you. If you don't love me enough to salvage what we have, then you're going down alone. I won't be here. And I won't be taking your name with me when Jacob and I leave. Do you hear me? All I've ever wanted was you, not this land, not your dead grandfather's dream. You decide what it is you want, Rory. And you decide tonight. Trevor's coming by tomorrow. If you don't want me, I'll be leaving with him."

While he stood, staring stonily ahead, Norah swept from the room and finally gave in to weeping as she rushed up the stairs.

"You look like a man who's had a rough night."

"Heya, Scotty." Rory looked up from his littered desktop and dredged up a smile for his brother. "Grab a seat. Can I get you something to drink?"

Dark brows rose in a smooth question. "It's seven o'clock in the morning. Kind of early, isn't it?"

Rory's smile took a wry bend. "Not for coffee strong enough to float a horseshoe. 'Bout all that's keepin' me going. You got that knife with you?"

"Why? You have to slice it out of the pot?" he asked, drawing the big blade.

"Naw. I need you to cut this off for me." He

brought his bad leg up, propping it on the corner of the desk. "Doan worry 'bout being gentle. It's killin' me."

Scott stared at his foot.

"Go on, Scotty. It's all swoll up in there, and I cain't muster the grit to give it a good yank. Cain't feel my toes."

"You want me to cut off—"

"My boot. What'd you think I was talking about?" He gave his brother a curious look. "Sometimes I purely wonder about you."

Appearing absurdly relieved, Scott gripped the mangled piece of boot leather and ripped through it with his blade. Behind him, Rory groaned and panted harshly, then gave an unrestrained sigh as the footgear was peeled away.

"That's better."

"It's not going to get better unless you stay off it," Scott warned, giving the toes a gentle massage. "I went through too much trouble to see you could wear a matched pair of boots. Don't make it a waste of my time."

"Yes, Mama."

Scott gave the sole of his foot a sharp slap and resumed his seat as Rory babied it with a pained glower. "You want to go hobbling around like a fool, I'll bring you over a pair of moccasins. They'll go easier on you."

"That'd be right kind of you, Big Brother." Gingerly, he lowered his foot and then poured them both a cup of steaming coffee. While he nursed his, he was aware of Scott's scrutiny. "Haven't seen much of you. Gena keeping you close to home?"

Scott gave a regretful snort. "I wish I could be there long enough to complain about it. I've been back and forth between the Cheyenne and town making talk with Samuels over the lands bill."

"That feller's got his fingers into everythin', don't he?" Rory drawled out in such a way that his brother's look intensified. After taking a minute to sip his coffee, the redhead canted up a nonchalant glance. "Whatcha think a him, Scotty?"

Scott leaned back with a thoughtful frown. "I'm not sure. He talks a good line. He seems sincere, but that doesn't mean anything. I've listened to a lot of smooth-talkers and no-doers. Haven't got a fix on him yet. Do know he's got strong political backing and an expensive campaign building up in the East. If he's a man of his word, he could get things done. If he's a puppet to his father, he's no good out here. What opinion does Norah hold of him?"

Rory studied his brother's impassive face, wondering what he knew. "Now that's a kinda touchy subject. Lemme jus' say she's got enough faith in him to cast a vote in his favor."

"Norah's a smart woman."

"Ummmm." Rory followed that noncommittal sound with a moment of restless fiddling with the papers in front of him. Scott waited patiently. "Scotty, I was wondering if you'd handle something for me, legal-like, I mean."

"I'm expensive."

Rory smiled. "But you're the best and I trust you. And you're the only one I know that'll take barter for a fee."

"Oh? And what do you have that I might want?"

"A whole lot of meals on the hoof for your daddy's relatives, if you're interested."

He was. And he was alerted by his brother's sudden quiet. "Rory, what are you planning?"

"I was thinking of sellin' the Bar K."

"You were thinking of—" Scott couldn't finish.

He'd been less surprised when Rory had asked him to cut his throat. He frowned. "You'd better start talking and making a hell of a lot more sense."

"I got debts up to my eyeballs, Scotty, and I can't see my way clear to pay 'em."

"If you needed money—"

"Hell, you ain't got no money. And what Daddy's got, he worked hard to earn. I can't go asking him to sink it down a hole that's got no bottom. It jus' ain't worth the trouble a hanging on no more."

Scott's eyes narrowed. "I don't believe you."

"I ain't askin' you to believe me. I'm askin' you to help me sell out so's I can—"

"What? So you can what? What else do you know how to do?"

Rory put his hands over his tired eyes, rubbing slowly. "I doan know."

"Rory, have you thought this out at all? What else have you ever wanted in your entire life except this place?"

He didn't answer He didn't have to. Scott saw it plain in the eloquence of his gaze.

"It's Norah. Is she making you sell? I can't believe she'd do that. Has she got any idea of what she's asking?"

"Doan lecture me, Scotty! I doan want to hear it. Not unless you want to tell me why you've all of a sudden decided to move to Washington."

Scott's jaw gripped tight.

"Didn't think so. Maybe it's time we all moved on to something else. I been up all night a-thinking on this. I'm tired. I'm mad as hell and scared spitless. My foot's hurtin' so bad I'm 'bout ready to tear it off with my teeth. All I want to know is if you're gonna help me. 'Cause if you ain't, I'll—"

Scott's bronze-colored hand settled over his knee.

337

His voice was quiet and firm. "Whatever you need."

Rory's breath expelled in a whoosh. The tense line of his shoulders collapsed. "I'm obliged."

Scott sat silent for a minute, trying to assimilate everything. Rory was serious. He really meant to sell. With a resigned sigh, he asked, "Do you have a buyer?"

Rory pushed the slip of paper at him. "Samuels has mentioned a right reasonable figure. I thought— What's a matter, Scotty?"

"Samuels?"

"That's right."

"But I thought you were set against selling to M.S. Consolidated because they wanted to chew everything up into little pieces."

"Still am. What you gettin' at?"

"M.S. stands for Martin Samuels, Trevor's father. He's been after this particular chunk of the Dakotas for a long time. Are you sure you want to give it to him?"

"But Norah said—" He stopped the words cold. Norah said Trevor was making the offer as a favor to her. But that was a lie. Samuels had been after the property for months, long before Norah came back to him . . . and insisted that he sell. Had they thought to get his grasslands if the motive was sweetened up just right? And just what was Norah Denby Prescott getting out of it?

Piece by piece, a very ugly picture arranged itself for his study.

Chapter Twenty-one

Norah spent a restless morning excluded from the doings behind her husband's study doors. She knew Scott was with him. She'd seen him briefly when Dawn had ridden over to spend some time with Jacob. He'd spoken to his daughter in a terse Lakota, and solemnly the child had nodded then had asked her if Jacob could spend the day at the Lone Star. Not sure why that request made her so apprehensive, she'd agreed. Scott hadn't spared her any sign of acknowledgment, just a bland stare before he closed the study doors behind him.

What were they doing?

What required all the secrecy of a war council between the two Prescott brothers?

Had it something to do with the conditions she'd slapped down before Rory the night before? She'd had plenty of time to consider them, herself. She wasn't being unreasonable. What she was, was scared. Rory's condemnation had shaken her to the soul with its unbending ferocity. His words had hurt her just as his deeds had hurt her. But she loved him. She'd borne him a child and had worn his name for eight years. Didn't that deserve one last chance? If he could get beyond the tethers of the past, she could forgive him anything. To start over, clean and fresh, she would live with him in a soddy or, she thought with a wry smile, in skins under the sky. If he would just once put her first, nothing on earth could drag her from his side again. If he cared for her as he once had, before he'd stumbled on the secrets of her past; if he'd meant it when he told her *Just you, only you*, he would make the right choice for all three of them. He just had to.

Because how was she ever going to walk away? If he called her bluff, how was she going to pick up that packed bag and walk out the front door? He had to love her enough not to force her hand.

Then, shortly after a lunch she couldn't eat, Trevor arrived. With him was Carter Clemens. Before they had a chance to do more than exchange cursory greetings, Scott came out of the study wearing his most stoic face.

"What's this all about, Prescott?" Trevor asked curiously. "What kind of talk requires the presence of my lawyer?"

Rory was going to sell. Norah sucked a quick breath. What else could it be? She'd hoped; she'd prayed, but she'd never quite believed until this minute. And relief made her knees so weak she could scarcely follow when Scott asked that they join him in the study. The inscrutable half-Sioux fell in step beside her, his hand pressing just for a second to the small of her back in a gesture of support. Then, without looking at her or speaking, he drew away to precede her into the study.

Rory was seated at his desk, and before it three chairs were arranged as if he were granting an audience. Scott, standing behind his brother, motioned for them to be seated. Norah hesitated. It seemed so distancing, that carefully angled chair. Instinct told her to go stand with Scott at her husband's side, but when she made a move toward him, Rory told her flatly, "Sit down, Norah. This won't take long."

Uneasily, she sank down into the chair. She was watching him closely, studying the hard lines of his face. She could have been looking back ten years into the face of Garth Kincaid. There was that same harsh, borderline ruthless quality in the set of his features, and suddenly she was afraid. It took all her gumption to say at last, "You've decided?"

"Yes." He drawled that out softly. "I've decided to give you what you came for, Norah. I'm having Scotty draw up the papers for our divorce."

"Di-divorce," she stammered blankly.

"Figured since you an' Samuels would be hooking up once this is done, we'd invite his lawyer to sit in so we could make it quick and clean. That all right with you?"

She was in shock. He'd chosen the Bar K. He'd chosen the Bar K! She barely heard his next words through the roar of panic in her ears. She felt Trevor's hand close over hers, and she lacked the strength to throw it off. No! Her heart was pounding. No! This wasn't what she wanted!

"I asked Scotty to draw up some papers; and if we can come to some agreeable terms, there's no reason we can't sign and get it over with."

Norah grabbed for a noisy breath. Her words were fractured. "But I don't want—"

"This ain't about what you want," Rory growled with a sudden rumbling fury. "It's what I want. After what you done . . ." He took a second to regain his control, swallowing hard and turning his narrowed eyes away from the very pale visage of his wife. "Scotty, you get on with the particulars."

Scott wouldn't look at her either. He addressed himself to Trevor and Carter like the polished lawyer he was. "We're fortunate that South Dakota has some of the country's most lenient divorce laws. I don't think there'll be any problem establishing Norah as a resident, not when the right palms are filled. I can see about getting a public trial waived since no one is contesting."

"I am." Norah's objection surprised them all. She couldn't believe Rory would be so incensed about finding her in Trevor's arms that he'd go to such extremes to punish her. Enough. It had been a mistake. A terrible mistake. She had to make him see that. She had to let him know how much this marriage meant to her. "I'll contest it." She tried frantically to catch Rory's gaze, but he wouldn't allow it.

"Why? 'Cause you can't get your hands on the Bar K?"

"The Bar K?" she murmured incomprehensibly.

"I doan want to hear it, Norah. I doan want to hear nothing. I ain't a fool. I let you walk all over me 'cause I loved you and I wanted to believe you could change. I was wrong. I'm making amends for it now."

Loved. She drew a tortured breath and readied to protest.

"No more!" he roared. "No more lies. I want you out of here, today. I want you off my land and outta my life."

"You can't mean—"

Scott spoke up softly, with a silken sobriety. "We

342

could make this very unpleasant."

"Listen to him, Norah," Trevor urged, chafing her hand.

"No—"

Scott's tone hardened as his palms rested on his brother's shoulders. "We can make it very ugly. We could publicize your adulteries; we could legally take control of all the monies in your bank account and any properties you might have and make it impossible for you to remarry. We have incontestable grounds of willful desertion. We could deny your share of guardianship—"

"No!"

That shattered her composure and her pride. She saw again Scott telling Dawn to take her son away—away from her—to the Lone Star where she might never see him again. She heard Aurora's threat and the rumble of Rory's fury. To the Prescotts, family was everything. But to Norah, Jacob was the only thing. He was all she had.

Distraught, Nora flew around the desk before Trevor could catch her. She was on her knees at her husband's feet, wet cheek pressed into one big hand. "No, Rory, please. Please don't try to take Jacob from me. You can't. Please don't take my son." As she sobbed shamelessly upon him, his fingers moved slowly, gently against her cheek. His words were just as soft, for just the two of them to hear.

"Don't, honey. I won't. I won't. You're his mama. He should be with you."

She gave a fragile little cry and wrapped her arms about his neck, hugging fiercely. He didn't move. His arms stayed at his sides. He could feel the hot dampness of her cheek next to his, and his eyes screwed up tight.

"Rory, don't do this. Please. I can explain. I'm sorry. I love you."

He jerked at that last claim, head turning away, body stiffening into unyielding stone beneath her. "Sit down, Norah. Let's just get this done."

"Please—"

Scott took her by the elbows, lifting her up and pulling her away. She leaned into him for a steadying moment and cast up a beseeching look. She thought she saw a softening in his expression, but it was brief and she knew any sympathy he had for her would not best the love he had for his brother. The Prescotts had cut her out of the family.

Weakly, she sagged into her chair, drying her face with the handkerchief Trevor provided. His hand was on her shoulder, rubbing gently, but she hardly felt it. She was looking at the twist of crisped wire on the corner of the big desk, the symbol of how everything good between them had become so distorted. It could never be right again. Because decent men didn't marry whores.

"It would be easier," Carter was saying in his whiny little voice, "if Mrs. Prescott filed. And more socially acceptable."

"Well, hell, that's my main concern," Rory drawled lethally. "Wouldn't want things to look bad when you go politicking, would we?"

"What grounds?" Scott demanded.

Norah stopped feeling sorry for herself. The blame was not all hers. "Adultery," she said very clearly.

Rory's palms slapped down on the desktop. "No. You look around; you ask around. You won't be able to find nobody that'll say I was ever—*ever* untrue to you. When I said my vows, I meant 'em!"

"I wouldn't have to look that far, and you know it!"

"I don't know nothing of a kind! Say it plain, Norah. Who you think I been stepping out with?"

It was on her lips. Temper and pride demanded she speak it. He was foolishly goading her to speak a truth that would destroy his family. She drew a tight-chested breath, trying to steel her indignant resolve. Then she saw the dark bronze of Scott Prescott's fingers where they curved over the cap of his brother's shoulder. And she knew she would say nothing. But she stared at Rory, a straight-on, hard stare that told him though she was protecting him with her silence, she knew the truth. Their gazes were locked for a long, challenging moment, sparked by anger and the hurt of betrayal. And then Rory looked away.

He raised an unsteady hand to pass across his eyes in a weary gesture. His voice was flat and somewhat ragged. "Go ahead and file. Say whatever you like. Claim I spent my nights warming every woman in Crowe Creek. I doan care. Tell 'em I beat you regular and was a roaring inebriate. There's a good word for you. Learned it from my boy. Tell 'em I failed to provide and neglected my husbandly duty. Tell 'em whatever the hell you want, just get it done. I doan care. Just do it. I ain't gonna remarry, anyway. Once was all I wanted."

He shoved away from the desk, wobbling up to his feet, swaying until Scott caught him by the elbows. For a moment, that firm support was all that kept him standing. He turned to his brother, murmuring hoarsely, "Can you handle the rest a this for me, Scotty?"

"I will."

Then Rory came from around the desk, limping so badly Norah had to grab the arms of her chair to keep from running to offer her assistance. He paused for a

345

moment, breathing hard and shallowly before releasing the edge of hard wood to make his way across the room unaided. It was a laborious trip, one that had tears bright in Norah's eyes as she watched him progress in such obvious pain. A pain that went far beyond the miseries of the flesh. He paused at the side of her chair, reaching out without looking to brush the back of his forefinger along her cheek. Then, before she could grasp his hand, he moved on, leaving her.

The rest of the meeting went by in a quick, business-like blur. Decisions were made between Scott and Carter and, for the most part, Trevor answered for her. She, Jacob, and Trevor would leave for Baltimore that afternoon. Carter would remain to finalize the paperwork and act as her proxy. Scott agreed to bring the documents to Baltimore for final signing on his way to Washington. She would have Jacob; Rory would have the Bar K. All they wouldn't have was each other. It sounded so civilized, so remote when discussed between two lawyers, almost as if it were happening to strangers. She was too numb inside to protest any more and was grateful for Trevor's intervention on her behalf.

"Time to go, Norah," he was saying as he lifted her out of the chair.

"I have to get Jacob's things together," she murmured in a quiet daze. "He's at the Lone Star."

"Rory's gone to get him," Scott told her softly.

It hit her then, the finality of it, and all her strength abandoned her. Her knees went to water. She couldn't catch her breath. Then abruptly, she was caught up in her brother-in-law's strong embrace. Trevor started to reach for her, but Scott's fierce glare warned him away.

"Wait for her in the hall," he advised with an inarguable forcefulness.

She hadn't meant to cry or to cling to Scott Prescott quite so desperately. As if he realized she was holding to him as a representation of all she had and was now forced to leave behind, he held her wordlessly and let her weep.

"*Ceye sni yo. Toskel ociciya owaki hwo?*" The sound of the low Lakota words was soothing; then he spoke them again so she would understand. "Don't cry. What can I do for you? I owe you a life, and I would repay you that debt if I can."

Norah gathered up the remnants of her will and stood back so that his hands were lightly cuffing her upper arms. She looked up at him, at the man who'd been her most dangerous enemy and was now her only friend.

"Take care of him, Scott. Don't let him lose everything because of his pride. He's a good man. He deserves more than I've been able to give him. Please see that he's all right." Tears threatened again, so she stopped speaking.

"I will."

"And Scott—"

"Yes?"

"Stay with your wife. She really does love you."

His expression clouded at the mystery of her words; but she said no more, simply stretching up to press her cheek against the warmth of his. When she came down, he took her healing forearm in his hand and guided her palm over his heart. His words came straight from there.

"If you need anything, *hanka*, either you or the boy, ever, you come to me and I will do what I can."

"How do you say thank you in Lakota?"

"Pilamayan."

"Pilamayan."

He smiled that thin, close-lipped smile. "Norah, I would have you know that Rory is my brother and I cannot stand against him, but I think he is wrong in this. I wish you well."

"Pilamayan." She touched a hand to his face and hurried to join Trevor Samuels before her resolve crumpled completely.

"Time to go, pard. Say your goodbyes."

"Already?" Jacob moaned as he glanced reluctantly at the hand of cards he was holding. He was about to make his bossy cousin eat her words.

"Now, Jacob."

The crack of her son's words brought Aurora from the kitchen. She took one look at him and cast her apron aside. "Go on and finish that hand, Jacob, but be quick about it. I want to talk to your daddy a minute."

Rory hobbled out onto the windswept porch and she followed, anticipating yet dreading what he would say. He waited for her to speak, leaning back against the rough log siding, choking on the swell of emotions. His expression was tragic.

"Is it today?" she asked at last.

Rory's composure crumbled. His features twisted up in the worst kind of agony. "Oh, God, Mama, how am I gonna say goodbye to him?"

Aurora put aside all her questions, all her animosity and mothering instincts to answer with the strength of experience. "You do it with a smile. You hug him; you tell him you love him, and you let him go."

348

"I can't."

"Yes, you can. It'll be just about the hardest thing you'll ever do but you'll do it." She was thinking of the son she'd sent away to the East to keep him safe from the inevitability of his heritage. And she knew exactly how her youngest son was feeling this very minute, as if his heart were being torn from his chest by the cruelty of circumstances he couldn't control. Smothering him with sympathy wouldn't help. She tried to remember what it was her husband had said to get her through the pain of parting.

"Rory, you say goodbye and you make it as easy for both of you as you can. You tell him that this is his home and where he'll always be welcome. You tell him you'll hold him in your heart till the day you die, and then you let him go. Save your grieving for afterwards. Don't let him see it."

"I'm ready, Daddy," Jacob called as he pushed the door open. He missed the quick hand his father scrubbed across his eyes before greeting him with a smile.

"Did you win?"

"Skunked her."

"Attaboy."

Dawn came out, sulky in her defeat. "Where did you learn to play poker, *Istamaza?* Uncle Rory taught me, and he's the best there is."

"My mama taught me," the boy claimed proudly. "She said it's all in the bluff."

"She'd know," Rory murmured huskily, and Aurora gave him a cautioning glance.

"I'll beat you next time, *Ist—*"

"Just what does that mean, what you keep calling me?" Jacob demanded with a flare of annoyance. Dawn grinned, as if she'd been waiting for him to get

349

riled enough to ask.

"It means eyeglasses."

"Oh." Not as insulting as he'd supposed. At least it didn't mean sissy.

"I'll get even with you, *tahansi*. And that means cousin." Giving him an affectionate punch in the arm, she swaggered back into the house, arrogance not at all hampered by her tender ankle.

"Jacob, you give your grandma a hug and tell her thank you for putting up with you."

Aurora gathered the boy close as he did as he was told. Reluctantly, she set him down and called into the house, "Ethan, Gena, Jacob's leaving."

Something in the quality of her voice brought them in a hurry. And one glance at Rory's unsuccessful smile confirmed the worst. Gena was quick to thread her fingers through his to absorb their shake and tremble while Ethan bent down in front of his grandson.

"Jacob, it sure has been a pleasure having you spend time with us. You take good care a your mama and you come on back as soon as you can."

Not understanding the enormity of his promise, Jacob vowed, "I surely will." He gave the big Texan a hard squeeze around the neck. Ethan stood with him and planted him down in Rosebud's saddle.

"How you doing?" Ethan asked his son in a low aside. Rory nodded, then slowly shook his head. A big hand clamped down on the redhead's shoulder, pressing hard. "You come on over for supper, you hear? I want to take a look at that foot you're so set on abusing."

"I will, Daddy."

"Hang on, son."

"Yessir. 'Bye, Mama."

She hugged him fiercely, holding his head to her shoulder for a long minute, then pushing him away with a stern, "Remember what I said."

"Yes, ma'am." And he stepped up behind Jacob, gathering the reins. "Say goodbye, Jacob."

The boy waved and smiled as Rory urged Rosebud into a loping canter, heading for the Bar K.

He listened to Jacob ramble on and on about his plans for besting Dawn at cards and for breaking Ghost to a saddle. Rory said nothing. He couldn't through all the sorrow thickening in his throat. Jacob was puzzled by his quiet mood. Until they pulled up in front of the Bar K's porch and he saw their luggage stacked in the back of Trevor Samuel's buggy. Then he understood everything. He twisted in the saddle to look up into his father's somber face. His words were brutally concise.

"You lied to me."

Then he was wiggling out of Rory's embrace, jumping awkwardly down from the little red mare to race to his elegantly starched and proper mother who awaited him on the porch in her travel cloak. He looked to her in panic, and she smiled softly, sadly.

"Jacob, we don't want to miss our train."

Norah watched as Rory climbed down gingerly from the saddle. He wouldn't look at her. His eyes were on their son. Then he walked stiffly up the steps and into the house.

Trevor took Norah's arm, having to tug gently to get her moving with him. He helped her up onto the cushioned seat and tucked a lap robe about her knees. When he put out his hand to Jacob, the boy balked, his be-spectacled eyes uncertain.

"Jacob," Norah called firmly, but he wouldn't budge.

351

"Tunska," Scott said softly as he bent down to meet that frightened gaze, man to man. "You listen to your mother and show her every respect. Be brave for her." Jacob swallowed hard and nodded. Scott smiled. "And don't forget where your family lives."

"No, sir. I won't." He gave Scott a tight hug and let his uncle lift him up into the buggy.

Just as Trevor was picking up the reins, Rory came out of the house, toting a large parcel under his arm. He deposited it in the back of the buggy. It was the bearskin. Jacob looked questioningly from the muzzle stretched wide in its harmless snarl to his father's cocky grin.

"That'll impress the hell outta 'em in Baltimore."

Jacob gave a small cry and launched himself from the buggy seat into his father's arms. Rory staggered but held tight.

"I don't want to go, Daddy."

"Shhh. Hush now. Doan go forgetting you're a Prescott."

"Can I come see you?"

"That'd be up to your mama." Rory's gaze lifted then, touching on Norah with a quiet, heartrending appeal. She managed a jerky nod and he, a fragile smile of thanks. "Sure you can, pard."

"And you can come visit me?"

"I doan think so. You write me, you hear."

"I will, Daddy. And you take care of Ghost."

"He'll be waiting for you."

"Don't shoot him."

"I won't." His big hand moved restlessly through the boy's dark auburn hair. "I love you, Jacob, and I'm damn proud to be your daddy." He pressed a quick kiss to the boy's temple and settled him back on the buggy seat, stepping back quickly to reinforce the

352

sense of separation. Norah's arm curled about the child's shoulders to anchor him in place beside her. Rory's gaze touched hers again, very briefly, and the loss welling up in the darkness of his eyes intensified to a glittery brilliance. Then he reached up for the brim of his hat, not in a salute but to tip it down to cast his face in shadow. And that's how Norah would remember him, standing, unsmiling, at the base of the Bar K's porch watching them drive away without a word of goodbye passing between them.

Chapter Twenty-two

No one respected the process of grieving more than a Lakota. Therefore, Scott was bound to keep his distance from the Bar K until he had a suitable reason. It wasn't a pleasant reason, but it was enough to send him to his brother's door with an excuse for the intrusion. He was worried. They all were. After that first silent evening he'd come for dinner, Rory had kept to himself at the Bar K, tending his own sorrows. Aurora, Gena, and Dawn chafed to visit; but Ethan put his foot down. Not until they were asked. And no invitation came.

"No," Scott said firmly as he rolled up into the saddle. "It's business, Gena."

"Business, my eye, Scott Prescott."

"You can't come. I'll tell him you said hello."

Gena sniffed at that paltry second best. "You tell your brother that you, Dawn, and I are coming for dinner tomorrow night and that he better be there to welcome us and he better be polite and sober."

Scott grinned down at her. "How could he possibly refuse such a genteel request?"

"You tell him. He needs his family. And we're going to be there for him even if we have to stuff our love down his throat."

Scott leaned from the saddle, catching his wife by the back of her head and pulling her up for a long, wet kiss. Then she gave him a push.

"Tell him!"

"Yes, ma'am. You're a tough woman, Gena Prescott."

"It's the company I keep." She slapped her palm down on the rump of his horse and watched him ride off toward the Bar K. Only then did the anxious tears appear in her eyes.

Scott expected the worst. But instead of finding his brother holed up behind closed doors into a bottle of rye, Rory was sitting on the porch swing with a cup of coffee. Though the snow was gone, the air was filled with the snap of approaching winter, not the kind of weather to invite a leisurely appreciation of the out-of-doors. But Rory appeared quite content in his bulky coat with his foot propped up on the swing.

"Heya, Scotty!" His smile broke wide and genuine in greeting. "Ain't seen you in a while."

"Forget where we live?" He tied up his horse and took the steps with a lithe stride.

"Naw, jus' been taking it kinda slow. Healing up." He gestured to his foot, but the vicinity of his heart would have been more accurate. "Mama send you to see if I was behaving?"

"Not exactly. But Gena did invite us over for dinner tomorrow night."

He grinned. "That's real subtle-like." He eased his foot to the porch boards and reached up. "Gimme a hand and I'll stand you to a cup of coffee. 'Less you're inviting yourself to more than that."

"Coffee's fine."

They walked side by side to Rory's study, Scott

slowing his pace to accommodate his brother's halting steps.

"How've you been?"

"I been doing."

And his study bore that out for the most part. No broken glass. No empty bottles. No signs of disarray. Just a heavy blanket tossed over the back of the sofa where he'd been spending his nights. Rory snatched it up, muttering, "Too hard to climb the stairs," in an explanation that wasn't necessary. He didn't want to be alone in the bed he'd shared with Norah.

"Feel up to some business?"

The softening of Scott's tone warned him. "What kind?"

Grimly, Scott drew out a stack of legal papers and set them on the desktop. Rory regarded them expressionlessly but made no move to look at them.

"That it, then?"

"I'll take them to Baltimore next week when I go, and she can file them."

A moment's hesitation, then a quiet, "All right."

"Sure?"

"Said so, didn't I?" That wasn't quiet or sure.

"Something else."

"What?" Rory growled.

"Heard from the bank that all the Bar K notes had been bought up by one party. They're almost due. Can you meet them?"

"No." There was no sense of agitation in that claim. Rory moved to the broad set of windows and stared out over the rolling hills burnished a late seasonal gold. The pads of his fingers rested lightly on the glass fogging it with their warmth. "Funny. I doan even care. I got no joy in this place no more. I'm tired a fightin'. Let 'em take it. It doan matter."

Scott stared at him, alarmed by the spiritless reply

but not surprised. "Grandfather built this place for you," he said quietly. He never called Garth Kincaid by the fond moniker of Major, and his tone never softened with anything near affection when he spoke of the family patriarch. It was only for Rory's sake that he spoke politely of the dead at all.

"I should have let him take it to hell with him. Then maybe I'd still have a wife and son. Let strangers try to make a go."

"Not exactly strangers."

Rory turned, curious. He took the paper Scott handed him and had only to see the letterhead. M.S. Consolidated. "Damn her greedy heart. She just won't let go."

"What was that?"

Rory wadded it in a convulsive fist and glanced at the divorce papers. "You say them ain't final yet?"

"No. Not until Norah files them. Having second thoughts?"

"About some things, yes. When you going to Baltimore?"

"Tuesday. Is there something you want me to tell her?"

"Tell her I mean to take back what's mine."

Norah was fastening glittery diamond clusters to her ears as she whisked into her son's bedroom.

"Schoolwork all done?"

"Yes, ma'am."

"I want you to turn right in when Bridget tells you to. No reading after lights go out, young man. How do I look?"

She made a slow turn for his somber inspection. Pale tangerine-colored silk skimmed her figure, it's Empire-style bodice scooping low from the edge of her shoulders and a side placket of heavy crystal beading emphasizing the long line of her legs before spilling out into a shimmering fantasy around the pooling hem. She extended her arms gracefully to show off the silver chiffon scarf draped from the tiny flutter of her sleeves to the beaded cuff of her gloves before whispering down to the floor. The finer points of her Madame Paquin gown were lost to his seven-year-old scrutiny. To him, it looked orange and sparkly and displayed entirely too much of his mama for his liking. Trevor Samuels would like it, though. That was enough to bring a scowl to his brow.

"You look very pretty, Mama," he claimed dourly.

"I see I shall have to teach you how to give a compliment so that it sounds like one. Give me a kiss. I have to go."

"Is Trevor waiting?"

She frowned at his sulky tone. "I thought you liked Trevor."

"I do."

"But?"

"He's not my daddy."

"Oh." Norah came to sit beside the gloomy-faced child. How long had it been since she'd seen him smile? Not caring if her gown creased, she gathered him into a close embrace. "Oh, honey, Trevor isn't trying to take your father's place."

"Yes, he is. He told me he was."

Norah's brow lifted in a cool arch. "Did he? Well, you know that isn't true."

"He said when you got married he'd make me into a Samuels and he'd be my daddy. I don't want to be a Samuels. That ain't my name."

She was too distracted to correct his grammar. It sounded alarmingly natural. She sat back, holding

358

him at arm's length. "No, it is not. You are a Prescott, and there is nothing wrong with being proud of that."

"Then why are you going to change your name?" Before she could think of a suitable reply, he asked, "Are you mad at Daddy?"

"No." A whisper was all she could manage. "I love your daddy very much. I always will." Her gloved fingers stroked his cheek. "And as long as I have you, I have a part of him with me. And I won't ever be lonely."

"But who will Daddy have?"

Her voice strengthened with that reply. "He has his family and his ranch."

"Should I be mad at him?"

"Why?"

"He lied to me, Mama. He told me I could stay with him, that we were family. You said it's bad to tell a lie and break your promises."

"Oh, dear." How to explain that one to a little boy with confusion in his heart? She thought hard and dug deep into her soul to find an answer. "Jacob, some promises you make because you love someone; but, no matter how hard you try, you just can't keep them. Your daddy tried. He did the best he could. He just couldn't keep that promise, no matter how much he wanted to. I know that's hard to understand, but someday you will. Don't be mad at him. He did the very best he could."

He did the very best he could.

Jacob hung his head to mumble, "I thought maybe he didn't want me around any more."

"Oh, no. That's not true, at all." She hugged him hard, feeling the dampness well up in her eyes. How could she tell him it was his mother Rory no longer wanted?

359

"Norah? Are you ready?"

"Just a minute, Trevor. Jacob and I were just saying good night." She sat back and looked from her glum son to the dapper man waiting in the hall. "Perhaps I'll stay home this evening. I haven't had much time to spend with Jacob—"

"Norah, you can't! There'll be important Party members I need to introduce you to. You know how Mrs. Parkinson adores you and your work for the Municipal Art Society. You can spend time with Jacob tomorrow. You don't mind, do you, champ? Oh, and don't forget we have a luncheon tomorrow with the Bowdoins, something about housing, I suppose. And dinner at the Thayers's."

"I can see that will leave me a lot of time for my son," she remarked dryly.

"You know how important these engagements are for us."

"For your career," she clarified crisply. At his pleading look, she conceded, "Yes, I suppose they are."

"Go on, Mama. I'm very tired anyway. You have a nice time."

Norah hesitated. "Are you sure, honey? It's just a party. There'll be lots of others."

But Jacob was already taking off his glasses, setting them on the nighttable before easing down under his covers. "I'll be fine, Mama." Then he canted a baleful glance up at her through the heavy fringe of his lashes, and her heart staggered. Dear Lord, that look was pure Rory Prescott. Trevor had to lift her from the counterpane and propel her toward the door. But the memory of that look lingered.

*　　*　　*

Norah glanced up from her conversation with Mrs. J. William Funck, the founding president of the Women's Suffrage Association and broke off in mid-sentence. She blinked and craned her neck, then she shook her head. She must have imagined it. For a moment, she'd thought she saw a black John B. Stetson hat in amongst the elite of Maryland. Her talk with Jacob must have rattled her more than she suspected. The last person she would ever find in Baltimore was Rory Prescott in his Dakota finery. But still, she was discomposed.

"Could you excuse me for a moment, Emma? I need to freshen up."

Then, as she turned, there was a slight part in the clannish gatherings. There was no mistaking it. The black hat, the broad shoulders, the thigh-hugging denims beneath a black evening coat.

Rory.

He'd come for her. Finally, he'd come for her.

And just as soon as that dizzying hope overwhelmed her, she recognized the small figure at his side. There, in the easy loop of his arm, was Gena Prescott.

The hurt of it was devastating. She was instantly blinded by disorienting tears. Out. She had to get out before anyone saw her and suspected something was wrong. Before *they* saw her. She whirled in a daze of despair and collided with a man in flawless evening-wear.

"Don't fall apart," he urged softly as his hands captured her elbows.

"Scott . . ."

"Do you want to sit down?"

She nodded, jerkily. Everything seemed suddenly dark and out of focus. She couldn't swoon at the unexpected arrival of her soon-to-be-ex husband, not here in front of all Trevor's society friends. The gossip would be deadly. Scott must have known that, for he was very solicitous and discreet in guiding her to a shadowed archway. She dropped onto a cushioned window seat, gasping for the return of reason.

"Would you like me to get you a drink?"

"What are you doing here?" she cried out softly. She was suddenly frantic and furious with this trio from South Dakota for flinging such an upheaval back into her life. For making her hope. "You have to go. You have to get him out of here, now."

"Afraid it will look bad?" Scott drawled silkily. Her tone put his back up out of habit. "Afraid the appearance of a husband will cast you in the role of adulteress in the eyes of this fine crowd? Rory's not here to play the wronged man to the embarrassment of your lover."

"Wronged man? I should think not. He wouldn't dare play the innocent party after the shameless way he's been carrying on with your—" Her hands flew up to cover her mouth as she realized what she was saying and to whom. She caught back the word, but it was too late to take back the insinuation. It struck Scott with the viciousness of a slap, and he recoiled with a harsh intake of breath.

"My what?"

What had she done? She scrambled mentally for a way to avert disaster. "Nothing, Scott, I'm just upset and I wanted to—"

His hand grasped the necklace she wore, sliding up until it tightened about her throat like a damning noose. Scott leaned in close. His eyes were hot as molten gold. "My what?" he repeated in a low hiss. "My wife? What are you suggesting, Norah? That my wife and my brother are lovers?"

362

The ruthless blaze of his eyes terrified her as the savage in his soul surfaced. She could imagine him capable of anything. "Scott, please."

"Are you asking me to believe that they've been intimate while I was away? That maybe I should ask my wife if the child she's carrying is mine or his?"

Norah's tearful gaze was his answer. Her hands slid over his in desperate entreaty. "Scott, Gena loves you. I'm sure it was just a mistake."

He was very still, realizing she was trying to protect him, that she'd said what she'd said out of belief, not maliciousness. "There was a mistake," he said softly.

"Scott, please try to forgive them. I'm sure they never meant to hurt you."

His free hand rose to brush the rush of dampness from one smooth cheek. His voice was very gentle. "But they hurt you, didn't they?"

With a quiet sob, she tucked her head, her tears rolling in a river of despair. Scott sighed heavily and drew her into his shoulder. "So that's it," he said softly, to himself. "Now it makes sense."

"I thought he loved me. I thought she was my friend," Norah sobbed wretchedly, grateful to unburden the awful secret at last. It hurt. It hurt terribly.

"He does, and she is. Oh, Norah, what a hard life you must have led. You haven't the slightest idea what it means to be part of a family, do you?"

"Rory's in love with her," she moaned in desolation.

"I know. That's why I trust their welfare to him. That's why I can place my wife and daughter in his hands and know that they'll be safe and cared for. The same way he gave you and Jacob over to me. I trust Gena with my heart, and I trust Rory with all that I love."

She squeezed her eyes shut as if to deny the memory. "But I saw them—"

Scott cut in quickly, confidently. "I don't know what you saw or what you thought you saw. But I know without the slightest doubt that you're wrong in what you believe. My brother and my wife have very deep feelings for one another but there's nothing in those feelings that threatens me or you. That's friendship, Norah; kinship, not desire. It's nothing like what Gena feels for me or Rory, for you. There is nothing you could tell me or show me that would make me believe Gena has been unfaithful to me. Her love is the only constant in my life. If you had the same kind of faith in my brother's love for you, you would never have left him. If you knew anything of love, you wouldn't be here with another man."

Norah listened to his words, believing because of his unshakable faith. No wonder Gena Prescott would willingly sacrifice plenty for simple skins and sky to be with him. Perhaps it was the ugliness of her past that colored what she'd seen, changing the tender comfort between friends into a sordid situation. But it didn't really matter. Not now. Because it didn't change the painfully obvious.

"But he doesn't love me. Not any more."

Scott laughed. It was an exasperated sound. "I didn't think there could be a bigger fool than my brother." He took her by the shoulders and held her away. When she wouldn't meet his eyes, he forked his thumb and forefinger beneath her stubborn jaw and forced her head up. "Norah, how could you be so ready to give your life, your very soul for him and not have a grain of faith in his love for you?"

"Scott, he can't forgive what I was."

"Are you sure it's Rory who can't forgive or forget?"

While she sat, stunned by the question, he used the pad of his thumb to wipe the wetness from her face. She stilled the gesture by catching that hand in hers and holding tight.

"You argue a good case, Counselor. You'd have a great future in politics."

He chuckled. "I don't think so. I have a bad habit of preferring the truth."

"And for making others face it." She stood, and he rose with her. Her kiss was warm and light against his bronze cheek. "I think you've just repaid your debt."

He seemed quite pleased with that as he cupped a hand beneath her elbow and escorted her back into the dazzle of their host's ballroom. Norah hung back slightly, not quite ready to face a certain couple. He gave her a prompting glance.

"Why are you here, Scott?"

"I'm on my way to Washington to see about accepting a position with the Office of Indian Affairs. Perhaps I can make more of a difference within the system than fighting it from the outside."

"And Gena? I didn't think she ever traveled with you."

"I heard some wisdom spoken by a friend, telling me to keep my wife close to me. I thought she might enjoy the socializing."

Norah repressed her comment. The smug Scott Prescott didn't know his wife as well as he thought.

"I have to flatter and bend some rather influential Commission members. With Gena beside me, I am less likely to pull my knife and begin carving on their miserable hides."

"I'm not without sources myself. Would you like some introductions?"

"Are you sure that wouldn't be a conflict of

365

interest?" He nodded across the empty dance floor to where Trevor and his father were involved in an intense discussion with several politicians. Carter Clemens stood on the fringe of the group. His features froze when he saw the two of them together.

"Nonsense," Norah claimed. "Trevor's beliefs are very much in line with your own."

"If you say so. And yes, I would like those introductions."

As they wound through the crowded periphery, the musicians began a sentimental tune and couples drifted onto the open parquet to turn in each other's arms. Norah studied her sleekly handsome brother-in-law. She didn't want to ask, but she had to know.

"Why did Rory come all this way? He didn't have to."

"You'll have to ask him, *hanka*. He didn't share his reason with me."

"But you did bring the papers."

He nodded solemnly. "But nothing is final until you sign them and file. Until then, you are my brother's wife and your place is with him. You called back his soul, Norah. Without you, he has no purpose on this earth. He belongs to you."

She smiled wryly at that. "Oh, Scott, we both know he belongs to the Bar K. And we both know it was the poultice that saved his life."

He smiled back, that thin, blank smile of mystery. "Was it? The Lakota would say it was your strength. They would say he returned to the one who loved him best. Of course, we are much too intelligent to believe such things or I would wonder why he was suddenly ready to sell his grandfather's ranch for you."

"He was?"

"But it must be superstitious nonsense, as you

366

said. Or you would not have cast him away for another who cannot love you half as well as my brother."

"I didn't cast him away," she declared angrily. "He was the one who asked you to draw up the papers. There is nothing I want more than to be his wife."

Several heads turned their way in curiosity. Norah glared them down until they flushed and went back to their own conversations.

"I never wanted to leave in the first place. It took me three years to find a reason my pride could accept to go back to him."

Scott's stare penetrated to her very soul. "Would you go back with him now?"

She hesitated. Her heart said a wild, unfettered yes, but her mind advised caution. "I don't know. It may be too late to go back."

"Well, there is one thing about us Prescotts: When we want something, we usually don't let anything get in our way of having it."

The music changed from sweet to sassy with the first notes of "Ta-ra-ra-boom-der-e." As the romping tune encouraged a lively dance, Norah watched her strapping, redheaded husband lead his sister-in-law out onto the floor. He was grinning wide, backpedaling Gena through the other couples at a rollicking tempo. She had to smile at the sight of the big, black-hatted Dakota cowboy stomping his way between the members of Baltimore's Social Register as if it were a Crowe Creek barn-raising.

"Scott, do you dance? I mean to something other than rattles and drums?"

He smiled. "I've been known to step to an adequate do-si-do on occasion."

"Good."

She grabbed his arm and dragged him onto the

367

dance floor. He was more than a passable dancer with his cat-like grace, and he moved with the same Western two-step scuffle his brother stepped to, setting them apart from the polished ease of the other dancers. He let her set their direction, though it was no surprise to him. Nor did he mind when she left him. Rory was spinning Gena around beneath his right arm when Norah lifted the left and made a neat revolution under the bridge it made. Smiling, Gena was quick to partner up with her husband, leaving Norah in Rory's arms.

He just stood there, his one hand captured in hers. his other dangling loose at his side. His stare was dark, intense and unreadable. For a moment, Norah feared he would walk away or, worse, continue his immobile stance until she was shamed in front of all. She didn't try to persuade him with a smile or a word but rather with the lightest of touches—her fingertips atop the high range of one shoulder, pressing gently as she took a step back. He followed. His hand came up to rest with a comfortable familiarity on the curve of her hip, guiding her through the throng of dancers the way he'd steer his horse with the pressure of his knees. He looked so wonderfully original in the sea of same and conservative formal garb. Though he sported a traditional black evening jacket and starched white shirt, a new Stetson crowned his bright hair and a pair of shiny new pointy-toed boots poked out from beneath his Levi Strauss's. No one would mistake him for other than what he was, a rough-edged cowboy, and he was arrogantly proud to claim it.

After a couple of fancy turns, she asked, "How's your foot holding up?"

"Dang near killing me, but I jus' can't say no to a spicy song and a pretty girl."

And then he smiled, not his great bursting grin but a small bend of closed-lips. Like Scott. She wanted more than anything at that moment to be in his arms, held tight against the large, work-hardened frame, caressed by the big, weather-roughened hands; but he didn't encourage her to come closer. He kept her moving at arm's length. So he could watch her through those dark, fathomless eyes.

Too soon the song was over. Rory kept his arm about the curve of her waist to steer her from the dance floor. He was limping, not badly but enough to betray the effort it was taking. What now? Norah wondered. She wanted to take him home with her. She wanted to spend the night making love to him. She wanted to greet Jacob in the morning with his father at her side. She didn't want to let him go, not for a second. But what did Rory want? He'd come all the way to Baltimore. Why? Her mind was spinning wildly trying to figure it. What could possibly drag Rory Prescott off his range? Scott's words kept returning, filling her heart with hope. For her. He'd come for her.

Those hopes tangled in confusion when Rory hitched her up short in front of Trevor and his father. Trevor's mild hazel stare demanded an explanation. But she wasn't interested in his reaction. Norah was looking up at the big Dakota cowboy. He took her hand and, even as she tried to curl into his side, he was pulling her away, pushing her toward the rigid Easterner. He fixed her fingers upon Trevor's arm.

"Here you go," he drawled with a deceptively friendly rumble. "Found her wandering. You'd best keep her on a shorter lead."

Trevor's hand instantly anchored over hers, holding her fast at his side when she would return to

Rory's. Her anxious gaze searched his impassive face, begging an explanation. And then she had it, point-blank and with a stunning velocity.

"You must be Mr. M.S. Consolidated." Rory put out his hand to Martin Samuels, offering with it his most innocuous smile. There was nothing benign in the smolder of his stare. Samuels took his hand warily, not sure what to expect of this seeming bumpkin with the razor-sharp glare. Then Rory continued with his affable speech, as if they were old and best of friends.

"I got to hand it to you. You are smooth. You just don't miss a trick. You wanted something a mine, and you just wouldn't take no for an answer. When you couldn't get me through my pockets, you found a way to stick between my ribs like a good sharp blade. You almost had me. I was almost ready to roll over like a stupid ole hound. You're a smart man. You hired on the best there is, but you forgot one thing. I already seen her at work. I've seen her ply her lies and sell her kisses. And I'm here to tell you, they're worth the price you paid for 'em."

Norah became a cold, rigid pillar at Trevor's side.

"It ain't Norah's fault. She done everything she was supposed to. And I was all ready to believe her. Imagine being taken in twice by the same lying pair of lips." He smiled. It hardened on his face into a grim parody of amusement. "She'll make a grand politician's wife. I hear tell there's a real need there for knowing how to twist the truth."

He glanced at her then but looked away too quickly, missing the way a glaze of shock melted to plaintive despair. He saw only the surface indifference in that expressionless daze, and it cut him deep, prepared though he was to see it. His smile bent into a cynical curve. "Yessir, you pay her well. Ain't nobody who puts herself body and soul into a job like my Norah."

"I've listened to about enough of this," Samuels said impatiently. "If you've a point, Prescott, make it."

"A point? Oh, yes. I come all this way to make a point. I wanted to meet up with you, to shake your hand and tell you how much I admire your style a business. You an' my granddaddy would have got along jus' fine. When a man tries to gut and hang me out to dry, I want to look him straight on when I tell him to go to hell."

"Now see here," wheezed Carter Clemens in shrill outrage.

"Shut up, you. I ain't talking to you." Rory took a menacing step closer to Martin Samuels, but the old man didn't waver. Gritty ole feller, Rory had to admit. "You keep your money and your paid whores. And you keep off my property. I'd plow every blade a grass under and spade the dirt straight down to hell 'fore I'd let you set foot on it."

Samuels wasn't intimidated. His tone was almost bored when he said, "Very nice speech, Mr. Prescott, from a man who doesn't know he's already lost. I happened to hold all the notes on your property; and when I collect, you have no means to pay them. I win, you see. I always win."

"You ain't never played a hand out against me." Rory smiled again, a wide baring of white teeth. "I got all I need to pay you off. See, my sweet wife Norah's been putting together a tidy little nest egg; and seeing as how what's hers is mine, I jus' helped myself to it." His smile fell and with it, all pretense of civility. "Your notes are paid in full, you sonuvabitch. You lose."

And with that, Rory Prescott stalked from the room with an arrogant staccato of Cuban heels.

Chapter Twenty-three

"The man is insane," Trevor declared. "What on earth was he talking about?"

Norah knew. All too well. Rory hadn't come to Baltimore to take her home. He'd come to take his revenge upon her. And a harsh, bitter revenge it was. She knew exactly what he meant by each and every hard word he'd spoken, and she knew why he'd come to the conclusion he had. He thought Martin Samuels had sent her to the Dakotas to seduce him into selling the Bar K. He believed it because that was the kind of woman she had been and the kind of work she knew how to do well. He believed it because she'd never convinced him of her love.

She'd spent four years of marriage reminding him of her discontent with what he could provide. She'd insulted his family and spurned his efforts by building her house. She'd run from him because it was easier than fighting for him. When she returned, it was with a lie for a reason. She hadn't told him she'd come home for him and what they had together. She'd forced their differences into his face at every opportunity, suspecting him of infidelity and giving him reason to believe it of her by carrying on

372

shamelessly under his roof. She'd hurt him and humiliated him, stripping him of his pride and his son. And when he'd taken all he could, in one purposeful stroke, he'd cut her off from everything: From the chance at a future, from the resources to survive, from the right to hold her head up with any degree of dignity. Though he was wrong in his reasons, he was right to have cause.

How did she go about telling him that she'd been wrong, too?

"The man is a fool," Martin Samuels amended harshly. "How dare he think he can speak to me that way. Carter!"

"Yes, sir."

The seething businessman turned to his aide and towed him away from the others with a crushing grip on one spindly arm. He made his words low, but that didn't detract from their force.

"I want that man destroyed. Do you hear? I want the pleasure of ruining him. How dare he spit on me in front of my son."

"I'll see to it, Mr. Samuels."

The old man smoothed down the creases of his evening coat as if by doing so he were brushing away the threat of Rory Prescott. "And the woman, she's become an embarrassment. If her husband has indeed stripped her of her wealth, what use is she?"

"She still isn't without influence. Sir, if I may suggest it, I have the means to control her and to see she is never indiscreet again. Your son fancies himself in love with her. If you forbid the relationship, he may resent you for it. Better you allow him his illusions but take precautions to see they're safe ones. By giving him what he wants now, you are insuring your power to get what you want later. Norah Prescott is no threat to him. And I'll see her husband is no threat to anyone."

Samuels considered the little man's words. Clemens was clever and he wouldn't make assurances without good cause. "Do it. But first, I want Prescott to receive a very clear warning. I want him to know he's about to be gutted and hung out to dry. See to it. No man curses me. Not to my face. No man."

"I'll see to it, sir."

Rory's fury was fierce enough to propel him down several windswept Baltimore blocks. It was the ceaseless pain in his foot that forced him to stop long enough to glance around, long enough for him to realize that he was lost. He couldn't remember turning off, but there was no sight of the place he'd been and he had no idea how to get where he was going. A perfect end to the evening.

God, he hurt. He was tempted to sit down on the dirty curb and howl in aimless misery. He'd been wrong to come here. He felt none of the spirit-lifting vindication he'd expected. Instead, he felt small and spiteful and wretchedly unhappy. All because she'd been able to dissolve his self-righteousness with a delicate touch.

Just seeing her soothed the savage rawness in his soul. Holding her had been exquisite heaven. He'd been so hungry for the sound of her voice he'd nearly cast all his plans aside. But seeing her there on Trevor Samuels's arm had unstrung his reason. She looked so at home in the glittery social setting and he was so obviously out of place. He'd almost slunk out the back door, but his pride held him firm. Now his pride had his heart in tatters and he felt like the meanest kind of fool. A bragging, strutting fool trying, always trying, to impress her with what a big man he was.

All he was left with was the bitter taste of truth: He might have salvaged the Bar K, but he'd lost Norah. He had an unwelcomed insight into the future: Sitting behind that big desk, ruling his kingdom all alone, just like his grandfather before him. The emptiness of it ached through him like the harsh slice of November air. How had everything gone so wrong? Why hadn't she been able to love him?

He started walking, favoring his throbbing ankle as best he could. He was walking blind without thought or destination, so lost to the dismals he never heard the soft approach of footfalls. Nor did he see the blackjack that caught the side of his head in a stunning blow. His next awareness was of cold, gritty pavement beneath his cheek and a circle of shiny shoes around him. He had a vague impression of rapid movement from one of them, and agony exploded in his face. He heard his nose break and felt the warmth of blood. Blackness surged up around him as he sensed more than saw another kick aimed for his mid-section. He grabbed his assailant's ankle, yanking hard, and was rewarded by a curse and the heavy thump of a good-sized man meeting hard ground with his rump. There was no way to protect from a stunning impact to his lower back. The pain was numbing, and his grasp on consciousness teetered. He curled up tight on that grimy sidewalk, remembering with a wry wane of reason the haughtiness of Norah's voice, *We don't hit in Baltimore.*

Then another voice intruded, low and lethal.

"Back off."

Rory heard a scuffle of confusion and uncertainty as those around him regrouped to face a new danger.

"Rory?"

He tried to smile. "Give 'em hell, Scotty."

The hired thugs, four in number, armed with weighty bludgeons, regarded the compact threat in evening wear and they grinned amongst themselves.

"Mind your business, buddy, 'less you want some of the same," one of the burly men growled.

"Serve it up," the swarthy gentleman coaxed with the beckoning of his fingers. It was an intolerable goad.

The one who spoke swung first, aiming his sap where the dark head had been a split second before. It whistled through empty space. Before he could check his swing, he caught the glitter of deadly silver. Pain scissored across his face as the blade opened a gash from cheek to chin before swiping low in a slash across his companion's tendons. The crippled man wailed lustily and the four of them reassessed the situation. Whoever this dapper fellow was, he knew how to handle a knife. From the way he was crouched and balanced for an attack, they weren't going to get the best of him without losing several pints of blood. It wasn't worth it. Their message was already delivered. No point in belaboring it.

As the trio of toughs faded back into the shadows of the street, dragging their howling companion, Scott wiped his blade on his pant leg and went to kneel beside his brother.

"How bad is it?" he asked tersely. Blood gleamed black under the street lamps.

"Golldangit, Scotty, I'm having the awfullest time imaginable."

The Lakota's smile flashed bright in relief. "Let me get you up and headed in the right direction."

"To think I let you talk me outta wearing my pistols. I thought you said cities was civilized places."

"The cities are. The people are the same all over.

C'mon. Grab on."

They managed to get back to the hotel and up to their adjoining rooms on the sixth floor. There, with the fearsome spill of blood wiped away, Scott surveyed the damage. Rory was slouched on the bed, bleary-eyed with discomfort and short of temper.

"Who were them fellers? Bent on robbin' me, you think?"

"No. I followed them from the party. They're Samuels's men. What did you say to send him after your hide?"

"Too much," Rory grumbled glumly. "I'm headin' for home in the morning. Sorry I spoilt you and Gena's evening."

"Aren't you going to speak to Norah first?"

"Scotty, we done said a lifetime a hurtful things to each other. I ain't got nothing left to say."

"She might have something to say to you. Besides, I thought you wanted to see Jacob."

Rory's sigh was poignant. "I doan know if she'll be of a mind to let me. Probably'll shoot me right off the front steps. Wouldn't blame her iffen she did."

"Rory, look up at me for a minute."

He lifted his head in question, and Scott took his face tightly between his hands. With palms pressing into his cheeks, he aligned his thumbs along Rory's battered nose and gave a quick jerk. Then he clamped one of his hands over his brother's mouth to seal in his howl of surprise. The city's leading motel didn't hold with screaming in its rooms. Guests trailing blood up their expensively carpeted stairs was bad enough.

"I didn't think you'd want to go breathing out of the side of your face for the rest of your life," Scott justified as he eased his hand away. Rory came out sputtering.

"You could warn a feller. Like I wasn't hurtin' enough already." He felt tenderly along the break. It was straight anyway, or would be once the swelling went away.

"See Norah."

Rory looked up at him sourly. "Like I said, I'm hurtin' enough already. I ain't gonna let her kick me, too."

"I'm going to kick you if you don't listen to me. That woman loves you. Don't you look away from me. I said she loves you, and that little boy loves you. What are you going to do about it? Toss them away? To the likes of Samuels and his son?"

Rory moaned wretchedly. "Scotty, let it alone. Norah, she ain't like Gena. She's not gonna make a cozy home for me and soothe my soul. She ain't quiet and gentle and sweetly deposed and turned toward forgiving."

"No, she's not. Gena's my wife, and she's just what I need. Norah's your wife, and she's tough and bossy and opinionated and smart and just what you need. When are you going to open your eyes and make use of what she is instead of whining over what she's not?"

"She doesn't want what I got to offer, Scotty."

"Doesn't want?" Scott stood, throwing up his hands as if to ask patience from his gods. "If she didn't want you, why would she have come back during the fire? Why would she have stayed for four miserable years doing without? Then come back?"

"She came back because Samuels paid her to, so she could get me to sell the Bar K."

Scott stared at him aghast. "That's the stupidest thing I've ever heard you say. Nobody paid her to follow me into the Hills ready to shoot me down for endangering your life. Nobody paid her to tear open her arm in sacrifice for your soul. She cursed the gods to bring you back to her. If you owe your life to anyone, you owe it to her. Why would she go through so much trouble if she didn't care?"

Rory was silent. He was processing what his brother told him. And it fit in with all the shadowed remembrances. He'd thought it was a dream: The old Indian chanting over him; the firm grip of Scott's hand over his; Norah's frantic, angry cries. *Rory Prescott, don't you dare leave me! I love you!* He'd heard her and he'd come back. He couldn't explain it. He just knew. She'd told him the wrapping on her arm was from a cut she'd gotten in the woods. If he looked, would he find a simple cut or the symbolic scarrings his brother bore?

A tapping interrupted his glum musings. Upon Scott's cautious opening, Gena slipped through the door and came to kneel in front of Rory. He leaned into the hand she put to his cheek.

"Are you all right?"

"Doan fuss, Sis," he rumbled, but his quiet sigh encouraged it.

Scott watched the two of them together from his stoic distance. He watched his wife's touch move tenderly along his brother's face and observed the small smile of response from Rory. An unbidden tension began to creep along his muscle groups. Once aware of it, he forced it away with a conscious effort of control.

"Gena, come on. Leave him to the bed he's made." He crossed over to grip her arm, urging her to her feet with a compelling strength. Her reluctance was plain, but she didn't resist.

"Go on, Sis. It's all right. You two go on and curl up all nice and cozy. Doan even think a me over here all by my lonesome. I'll be fine." His weighty sigh

379

turned Gena to pudding.

"Oh, Rory." She leaned down to kiss the cheek he offered up; and seeing his satisfied smirk, Scott gave a snort of disgust. He hauled his wife back up and held her securely against his side.

"Get your own woman, fool. You know where to find her."

Rory scowled up at him. "Scotty, you got no mercy in your soul."

"What I've got is a woman who loves me to warm my bed, and I'm wise enough to know how fortunate I am. What you've got is too much pride and cold sheets. I don't feel sorry for you at all. Good night. Oh, and you'd better order up some ice for your nose if you want to see tomorrow. 'Course you've blundered through half your life blind, so you're probably used to it."

"Go on an' kick me again, Scotty. Everybody else has." He tottered to his feet and looped an easy arm about his brother's shoulders, pulling him in tight for a crushing hug. He used his other arm to include Gena in that affectionate circle. "Danged if I know how you put up with him, Gena-honey." He kissed her temple and pushed them both away. "If you ain't gonna feel sorry for me, you might as well leave," he grumbled with a surly petulance. Then he grinned wearily. "I'll see you in the morning."

Scott clapped his hand behind the redhead and shook him gently. "Think about what I said. And get that ice."

Smiling, Rory growled, "Git outta here."

Once in their own room, Gena reached for the lights; but Scott stilled her hand, drawing her into his arms instead. His kiss was long and lavish, and

380

she melted into it with a contented murmur.

"It's good to have you here, *cante skuya*. I've spent half our married life in rooms like this one without you beside me. I've missed so much."

Her answer was a soft, "I love you, Scott."

"It won't be like that anymore. I'll have you and Dawn and soon the baby with me. We'll be a family."

"We were always a family," she corrected gently as her fingertips traced the sharp angles of his face.

"I don't want to lose you, Gena. You are the most important thing in my life." His arms tightened almost to the point of discomfort. He was thinking of her hand on his brother's cheek. He shook that image away.

"Lose me? There's no danger of that."

"Gena . . ."

"What?" When he was silent, she leaned back so she could look up into his face. It was dark and shadowed except for a faint glimmer of outside light that reflected in the gold of his eyes. "What is it?"

"Why—nothing. It's nothing. Just foolishness."

"What?"

He took a shallow breath and plunged in. "Why would Norah think you and Rory were . . . lovers?"

She gasped in shock then was still. "Is that what you think?" she questioned softly.

"No. No, of course not." She could feel him knotting up with apprehension in spite of his bold words. She rubbed his shoulders and his arms, provoking him with a chiding smile. He ducked his head, shamefaced, and murmured, "I would hear you tell me I have nothing in this world to worry about."

"Scott." She cupped his chin in her hand and angled his gaze to meet hers. "You have nothing in this world to worry about."

"I'm sorry, Gena. I don't know why I had to ask."

She stretched up to silence him with a forgiving touch of her lips, then rested her head on one broad shoulder. She smiled with a degree of deviltry and told him, "I can see where you might be concerned. He does have the most devastating kiss."

"Should I be concerned enough to go next door and cut his heart out?"

Because she wasn't completely sure he was joking, Gena calmed him with a caress and a firm, "No. Besides, he's already done it to himself over Norah. Are all men so foolish or just the ones in your family?"

Scott made a disgruntled noise but squeezed her tight.

The kiss. If Norah had somehow seen it. . . . Gena frowned. "No wonder she's been so cool to me. And I'm almost sure she overhead Rory and me talking about the baby. She could have misunderstood."

"What?"

Now it was her turn to be uneasy. "Different things."

"Things you can speak about to my brother but not to me?"

She hugged him fearfully close. "Oh, Scott, I was afraid you'd think I was using this pregnancy to force you to take the job in Washington."

"But, Gena, that was my choice."

"Would you have made it if I weren't carrying this child?"

His silence was her answer.

"Scott, I don't want to take you from the things you love. They're the things I love, too. I don't want to live in Washington, going to affairs like this every night. I don't want to see you mourning for the loss of your freedom and your people."

"I wouldn't—"

"You would. You wouldn't say as much, but I'd know it in my heart and I would always feel to blame."

"But, Gena, I haven't been there for you. My brother held you when you gave birth to our daughter. My parents comforted you when you lost our babies. I have never been there when you needed me. How can you not blame me for that?"

She stroked his taut cheek and kissed him. "I don't."

"Am I making a mistake in considering this job?"

"What does your heart tell you?"

He took a moment to reach down deep, and then he told her, "It tells me to go home. To where my family lives and my spirit roams. It tells me I am the luckiest man alive to have a wife such as you and that I am a fool for not having asked you how you felt about this move. And it tells me if you ever kiss my brother on the mouth again, I should beat you soundly in proper Lakota fashion."

"I'm not afraid of you, Scott Prescott." Her fingers had begun a tempting massage beneath his starched shirt front.

"You should be," he warned, then he negated that caution with a hard, plunging kiss. When he leaned away, Gena smiled up at him as she led him further into the room, to where their bed was turned down and inviting.

"Like I said," she purred. "You have nothing in the world to worry about."

It took him a minute or two to figure out how the telephone worked so he could call down for some ice. Once that was done, Rory stripped to the waist and washed up, feeling better until he caught a glimpse of his face in the mirror. Damned if he wasn't going to look like a raccoon by morning once the blacking settled in beneath his eyes. His face ached. His ankle throbbed. His mind spun with indecision. It was going to be a long, long night. Thinking maybe he should order up something medicinal by the fifth, he was about to reach for the telephone when there was a knock on the door. He hobbled over and squinted out at one of the Rennert's liveried employees.

"Your ice, Mr. Prescott."

"Thanks, son. Set it over there." He limped to his dressing table to fish for some coins, tipping the boy generously enough to earn a broad grin.

"Thank you, sir!"

Rory fetched a towel from the bathroom and was ready to make an ice pack. Then he frowned. The hotel surely had the oddest way of supplying ice. They sent it packed around a magnum of champagne.

"Danged if they didn't feel sorry for me after all," he muttered, tipping the chilled bottle toward the room next door. He popped the cork and took a long swig before scooping a handful of shaved ice into the towel and holding it over his sore features. He studied the bottle, unable to repress a warmhearted grin. He remembered all the trouble a beautiful lady in Deadwood had started by sending a bottle of bubbly to his room. He'd been out of his mind crazy about that woman.

He still was.

It was then he noticed that beside the champagne bucket stood two long-stemmed goblets. Two. He stared at them for the longest time, his heart leaping up to bang in his throat. He nearly tripped over his own feet in his haste to answer the next knock on his door. For a moment, all he could do was gaze at the woman who stood outside his door in her shimmery gown with her expression set stubbornly and her grey eyes glimmering wetly. She wasted no time tearing into him.

"Before you say anything, Rory Prescott, I'll have you know I don't care a rap about your ranch or your money or anything else, except you. You probably won't believe me, but I'm going to tell you anyway. I had nothing to do with any plan to steal the Bar K out from under you."

"I know."

"And furthermore, I don't appreciate you . . . You know?"

"I'm sorry, honey. I didn't mean to ruin your speech. It was a good one, too. I can always tell by the way your eyes get all fired up. Why doan you step in outta the hallway and finish it for me?"

She hesitated.

"I'll share this here bottle a champagne with you if you'll help me pull off my boot."

His beguiling look melted her stern expression. At her small smile, his grin broke wide and he ushered her inside, shutting the door on the outside world.

"What do you mean, you know? How do you know?" she challenged testily, not ready to give up her argument so soon.

"You might say Scotty kicked the truth into my thick head."

Norah's temper blew up like a thundercloud as her touch eased along the break in his nose. "Scott did this to you?" That was a low, dangerous rumble.

"Whoa now, honey. Scotty didn't lay a hand on me, and I doan think he'd much cotton to you a-coming after him with a gun. Not a second time, anyway."

"He told you."

"Why didn't you tell me?"

Norah took a nervous step back from him, suddenly all too aware of his bare chest and brawny arms. Her emotions surged with wild palpitations. "The time wasn't right for it. And I was too busy being angry with you for something you didn't do."

"Hell, I did enough things to earn that. I wish you'd told me." His voice lowered to a husky timbre. Very gently, he pushed down the elbow-length gloves, baring the vicious-looking web of scarring along the fair white flesh of her inner arm. No sight had ever horrified and humbled him quite so completely.

"Dear God, Norah," he whispered thickly.

"It had to be a sacrifice from the one who loves you best. Scott was ready to offer up his fingers." She tried for a smile, but it snagged painfully and wavered.

"Hell, Scotty's a Lakota. He'd offer up both arms and legs for me without blinking an eye."

"So would I."

He swallowed, suddenly having a difficult time keeping his breathing regular. His fingertips grazed restlessly up and down her arm, and he couldn't look away from the inviting warmth building in her gaze.

"You want some of this?" he asked distractedly, gesturing toward the champagne.

"No," she murmured throatily. "I want some of this."

Her hand curled behind his neck, drawing him down for a soft, reacquainting taste of heaven. The tip of her tongue traced delicate patterns along the part of his lips until a groan rattled up from inside him.

"Take all you want," he whispered obligingly. "Seems I owe you one from that time in the barn. I'm truly sorry about that, Norah-honey. I was being a crazy jealous fool."

"Just one?" she queried saucily, completely ignoring his apology.

Rory grinned. "Well, now, darlin', we got us all night." Then he paused. "Doan we? Can you stay? I mean, is someone with Jacob?"

"Jacob's fine. Our housekeeper is there. He won't even know I'm gone, and you can be there in the morning when he wakes up."

"I like that idea a whole helluva lot." He sucked in a quick breath as Norah's hands worked open the front of his denims with an impatient skill. "Honey, boots first," he reminded her a bit breathlessly.

"I'm getting there," she countered wickedly as her hands pushed in next to hot skin. She kissed his mouth, his chin, his neck, his chest, working her way progressively lower until he forgot about the boots and the pain in his face.

Until he forgot damned near everything.

Chapter Twenty-four

Scott Prescott eyed the gentle feminine rounding of the covers beside his brother and frowned. He'd been worried that discomfort would keep Rory up all night, but from the looks of the empty champagne bottle upended in a bucket of water at the bedside and the intimate proximity of his companion, he probably hadn't felt the slightest pain. Yet, Scott vowed fiercely.

"Hang you, Rory, for making a liar out of me," he muttered furiously as he circled the foot of the bed. "I go out of my way to get you and Norah back together, and you go and hook up with some cheap piece of goods. Norah's going to send you back to the spirit world with one shot; and if she doesn't, I will."

He snapped the back of his hand against the woman's buttocks and snarled softly, "Get up out of there. How much does he owe you?"

"He owed me three years, and you owe us a little more privacy."

Norah's annoyance was tempered by the look of sheer amazement on Rory's brother's face. She'd never imagined the unflappable Scott Prescott could look so totally undone as he did standing at the edge of the bed with his chin hanging down to his chest.

"'Morning, Scotty," Rory muttered into his pillow. "The two a you mind keeping it down a little? I was trying to get some sleep. Norah-honey, tell him to go away."

"Go away," she repeated as Scott's jaw slowly shut and he blinked with a comic disbelief. Then the shock wore off, and he grinned with pure delight.

"I'll be damned."

"I'll see to it personal if you doan git outta here."

Smothering his smile, Scott said in his own defense, "Gena made me come check on you. She was afraid you might be suffering."

"You can tell her I survived the night quite nicely, thank you for askin'."

"We were heading down for breakfast."

"Go on without us. I'm having breakfast with my boy."

Scott gave the two of them a long appraising look and nodded to himself. Then to Norah, he said, "Sorry about the swat on the—"

"No problem."

Rory's bright head lifted off the pillow. "On the what?" he rumbled.

"I'll let you explain it to him, Norah." And Scott bowed out of the room quickly, grinning all the way.

"On the what?" he demanded, rolling over to confront his wife.

"Oh, my God!"

Her sound of dismay alarmed him. "What? What?"

"Oh, your poor face!" Her fingertips sketched the dark crescents rimming each eye.

"I seem to recall a plan to put ice on it, but I got distracted somehow." He grinned and she smiled back, smugly.

"Yes, you did." Her kiss was soft, sweet. "You never did tell me what happened last night."

"What part a last night were you wondering over, honey?" His dark eyes provoked a chuckle from her with their hot simmer of mischief. "It doan matter right this minute. All that matters is you're here and I'm having breakfast with my family. Everything else can wait."

And she was in total agreement.

"Daddy!"

Jacob came flying down the steps right into Rory's arms. Hugging the boy to him, Rory murmured happily, "Howdy, pard. Where's my coffee?"

"I'll go fetch you some," he offered eagerly, wiggling to be set down.

"Just a minute." Rory took another second to appreciate the feel of him in his embrace, then put him down.

"What happened to your eyes?"

"Musta happened when I put my foot in my mouth. You were getting me coffee?" As he scampered off, Rory looked around him. "Some place."

"Do you like it?" Norah asked, slipping her fingers between his as they stood side by side in the foyer.

He took in the austere style of the crate-like Mission furniture, the Morris chairs, the fringy portieres hanging in the archways, the artificial flowers displayed under glass bells, and the print of *The Burning of Rome* gracing the wall. It was stylish and posh. It was the home of a stranger; and, feeling very uncomfortable in it, he answered honestly. "No. But I bet it cost plenty."

"You don't want to know," she replied dryly.

"What's this?" He clomped into the parlor and

stroked his hands across the top of her phonograph in curiosity.

Smiling, she moved him aside. "Here I'll show you." As it began to play "Come, Josephine, in My Flying Machine," she watched a boyish wonder light his features with animation.

"Oooh, I gots to get me one a these."

He turned to study the contraption more closely, and her gaze shifted down to appreciate the sway of his hips rocking in time to the tune. Just as she was about to place her hands on that tempting snug denim, Jacob came clamoring into the room.

"Here you go, Daddy. Are you going to join Mr. Samuels? He's waiting in the breakfast room."

"That so?"

"Trevor's here?" Norah asked in obvious dismay. She was watching Rory. She hadn't wanted the mood between them to end so soon.

"Honey, why doan you go on up and get yourself dressed, and I'll go make some talk with Samuels."

Norah hesitated. She couldn't go meet Trevor in last night's crumpled evening gown, but could she trust her husband not to slay him in her absence? "Rory . . ."

"I'll show him where it is, Mama," Jacob offered, tucking his hand inside his father's much bigger one.

"I won't be a moment," Norah vowed and hurried for the stairs.

Jacob smiled up at his father and tugged him forward. "Boy, am I glad to see you. Mama doesn't know it, but I always wait up when she goes out in the evening, just until Trevor drops her off. Last night was the first time she didn't come home, and I got kind of worried. I guess she was with you, huh?"

"Yep. I was taking good care a your mama." *Lord bless you, Jacob Prescott, for answering that ques-*

tion for me. Trevor Samuels hadn't been spending his nights under this roof with his wife.

Trevor was surprised by Rory's appearance but not his presence. When Norah had disappeared from the party with the elder Prescott brother's wife, he'd guessed where she was going; and when he'd arrived at the townhouse earlier to be told she wasn't home, he'd known why. She'd gone to Prescott's bed. And now he was here bold as brass to rub it in with his smug smile and smoldery-eyed stare. Well, he wasn't going to be discouraged. They were on his territory now and, here, Rory Prescott was the stranger.

"My, but you look the worse for wear," he said mildly as the big cowboy took a seat.

"Forgot they had rats in cities. Big 'uns, too. Fell over some on my way back to my hotel last night. But you wouldn't know nothing about that now, would you?"

"No, I'm afraid not. Jacob, why don't you go find Bridget? Perhaps your father would like to have some breakfast. Tell her I'll just have coffee, as usual." He was quite pleased by the set and grind of Prescott's teeth as Jacob hurried off. As soon as the boy was out of earshot, he dropped the polite mask. "Why are you here? Haven't you done enough to hurt Norah? Why can't you just leave her alone?"

"Can't see that it's any a your business. As for my leavin', you can ask her if she wants me gone."

"My concern is for Norah and Jacob."

"So's mine, seeing as how they belong to me."

"Not for much longer." The cowboy winced at that, and Trevor decided to drop the polite emotional appeal. "Look around you. This is the home she's made for the two of them, a home I've been welcome in for a year now. You don't fit in here. Norah and I share the same friends, the same interests, the same plans. I bet you don't know the slightest thing about her outside of the bedroom."

Rory bristled at that, but Samuels went on smoothly.

"I know what it is she sees in you. It shames her that she cannot seem to control it. But on other levels, do you have anything in common with your wife? I think not. Did you know she serves on a half-dozen charitable committees and has raised a small fortune for the betterment of this community? Did you know she's had moving editorials published in both the *Sun* and the *News*? She's a member of the best women's clubs in Baltimore and a sought-after guest in every fashionable drawing room. What do you offer her, Mr. Prescott? What kind of intellectual stimulation and worthwhile pursuits? You really don't expect her to give up all this to sit in that big lonely house waiting for you to come in from your cows, do you? And what about Jacob? You have to steal money from your own wife to pay your bills. How are you going to provide any kind of security for that little boy? Would you have him shoveling manure in stalls or making a future for himself at a fine school? If you love them, how could you possibly demand that they surrender all that they have to settle for what you can give them? I can supply them with what they need, with what they deserve. How can you argue with that in good conscience?"

Rory stared at him across the crisp white table linen and drawled very quietly, "They're my family. They love me, not you."

"And you think it's that simple?"

"I know it is."

At that moment, Jacob came racing back into the room, darting straight for his father. He clambered up on Rory's lap and looped his arms about the big rancher's neck, smiling up at him with such un-abashed affection, the redhead's chest plugged up solid with emotion. He rumpled the boy's hair then took off his new Stetson and planted it firmly on his son's head.

"Well, lookee there. Almost fits."

"Does that mean I can start doing your books for you, Daddy?"

"Probably couldn't make more of a mess in 'em than I have. That'd be up to your mama, son."

Jacob's smile faded slightly. "You are taking us back with you, aren't you?"

"That'd be up to your mama, too."

He looked up to see Norah standing in the arched entry. No one could look as drop-dead gorgeous in the tight complication of clothing as his wife. She was every inch elegant, and he was as awe-struck as the first time he'd laid eyes on her. She stood poised like a fashion doll, her gaze going cautiously between him and Trevor. The Easterner bounded up, his hands on the back of the chair beside him, inviting her to sit at his side. Because Jacob was on his lap and his foot pained something fierce, Rory didn't stand. But he commanded her with his stare.

Don't you go to him, Norah. By God, you're still my wife. You come here to me. Come here!

She received that arrogant order from him with a slight stiffening of form. Her grey eyes narrowed in objection, and she was readying to turn toward Trevor in defiance of his challenge. Then, Rory softened his look, letting his expression ease from its tense lines, letting his dark eyes grow lambent and his smile loosen in a seductive curve, beckoning.

C'mon over here to me, Norah-honey. Come over here where you belong.

And she did. Without pause. As if Trevor had

suddenly fallen off the face of the earth. Drawn by the warmth and promise of his gaze just as she'd resisted his cold command. Responding because he wanted her, not because he owned her, and he would never again forget that. He reached up a hand, and she meshed her fingers through his as she took a definitive stand behind his chair. He let his smile convey a surprisingly humble gratitude, but when he looked across the table at Trevor, that look hardened with a gloating triumph.

See, I told you how it was that smug look said, but Trevor refused to relent.

"Norah, you haven't forgotten our luncheon with the Bowdoins, have you?" he murmured casually as he resumed his seat.

"What?" She'd been toying with the bright hair at the nape of her husband's neck and missed what he was saying.

"The Bowdoins?"

"Oh. Of course. That was today?" She sounded distressed by the reminder, and Trevor pressed gently.

"Yes. They're expecting us. Remember? We're going to get their pledge for housing funds?"

"Yes. Ummm . . . Trevor . . ." Her fingers were rubbing lightly along Rory's neck in a distracting caress. And because her reluctance was so obvious, he was inclined to be generous.

"Honey, if you got plans for today, it's all right. I understand. Jacob can show me around. He doesn't have school on Saturday. You go on and take care of your business. We'll be jus' fine."

And his confidence was the worst kind of threat to Trevor Samuels. It meant he hadn't the slightest worry over his place in his wife's life.

"Well, then," Trevor announced with a clearing of

his throat. "I guess I should be going. I'll be by for you around elevenish?"

"Fine. Jacob, could you show Trevor out, please?"

That clearly wasn't the escort he had in mind, but he smiled tightly and kept his protest to himself. He hadn't given up yet.

When they were alone, Norah slid around to take her son's vacated place on Rory's lap. Her palms stroked over his cheeks with a restless longing.

"Are you sure you don't mind? I can cancel. It's not really important."

He caught her hands, holding them still, holding her attention with the sudden gravity of his stare. "Norah, have you ever been unfaithful to me?"

"No."

Everything inside him shivered loose at one time. He took a raspy breath and swallowed hard. His voice was very quiet. "Then I doan mind." And his eyes slid shut as she bent down to kiss him.

"C'mon, Daddy," Jacob burst in with his childish enthusiasm. "We've got a lot to see." He tugged on Rory's hand until his father sighed and reluctantly swatted Norah on the bottom to move her off his knees.

"Jacob, don't wear your father out," she warned sternly. And the simmering look she gave the big cowboy stated plainly that she wanted that privilege for herself.

"I won't, Mama."

But he did. In his youthful exuberance, he tried to show his father everything Baltimore had to offer in the span of one day. While western footgear wasn't designed for city sidewalks, Rory enjoyed himself too much to complain. He delighted in riding on the electric streetcars and was awed by the press of the crowds. Nothing in his travels to Deadwood or

Cheyenne prepared him for an eastern city. Jacob had to drag him away from the storefronts and had to jostle him hard several times to keep him from stepping in front of a snorting motorcar. The boy was impressed to hear that he'd once driven his mother about during their courting days, but Rory grinned and refused to elaborate when Jacob pressed for details. They visited the park, a vaudeville show, and an amusement park where Rory was chagrined to find he couldn't hit the broad side of a barn in the shooting galleries. It was going on four o'clock and Rory was going on the last of his reserves when they returned to the townhouse.

As Jacob scrambled upstairs with his purchases, Rory was able to vent his distress. With a heartfelt groan, he hobbled into the parlor and eased down onto one of the uncomfortable chairs. Using the heel of his right boot as a jack, he worked off his left, gripping the arms of the chair and his jaw with a sweat-popping concentration. As it gave, he sighed with relief. His ankle was pounding, protesting the long walk on hard byways. Dragging it up onto a low stool, Rory let his head fall against the back of the chair and his body go limp.

"I can't tell by looking at you if you had a good time or if I should call for an ambulance."

"Gimme a minute. You may have to call in an undertaker." Rory rolled his head upon the hard wood to grin weakly at his wife. She smiled back, but kept her hesitant distance. A tenuous mood settled between them, and Rory ventured very softly, "I had a right fine day. And I thank you for lettin' me have it."

"I'm sure Jacob enjoyed it every bit as much."

The tension grew. It was awkward and uncomfortable but not a destructive tension. Rory shut his eyes for a moment, trying to whip up the strength to move. He didn't want to. He didn't want to face the fact that he had divorce papers ready to give this woman in his hotel room. One night of soul-shattering lovemaking didn't change that. But a lot of words might. He just wasn't sure which ones to use.

"From the looks of all the bags you left in the hall, you must of visited every department store in town," Norah was saying.

He grinned. "Just about and they were surely something to see. Why they had things I ain't never seen 'cept in catalogs. They had this little trolly-like thingamabob that took my money and brought me my change and—" He broke off. She was smiling at him, and he flushed. "Well, I ain't tell you nothing new," he grumbled, feeling suddenly the worst kind of country hayseed in her sophisticated eyes. Probably Jacob thought so, too, he figured glumly, thinking back on how he'd gushed about the wonders of the five-and-dime over a five-cent Coca-Cola. "I'd best be going."

Norah came to him then, dropping her wary pose as she sank beside his chair. She used both of her hands to hold him down in it. "Catch your breath and tell me what you bought."

With her so close, it was hard to think of anything as abstract as leaving. Rory smiled and eased back against the cushions, basking in her attention.

"Well, lemme see. I got Daddy a pyrography set—that's one of them things that burns lines in wood." Norah nodded, smiling to encourage him. "An' I got Dawn a magic lantern with colored-glass slides in it. An' Mama a phonograph. She's gonna love that. An' I got me a Brownie camera. Purely amazing thing for a dollar. I already done took a batch a pictures of

Jacob when we was at the park. He was riding on this fat ole pony—the sorriest excuse for horseflesh you ever did see—an' I—"

"I love you, Rory."

"—an' I got Jacob a deck a cards so's he can practice up to show Dawn a thing or two when he comes home to visit me." His voice dwindled off; and, for a moment, he sat staring at the brightly patterned rug, not saying anything, not looking up at her. His rhythm of breathing grew increasingly erratic until his chest was jerking with it.

"Did you hear what I said?"

He nodded slightly but still wouldn't look up, not until Norah's hand curved beneath his jaw and lifted. His dark gaze had liquified into a yearning so intense it took her breath away to see it. She began to bend, leaning down toward the temptation of his softly parted lips.

"There you are, Mama."

Norah jumped back, and Rory dashed a hand across his eyes.

"Trevor's here. You ain't going out tonight, are you?"

"Aren't," both parents corrected at the same time. When Norah glanced at him, bemused, Rory grinned sheepishly.

"Cain't have my boy soundin' like no ignorant cowhand," he explained.

Norah smiled, unable to take her eyes from him as she instructed Jacob to show her guest into the sitting room.

"Awww, Mama. Do I have to? I was fixing to talk to Daddy."

"You do what your mama tells you."

"Jacob, I need to talk to your daddy for a minute. You go on."

"Sheeeooot." The tow of his shoe scuffed at the rug indignantly, but he shuffled off to do as he was told.

Rory was grinning crookedly. "I musta given my mama a whole lotta grief when I was his age."

"And she loved every minute of it," Norah guessed rightly. Then she sobered. "About tonight."

"You doan need to explain nothing to me, Norah. You got your own life here. I ain't gonna get in your way."

"You're not. I want you here. It's just that I've made these commitments and—"

"Honey, I said it was all right."

She looked unconvinced. She took up his lax hand, pressing her cheek into its rough palm. "Come with me."

"What?"

"Come with me tonight. It's a big dinner party. I've invited Scott and Gena to join me. I promised Scott some introductions and—"

"No, honey. I won't be no third wheel."

"Rory—"

"'Sides, I doan think I could stand up let alone hold out for no fancy mix and mingling. I'll jus' hire up one a them hacks to take me back to the hotel and spend the evening soaking my foot. I can't put my boot back on."

"Soak it upstairs," she suggested impulsively. When he opened his mouth to protest, she hurried on. "Stay. Please. You can have supper with Jacob. I know he'd love it. I won't be out late. Be here when I get back. Please."

"Norah-honey, I—"

"Rory, please."

He searched her beseeching gaze then relented. "Awright."

She touched her lips to the heel of his hand and

stood. "I'd better get ready." Still, she stood there, hanging onto his hand until he pulled it away.

"Go on."

She returned to say good night; and, as he struggled to stand, she hurried to him instead, easing him back into the chair with the pressure of her palms. She was a vision in soft peach satin trimmed with creamy lace and velvet ribbons. His smoldering gaze of appreciation altered when he saw her hat.

"Did you shoot an' stuff them poor little things up there yourself?"

Norah reached up curiously, then remembered the stuffed doves adorning the poufs of lace. She laughed, a low ripple of sound that moved over him like a heated caress. "Would you rather I didn't wear it? I could go wrapped in a bearskin."

"That an' nothing else," he suggested huskily as he caught the edge of her skirt and reeled her in close. "No, honey, you look jus' fine. Jus' fine." His hand moved up and down her thigh, shifting the satin along her leg. "An' I'm gonna enjoy taking it off you, later."

He felt her shiver with anticipation, and his mood was much appeased. Her hand slid over the top of his, redirecting it slightly. She rocked against his palm.

"I don't have to go."

He laughed and retrieved his hand from the hot contour of her body. His smile was pure provocation. "You jus' remember what you got waiting."

She knelt in a pool of shimmery fabric, her gaze intent upon his. "You will be here?"

"Yes, ma'am."

"Norah, are you ready to go?"

Rory's smile strained at the sound of Trevor's voice, and he turned his head a slight degree so that her kiss took him on the cheek instead of the mouth. Chagrined, Norah rubbed the smudge of lip rouge off with her thumb.

"I won't be late."

"G'night," he murmured noncommittally.

She grabbed his head between her hands so he couldn't move and savaged his lips with a hard shock of passion. Panting lightly, she told him, "It's going to make me crazy thinking about you." Then she was gone before he could reply.

The first people Norah sought out in the glittering affair were Scott and Gena Prescott. With Trevor and Carter in tow, she crossed to the handsome couple and stretched up to embrace the stoic half-Sioux. She could feel his recoil of surprise, but he was quick enough to understand her motive. What better way to establish their alliance to this room of politicians and bureaucrats?

"Where's my brother?" he asked quietly as she pressed her cheek to his smooth bronze one.

"Soaking his foot and probably enjoying his evening much more than we will be."

He laughed at the truth of her wryly spoken statement. "I'm sorry about the misunderstanding this morning."

Norah stepped back and smiled. "No, you're not."

He grinned, an attractive slash of white against his copper skin. His arm went purposefully around his wife's waist, drawing her in close so the two women couldn't avoid speaking.

"Hello, Gena," Norah began with a cool formality. Then she saw the tender emotion swelling in the other woman's eyes and realized Scott had told her everything. Color climbed hotly in her cheeks along with a terrible embarrassment. But Gena refused to let her suffer from it. She reached out to draw her sister-in-law into a warm enveloping circle, hugging close, bridging too many things to mention aloud with that embrace.

"Norah, Rory is so in love with you, no other woman even exists for him," Gena whispered forcefully for her hearing alone.

"I know. Forgive me for being so foolish."

Gena leaned back, smiling delightedly. Then she glanced at Trevor, who lingered by Norah's side, and asked in a low voice, "Then the two of you are back together?"

"We're working out the details," was all Norah could admit. But it was enough to satisfy the pretty blond. She hugged to her husband's arm happily and simmered sweetly when he drew her thumb down her soft cheek.

"Will you allow me to talk business now, *mitawicu?*"

"Go ahead. I'm content."

Scott put out a judicious hand to Trevor Samuels and nodded to his lawyer. "I've come to collect on your promises to my people, Samuels."

"I'm sorry, Mr. Prescott," Carter interrupted smoothly, "but what promises might those be?"

Scott gave him a cool, severing glare, then looked again to the elegant Trevor Samuels. "Are you suffering from an equally poor memory and lack of conscience?"

"I told you I don't break promises," Trevor assured him.

"What he means," Carter asserted quickly, "is that he understands your concerns and will see them channeled through the proper chain of—"

"Red tape," Scott finished for him. "I'm very

familiar with the trail. It's vague and shadowy and has a very abrupt dead end." His hard eyes challenged Trevor. "I had thought better of you."

"Trevor," Norah spoke up as she wound her arm through his. "What exactly did you promise Scott?"

Scott answered. "He promised to stand behind my push to repeal the Burke Act."

"Mr. Prescott," Carter cut in. "Your protests are quite misguided. Mr. Leupp, of your Commission of Indian Affairs, heralded that bill as one that would end the restrictions keeping your—people from taking their place as citizens."

"What it does, Mr. Samuels," Scott continued, ignoring the little lawyer, "is perpetuate the lie of the Dawes Act as a device for expropriating Indian land. When Congress granted the Commission the power to sell land held in trust for the Sioux, it made itself into a puppet of rich merchants like your father who pressure for control of the best lands then sell them off for dry farming. It's the blindness of reformers like you, who mask your good deeds with misinformation about my people, that do the most damage."

"And fanatics like you who hinder progress," Carter concluded thinly.

"Gentlemen, please," Norah interjected as a cool voice of reason. "This is a dinner party, not a debate."

"Yes," Trevor agreed, then said quickly, "and if you'll excuse me for a moment, I must go say hello to the Thayers." As he left, Carter trailed after like an obedient pup.

"Let me talk to him," Norah advised, placing a calming hand upon Scott's seething chest. "Back down or you'll get nothing accomplished. Gena, keep him away from anything sharp until I get back."

Trevor smiled down at her tightly when she returned to his arm. "I thought I'd been deserted," he remarked dryly.

"Just smoothing ruffled feathers."

"That's what I adore about you, Norah. Always the soul of diplomacy." He lifted her hand for a fond kiss, pausing when his gaze caught on the gold of her wedding band. Then, determinedly, he tucked her in close to his side.

"What did you promise him, Trevor?"

"Oh, the usual. That I would help if I could. That I would push where it was needed."

"And?"

"And?"

"Are you?"

"I would like to, Norah. I believe he is just in his grievances. I'm just not certain it would be wise of me, politically, to intervene at this time."

She braked abruptly in the center of the room and stared at him. "I beg your pardon? Would you clarify that for me?"

"Carter feels—"

"Carter? You mean your father."

"Nonsense, Norah. He doesn't influence my decisions."

"Doesn't he? If not, then take a stand on this, on what you believe is right."

Trevor vacillated, clearly uneasy with her demand. Ever the politician, he chose to skirt the issue by forcing another. "How can I make any kind of a stand when I'm half out of my mind wondering where it is you'll decide to be?"

"There should be no question of that, Trevor," she answered. "I stand with my family."

Chapter Twenty-five

"After all they've put you through? Norah, how could you be so blind?"

But while talking with the suave politician, staring up at him, blindness was slowly falling away. "You used me."

Trevor looked confused. Before he could placate her with any silky explanations, she continued with a more aggressive understanding.

"Oh, I know much of my charm for you has been the fact that I know whom I know and that I have—or rather had—an extensive bank account. That, I didn't mind. And I didn't mind helping you with your speeches and greasing the wheel of your campaign with words in the proper ears. That's business and I understand business. I can also see that a wife who can organize your social schedule and can entertain your political constituents would be of more value to you than a woman who stirs you to great passion."

"Norah, please," he whispered in a shocked voice, glancing about to see if anyone were listening. He looked very uncomfortable with her words; and she realized it was because they were intimate and they never had been, not on any level.

"But I wouldn't have minded that, either, Trevor. What I do mind is what you did in South Dakota. You used me. You dug up that information about the Bar K finances and you used it to drive a wedge between Rory and me. You couldn't lose, could you? If he'd sold the Bar K, your father would have had the ranch. If he said no, which he did, you were sure you'd have me. But I think I'm giving credit to the wrong person. Carter must have masterminded it. You just used the weapons he gave you. You didn't count on Rory being man enough to stand up against your father, because you never were."

He was staring at her, aghast, features pale with a distraught helplessness. She no longer found it endearing. She found it flaccid.

"I'm sorry, Trevor. I truly like you. You've been wonderful to me and to Jacob. I admire ambition, but I cannot be with someone who condones irresponsible ruthlessness to get what he wants. Compassion and compromise are noble traits, but they aren't weakness. I'm sorry, Trevor, but I no longer have any respect for you." That said, she marched away, back to join the Prescotts, back where she belonged.

Dang but the city was cold and lonely at night.

Rory let the curtain fall back in place. There were no stars, no natural lights above. Just a gritty haze cut by the blaze of man-made brilliants. There was no space. Houses, crammed in together, elbowed out trees and grass and even ground with its covering of artificial surfaces. Noisy, too. Motorcars sputtered and blared their horns; streetcars still clamored, and the to-and-fro movement outside the house was ceaseless. It made him edgy. It made him homesick. It made him wonder how on earth his brother had survived all those years in school.

He prowled the downstairs rooms, and his agitation increased. It was her house, only this one was worse than the mansion on the Bar K. In this one, there was no evidence that he'd ever existed. It was a testimony of how well she'd done for herself without him. And unbidden, Trevor Samuels' words returned as food for doubt. Had he any right to take them from this? He wasn't of the city, but Norah was. She understood its rhythms and thrived on its hectic pace. Jacob was her son. Did he have anything back in the Dakotas that could come close to this? No, not for a thousand miles in any direction. He'd never understood her unhappiness until he, as Scotty would say, had walked in her moccasins for a day. His feet hurt. And he was damned discouraged.

Figuring Jacob would be ready for bed, Rory climbed the stairs with halting difficulty. At the top landing, he hesitated to catch his breath and his bearings. Before dinner, he'd soaked in a big, old tub at the end of the hall. The door was closed, so he assumed the boy was still in there splashing. Jacob's room was on one side of the stairs and Norah's on the other. He didn't know which was which and going back down was out of the question. He chose to go left out of a desperate need to sit down and had only to step across the threshold to be enveloped by Norah's presence. He closed his eyes and breathed deep, drawing in and savoring the scent of violets and powder and crisp starched fabrics and bedlinens. His anticipation for her return spiked hotly, then eased to a simmer. He was about to leave when curiosity held him, prompting him to turn on the light to take a quick look around.

Nice. Stylish but not cluttered, just like Norah. Not a man's room but not uninviting either. There was a fireplace framed in warm tiles and a big stretch of open floorboards right in front of it to tempt his imagination. He was still grinning to himself when his roving gaze touched on her nighttable. All it bore were two pictures. One was a close-up photo of a stiffly posed Jacob. The other was the sketch Gena had done of him, Dawn, and Jacob at the stream the day they'd caught Jacob's fish. He crossed over for a closer look. It was good. He'd been captured in full, cheeky grin with his arms about his son. And Norah had kept it here, at her bedside.

"Whatcha doing, Daddy?"

He gave a guilty start, then smiled. "Jus' looking at your Aunt Gena's drawing."

"Nice, isn't it? She gave it to me, but Mama said I got the bearskin so she wanted the picture. Doesn't even have my fish in it," he pouted, then immediately brightened. "Hey, come down and see my room. I've got all sorts of keen stuff."

Rory ran his fingertips along the frame pensively.

"C'mon, Daddy!"

Keen stuff, he'd said. Rory gazed about the boy's room in amazement. He would have thought he was in heaven if he'd had half of the things Jacob stashed on every surface and shelf. His own childhood toys had consisted of a horse, a rope, a fishing pole, figures Ethan had whittled—and acres of grass, streams, hills, and trees. And for his first ten years, his brother. He guessed city boys needed more material pleasures to make up for the lack of space to let their imagination roam wild. The only thing he could claim he'd given his own son was the big bearskin stretched out on the floor.

"Well, ain't this somethin'," he remarked, then sat

down on the bed to ease his foot while Jacob proudly displayed his collection of stamps, streetcar transfers, and baseball cards.

"Have you ever been to a baseball game, Daddy?"

Rory shook his head, smiling softly.

"I'll take you to one, someday."

Someday. Rory's smile tightened.

"And this is a model steam engine. It really works, too. Trevor—Trevor helped me put it together." He cast a shy glance at his father, then hurried on. "And Mama bought me this chemical set, but she won't let me play with it until I'm older. She makes me take piano lessons. Did Grandma ever make you do that?"

"No. I think I'da run away from home first. I can play a harmonica, sorta. Scotty taught me when we was little."

"Really?" Jacob looked impressed. A harmonica was much more appealing to him than the big, old parlor piano where he took his torturous lessons for fifty cents an hour. "And here's my kite. *I* picked out all the colors, and Trevor—" He broke off, looking embarrassed once more.

"Jake, doan go hanging your head like that. You ain't got nothing to be ashamed of. He was here to do them things with you. I wasn't. That's not your fault."

"I wish it had been you," he murmured quietly with a candor that tore Rory's heart in two.

"So do I." He swallowed down the wad of regret and smiled. "You gonna show me how to fly that thing?"

Jacob's animation returned. "Sure. Tomorrow if we've got the wind for it. Kite weather's in the spring, though. I was hoping to find some arrowheads for the tail, but—"

Rory poked at the grizzly's head with his toe. "But you got distracted by our friend here. I'll have Dawn

410

round you up some and send them." *Send them.* A terrible sorrow rose up from his soul. He hoped Jacob wouldn't catch on to his words, but the boy was smart. He stared at his father through bespectacled eyes, that gaze fearful and uncertain.

"You're not leaving, are you, Daddy?"

"Son, I can't stay here. I gotta go home. If I didn't, who'd look after Bud and Ghost and keep your cousin outta mischief?"

"Oh." He stared glumly at the floor. Then with a double-barrelled directness, he asked, "Are you going to let Trevor be my daddy?"

Rory pulled a tight-chested breath. "I'm your daddy. And you're a Prescott."

"That's what Mama said, too."

"Did she?" All tension inside him eased. "Hey, time for you to be under them covers."

As he scooted underneath them, he asked, "Will you read to me for a while? Mama always does."

"Well, now, I ain't much for readin' out loud but . . ." How could he say no to that clean-scrubbed face lifted up to him? He remembered many a night from his own childhood, the four of them on the front porch watching the stars wake against the distant sky, Scotty dozing on their mama's lap, and him with his head lying on his daddy's chest, feeling the comforting rumble of his voice as he told them a story. Nothing came as close to being perfect in his life as those precious nights embraced by his family's love, except waking up to a cool, silver dawn with Norah pressed up against him for shared warmth. Or the happy innocence of his son's expression as he shoved over to give him room beside him at the headboard.

"Awright. Whatcha want me to read?"

Jacob fished under the edge of his bed and

produced a well-worn dime novel. "This one." Rory opened his arm, and he nestled in contentedly, passing his father the book. The big cowboy eyeballed the cover depicting a muscular fellow in scanty athletic clothes breaking through the winners tape at the end of a race. Several rather well-endowed cheerleaders were bouncing on the sidelines. They had on short skirts. No wonder his brother had liked college.

"Who's this feller?"

"He's Frank Merriwell. He's my favorite. He's an All-American hero. He doesn't drink or smoke or swear or treat women with disrespect."

"Doan sound like nobdy I'd like to know. Bet he can't rope a steer or ride a bronc."

"Oh, Daddy. He's just a pretend hero, not like you."

Mollified, Rory gave the book his attention. "Let's see what this feller Frank does for a livin'. Says here he's a prep-school hero who goes to Yale—Scotty ain't gonna like that, him being a Harvard man." Jacob grinned encouragingly. "Says he stands for virtue being its own reward. Maybe, but that doan pay the bills."

"Daddy," Jacob complained, but he was still smiling.

"Says he personifies the American ideal and is pure of heart. Doan sound like nobody your mama'd like to know, either."

"Read."

Rory squinted hard at the printed page. "Awright. Says he's a paragon of athletic prowess. Whatcha suppose that means?"

"He's good in sports."

"Oh. Why didn't they just come out and say that, then? Prowess? What's that mean?" Jacob shrugged.

Rory recalled Norah praising him for his virile prowess, and he scowled. Was this the kind of book he should be reading to a seven-year-old?

"Your eyes bothering you, Daddy? You've got them scrunched up something fierce. Here. Try these on."

Out of curiosity, Rory fit Jacob's spectacles on the bridge of his nose and then he made a small sound of amazement as the words popped into focus. He looked over the rims then through the lens several times, surprised by the way things went from a muted blur to sharp detail. "Well, I'll be," he muttered. "Mind if I borrow these to read this here story?"

Jacob shook his head and burrowed up against his father's side.

And that was how Norah found them hours later.

It was a dreadful evening. Norah had never been so glad to shut her front door upon Baltimore society. Dinner had been a laborious endurance of Trevor's baleful glances. She couldn't miss the wounded looks as she squired the Sioux lawyer through the echelons of Baltimore's rank and file in much the same way she had him. Scott was suave and polished, Gena sweet and endearing. Norah's elite friends were enchanted. But as the evening wore on, all she could think of was Scott Prescott's redheaded brother waiting in her home and she couldn't wait to leave.

None of the lights were on downstairs, but Rory's coat hung by the door to calm her alarm. If he was waiting upstairs, the possibilities were even more intriguing. Puzzled, she followed the spill of lamplight to Jacob's door and stood at the threshold for long minutes soaking up the sight of the two of them. Jacob was tucked into the bend of her husband's arm, his own thin one banding the big cowboy's middle. One of Jacob's dime novels lay open upon Rory's slow-moving chest, and her son's eyeglasses rested beneath the swollen break in his nose. Both of them were fast asleep.

Moving quietly so as not to wake them, she crossed to the bedside, leaning over to kiss Jacob's soft cheek. Then, smiling to herself, she eased the book out of Rory's slack hand and removed Jacob's glasses, putting both on the bureau top. Looking down on the slumbering redhead, the uncomplicated love she felt for her son deepened and expanded into richly shaded emotion. She wanted to kiss him good night, too; but a simple bussing of the cheek wasn't going to be enough, so she didn't. He looked too done-in with his battered nose and radiating bruises. He never did tell her who or what had hit him. He'd said it wasn't Scott. She should believe him. She would believe him from now on.

Carefully, she drew the quilt up from the foot of the bed until it covered the two of them snugly. For a moment she leaned close, savoring the scent of just-washed boy and warm, clean man. With an effort, she switched off the light and returned to her own room where she slipped into her nightclothes and into her bed, alone. It wasn't how she'd planned to end her evening, but she wouldn't complain. Rory was here, beneath her roof; and, for now, that was more than enough.

She closed her eyes and drifted for a long moment, letting her imaginings fill with the memory of Rory Prescott's scintillating kisses. And then he was kissing her, softly at first, then with increasing fervor as she stirred in response. Her bed dipped with his joining weight, and she was smiling when her eyes opened. A warm, mellow glow bathed his features in a wash of bold bronze and dusky shadow. He'd made a fire, she realized in some surprise. She wasn't aware that she'd fallen asleep.

"Why didn't you wake me up when you got home?" he complained huskily as he settled over the top of her in an intimate press. He was partially dressed, having stripped down to his denims. He carried most of his weight on elbows and knees so she could feel him and not be crushed beneath him.

Norah freed one of her hands to brush his bright hair back from his brow. A wonderful tenderness jockeyed the excitement aside as she replied, "You looked like Jacob had worn you down to the bone. I felt sorry for you."

"He's a helluva little guy."

"I wanted to give you more children, Rory."

He was surprised into complete stillness.

"I'm so sorry," she continued quietly. "You never said anything, but I knew how hurt you were. I know how hard you tried not to blame me, but it was my fault. I insisted we move into town. I wanted that baby so bad, but I was scared of having it alone at the Bar K. You were so good to me and you never complained about making that ride back and forth everyday, but I could see what it was doing to you. Part of me was relieved when I miscarried, because then we could go home and you wouldn't have to work so hard anymore. I don't think God ever forgave me for being glad."

"But I do. I do, honey. Why didn't you ever tell me how you was feeling?"

Once it started, there was no holding back the stream of anguish seeping from the corners of her eyes. "Because you were never there, Rory; and when you were, we never told each other anything."

The truth of that struck hard. He'd been so busy

working to please her and loving to appease her he'd had no time to simply care for her the way he should have. He'd concentrated on all the wants and forgotten the needs. He'd been twenty-years-old when fate forced him into the shoes of a man three times his age. He'd never had time to explore the joys of being a husband or a father. Because he had been afraid to hesitate, he'd plunged right in over his head and, for eight years, hadn't been able to break surface.

"Norah, when you left that first time, you told me it was because I didn't need you. I know I didn't say it proper or probably even show it; but, honey, having you and Jacob was the only thing that kept me going. I couldn't have gotten up day after day to do the things I had to do if it wasn't for the knowing that you was there for me to hold to when I got home at night. When you left me, I was outta my mind for the longest time. I spent every night in town, inside a bottle, scared to go home to nothing. I'd a kilt myself if Daddy hadn't come after me and kicked my butt but good. He tole me that nobody who loved me as much as you did was gonna stay away forever and that I'd better make damned sure that I had something worth you coming home to. Come home with me, Norah."

"Rory, you should find yourself someone who'd take care of you and give you children. Someone like Gena."

"Gena's my brother's wife. You're *my* wife. I don't want nobody but you. You gave me the finest boy a man could ever ask for. Any time I get to hankering for more kids, all I have to do is put him and Dawn in a room for an hour and wait for 'em to get scrapping. Cools a man's desire for a passel a kids right quick."

When she responded with a faint smile, he leaned down to brush away her tears with the softest of kisses; one to the corner of either eye, then to the yielding cushion of her mouth. She made a quiet, vulnerable sound and cast her arms around him. When she made it clear with arching shifts of her body that she was interested in more than tender kisses, Rory lifted up, grinning.

"C'mon."

Norah frowned. "Come where?" They were already in bed. What more could he want? But he rolled off her and off the mattress to tug her hands.

"C'mere."

Perplexed, she scooted after him, leaving the inviting sheets. And then she saw what he had in mind.

He'd built the fire up to a cheery warmth. Before the hearth, sprawled Jacob's bear rug.

"I couldn't think a nothing else after you mentioned wearing it. All I kept picturing was your bare skin on this here bearskin. What do you think?"

"Hmmm." She knelt down on it and sank her fingers deep into the pile. "Oooo. It's thick. Nice. Come see for yourself." Her arms reached up for him. He filled them in a heartbeat. After sharing a long, lapping kiss, he stretched out beside her.

"Feels a lot nicer being on the outside a him than it did on the inside."

He leaned over her, kissing her lips lightly before thrusting his tongue between them. After a very thorough examining, he remarked, "Now that was pretty nice in there." His hand skimmed down her nightgown, the roughness of his palm creating a soft whispery growl as it rasped over the fragile silk. Then she gave a luxurious purr as it made the return journey along sleek inner thigh to plunge within the anticipating heat of her body.

"Oh, yeah. This is nice, too." And he continued

417

the movement until her breathing began to labor. Then, he withdrew.

It took him a scant second to shuck out of his Levis, then he was pressing in hard and hot all the way up to the walls of her belly. Norah moaned his name and hung on tight. "Oh, now, sweet darlin', that is right nice. What'd you think?" He punctuated his question with a slow draw and hard thrust that had her groaning. "What? Didn't quite catch that."

"Very nice," she agreed breathlessly.

"Must be due to my virile prowess," he gloated, then, after a second of thought, he frowned. "What kinda books are you letting Jacob read that they talk about such things right there on the cover? Why I never—"

She pulled his head down and kissed him hard to shut him up. "Now, what are you talking about?"

"Prowess."

She smiled. "That means exceptional bravery or extreme skill."

He thought for a minute then grinned wide. "I think I like that. Yes, I do. Thank you very much." And he meant to take his sweet time living up to it.

Norah sighed as his fingertips flirted around the pucker of one breast.

"This is right pretty," he mentioned casually as his thumbs edged her nightdress away from both aching peaks. "I ain't never seen you in something like this." He lowered his head and began a delicate suckling.

Her body undulated beneath his. "That's because it's a trifle immodest for your family and our son. And when it's just you and me, you never leave anything on me long enough to notice what I'm wearing."

"That ain't so." He shifted his hips, and her fingers grabbed for his hair. He had to chase the rapid movement of her breasts before enjoying another taste. "Come home with me," he whispered gruffly, speaking with his mouth full. He'd begun a slow, easy rocking that had her thrashing with impatience.

"Rory . . ."

"Honey, I want you. I need you there. Come home with me."

Her breaths were coming convulsively. "Rory . . . oh, God."

"Norah, please."

"Oh, Rory!"

He rode out the hard, shaking spasms, losing himself somewhere in the middle of them. But he didn't get his answer. And when he pressed for it as they quieted, she smiled up at him and murmured, "Honey, you've all night to convince me to say yes. You're off to a good start."

Somewhere closer to morning than midnight, they fell asleep entwined before the fire. It seemed as though only seconds had passed, but it must have been more because when Norah opened her eyes, the fire had burnt down to soft coals.

Rory was tossing beside her in his sleep, breathing in hard, uneven pants. His restless movements were what had awakened her. She rubbed her palm along his shoulder. It slid on sweat.

"Rory?"

"Jacob, run!"

The sudden cry scared her and startled him awake. Rory rolled up to hands and knees and scrambled backwards off the rug where he crouched, staring down at it in a glaze of horror.

"Rory? Honey? It's all right. You were just dreaming."

"Oh, God." He dropped down on his rump on the cool floorboards and hugged his knees, shaking all the way to the soul as Norah slid over to embrace him. He didn't respond to her, shivering hard enough for his teeth to rattle together. He stretched out a toe to cautiously nudge the tanned hide.

"It's cold down here. Come on. Rory, come on. Climb up into bed." She tugged on him until he rose up and crawled under the covers, huddling to himself until she slid in close. Then his arms curled around her tight enough to crack bone. When he spoke, his voice was low and hoarse.

"When I looked up and there was Jacob with that big old gun, just a little feller who'd never shot at nothing in his life, chasing down that grizzly bear, I yelled at him to run, but he wouldn't. He wouldn't, Norah. And I just knew I was gonna see that monster eat up my little boy right in front a me and there wasn't nothing I could do, nothing I could do."

She knew exactly what he was talking about. It was the same impotent terror she'd felt watching his life slip away in the *wakan's* tipi. She kissed his damp brow, hugging him tight, pushing that taste of horror away.

"Norah, I swear to you I will never, ever let any harm come to you and Jacob. I swear it on my life."

Norah closed her eyes, letting his kisses adore the curve of her lips and the arch of her throat. She let him mold her passions with the movement of his hands, from stroking forays over her breasts and belly to purposeful revolutions between the welcoming spread of her thighs. Instead of urging a hot flare of emotion, he built a slow fire, one that would burn steady and last a lifetime. She encouraged him with the soft brush of her lips beneath his blackened eyes and on the sore bridge of his nose, at his temple where gashes were still healing, below his ear where his mama had once made one of her many neat seams. He had more scars on him than a Dakota map had byways, and each one had shaped the direction of the man he was. She could travel them by memory because each one was scored upon her heart, as familiar to her as the scars made by her past. Both of them were marked by those deep reminders of what they'd managed to survive. She saw his as badges of courage and determination. How, she wondered as the first warm ripples of sensation swept over her, did he view hers?

"Come home where you belong," he whispered seductively as he settled in between her knees. His rough palms moved up and down her thighs before curving around the softness of her bottom, lifting her to meet the strong press of his possession. He sank inside her slow and deep, with the surety of a man who knew he was home and was confident of his greeting. Norah invited him to stay with a small cry and a lingering sigh. Her hands roved along his broad shoulders, down his muscle-hardened arms, up his chest to finally mesh behind his head. She said his name, loving him so much it hurt. As he began to move, they were both aware of how different the tempo of their lovemaking was—not an urgent, proving passion, but a quiet, compelling intimacy. Norah responded to it with a shattering bliss, pulling his head down into the cove of her shoulder, muffling her completing cries in the thick red hair. She felt his quickening breath blow hot upon her bared neck and heard its harsh intake. Then there was a wonderful, trembly silence.

Rory followed those satisfying shudders with a long thorough kiss. His tongue searched the inside of her mouth as if in desperate need of every scrap of

421

sweetness she had hidden there. His hand vee'd beneath her chin, fingers clamping hard along the line of her jaw as he thrust deep, deeper, until a wild moan of abandon rose up from her throat. His grip gentled to a light caress of her cheek and his kiss eased, tongue withdrawing with a last flicker that coaxed hers to follow across the junction of their lips. At last, he lifted up slightly to revel in the sated splendor of her expression.

"I love you Norah. Will you come back to the Dakotas with me?"

"Yes."

And he smiled, that slow, spreading, sassy smile. "Hot damn."

Chapter Twenty-six

He woke up at a surprisingly early hour, not exactly sure where he was until he felt the warm press of woman up against his flanks. Then, he figured it didn't much matter.

Grinning to himself, Rory rolled over and allowed a few long minutes just to appreciate the sight of his wife stretched out naked like a lithe glossy barn cat absorbing sunshine. Want stirred inside him despite his contentment. Love unfurled deeper still as he bent down to lightly kiss her lips.

"'Morning, honey."

"Time's it?" she muttered groggily as her fingers toyed blindly with the rough burr of his cheek.

"I d'know." He squinted at the clock on her bureau. "Seven."

"Oh, Rory," she groaned, flopping over onto her belly. "Go back to sleep."

"Can't," he murmured as he trailed a string of kisses along her shoulder blades. "I'm wide awake."

"I'm not and I don't want to be," she grumbled irritably.

"Mind if I take advantage of you whilst you're sleeping?" His palm rubbed over one of her per-

423

fect buttocks. Damn but she was a fine looking woman!

"Go ahead," came her discouraging mumble.

"Well, now, honey, that doan sound all too invitin'."

"Then go find yourself somebody else."

"Might jus' do that."

She rolled over to find him grinning down at her with an impossibly arrogant expression. "You do and I'll have your hair stretched out in front of that fire, too."

"Yes, ma'am." He leaned down to kiss her again. Her response was slow and sleepy and very sensual. And then she was yawning in his face. He laughed. "Go back to sleep."

"Ummmm." She rolled away from him and tugged up the covers.

"Honey, I'm gonna head on over to the hotel and grab up my gear. No sense me paying for a room. Is there?"

When she didn't answer, he frowned slightly.

"Norah-honey?"

"Ummmm? I love you, too, Rory." That weary little rumble wasn't the exact answer, but it was close enough to snatch at his heart.

"Be back in a bit."

"Ummmm."

He dressed quickly and took a second to peek in at Jacob, who was still burrowed under his covers like a prairie dog, before heading downstairs to hunt up his boots. Clapping his hat on his head and bundling his coat around him, Rory took stock of things from the front steps. It was cold out and quiet. Sunday, he realized with some surprise. Since his foot had stopped complaining and it felt so good to be out in the air, he decided to test his bearings by setting out aground. Scotty'd be up and maybe he could get his brother to stand him to a cup of coffee. He was painfully short of funds after yesterday's extravagances. But he had just enough to buy three tickets to the Dakotas, and that made him a very rich man.

He'd gone a couple of city blocks when he noticed a closed horse-drawn cab had pulled up alongside him. He didn't pay it much mind until he was fixing to cross a street and it swerved in to cut him off. The door opened toward him.

"Mr. Prescott, might I offer you a ride."

Rory stepped back up onto the curb, his senses alert to danger. "I doan think so," he growled warily.

"I'm afraid then that I'll have to insist."

And the bore of a handgun backed up the invitation.

It was nine-thirty when Norah finally climbed out of bed. She took a long, hot bath, luxuriating in suds that pampered her overworked muscles, smiling as she thought of the reason for her exquisite lethargy.

Lord above, she loved that man!

It was hard to concentrate on concrete things, like closing up the house, whether or not to sell it, what amongst her things should she pack, taking Jacob from school. The feel of Rory Prescott's touch kept intruding. She wasn't naive enough to think that all their problems had disappeared in the span of one splendid night, but she had solid reason to hope. They'd talked more in those few hours than they had in years; communicated with words, not with shouts, not just physically; and the bonding closeness was back between them, strong and sure. She wanted Rory Prescott, as her lover, as her husband, as the father of her son; and she was willing to work hard to have him. He'd started to open up the doors of acceptance in his heart; and when he'd forgiven her, she'd found she could forgive herself. And there was a wonderful freedom in that.

Dried and dressed, she went downstairs to accept a hug from Jacob, whose first question was, "Where's Daddy?"

"He went to get his things at the Rennert. He's probably having breakfast with your Uncle Scott and Aunt Gena."

"You mean he's moving in here with us?"

"Would you like that?" she teased with a smile.

"Like it? That'd be great!"

She knelt down to hug him again when there was a quiet knocking at the door. Pressing a quick kiss on her son's brow, Norah went to answer it and was plainly surprised to find Trevor Samuels on her front step.

"Good morning, Norah."

"Mr. Samuels."

He winced at her cool tone but proceeded bravely. "Might I come in for a moment? I would like to speak to you."

"I don't know that we have anything to say."

"Norah, please."

Because she could never harden her heart to a look of abject despair, Norah held open the door and Trevor slipped in, hat and humility in hand. He was met by Jacob's unswerving glare.

"Hello there, son."

"I'm not your son," Jacob growled with enough prickly rudeness to earn himself a harsh glance from his mother. Without another word, he turned and ran up the stairs, leaving Norah stunned by his atypical outburst. Trevor was not offended, however, and was quick to possess himself of her hands.

"Norah," he began in a crooning whisper. Immediately rigid, she tried to pull away.

"Let me go, Trevor. My husband will be home any minute, and I don't think he'd like seeing me pawed in his front hall."

"I see." He dropped her hands and took a reevaluating step back. "You've gone back to him then." He said that with a tragic inflection, as if she had broken his heart.

"I love Rory. I was wrong to think I had any kind of a life without him."

"But does that mean we can't be friends? Norah, I have so much respect for you, and I realize I have far to go to earn yours back. Please let me try. You can't be so cruel as to shut me out completely."

"Oh, Trevor. Don't be so dramatic. I'm not all that angry."

"Then prove it. Go to this morning's service with me. Your husband can go, too, of course."

Her eyes narrowed thoughtfully. "And of course this has nothing to do with bumping into some of my acquaintances afterwards and the fact that you need boosters to officially begin your campaign."

"Do you mind terribly, Norah?"

The fact that he didn't deny it, softened her resolve. "All right. This once. I would like to see you get a spot on the ballot."

"Oh, my dear Norah. You've made me the happiest of men." He grabbed up her hand to press grateful kisses upon it.

"Stop that!"

They looked in surprise to a glowering little boy braced in the center of the staircase. He didn't back down beneath his mother's reproving gaze.

"Wait for me outside, Trevor." He nodded and

427

when he was gone, she turned to face her son with a cool, "I am not pleased with your behavior, young man. Go get your coat. We're going to church with Mr. Samuels."

"I'm not going with him. And I don't think you should, either. Daddy won't like it."

"Your father does not dictate who I can have for friends, and neither does an impertinent seven-year-old."

"But this is Daddy's house—"

"This is not your father's house, nor will it be. He's going back to the Dakotas, and we—" She broke off abruptly. "I don't have time to argue with you, Jacob. We will discuss this when I get back. We have some things we need to say to you. And in the meantime, you had better be thinking of an appropriate apology in your room. Is that understood?"

He stared at her for the longest moment, tears welling up in his somber grey eyes. Then he fled, and she could hear his door slam overhead. Wondering what had gotten into him, she sighed in exasperation as she slipped into her cloak. Hopefully Rory would be back soon to talk some sense into him.

Draped across his bed, Jacob quivered with silent sobs. What had happened? He didn't understand it. He thought things were going well between his mother and father. Then slick ole Trevor Samuels started in slobbering on his mama's hands and suddenly she was packing his father off to the Dakotas without them. Did that mean she was going to marry Trevor after all? He swallowed hard, trying not to think of it. If his mother remarried, maybe his father would, too. Maybe he'd have other children with his new wife and forget all about the one he had back East. Panic rose inside him in shivery waves.

He heard the clatter of bootheels in the front hall. Jumping up, he scrubbed his eyes dry and went running.

"Daddy!"

He was halfway down the stairs when he saw his father's expression. It stopped him cold as death. He didn't need to hear him to speak to know he'd come to say goodbye. Well, he wouldn't listen! He whirled and started to scramble blindly for his room.

"Jacob! Wait!"

Rory caught him, dropping down on the steps with the trembling child clutched to his shirt front, holding him for a long emotional moment before he attempted to speak.

"I'm sorry, Jacob. I'm sorry. I never wanted to hurt you."

"Then why are you going?"

"I have to, son. I—I can't explain it, so's you'll understand. I love you, Jacob—you and your mama—more than anything in this world. Doan you ever—*ever* forget that!"

Jacob banded his father's neck with his arms, hanging on with all his might. "Don't go!"

"I have to."

"Take us with you!"

"I can't. I want to, but I can't. Oh, God, Jacob, please doan make this any harder. Listen to me. You listen. This is important." He held the whimpering boy away from him, giving him a sobering shake. "Jake, you listenin'?"

Finally, he nodded. There were tears in his father's eyes, and that shook him worse than anything he could think of. "I'm listening, Daddy," he said in his bravest voice.

"You give this to your mama." Jacob glanced down at the official-looking papers, taking them unwillingly. "You tell her that I love her. She ain't gonna believe it, but you tell her anyway. An' you tell her I made a promise and I'm paying the price. Can you remember all that?"

"Daddy . . ."

"Can you remember?."

"Yessir."

"Now you give me a hug and kiss. I gotta go. My train's leaving in a half-hour."

Jacob hung on fiercely and wouldn't let go until Rory pried him away.

"Take care of your mama, Jake. She's gonna need you bad." He took off his black Stetson and fit it onto the boy's head. "There, son. You just growed into that. I love you." He cupped one cheek in his palm and planted a hard kiss on the other. Then he went down into the foyer without a backward glance to pick up the things they'd bought while they'd spent the day shopping.

"Daddy?"

Rory tensed but didn't turn. He bundled up his things and opened the front door.

"Daddy!"

He stepped out and closed it quietly behind him.

Jacob sat stunned on the stairs for a long while, dampness from his eyes blotching the papers he clutched to his chest. Finally curious about them, he took a look. The words were long, and he didn't understand but half of them. One of them scared him, though he didn't know why. D-i-v-o-r-c-e-m-e-n-t. He sounded it out. It sounded ugly. For a long time, he sat huddled on those steps, crying silently in his confusion, wondering what had happened to his world.

*   *   *

"Rory? Jacob?"

Norah removed her hat pins in front of the hall mirror, then frowned at the silence. Perhaps Rory hadn't returned yet, but the thought of her son refusing to answer in a sullen fit of temper annoyed her in the extreme.

"Jacob, answer me!"

It was as if the house were empty. Bridget didn't come in on Sundays, so she and her son always went out to dinner together. It was something they looked forward to each week, something she looked forward to including Rory in today so they could tell their son over lunch that they'd all be going back to the Bar K together. And she would not let Jacob spoil her plans with his petulance.

Irritably, she climbed the stairs and pushed open her son's door.

"Jacob Prescott, are you hard of hear—"

He wasn't there.

Something was wrong. She felt it prickle along her nerve endings like a chill. She saw some folded papers on his bed at the same time she noticed his cupboard was ajar. She picked up the pages as she nudged open the door. Jacob's travel bag was missing and so were half his belongings. Numbly, she looked to the papers in her hands for an answer.

Petition for divorcement. She read it and reread it with a blankness of mind and spirit. She didn't understand. Then she opened the note tucked in with it, recognizing her son's big block letters.

"Oh, God."

Gone home with Daddy. We love you. Jacob Prescott.

The strength went out of her legs and she felt the bounce of her son's bed beneath her. Rory was gone.

He'd gone back to the Dakotas without her. And he'd taken Jacob.

Her paralysis didn't last long. She leaped up and raced downstairs for her parlor telephone. In a frightfully calm voice, she asked for the Rennert Hotel and listened with a deadened horror to the desk clerk saying all three Prescotts had checked out that morning.

"This can't be happening," she moaned aloud, pacing aimlessly from room to room like something trapped and afraid. "Rory. Rory, why? I don't understand. How could you do this? How could you do this to me?"

"Mrs. Prescott?"

She whirled with a gasp of alarm to face Carter Clemens.

"I didn't mean to startle you. I knocked, but you must not have heard."

She stared at him expressionlessly.

"He's gone, you know."

"W-who?"

"Your husband."

"What do you know about that?"

"Why, I know everything about it. I arranged it."

"You—"

"Please, Mrs. Prescott, won't you come into the parlor and have a seat? You look quite pale."

She let him lead her to a chair, and she sank down strengthlessly. "What did you do?" she demanded in a stricken tone. "If you've hurt Rory—"

"Violence doesn't work with men like him. I'm afraid I discovered that rather tardily."

"You—" Understanding began to dawn.

"Yes. Or rather I had it done. But he's a stubborn man, and then there's his brother. Another difficult problem. But I say, one problem at a time. Did you know that Trevor was actually going to withdraw from politics after your little tiff last night? He had a very unpleasant discussion with his father. Mr. Samuels was not at all pleased, so I was put in the uncomfortable position of having to take care of things. You see, Mrs. Prescott—may I call you Norah? You see, Norah, Trevor wants you as his wife. He doesn't believe he can have any kind of successful career in office without your guidance; and, personally, my dear, I think he's right. So I arranged things. That's what I do."

"What did you do to Rory? What did you do to make him leave?"

"Why, we had a very long conversation, and I found him surprisingly reasonable. I merely asked him what kind of mother you would be for his son if you were in prison."

"What?"

"George Kary, Davis Green, Lawrence Main, Ansel Goodwin, do those names mean anything to you?"

My God, he'd done his homework. Those were the names of some of the men she and Cole Denby had bilked of their fortunes. Confusion gave way to a mounting fury. "How did you find out about them?"

"Oh, my dear, when Trevor expressed his interest in you, I did some very thorough checking. I uncovered some, shall we say, unsavory details. But you needn't worry. I covered your tracks quite well. Your secret is safe with me. For the moment."

"So you blackmailed Rory into leaving me." Those words came out hard, as if she'd had to drag them up from her throat with a block and tackle.

"I told him that with the evidence I had, I could see to it you were an old woman by the time you got out of jail; that if he didn't leave quietly, without a fuss, I would take what I knew to the nearest constabulary and have you arrested. I also informed him that there was a good chance that he could be implicated for harboring a fugitive from justice and could well lose everything he has. And then how would he raise that precocious little boy?"

"Does Trevor know anything about this?"

"Oh, good heavens, no. He is much too above this sort of reality. Poor Trevor suffers from too much conscience, which is why he needs us, Norah, dear."

Norah's mind was working frantically. Rory had left to protect her. He hadn't even said goodbye. But then Carter must have arranged that, too. He would have known she'd be out of the house when Rory came to deliver the divorce papers. But Jacob had been home. Did he know about Jacob? Suddenly she was very glad she didn't have the boy with her. She could maneuver better alone.

"So," she demanded coldly. "What is it I'm to do to stay out of prison?"

"Why marry Trevor, of course. I had to promise your husband that you and the boy would be very well taken care of. I think he means to have his troublesome brother check up on your welfare. He must really love you." He said that last with what almost sounded like a trace of humanity.

Yes, he does, she thought savagely to herself. *And he's going to make sure you are very, very sorry.* But that would have to wait. Now was the time for caution.

"I assume there is more to this little bargain."

"Yes. We will want you from time to time to influence Trevor in our favor."

"Our, meaning his father's."

"You're very smart. As I've stated, Trevor has an annoying amount of good intentions. Like that

434

business with your brother-in-law's heathen brethren. Mr. Samuels was very upset when Trevor decided to press their cause. He has his sights set on developing that land. The Prescotts have inconvenienced him considerably. Perhaps down the road, you can be of help in that area, too."

Her voice was precise and unwavering. "I will never ever do anything to stand against my family. Besides, Trevor would see through that in a second. He knows how I feel about them."

"Ah, yes. Clever. I hadn't thought of that. Very good, my dear. We shall work well together. It won't be a difficult duty. Mr. Samuels is prepared to be very generous."

"Mr. Samuels can go to hell."

Carter's eyes slitted, and his nasal voice grew thin. "I wouldn't say that to his face if I were you. I would hate to have to dispose of you after all the trouble I've gone to."

And Norah saw in that second how wrong she'd been to ever believe Carter Clemens harmless.

"I would like you to leave now. I have preparations to make."

"Oh? And what might they be?"

"For my wedding, of course."

"Of course." The little lawyer smiled narrowly. "Smart and beautiful. You are just what Trevor needs."

"Get out. I won't have you in my house."

For a moment, she feared she might have overstepped herself. The spindly man went so rigid he trembled. Then he smiled again. "I don't blame you, Mrs. Prescott. We'll speak again, soon."

As soon as he left, Norah raced up the stairs. Carter Clemens didn't know her. She would rather rot in jail than live a sham at Rory's expense. Of course, being the big courageous fool he was, he would shoulder all the burden of her future without complaint. But she wasn't ready to make a stoic sacrifice. She was going home. She would make her stand at the Bar K with her husband, son, and family. She needed Rory's strength and Scott's counsel. Perhaps she could make some kind of restitution with her old victims. Scott would be able to arrange it. She would trust him with her life, just as she trusted his brother with her love. And, at least, if worse came to worse, she could say goodbye to Rory in person.

How to get out of Baltimore? Clemens would be watching. She wouldn't underestimate him again. She never made mistakes twice. Then she smiled. He didn't know her. He knew only the sophisticated lady who lived in a fine townhouse, not the desperate schemer who used trickery for a living. He wouldn't expect her to move so fast and not right out from beneath his nose.

Calmly, she went downstairs and picked up the telephone.

"Trevor, I've been thinking of how much I would like to attend that little gathering at the Gaithers's tonight. Do you think you could escort me? It couldn't hurt to become an intimate of George's now, could it?"

It was dark. All he could see out the window was his own grim reflection. Cold company on this long night. At least Scott and Gena were sleeping in their seats across from him so he didn't have to endure their questioning stares. It was hard holding together in front of them, but it was better than coming apart like a poorly made saddle after a good soaking rain. He could feel the edges unraveling as strain and distance took their toll. He'd be a mess of loose ends by morning if he didn't get some sleep, some relief from the awful ache inside him. He needed to be home. He'd feel better there. Here, on this westbound train, the sense of what he was leaving behind was too acute. He'd be better when he got home.

He leaned his forehead against the cool glass and shut his eyes. The rocking of the car should have soothed him, but all it did was shake the scrambled emotions around. Thank God for Scott and Gena, or he'd have gotten on the wrong train and ended up in the Carolinas; he hadn't been able to see a damned thing through the grief blurring his eyes. And thank the Lord for their silence, uneasy though it was. When he told them he was leaving, he must have scared Gena half-to-death with the look on his face, because she'd grabbed onto his brother and announced that they were going with him. He refused to tell them anything. Maybe he should have confided in Scott, but he was so torn up inside and so scared for Norah he couldn't think straight. What if something he did landed her in prison? He'd never be able to live with that or look his boy in the eye again. At least he knew they'd both be safe and cared for. That was some consolation to his mind, but it did absolutely nothing for the devastated condition of his heart.

"Daddy, I'm cold," came a little voice at his side.

Unthinkingly, Rory lifted the armrest between the two seats, raised his arm and said, "Tuck in here, pard." It was the feel of the shivering figure burrowing close against his side that finally reached him. "Jacob? Oh my God."

For a long heartbeat, he just grabbed the boy and squeezed him tight. Then reality intruded. "Jacob, where's your mama?" He looked around at the half-

437

empty car, heart pounding hopefully.

"At home," came the small reply.

"In Baltimore? How'd you get here? Answer me."

"I climbed on the train when no one was looking. I've been hiding out back with the bags, but it got cold and dark and I got scared."

"Doesn't your mama know where you are?"

"I left her a note."

"A note? Oh, Godalmighty. She'll be outta her mind with worry. How could you have done such a thing? Jacob, what were you thinkin'?"

The boy sat back in his seat, lip quivering, eyes welling up miserably. "I'm sorry, Daddy. I didn't mean to make you mad. I thought you'd be glad to see me."

"Awww, hell. Oh, Jacob, I am glad to see you, son. C'mere." He pulled the boy onto his lap, hugging him close, wrapping him in the warm folds of his coat. "How we gonna get you back to your mama?" he thought out loud.

"I don't want to go back."

"What do you mean?"

"Mama told me that as long as I was with her, she'd have a part of you and wouldn't be lonely. I figured since she's got Trevor, I should be with you so you wouldn't be lonely."

"That right?" The two words came out so thick they were almost unrecognizable. He cleared his throat and said gruffly, "Well, I guess you'll have to come home with me. I can't send you back on the train all on your lonesome. We'll have to wire your mama as soon as we can so's she'll know you're all right." He took his Stetson off the boy's head so he could press a kiss atop it. "Till then, we can keep each other company. That awright with you?'

"Yessir, Daddy," Jacob murmured, snuggling up

happily against his father's chest. Everything was going to be fine. When his mother found out he was gone, she'd come running after him, lickety-split. Then the three of them would be back together. He'd let his daddy take care of things from there. He was going home.

Chapter Twenty-seven

She was only eight hours behind them. Knowing that made the trip easier for Norah. She'd planned it uncomfortably close in Baltimore. She'd fled out the Gaithers's servants's door while Trevor was waiting for her to powder her nose and had gone directly to the train. She had her bank-account books, Gena's drawing folded into a small square, and the divorce papers. She wouldn't leave them behind. As a further precaution, she took the ten-o-five to New York and, from there, headed straight west. And she didn't sleep or stop looking behind her until the scenery turned Dakota gold. Then she closed her eyes and dreamed of holding her husband and her son. When she awoke, it was to the familiar.

Having spent the earlier part of her life running ahead of the law, she knew how to be careful in case Carter had wired ahead to plan an unpleasant welcome. He would be searching the trains for a woman and a boy. He couldn't be sure she would head for the obvious place, her family, so he had a lot of ground to cover. That meant it would be easier for her to slip through. She got off at the station before Crowe Creek. There, she meant to hire a rig and travel to the Lone Star. And, if Aurora Prescott would let her in, all she had to do was wait for Rory to come for her. He would keep her safe.

Cheyenne Junction was a dirty little place on the former fringe of reservation lands. It was hardly more than a trading post and, after a few inquiries, she was dismayed to find there were no buggies or horses for let. It was a distance to the Lone Star, but she would trade for some sensible shoes and walk it if she had to. Then a familiar face caught her attention. She recognized one of the swarthy Indians across the rutted street as High Hawk, Scott Prescott's friend, and saw hope. He and three others were loading supplies into a shabby buckboard. Not the best transportation, but better than blisters.

The handsome Sioux brave looked at her warily when she asked him for a ride to the Prescott ranch. He exchanged several minutes of low incomprehensible gutturals with his companions while she waited, shivering in the chill of an overcast afternoon; then he turned to her with a thin smile and extended his hand to help her up onto the rickety seat. He drove the wagon, and the other three flanked them on horseback. She was too relieved to pay much attention at first. Then she noticed they were headed in the wrong direction.

"This isn't the way to the Lone Star."

There was no response from the stoic Sioux.

"Wait. Let me off here." She tried hard to keep her voice level, to betray none of her sudden alarm.

"You will come with us, woman of *Pehin Luta*. I should not like to hurt you, so you will do as I say."

Norah swallowed hard and demanded, "What do you want?"

"You are friend to him who has big voice in Washington. He has spoken to us falsely; but now

441

that we have you, perhaps he can be made to keep his promises."

Trevor. She sat stiffly on the seat of the buckboard. This had to do with Trevor and the Sioux land. And she was right in the middle as a bargaining tool. She had only to look at the man's taut features to know he could not be pleaded with. His was a hard face, and his was a desperate situation. She stayed wisely silent. She'd stepped from the frying pan into the fire, and now all she could do was endure the heat. Until Rory came for her.

They took her to a small shack and provided her with a thin blanket and some water but no light or food. She slept on the cold dirt floor, alone, not yet afraid but shaken by hard chills and much worry. She was just stirring in the grey haze of dawn when she heard the angry hiss of spurs and a loud, fearsome bellow.

"Git the hell outta my way! Norah?"

"Rory. Rory!"

The door banged open, and she cringed back from the harsh slap of daylight. Then a big shape blocked it out and he was down beside her on his knees, his arms around her, the hard beat of his heart thundering beneath her cheek.

"You awright, honey? If them savages so much as laid a finger on you, I'll—"

She put back her head and he was kissing her, hard and hungrily, his mouth ravaging hers, his hands rough yet so very tender in their restless inquiry. Then he held her with a tight possessiveness, crushing her to his chest, pressing her face into the warm hollow of his throat.

"Norah, are you all right?"

Scott's voice. For the first time, she realized they weren't alone in the little room. She peered out of the

442

safety of Rory's embrace to see Scott and High Hawk and two other Indians. The two braves were well armed. The Prescott brothers weren't. It was then she realized Rory wasn't here to rescue her.

"I'm fine," she answered in a strong voice. "I'll be better at the Bar K."

"We're doing what we can, honey," Rory whispered huskily against her hair.

"How did you find me?"

"Them Indians showed up on the doorstep of Lone Star to tell Scotty they had you and for him to get word to Samuels about some kinda deal. He wouldn't talk to them until we seen for ourselves that you were all right, so they brung us out."

"Jacob?"

"He's with Mama and Daddy. I'm sorry he gave you such a worry. I didn't know he was with me."

"It's a good thing he was."

"An' I didn't know you was gonna follow."

"Did you think I wouldn't? Did you think I would give up everything I want? We've got a lot of things to talk out; but first, take me home. Oh, Rory, I just want to go home with you."

"Shhh. You let Scotty do the talking for now."

And as long as his arms were around her keeping fears at bay, she was willing to stay silent.

"This is not the way, my brother," Scott told High Hawk in brusque Lakota.

"We have tried your way, Lone Wolf. There is no pride in it. We are kept like camp dogs on a short leash. It is not the way men should live. I should not have to tell you these things."

"I know them," Scott admitted grimly. "What do you hope to gain by taking my brother's wife?"

"We will use her to bring Samuels. He will keep his word to us and restore our lands. His father will not crowd our families into the mouth of starvation."

"And if he does not?"

"She dies."

Scott's expression didn't alter. "Then you will die."

"So be it. There is no honor in living the way we do. We will bring glory in our deaths. We will make a noise that they will not be able to ignore in Washington. They will not care if a handful of Indians die—but a white woman of the East, that they will notice. And then perhaps you can make them hear your words."

"They will curse your names. *I* will curse your name. Do not do this. She is of my family and my heart."

"This saddens me, but I can see no other way. You will send word. You will bring Samuels to speak with us. The woman of Red Hair will be safe as long as you do not interfere. If you do not do as we say, she will be dead before you can reach her. You know I do not lie about this."

Scott glanced over at his brother and the woman cherished in his embrace. Then he turned back to his childhood friend. "I will do as you say. I am trusting her to your care. Do not fail my trust or there will be no honor in the way you die."

High Hawk nodded. "You go now."

"Rory."

"Gimme a minute, Scotty."

"Now."

Norah clung to him. She couldn't help it. She couldn't bear the thought of their separation. All her courage failed when faced with surrendering his strength. Her fingers curled in his coat. She was shaking. Then Scott was pushing them apart.

444

"Rory, we've got to go."

"I can't, Scotty," he growled without sparing him a glance. "I can't leave her here like this." His stare was swallowed up in the soft grey of his wife's gaze.

"They'll kill you."

"Let 'em."

That alarmed Norah enough to restore her pluck. She straightened, but her hands were still on him, touching his sleeves, his collar, the sides of his face. "Go with Scott. I'll be fine. Please, Rory. Jacob will need you. I'm not afraid." She smiled to show him that was true. But it wasn't, not really. She was terrified of never being this close to him again, of never being able to tell him what resided in her heart. So she wouldn't wait for a better time. "I love you, Rory."

He made a low, pained sound and mashed her tightly into the hard wall of his chest. He looked frantically to Scott for reassurance. "They ain't gonna hurt her, are they, Scotty?"

Scott looked him straight in the eye and lied to him. "No. It's just to get Samuels here. Then they'll let her go."

Rory believed him and sagged with relief; but Norah, who was watching the subtle shifts of emotions shading the golden eyes, saw the truth there. She wasn't going home. At that instant, Scott's gaze touched on hers and he knew she knew it.

"He's right, Rory," she said with a remarkable calm. "They have no reason to harm me, and I won't give them one. Now, please go. And listen to your brother."

Contrarily, he caught the back of her head in his hand and pulled her to him, kissing her searingly. When he would draw away, she pursued him, desperate for the taste of his mouth, wild to

445

experience all of him that she could in these last short moments. He shrugged out of his coat and bundled her in it, using his grip on the lapels to trap her in close to him for another long kiss. She put all the feeling she had for him in that kiss, fighting down the apprehension, the dread, so that he would only taste the love and longing.

"I'll be back for you. I love you, Norah. I swear to God I won't let nothing happen to you." Then he let her go and started for the door, pausing in front of High Hawk. He stared long and hard at the Indian, his expression as ruthless as the Badlands. "Any of you harms a hair on her head, I'll be coming for you. Count on it." With that, he stalked out.

Not having to pretend bravery anymore, Norah wrapped her arms around Scott Prescott's neck and let the tears go in a rush. "Take care of them for me, Scott. Don't let him know I was afraid."

"*Kopegla sni yo.* Do not be afraid. You have humbled the spirit world with your courage. I won't be far away. I'll see you're safe. I swear it on my love for my brother and my unborn child." Then he smiled at her, that thin, flat smile, and he told her very quietly, "I should not like to kill my friends, but I will if it is the only way. I owe you a life. Trust me."

She looked deep into the gold of his eyes and found strength there, enough to let go of his hands and to say with a soft belief, "I do." Then, he, too, was gone and all she had to cling to was the warmth of Rory's coat.

Aurora stepped out onto the cold darkness of her front porch. She was about to call her younger son in for supper when she heard him speaking soft and low to the shadows of the yard beyond. She hesitated because there was no one there and, hearing his first few words, she knew he wasn't addressing anyone she could see. Held silent by a throat-clutching tenderness, she waited, not interrupting, as he spoke his piece.

"It's me, Rory Prescott. I hope I ain't bothering you. I know I been asking a lot lately but—oh, sorry." He swept off his hat and twisted it in his hands. "I ain't trying to be bold or nothing standing here on my hindlegs, but my knee won't bend and if I was to get down on 'em, I'd like to never get back up. Where was I? Oh, yeah.

"I figures you got a reason for everything you do. I guess you took her away from me for all them years so's I could do some thinking and me, being the prideful fool I am, I wasted 'em. But I know what you was getting at now and I'm asking—I'm beggin'—for the chance to make good on what I learned. I ain't one a your smartest creatures and I know you been patient with me and I 'preciate that. I know I can get it right. I got the best kind of examples in my mama and daddy and in my brother and his wife. Alls I'm askin' is for you to see fit to bring her back to me an' I'll do the rest. I'll keep them promises. You let me come back when she called. I'm callin' now. Please let her come back to me." His voice had lowered to a husky vibration; then, after a moment's silence, he cleared it gruffly. "Well, thanks for hearing me out. I'll let you get back to things. I'm obliged for the time."

"Amen."

Rory gave a start and looked around. He gave his mother a fragile smile. "Think He was listenin'?"

She came across the porchboards to slip an arm around his middle. "He's heard me for thirty years. You two boys have been coming home to me, worse for wear but in one piece. I'll put in a word for her, too."

He draped his arm along her shoulders and hugged her to his chest, letting her ride out the heaviness of his sigh. When he'd come back from seeing Norah that morning, he'd come clean with everything that had happened in Baltimore. His mother hadn't had much to say then, so he wasn't sure where she stood; but he needed, badly, to know his family was behind him. He spoke somberly, from an aching heart.

"Mama, I know you and Norah don't get on well. I've sorrowed over that plenty. I know you think she's good for nothing but grief, but she's Jacob's mama and I love her more than anything. What she was, that's over and done with. I've put it behind me and I know it's a lot to ask, but I'd really be beholden if you could forgive her—"

"Hush, now." Her fingers touched his lips. "I don't see that there's anything to forgive. If Norah were the woman I thought she was, she would have run far and hid well to save herself. But she didn't. She came here for help, to you, to us, and we won't let her down, will we?"

"No, ma'am." A whole world of relief swept over him.

"Where's your brother?"

He nodded toward the horizon. "Out there somewheres keeping watch over Norah. Wouldn't let me come with him. Said I was about as stealthy as a bull moose and that they'd hear me a mile away. He's right." Rory gave another unhappy sigh. "If Scotty doan want to be seen, he won't be. Alls I got to do is wait an' worry."

Aurora rubbed his arm consolingly. "They won't mistreat her, Rory. The Sioux respect women. She's

448

safer with them than in the hands of most white men.''

"Glad to hear that.''

"Come inside. Dinner's ready, and Jacob's wondering if something's wrong. He needs his daddy.''

"An' I need his mama,'' he answered quietly, looking out toward the far plains with an unspoken anguish.

Trevor Samuels and Carter Clemens arrived three days later. Scott came in from his vigil to meet them at the train and escorted them to the Bar K. There in his brother's study, he laid out the Sioux demands in an expressionless voice while Rory stared silently into his hundredth cup of coffee. Trevor listened carefully, with concern, then brushed it aside with a casual, "Surely they're bluffing. They wouldn't harm Norah.''

"The Lakota don't bluff. They don't play games and they don't lie.'' Scott laid it out coldly, then put a gentle, bracing hand on his brother's shoulder. "If you don't do exactly as they say, they'll kill her without mercy, without thought.'' He felt Rory jerk, and his fingers tightened. "You're not dealing with politicians here. These are hard, desperate men who have nothing to lose. They would give their lives happily if they thought it would advance their cause. They won't let personal feelings get in the way of what they have to do. That's the way they're taught from birth. You can't reason with them; you can't bribe them; you can't frighten them. That's why the Lakota were the most feared warriors on the plains. That's why their culture is being crushed by men like you. You had better take them seriously unless you want that woman's blood on your hands.''

Trevor, pale, was convinced of the gravity of the situation. "What do they want from me?"

"More than words."

"This is madness," Carter Clemens wheezed.

"What would you have me do? Just walk away and leave her to suffer for my empty promises?" Trevor argued tautly.

"That would be the prudent thing. This is not your concern. You mustn't put yourself and your career in jeopardy. Your father would not stand for it."

"Do you think I'd put my career before the life of someone I care about? I'm not my father."

"No," Carter agreed. "You're not."

"What if I give them my written guarantee that my father will not purchase their lands for development? Would that appease them until I can take up their cause in Washington?"

"I don't know. It might."

"When can I speak to them?"

"I'm sure they already know you're here. It won't be long."

He nodded grimly. "I'll do whatever I have to." He pushed back his chair. "I think I'd like to freshen up before I go to the bargaining table."

When the two brothers were alone, a thick silence settled. Scott waited for a reaction; and when it came, it was like a tornado dropping out of the sky. Rory gave a sudden cry of pent-up fury and swung hard. The back of his knuckles took Scott in the jaw, slamming him against the bookcase, shivering the glass in the doors with the sheer force of the blow.

"Goddammit! You lied to me!" he roared, coming up out of his chair in a blind rage. Scott cradled the side of his face in his palm, making no move to protect himself. His expression was stark, but he understood. Rory's fists balled up in his shirt front. "Why did you tell me they wouldn't hurt her? I oughta—"

And abruptly, his anger blew out, leaving him harmless and deflated. With a soft, wailing moan, he leaned into his brother, too broken with despair to do more than ask, "Why'd you lie to me, Scotty?"

Holding the bright head against the hollow of his shoulder, Scott replied tonelessly, "What good would it have done for you to know? I lied to give you three days of peace. Norah made me promise to take care of you."

"She knows?" he cried in anguish.

"Yes."

"Oh, God." He was reeling and heartsick, picturing his wife alone, afraid, expecting to die for a cause that didn't concern her. All because she'd come back to him. He shoved away from Scott, scrubbing his face savagely on his sleeve. A hard determination carved his features and glinted darkly in his eyes. "I ain't gonna let it happen. I ain't gonna give up this easy. Nobody's taking what's mine from me. Not whilst I can pull a breath." He slowed his harsh panting and studied his brother's face. "I hope you got somethin' going on up there in that head a yours, Big Brother. You know these folks, Scotty. Are they like to give her back if Samuels doesn't do what they ask?"

Scott put his hand upon his brother's shoulder and said, with brutal honesty, "No."

"Then I guess we'll just have to take her."

It was the longest night he could ever remember. Rory lay awake in the big bed he and his wife had shared too briefly. He wondered how Norah was faring—if she were warm, if she'd been fed, if she knew how desperately he loved her. He tried not to think of what the next day would bring. He tried not to dwell on a future without Norah. He kept his thoughts reined in tight, but he was restless and anxious to be doing something—anything—to relieve the tension. The waiting was the worst, the waiting and not knowing.

"Daddy?"

He propped up on his elbows and mustered a smile for the little figure in the doorway. "Howdy, pard. Can't sleep?"

"Why are Trevor and Mr. Clemens here?"

Rory thought a moment and couldn't come up with a convenient lie to explain away the two men sleeping uncomfortably on the sofas down below. Nor did he want to. "C'mon over here, Jacob. We need to make talk, man to man."

The boy came to him slowly, with a reluctant dread. He knew something was terribly wrong. He'd watched it building in his father's face all day, massing like gloomy, dangerous storm clouds on the far Hills. It had something to do with his mama. He crawled up onto the bed and snuggled into the hollow beneath his father's arm.

"Jacob, there ain't no easy way to say it, so I'll put it plain. Your mama was on her way here to be with us. She was grabbed up by some unfriendly fellers who mean to use her to get their land back from Trevor's daddy. It's all kinda complicated, but me and your Uncle Scotty plan on fetching her back safe. I didn't say nothing 'cause I didn't want you to worry. Guess I was wrong to keep it from you. She's your mama and you got a right to know."

Jacob swallowed manfully, his grey eyes somber in

their study of his father's. "She won't get hurt, will she?"

"I doan want nobody to get hurt."

"Why'd you run out on Mama and me in Baltimore?"

"Doan you know no easy questions, son?" When Jacob's steady look demanded an answer, he sighed. "A long time ago, long before your mama met me, she had to make some real hard decisions. Some folks'll tell you they was the wrong ones, but I doan know. Your mama didn't feel like she had any choice. Anyway, some of the things she did, well, son, they broke the law."

"Mama?"

"Hush a minute and hear me out. No, not your mama. It was a scared little girl who got backed into a tight corner and she had to fight her way out. Back then, she didn't have nobody to care for her an' love her like she does now. She made some bad mistakes and, for a long time, I was mad at her for making 'em. But, Jacob, all of us make mistakes and we ain't got no right to hold them against another when they're sorry and they do all they can to make it right. Your mama's made it right, and it's time we laid it to rest. Doan you ever-ever think nothing bad about her. She's the finest, bravest lady I've ever known, and I'm right proud to have married her."

"Can I stay here with you for awhile?"

"Sure can. Now settle on down and get some sleep."

"Yessir, Daddy."

Rory closed his eyes, able to find a degree of peace in his troubled soul. He believed the words he'd spoken to his son, and they soothed. Jacob's presence made Norah seem near and, for a time, he actually slept. He must have, because Scott's voice jarred him from it.

"Rory."

He slid his arm out from under Jacob's head, careful not to wake the boy. He could make out his brother's silhouette against the deep indigo of pre-dawn. He reached for his pants as he asked, "We ready?"

"I'm to take Samuels to Willow Canyon at first light."

"They'll have Norah there?"

"Yes."

"Damn, that place is a bottleneck. Only one way in."

"Two, if you go around."

"Around? Scotty, that's close to fifty miles over some God-awful territory," he growled, grabbing up his shirt and yanking it over his head.

"There's a full moon. A man riding hard might make it."

"I will." He shoved into his boots, too preoccupied to even wince. "If I was to take two horses and ride 'em right into the ground, I could circle back and get under cover."

"Take Ghost."

Rory glanced back at Jacob as he sat up. The boy was sleep-rumpled, but his grey eyes—his mother's eyes—were alert and insistent.

"Awright." He stood, fully dressed, and turned to his brother. "Let's get this done."

Scott gave a single nod.

"Jacob, you go fetch them spectacles a yours and bring 'em down to me," he called as he strode to the door. By the time, Jacob padded barefoot down the stairs, he found his father feeding rounds into his Winchester.

"Here you go, Daddy."

"Thanks, pard." He tucked the glasses in his shirt-

454

pocket and knelt down to hug the boy. "You know any good prayers, you be saying 'em for your mama." He gave his son a quick kiss and straightened. "Scotty, you be careful. I ain't interested in raising that little baby-to-be of yours, so keep yourself safe."

"You, too."

Rory reached out to catch him by the back of his dark head, pulling him in close. Their embrace was strong with feeling but necessarily brief. "Watch your back, Big Brother. All our enemies ain't wearing feathers."

Scott nodded, taking his meaning wordlessly.

Clapping on his hat, Rory touched fingertips to Jacob's warm cheek, then he strode for the door. Moments later, there was the sound of rapid hoofbeats, then the silence of the night settled once more.

He rode hard, not sparing leather as he whipped his little mare into a full gallop. It was a dangerous ride over rocky, rutted ground that was all but invisible in the darkness. A misstep could snap a cannon bone and a neck without a whisper of warning. Rory leaned low into Rosebud's mane, crooning softly, "C'mon, Bud. Gimme all you got. Attagirl."

It was a race against minutes, each one notching dawn a little closer to the edge of the horizon. Rory pushed relentlessly until he felt Rosebud flag with exhaustion. He patted her lathered neck, murmuring, "You done me proud, Bud. Now go on home."

He twisted in the saddle, pulling Ghost over close beside the mare so that they matched stride for stride. Bunching his thigh muscles, he jumped. Leather struck the wind out of him as he smacked it with his belly, but he had a firm grip on the horn. Ghost snorted wildly and began to shy. Too late to do anything other than hang on. Rosebud had already veered off and was loping back toward her warm stall at the Bar K. With a fog of curses clouding the pre-dawn air, Rory fit his foot and levered up and into the saddle, gathering the reins to his fresh mount with an authoritative strength.

"C'mon, you Son of Satan. Let's see you run."

Had any of the Lakotas seen them skimming the Plains, they would have mistaken the flash of silvery hide for one of their restless spirits. The stallion was strong and fast, gobbling up miles with a churning rhythm while Rory goaded with his heels. He didn't ease up until they began to climb. It was still dark, and the cowboy had to rely on the animal's instincts as it picked its way up the rocky grade. When they neared the top, Rory swung down, landing poorly on uneven ground. His bad leg crumpled. Reins dropped as he hugged his knee reflexively; all he could see was his Winchester in the saddle boot on the back of a half-wild horse he'd just let loose.

He reached for the dangling reins. Ghost half-reared and then, miraculously, stood. Rory dragged himself up, murmuring quietly, hobbling awkwardly as his fingertips brushed saddle leather. He jerked the rifle free and jumped back, expecting the animal to charge. But Ghost stood, as still and steady as a prime cutting horse.

"I'll be damned," he mumbled and gave the damp neck a grateful stroke. "Maybe you an' me'll get along after all."

Taking up the reins, he led the horse the rest of the way so their approach would be quieter. He tied off the reins on some scrub brush then eased to the top of the rise. The valley below was in heavy blackness, so he lay down, long and low, to wait.

It seemed like hours but couldn't have been more than minutes before a watery daylight began creeping down the canyon floor. With breath suspended, he lifted up just far enough to peer over the broken rim of rock—and froze, entrails knotting up in a painful twist. There, in weak dawn shadows, stood Norah in the back of a buckboard, her hands bound, her neck angled oddly to accommodate the rope pulled taut around it. A rope securely tied to an overhanging limb.

Rory tore his gaze from his wife with difficulty. He had to be alert. Scott would be arriving at any moment. He counted three Indians, High Hawk among them. He'd thought there were four.

And then he heard a snort from Ghost and the restless clatter of hooves on stone. Distracted by the sound, Rory turned back in time to catch the glint of first light off the blade arcing down for his throat.

Chapter Twenty-eight

For the last four days, Norah had eaten little and slept even less as the Lakotas moved cautiously from place to place. The only thing that kept her sane was the sense of Scott Prescott close by her and the hope of feeling her husband's embrace.

She never saw Scott, but she knew the Indians felt him, too. It made them restless and wary and ever on guard. Each time one of them slipped away, she held her breath until he returned, alone. She spent countless hours thanking God that, though the elder Prescott had spent years in the East, his heritage had never been bred out of him.

She didn't speak to her captors, and her stoic silence seemed to impress them. They kept to their Teton tongue, and even High Hawk, whom she knew spoke English, didn't address her when he thrust her scant meals at her once a day. For the most part, she wasn't afraid, just cold and tired, until late the second night when two of the braves split a bottle of whiskey between them. High Hawk was away from their lean camp, out stalking his old friend in the shadows, she guessed. Talk grew bold and laughter harsh and soon she was aware of glittering stares turned in her direction. They were looks she recognized and she stared them down without betraying her inner terror. One of the men, of homely face and less years than the others, strode toward her, squatting down to study her with lustful interest. She glared back. When he reached for her cheek, she jerked away. His hand caught in her hair, twisting hard, but she refused to cry out.

"Let me go."

He smirked at her, amused.

"My husband is *Pehin Luta,* brother of Lone Wolf. I brought him back from the Path of Spirits when your *Sinte Gleska* could not." She pushed up her sleeve and the brave stared at her scarred arm, his features motionless. "You harm me and he will come for you in the night and snatch your soul away. You will roam the earth for a bodiless eternity and I will spit on you."

She didn't know if he understood the words, but the tone of contempt was universal. His face mottled and he drew back his hand. Norah braced for the blow.

"Henakeca!"

The brave backed off as High Hawk approached from the darkness. Terse words were exchanged and, from the haunted look the younger man gave her, Norah assumed High Hawk had interpreted her words. He scuttled back to his companions.

"You are brave, woman of Red Hair, but also foolish. Beware of frightening men as if they were children. They tend to strike at what scares them rather than run away."

Perhaps, but none of the men came near her again, not until the fifth morning when she was dragged up in the darkness to have her hands bound behind her back. There was a tension in the Lakotas, and she

459

knew that the end of the morning would find her back at the Bar K or dead. She tried not to think of it as she was pushed into the wagon and borne off into the night.

When they tightened the rope around her neck, she didn't struggle. It took all her control just to stand tall and act unafraid. As High Hawk regarded her, he smiled thinly and nodded.

"You make good woman for Red Hair, brother of Lone Wolf. Let us hope we can send you home to him."

It wouldn't do any good to plead for her life. She saved her breath and began to strain her eyes down the length of the canyon as day broke, eager for the sight of her husband. She recognized the man on horseback as Scott Prescott by the way he rode with head bared. The two men in the buggy were Trevor and Carter. But where was Rory?

High Hawk advanced with his rifle cradled casually in his arms. The other two held theirs at ready while Scott rolled down off his horse and came forward with low words of Lakota greeting. They talked for a moment. She watched her brother-in-law gesture at the men in the buggy and to her. High Hawk was watching the high walls of the canyon. And then there was a shot from high above, followed by an undulating Sioux victory cry. Norah didn't understand until she heard Scott's anguished wail as his features crumpled in an agony of distress. Rory. Now she knew where Rory was. Or where he had been.

She almost saved them the trouble of jerking the wagon out from under her. Her knees gave strengthlessly, and darkness pooled about her senses. She was aware of a strong embrace catching her, steadying her, and Scott's quiet voice.

"Norah. Easy. Easy."

High Hawk waved down the guns of his companions. He would not interfere with his friend's comforting of his brother's widow.

"Rory! They've killed Rory!" she sobbed into his shoulder. Great spasms of weeping shook up from her soul.

"Shhh. Rory's fine." His hands were on her wet cheeks, stroking them gently. "He's all right," he vowed softly.

"How do you know?" She searched his face, hungry for belief.

"Because I taught him that yell when I was eight-years-old, and he's still lousy at it."

She gave a whimpery little cry and sagged against him. "Oh, Scott, I want to see him again. I want to go home."

"Shhh, I know." His kiss was a warm touch of confidence upon her forehead. "Be brave." Norah took a deep breath and nodded.

Scott jumped down from the wagon and stalked to where his childhood friend waited impassively. His golden eyes were hard as agates.

"We finish this, and then we finish things between us."

High Hawk nodded stoically, accepting his responsibility for the other's loss and right to retribution. He had liked Red Hair and was not feeling good about what had been done, necessary as it was. There was no point in delaying business with more words or sympathy. "What is Samuels prepared to do to earn back the woman?"

Trevor climbed down from the buggy and motioned Carter to do the same. "Free her first, then we'll talk."

"No. Too much talk already."

461

"All right. I've brought a signed paper stating that my father will not push to buy your land."

"A paper. Tell them what use we have for such signed papers, Lone Wolf."

"This one will stand in a white man's court," Scott swore. "You have my word on it. I'll see it does, even after I've killed you."

High Hawk gave him a wry smile. "Strong words, *iyeska*. But are they true words?"

"Show him," Scott instructed curtly.

"Carter, give me the papers."

"No."

Trevor turned to look at the little man in surprise.

"I won't let you do this. I won't let you ruin all that your father has worked to do. Not for the likes of that whore."

Scott took a stiff stride forward, but Trevor stopped him with the brace of his forearm.

"You had better explain that," the Easterner commanded.

"Ask him. He knows what his brother's wife was. She used her—charms to steal good men blind. I found out all about her. I've got all the proof I need."

"Where? Show me."

"It's in my safe box in Baltimore. You fool! You incredible, weak fool. That woman was never interested in you. She wanted the man I could have made you into, the man your father wanted. Get in the buggy, Trevor. For once do something worthy of the name Samuels."

"I won't walk away from her. I don't care what she was."

"You'd throw it away for nothing? What a waste! It would destroy your father to see what a failure he raised. After all he's done for you, for me, I won't let

462

you disgrace him. Better he remember you with pride then to damn you with the truth." Pale eyes gleamed behind thick lenses. He climbed down from the buggy, eyeing the bland faces of the Sioux before crossing to his mentor's son. The time had come to prove himself, to show Martin Samuels how deep his regard and gratitude ran. "This can still work to our advantage. The outcry against the Sioux would result in the stripping of their land . . . if you and Mrs. Prescott were killed by them."

There was a small report of sound, not even as loud as the backfire of an automobile. Trevor Samuels's eyes rounded with surprise as a bright spot of crimson flowered on his shirt front. Then he crumpled without a noise.

Before the Indians could react to the unexpected violence, Carter thrust his palm gun up into Scott's face. At such close range, even a small caliber revolver would do a killing damage. Scott didn't move.

"Of course," Carter said almost pleasantly, "that means you'll all have to die. Goodbye, Mr. Prescott. You, I will not miss, figuratively or otherwise."

"No!" Norah's scream blended with the roar of the shot.

Rory countered the Lakota's attack, halting the downward plunge of his knife with the block of his rifle stock. His other hand stabbed down for his pistol belt, jerking one of his Colts free and discharging it directly into the Indian's chest. Blinking against the burn of powder, he rolled out from under the sagging weight of the dead man and cautiously looked below. They'd heard the shot. They were all looking upward. He had to think of something fast or everything would go straight to hell along with the ugly Indian he'd just sent. He hadn't practiced a good Lakota war cry for twenty years when he and Scotty used to use it to scare Kincaid cattle. He wasn't even sure he could do it. He cupped his mouth and let go with the warbling yell. The canyon walls eched and distorted it until hopefully only Scotty would recognize it as his own. Then he waited, watching the tableau playing out below him.

Someplace deep inside was registering the fact that he'd killed a man. He'd fought plenty and broken a few bones, but he'd never buried anyone; and the horror of it lodged an acrid taste in the back of his throat. He swallowed it down. No time for it now. Carefully, he stretched out on his belly, sighting the Winchester over the brace of his forearm. He beaded it in on High Hawk; but to his dismay, he found he was aiming at a vague blur. He couldn't hit what he couldn't see. He gave a soft curse then remembered Jacob's glasses. Praying they hadn't been smashed in the tussle, he pulled them out of his pocket—in one piece. Settling them on the bridge of his nose, he sighted again and smiled grimly as the handsome Indian came into crisp focus.

"All right, Scotty, I gotcha covered. Get ready, Norah-honey. We got a whole long night a loving ahead of us."

The shot took him by surprise. He lifted up from the rifle sights when he saw Trevor fall. For a moment, he was stunned, then quickly he hunkered back down to business. It was an impossibly long shot for a good marksman, which he wasn't. A man didn't have to be gun-handy to bring down a coyote with a shotgun and he'd never seen the sense in plinking tin cans off a fence post. But when he squinted down that long barrel as Carter Clemens

464

shoved his pistol between his brother's eyes, he said a brief prayer and squeezed with his forefinger.

The bullet ripped through Carter Clemens's throat, ending his threat in less than a pulse beat, but not the danger. Scott snatched for the knife he carried in his boot, yanking it free just as High Hawk pulled his. In his periphery, he saw the buckboard surge forward as Norah's cry and the sound of the rifle spooked the horse. She started to fall backwards. He had a split second to make a choice between saving his own life and hers. It didn't take him half that long to decide.

As a child, he could pin fleas jumping off camp curs with the flick of his blade and there was nothing wrong with his eyesight. He gave a quick fling and the fibers of manila parted just as Norah pulled them taut. She fell hard but unharmed to the ground. It was then High Hawk struck with his blade, burying it deep as Scott's arm, extended in the act of throwing, left his chest exposed.

High Hawk rode his friend to the ground, struggling to wrestle the knife from muscle and bone. Before he could, Scott's knee drove up hard, punching beneath his ribs to bowl him over. Then Scott was on his feet, wobbling, reeling, clutching at the protruding blade with stained fingers. He heard two more shots and was dimly aware of the other Lakotas falling. Then there were just him and High Hawk.

And from far above them, Rory was muttering fiercely, "Scotty, dammit, move! I can't get a shot!"

Scott was staggering. The pain was terrible, but not as fearsome as his anger. This man would have seen his brother killed and his sister-in-law hanged.

This man who was his friend. The thought of it infuriated him beyond physical agony. He grasped the hilt of the knife and jerked hard, crying out when it came free. He had to hold it in his left hand. His right was hanging useless. Despite his strength of purpose, unconsciousness was coming up fast, so fast he couldn't defend against the hand that gripped his wrist and wrenched the knife away. He went down to his knees. High Hawk had a handful of his hair, tugging his head back, baring his neck for the cut of the blade. And suddenly he couldn't see anything but his wife's face.

"Oh, God, Gena, I'm sorry," he gasped hoarsely as his eyes rolled back to white.

Slowly, his friend lowered the knife and drew the lolling dark head to rest upon his shoulder. High Hawk sighed and smiled tightly as he spoke a suddenly realized truth. "Ah, Lone Wolf, *mitakola*, yours is a voice of reason we cannot afford to lose."

By the time Rory rode Ghost down to the valley floor, Norah was kneeling awkwardly beside a slowly stirring Trevor and High Hawk was tending his brother's wound. He tumbled off the tall silver stallion, knee catching, dropping him down on all fours so he had to practically crawl the last few feet to grab his wife up in his arms.

"Rory."

He didn't answer. He was kissing her. Finally, he broke away long enough to turn her and untie her bonds. Then her arms were around his neck and they held to each other.

Trevor surprised them all by sitting up. He was hurt and woozy with blood-loss. The bullet had ricochetted off a rib, missing everything vital, but he felt as though his chest had been kicked in. "Norah, are you all right?" he asked raspily. He glanced back

466

at the inert body of his former aide, and shuddered with the shock of it. He'd never suspected.

After kissing her husband's rough cheek one more time, she turned to the injured politician and hugged him carefully. "That was a very brave thing you were willing to do for me."

"And I promise to do more. When I get back to Baltimore, I'm going to see my father stays the hell out of South Dakota. Then I look foward to meeting with Scott when he's up to it to draft some new proposals. Whatever else you might think of me, Norah, I am a man of my word."

"I think you're a fine man, Trevor. I always have."

He smiled at that, truly pleased. "And you have a good family here. I can't see any reason to disturb that. You have my solemn vow that whatever Carter has stashed away in his safe box will never surface. I hope I can always count on your friendship."

"You know you can," she pledged quietly. Then she joined Rory at Scott's side. She took up her brother-in-law's bloodied hand, kissing the knuckles gently. "I'm not going to have to wrestle the spirit world for you, too, am I?"

Scott grinned weakly, and his fingers squeezed hers as awareness waxed and waned.

"Glad to see you live, Red Hair," High Hawk told Rory with a somber sincerity.

"Kinda glad about that myself, no thanks to you."

"You have good woman, *Pehin Luta*. You should be proud."

"I am. You'd best git afore I remember that I want to kill you. Take back your dead and tell their families I will bring them beef and plenty of goods to pay my respects and grieve for their souls."

"I will." He stood and stoically went to see to his companions.

Golden eyes flickered open again, focusing slowly. "Heya, Scotty."

"Rory." He swallowed with difficulty and drew a couple of shallow breaths before speaking. "Glad to see you were watching your back."

"Tole you to watch yours, too, didn't I?"

He smiled faintly. "Gena's been looking for a way to keep me home for a while. Don't think this was what she had in mind."

"Doan think she'll care as long as I ain't bringing you in toes first. We'd best be getting the two of you over to the Lone Star so Daddy can start in patching." He brushed back his brother's damp hair with a gentle hand. "Thank you, Scotty. I owe you."

"No," he mumbled, pressing Norah's hand. "Just paying a debt."

Rory was sitting at his big desk, expression pensive, when he looked up and saw her standing at the door. His look immediately heated with welcome.

"Jacob all tucked in?"

"He wants you to come up to read to him. I told him you were tired."

"I ain't that tired." He smiled up at her as she settled upon his lap with her wrists locked behind his head. She smelled invitingly of her scented bathwater, and the silky movement of her robe made another kind of invitation. "I ain't tired at all."

"Well, I am," she sighed. Her gaze grew smoky. "I want to go to bed—with you."

"Well, now, you won't get no argument from me."

The picture frame on his desk caught her eye, and she smiled softly as she lifted it. "This is Jacob. Is this

468

one of the pictures you took in Baltimore?"

"Figured it was 'bout time I put something in there. The Major had a picture of my mama the way she was before she fell in with the Sioux. Always liked that picture, but it was kinda sad, you know, 'cause he'd stare at it for the longest time, jus' looking back. I doan want to look back no more. I got too much up ahead." He picked up the coil of crisped wire and dropped it into his brass wastecan. It made a very solid thump, like a heavy book closing.

"What shall I do with these?" Norah asked quietly, drawing the divorce papers from the pocket of her robe.

He was looking up at her, his dark eyes intense. "Think you could stand being married to a dumb ole bow-legged cowboy who's flat broke?"

She ripped the document in two and let it follow his past into the trash. "I think so."

"What'd you think, Norah-honey, could you see me as a farmer?"

She tilted her head from side to side as if considering that picture, then shook her head. "No. Sorry. I see a rancher. One who knows cows and grass and how to get the most out of them."

"I got no money, Norah."

"Yes, you do," she corrected, running a fingertip over his lips. "You've got lots and lots of money. Cole Denby's been investing it for you all these years. Take it and laugh in his face."

Rory smiled, a slow spreading smile. His pride wouldn't stand for having charity forced upon him. But taking what was owed him, now that was something altogether different. "Awright. Just as long as I doan have to thank him." He grew suddenly sober, his gaze deep and simmering. "I made a lotta mistakes with you and Jacob, and I'll probably make a lot more seeing as how I'm not too bright."

She smiled, running her fingers through the fiery thatch of his hair. "True."

"I'd really like another chance to make good on them promises I made you."

"Forget the promises and tend to the vows, Rory Prescott," she murmured, bending low to leisurely sample the curve of his mouth. His big hands fit around her waist, moving slow, easing up a rib at a time until they cupped the generous underswell of her bosom. "I love you, Rory," she whispered huskily into the part of his lips.

"Hey, Rory." There was a rattle of spurs and a brusque knock.

Norah sighed and settled back into the curl of Rory's arm as he called, "What is it, Cyril?"

"That mean ole silver horse a your boy's took a big bite outta Sammy's arm."

"Maybe he's hungry. Grain him good. He saved my bacon today."

"What about Sammy? Doan you want to come take a look?"

Rory turned a smoldery dark-eyed stare upon the woman in his arms and muttered, "Take care of it, Cyril. What the hell do I pay you for? Run him on over to my daddy. My mama makes a nice seam. I got me a story to read to my boy."

Cyril lingered, jaw hanging.

Rory gave him an impatient glance. "Well, go on," he growled. "'Less you want me to find someone with a little more gumption to be my foreman!"

"Nosir!"

Norah was smiling. "The poor man. Maybe you should have—"

"I ain't interested in seeing nobody's naked body

470

parts but yours. Wanna help me tell Jacob a story?"

"Something that has to do with prowess, I'm sure," she purred contentedly.

"I was planning on saving that story for you, honey. 'Lessen you're tired of hearing it over and over again."

"I never get tired of the way you tell it."

"That so?"

"Daddy!" came a youthful bellow from upstairs. "I'm waiting!"

"Reminds me a somebody, but I can't think of who," Rory admitted with a sassy grin. He shifted her so she was straddling his thighs, his palms moving up and down beneath her gown, creating a callused friction on her bared legs.

"Rory Prescott, are you trying to make things—difficult?"

"Why, yes, ma'am."

"Daddy! What's taking you so long?"

"Daddy, what's taking you so long?" Norah echoed as her tongue stroked lightly along his lips. Her hands eased down into his lap.

Rory sucked a quick gasp. He seized his wife's smiling face between his hands and kissed her breathless.

"What about Jacob?" she panted at last.

"Let him wait," came her husband's rumbling growl.

Epilogue

"Ora, sit on down before you pitch outta the buggy right onto your pretty fanny."

"Ethan Prescott, watch your tongue. There are children present."

"I'm hardly a child, Grandma," Dawn advised coolly from where she lazily sat in her saddle. "I'm almost seventeen-years old."

And glancing up at her, Aurora couldn't argue. She was a fetching young lady. With her buckskins hugging promisingly in all the right places and her flaming hair braided away from the chiseled perfection of sun-kissed features, no one would mistake her for a child.

"I'm not a child either," pipped up Noah Prescott with all his seven-year-old wisdom. "I know what fanny means."

"And your grandma's still got a nice one," Ethan claimed with a wide grin, his palm patting to prove it.

"You're worse then they are," Aurora scolded as she resumed her seat, but her fingers laced through the big Texan's excitedly. "When's the train due in?"

"What time you got, Gena?"

472

She checked her lapel pin. "Four."

"Any time." He glanced over her shoulder and shook his head. "I was beginning to think they weren't gonna be here to meet their own boy."

Aurora turned and smiled to see a buggy racing recklessly down the main street of Crowe Creek, scattering pedestrians like settler's hens. "Doesn't that boy know any speed but full out?"

"Heya Mama, Daddy, all. Looks like we just made it. Norah had to try on everything in her closet. Not like the boy's forgotten what she looked like since Christmas."

"Rory Prescott, you know perfectly well I'd have been ready on time if you hadn't—" Norah broke off abruptly, then concluded rather primly, "distracted me."

Rory grinned broadly and Dawn made kissy noises until her mother gave her a sharp look.

"Young lady, you'd better be practicing your manners if you plan to go to Washington with your father this fall."

"Yes, ma'am," the girl murmured contritely, then winked at her uncle the moment no one was looking.

"I sure doan envy Scotty that trip. He'll have her on a short lead in one hand and his big ole scalping knife in the other."

"Why don't you come with us, Rory?" Dawn pleaded prettily.

"Steppin' betwixt you an' your daddy? Unuh. Think I'd be standing within striking range when he gets to wondering where you got all your ideas about sparking with boys? No, ma'am."

"Dawn's gonna lasso herself a husband," Noah claimed with a gravity worthy of the father he so resembled. "She told me so."

"I did not!"

"The two of you stop it," Gena said sternly. "I won't have you tussling in the dirt when your father gets here."

"Wouldn't recognize 'em as his if they weren't. C'mon down here, Norah-honey. Let's get us a front-row seat. Didn't know so danged many Prescotts were gonna be here."

Rory hopped out of the buggy and stretched up his hands, fitting them under his wife's arms. Instead of swinging her to the platform, he brought her in close so she was flush against his chest, then let her down leisurely. She linked her hands behind his neck and matched his smoldering gaze all the way down. His voice pitched to a low, husky murmur.

"We didn't have to hurry. It ain't like Jacob can't find his way home."

A blast from the train whistle interrupted his suggestive smile and Norah hurried down the platform, Rory ambling more slowly in her wake, favoring his knee. His arm eased around her shoulders as they waited, and hers circled him low so that her hand rested firmly on the snug seat of his denims. For a moment, they were enveloped in a rush of smoke and steam, and he took advantage of the concealment to tip up her chin and grab a wet kiss. By the time the mist cleared, she was cuddled up against him as if they'd been married a month rather than sixteen years.

"Heya, Scotty!" Rory opened a space between them to draw in his brother the moment he stepped down from the train. He had a hard embrace for Rory and a quick kiss for Norah while his golden stare sought out his wife. Then his tense posture eased. "Hell, doan let us keep you," Rory grumbled, giving him a push toward the Lone Star buggy.

"Howdy, Mama." Scott stretched up a bronze

cheek for her kiss and reached around her for his stepfather's hand. Then, catching Noah as he jumped at him from the buggy, he stopped before Gena. *"Cante skuya,* you should not have come all this way. Not so close to your time."

Gena bent awkwardly over her rounded belly to kiss him with an enthusiastic longing. "I couldn't wait to see you. How was your trip?" She caressed his face and stroked through his short black hair as she spoke.

"Long and lonely. It's good to be home. I'll be glad when you can travel with me again. How do you feel?" He spread his finger wide over her abdomen and waited for the hard punch of life to meet his palm in welcome.

"Like I'm too old for this sort of thing." But she was smiling as she said it. "Your father says I'm healthy as an ox."

"C'mon, Daddy. I brought you a horse. Kick out of those shoes and get some grass between your toes."

Scott looked to his daughter and the smile froze on his face. *Wakan Tanka!* When had she gotten so beautiful? She'd always been a pretty child, but the sudden maturation from lithe youngster to supple female struck him right between the eyes. And his father's heart seized up in alarm. He wasn't going to get a lick of sleep when he took her to her first big city.

"Hau, Wihinapa. Leci u wo."

She rolled down off her horse and came to him, beaming like the sunrise her grandfather had named her for in the Lakota tongue. Her arms flung about his neck. "It is good that you're home, *ate.* Where's Jacob?"

"He's checking on the gift he bought."

"For me?"

He held her away and pinched her chin. "Since when do you look forward to gifts from boys?"

"Jacob's no boy. He's my cousin. And besides, he always brings nice things."

Scott couldn't resist her grin. He wondered wryly if any of the young men back East would be able to. He glanced up at Gena to find her smiling down at him in understanding sympathy. He reached up, and their fingers twined together.

"Heya, Mama!"

Jacob Prescott swung down out of the baggage car with an easy grace and strode across the platform to snatch his mother up for a gigantic hug. At sixteen, he was taller than she was, the image of his father and grandfather—a ruggedly handsome Prescott with his mother's extra polish to smooth the rougher edges. He regarded her with his daddy's grin and said, "Promise you won't be mad at me."

"Why?" she hedged warily. "What have you done?"

"Promise?"

"All right. What? You're not quitting school, are you?"

"Naw, nothing like that. Hey, Daddy!"

Rory swept him up in a crushing embrace, squeezing until their ribs groaned. "Howdy, pard." When Jacob stepped back, grinning wide, Rory took off his Stetson and clapped it down on the boy's head. Then he stood stock still. "I'll be. It fits."

"It was bound to one of these days, Daddy. Remember your promise. Get your books ready. You got yourself a first class account manager, at least for the summer."

"Well, awright!"

Norah smiled at the two of them. She noted her husband's relief. He never said as much to her, but he

476

was always afraid that someday their son would come home and express no interest in the running of the Bar K. Norah didn't think that would ever happen. Jacob was a Prescott and a Kincaid. He couldn't help what was in his blood. Jacob was already loosening his tie and tight collar and his manner of speech, easing into becoming his father's son instead of his mother's pride and joy. And she didn't mind it. As long as he stuck to his schooling. It gave her a reason to drag Rory East several times a year; and, as long as he didn't have to stay longer than a week, he was grand company. Especially at night when he didn't have the running of the ranch to occupy his thoughts and would relax to become all hers. She had him completely for those few precious weeks and, for the rest of it, she'd learned to share him. And she'd even learned to get along with his mother.

There was a commotion by the baggage car, and Jacob tugged his father's arm excitedly. "Daddy, come see what I got you."

Smiling curiously, Rory looked where he was told, and his dark eyes grew round with awe. "What is it?"

Jacob gestured to the machine one of the baggage handlers was two-wheeling down a ramp. "It's a motorcycle."

"Hot damn! Norah, will you get a look at that!"

She was looking and not fondly.

Rory gave it a reverent once-over with his eyes and then his hands. "This is some gift, Jake." Then his gaze narrowed and he looked at his boy straight on. "How'd you come by the money for this, son?"

He shifted for a minute, peering toward his mother over the steel rim of his glasses. "Well . . ."

"Spill it!"

"I sorta met up with Uncle Cole, and he gave me the money."

Norah grabbed for Rory's arm, hanging on tight as his every muscle went rigid.

"You what?"

"Oh, he was real nice and all and wanted to be remembered to Mama."

Rory's jaw grated hard enough to rend stone. "Take it back."

"Daddy . . ."

"You heard me."

Jacob hung his head, then very slowly canted his glance up through the fringe of his lashes in a woebegone look that Ethan and Aurora Prescott recognized in an instant. "I'm sorry, Daddy. I didn't mean for it to make you mad. Uncle Cole wanted me to buy something fancy like jewelry for Mama, to irritate you, I think, but I bought this for you, instead. I thought you might like the idea that it galled him something fierce."

The unyielding line of his father's mouth twitched. Gradually, the harsh angles eased and the dark eyes roved over the tempting gears and handlebars. "Did it now? Well, I guess the sonuvabitch owes me a good present. Start 'er up, Jacob."

"Yessir, Daddy!"

With a hard kick, the machine roared to life. The horses balked, and Dawn and Noah were popeyed.

"Ain't that something!" Rory crooned, mesmerized.

"Rory Prescott, you are not getting on that thing."

"Awww, Norah-honey . . ."

"Don't you honey me. You're not wearing your eyeglasses, and you'd run smack into the first tree you came across." She tensed when he turned to her, soulful-eyed and smiling sweet.

"Honey . . . Jacob brought it all the way out here just for me."

478

"You'd break your fool neck."

"No, I won't," he cajoled, stepping close and angling in so he brushed against her. His thumbs stroked under her taut jaw, lifting it so his mouth was provocatively near hers. "I'll be careful. Please?"

She scowled, and he began to grin wide, sensing she was weakening.

"I can take him for a ride on the back, Mama," Jacob suggested helpfully. "I leaned how to drive it in Baltimore. Me and Uncle Scott figured it out, and—"

Norah slashed a glance across the platform to Scott, who was taking off his shoes and socks. "Uncle Scott?" He smiled at her, guiltily.

"Well, hell, Norah, Scotty's been on it and it ain't killed him!"

"*I* just might," she muttered.

"C'mon, Mama. I won't go fast."

"Well . . ."

"Oooo, I love you, honey." Rory swooped down for a quick kiss then, as he drew away, paused. His hand cupped her cheek and he came back down for a long, tongue-tangling thank you. She melted like hot wax.

"C'mon, Daddy. You can do that later."

Rory smiled down at his sultry-eyed wife and told him, "Son, you doan know nothing about women. You take the time when it presents itself. Or when you got the time, you ain't got nobody to spend it with."

"Don't have."

"What? Oh. Yeah."

Jacob straddled the seat and strapped on a leather helmet. "Hop on, Daddy." When Rory settled on behind him, he warned, "Whatever you do, don't use your spurs."

"Jacob, don't let your father break any bones!"

"I won't, Mama. Just in case, I've decided to go into medicine," he announced, fitting the goggles over his eyeglasses. "That way, I can pick up the pieces."

"Bought time," Ethan breathed in relief. "Now I can finally retire."

Jacob revved the motor and Rory grabbed onto him tight with one arm, gripping his hat with the other.

"Race you to the Bar K," Dawn challenged, setting her heels back sharply so her mount jumped forward.

The motorcycle gave a jerk and roared to life, speeding down the street in a cloud of smelly exhaust. Scott gave Gena a quick kiss and skimmed over the rump of the horse Dawn had brought for him, landing in the saddle. Throwing off his coat and hat, he headed in hard pursuit.

"Well, Ora, we'd best be following in case any of 'em need to be picked up offen their rumps. You coming, Norah?"

She tried to hold to her stern disapproving look, but as her eyes tracked the zigzagging path her son and husband made across the Dakota plains, she caved in with a smile.

"Right behind you." She climbed up into the buggy and picked up the reins, still smiling, still watching them tearing up the dry ground. "Be careful, you crazy fool. I've got plans for a lifetime, and I need you whole."

And in the distance, the motorcycle trailed dust and Rory Prescott's loud "Whooee!"